TOOTH & NAIL

H. Carrington

Tooth and Nail

Copyright © 2025 H. Carrington

All rights reserved

The characters and events portrayed in this book are fictitious. Any similarity to real persons, living or dead, is coincidental and not intended by the author.

No part of this book may be reproduced, or stored in a retrieval system, or transmitted in any form or by any means, electronic, mechanical, photocopying, recording, or otherwise, without express written permission of the publisher.

ISBN-13: 978-1-0685166-2-7

Cover design by Dawn Southcombe (Dawnie-Chan)

Acknowledgements

Some things are better left unsaid. Gratitude isn't one of them.

Family is complicated. It's easy to complain about those closest to you. I know I have. Then you go into the world, and you find out about all the other families. Turns out, I'm lucky to have mine. This book probably wouldn't exist without them.

Parents, siblings, and niblings, I love you all. Thank you for loving me.

Friends aren't any simpler. You get to choose them though, so there's no one to blame but yourself. Thankfully, I don't regret mine. Most of the time.

To my Beta team (TS, KT, and PW)...
To my Gamma team (TJ, JP, and RS)...
To my production team (RL and DS)...
To those where life got in the way (RB, ED, and CW)...
To the crews of the *El Saviour*, the *Defiant?*, and the *Past Tents*...
To those notable others who made sure I'm standing here now (DB, MB, CD, JS, RW, RW)...
To whoever I've forgotten that I'll owe thanks and apologies to later...

Just like stories, everything's been said before. Just maybe not by each of us. This book wouldn't be the same without you. You're more appreciated than perhaps you know.

And finally, there's you, **the reader**.

Maybe you're someone I've thanked already. Maybe you're gonna put this straight back on the shelf and never think about it again. Maybe you'll read cover to cover.

Whoever you are, thank you for picking up my book. I'll try to make it worth your time.

Dramatis Personae

The Konreig Empire

The Imperial Court
Acquiel, Toland – *Tarnese noble, Tolinacious' son*
Acquiel, Tolinacious – *Imperial Governor of Tarnon, Toland's father*
Konreig, Rufenrich – *Emperor, Heizl and Thaun's uncle*
Konreig, Thaun – *Crown Prince, Heizl's cousin, Rufenrich's nephew*
Strahl, Dasimir – *Imperial Governor of Kragiv-Stal, Jilia's father*
Strahl, Jilia – *Stalian noble, Dasimir's daughter*

The Imperial Guard
Halig – *Captain, Imperial Guard, Second Army*
Klaus – *Private, Imperial Royal Guard*
Vandel – *Imperial Champion*

The Spire
Ciarra – *Spire Mage Fifth Class*
Fitzerin, Heizl – *Spire Mage Third Class, Thaun's cousin, Rufenrich's niece*
Graylen, Hastigr – *Spire Highmage*
Korten – *Spire Highmage*
Ortharn, Lena – *Spire Mage Third Class*

The Forge
Acquin, Sigren – *Imperial Shadow*
Amdon, Zecht – *Imperial Shadow*
Frida – *Imperial Shadowmaster*
Termal – *Imperial Shadow*

Non-Imperial
New Thala
Elhin – *Melech*
Renyar – *Patriarch of Thala, Remar's prophet*

Norjhost
Naqtuqa – *Norjan Warleader, Okuaak's brother*
Okuaak – *Norjan Shaman, Naqtuqa's brother*

Other Named Individuals
Aepoli – *Seorsan Inquisitor (deceased)*
Aurus – *Spire Highmage*
Cylarid of Oaks – *Yrgol elder, Bara of Oaks*
Daen – *Seorsan High Inquisitor (deceased)*
Daylen, Filip – *Kauylan noble, Reiget Trade Guild Shareholder*
Dwysil – *Seorsan academic*
Gildur, Dallan – *Imperial Baron, Former Imperial Champion*
Henlech – *Hastigr's former apprentice*
Gerwulf – *Imperial Guard, Second Army*
Goland – *Uloric priest*
Hildrun - *Imperial Guard, Second Army*
Ikkad – *Thalan Melech*
Jalor – *Thalan informant*
Konreig, Eraenie 'Erin' – *Rufenrich's younger sister, Heizl's mother (missing)*
Konreig, Myron – *Rufenrich's elder brother, Thaun's father (deceased)*
Kraze 'The Scathed' – *Oesel pariah*
Kwen – *Legendary Trissk'thalan tyrant*
Kuhlner, Rhaekeiran – *Former Imperial Governor, royal claimant (deceased)*
Märchen, Archimand – *Historian*
Marsowy – *Stalian linguist*
Orecalin, Aidan – *Spire Highmage*
Ortharn, Nennein – *Spire Highmage, Lena's grandmother*
Paluch, Myron – *Historian (missing)*

Pohl, Erna – *Imperial Shadow*
Razeen – *Thalan Melech*
Remar – *God-king of Thala, Bringer of Fountains*
Steinar – *Self-proclaimed 'Champion of Fjarl'*
Ulva – *Norjan shaman (deceased)*
Vinen – *Thalan Melech*
Yu Zhi – *Daqini Imperial Calligrapher*
Zarrek, Larren – *Tszerrichan Lairz, Scholar (deceased)*

Tooth and Nail – Prologue

"Some gods do not die; they break."

Highmage Hastigr Graylen
(309 I.Y.)

Families were complicated. It didn't matter if they were bound by blood or covenant, few things could be said to be so twisted.

Klaus sighed. He should've felt happy. His commander had finally recognised all his hard work. This was it. He'd dreamed about the Royal Guard since he'd been old enough to play soldier.

Instead, he now worked his first rotation. Klaus hadn't realised how much emphasis the royal family put on the *guard* in *guardsman*.

With one foot falling in front of the other in an unsteady, arrhythmic pace, he made his rounds. Others might've preferred a more even march, but he'd always found the innate unpredictability of his stride kept his mind sharp.

He didn't know how to feel. When he finished patrolling the miles of corridors and passages beneath the Emperor's palace, command would reward him with time with his family. Some of it, anyway. His wife and friends had assured him he'd enjoy it, but he couldn't help but question their faith.

His sister had contacted him without warning a few weeks before, suggesting their reunion. He hadn't spoken with her since before he'd enlisted. She hadn't approved of his chosen path, but then he hadn't thought much of hers either. Neither of them really got along with each other, truth be told.

For the life of him, Klaus couldn't work out why she wanted to speak with him now, or their brothers for that matter. With one missing on some misadventure, and the other locked within the Spire, he couldn't remember the last time he'd seen either of them. Whenever it was, they'd got along with one another about as well as they did now. Too many differences between them all, and too many years apart.

In spite of all that, it'd be good to see them again. If they could keep themselves from arguing, he might even have fun. He'd never admit it to their faces, but Klaus regretted how they'd parted. He couldn't give up an opportunity to clear the air between them. After all, they were the only family that he truly had.

His uneven steps led him to the Palace's Great Hall. As a simple soldier in the Imperial First, he'd have struggled to picture such a place. Tainted by the few details that had made it down to the rank and file, his imagination had painted luxury beyond reckoning. Such naive dreams didn't do the chamber justice.

Balconies, art, and plush furnishings lined every wall. Blues, greens, and gold covered every surface. Carpets as deep and lush as meadow grass extended before him. A single square foot of that fabric probably cost more than he'd made in a month at his last posting.

Rumour had it that the Emperor planned some announcement here for the next day. He'd end up on watch for that too, if he was lucky enough to attend at all.

Checking his sheathed sword out of habit, he skirted the room as he continued his round. Though his gaze took in the fabric of tapestries and the marble busts of unknown men and women, Klaus held himself back from touching anything. If he was going to ask for leave to see family, he didn't want to risk drawing notice from his superiors for the wrong reason.

Something moved at the corner of his vision, and he spun to face it. That hanging had moved, he was sure, though it hung down straight and motionless now.

One hand on his blade, he edged towards the tall lengths of expensive blue fabric. Wincing at the drape's delicate touch, he flicked it back. Nothing but an empty alcove.

Moving his hand away from his sword's pommel, Klaus let out a relieved breath. The wind must've played a trick on him. A weary mind could paint many pictures.

As he turned to continue his rounds, a slender, gloved hand locked over Klaus' mouth and nose. His sword never left its scabbard, the attack coming before he could react. Something sharp and hot sliced through the leather padding under his arm, breaking flesh and penetrating deep within him. Twice more it drove sideways into his chest, cutting vital organs, before Klaus felt its sharp caress across his neck.

The unseen attacker's grip didn't falter as his struggles weakened. Where the blade had stabbed him, his body grew cold. A strong hand pushed his arm away as Klaus made a final, desperate effort to break free.

As his strength faded, and the figure lowered him to the ground, he caught a glimpse of his assailant. Clad head to toe in dark cloth and leather, with a hood concealing their face in shadow, it could've been anyone. He couldn't even bring himself to cry out even the weakest of alarms as they reached down and wiped their blade clean on his uniform.

First swirls of dimly recognised colour, and then darkness swarmed the edges of Klaus' vision. As it closed down to a narrow point before disappearing completely, a single wry thought rose within him. Thank Hein, dying would be easier than reconciling with his family.

* * *

As it tilted back, the chair – some modern copy of a master's design – creaked in a most satisfying manner. Across the Hall, the assassin glanced around as if hearing the sound before returning to their task.

With his scuffed and worn boots resting on another seat, Haber laced ringed fingers behind his head and watched the figure work. Over the centuries he'd grown accustomed to such questionable actions, and so too, it seemed, had the hooded killer. He cocked his head, watching as they wiped clean the blood splatter and hoisted the fresh corpse across their shoulders. There was a certain reward in watching the competent at work.

For the briefest of moments, Haber considered following as the murderer moved to dispose of Klaus' body. The guardsman had had his own story – loves, habits, and flaws – but now he lay dead all because he'd stood in someone's way. It could've been anyone stumbling upon the killer, but a promising soldier had paid with his life. That poor guardsman; it was never just the wind.

No, following the assassin wouldn't benefit anyone. Haber had never pursued the divining of people's fates like some he'd known. Visions of the future spoiled all the fun. Still, he'd developed a certain instinct when it came to such plots. This single dead man didn't matter anymore.

Oh, sure, he could've spun Klaus' image around himself and taken his place. Haber had done it before, borrowing a spark of an erstwhile sibling's power to shape the illusion. It might even prove a worthwhile distraction for a while, but he wasn't sure how close to these events he truly wanted to be.

Stretching, he rose from the chair. Carefully returning it to its original resting place, he adjusted his elegant shirt and crossed the room. Wandering over the carpet and ignoring the spot where the Imperial had died only moments before, he walked to where the guardsman had disturbed the assassin from their work. Adjusting his black trousers, Haber crouched and tilted his floppy-brimmed blue and orange hat to one side to better inspect the flagstone.

Where the assassin had had to lever and labour, Haber slid a hand along one worn edge and raised it as easily as if turning a page.

His eyes shifted and danced across the tightly packed rubble before settling on the tiny cluster of desert rose. Nestled in a dusty depression, its sandy, crystalline shards protruded in a flower-like pattern.

This was what had drawn him here. The strange stone radiated sorcerous power. Someone had spent a great deal of time, effort, and essence creating it. Few had the talent to craft beacons like it anymore. He'd checked in on them all at one point or another over the years. For all his desires to be free of others' expectations, such oversight was what he'd agreed to in the first place. One shouldn't ignore such responsibilities.

Replacing the flagstone, hiding the crystalline beacon once more, Haber stood. The temptation to investigate further, to witness whatever would unfold, grew within him, but it wasn't his time yet. This plot had to unfold further, he was sure of it.

Turning on the balls of his feet, he walked away. He'd sensed others here in this palace that he didn't wish to cross paths with. Neither of them – the brute or the apprentice – had forgiven him for the part that he'd played in this small world's history. They should've thanked him and the others anyway; neither would've existed if he hadn't accepted that responsibility so long ago. Still, that was a story common in all men. No one appreciated what came before them.

Pausing at a tall window of frosted glass, Haber looked up. Through the twisted crystal and the silver clouds of night beyond, a blue-green light reached him. Few mortals would've spotted the Comet, but he wasn't like the other players in this game.

"Well," Haber whispered to himself with a slight shrug. "It's about time."

With an amused smile, he took three long steps and was gone. For all his interest to see what came next, experience dictated that remaining there could cost him dearly. The power of a god was nothing when compared to that of a story.

Tooth and Nail – Chapter One

> *"Body who cut the Horn,*
> *Mind to tell their parts,*
> *Heart that fell forlorn,*
> *Soul who took the Heart."*
>
> Traditional rhyme, New Thala

23rd day of Indern, 406th Imperial Year
17th Year of Emperor Rufenrich Konreig's Reign

Like a sword returned to its sheath, few great events began with the setting sun. Weary light hiding from view was a poor herald of history. Ambition, whether divine or mortal, cared little for such omens.

Golden light bathed the city, as alluring as the wealth so many desired. Long shadows reached out along the stone-lined streets and up whitewashed walls. With their backs to the Imperial Palace's pale shape, people rushed about their business, ferrying goods and knowledge to and fro.

Higher still than the Emperor's seat, thin clouds drifted against the darkening sky, the dying embers of day lining their flanks. They hinted at autumn rains, though none seemed eager to follow through just yet.

Beyond even those heights, a single point shimmered with blue and green. Stars had yet to risk the evening expanse, a meagre handful clinging to the eastern horizon. More would join them soon to illuminate the night sky, if twilight allowed.

Emerald and sapphire danced and fought within the glimmering star. It had hung overhead a few nights now, its presence noted only by a handful of scholars and mages. Over the coming days, more faces would turn skywards to study its passing. Some spoke of its arrival, less than once in a generation, but most had heard tales of the Comet from their parents. An arcane curiosity to distract them from their lives for a few weeks, to be forgotten once more before winter reared its head.

The strands of their attention reached towards it now. Whether noble or nobody, people's emotions and thoughts differed little. Imperfect nostalgia, day-to-day stresses, unrealistic expectations, and simple beliefs – most people had more in common than they cared to admit.

Those same threads wrapped between one soul and the next. Envy, suspicion, and desire mingled as easily as love, pride, and hope. Men and women alike thought of themselves and thought of others, unwilling to recognise the intricacies of interwoven emotion that wound them all together.

Only a rare individual spared the time to reflect on how others thought and acted, rather than just their own place in it.

One such person slowly opened hooded eyes. She winced as lamplight and noise shattered her focus, drowning out the sorcerous strands that spanned all things. Clamouring voices smothered the efforts of musicians as the muddied noises rose to her spot upon the balcony.

Ignoring the ignoble rumblings in her belly, she looked down upon the party's many guests. The noise of a hundred pampered mouths clamoured from wall to wall, filling the air with fledgling rumours. Lords and merchants, children and the elderly, anyone worth knowing now attended the feast.

She'd made it here, at least. In the company of the Empire's elite, few would complain. The finest foods, the most talented entertainers, the most influential and eligible individuals.

Leaning on the gallery's stone railing, she hid her grimace as she glared down at the assembled nobility. In spite of all her efforts, they still kept her at arm's length. It shouldn't surprise her. They treated the rest of the servant staff much the same.

Oh, sure, she carried a mage's sigil, and could claim to number among the Empire's most powerful individuals. It made little difference to the nobles below. She could read their instincts, twist their emotions, even warp their perception itself. They saw only a dangerous person who should be avoided at best and chained at worst.

Even her colleagues, other mages serving the Emperor, viewed her with suspicion. Most of them, anyway. Succeeding her own way, away from classes and their dusty old techniques, had made her few friends at the Spire.

Most there didn't care for how hard she'd had to work to garner the respect she now clung to. She could count the number who tolerated her differences on one hand. Instead, they saw her name and cried favouritism. How else could someone who failed every core lesson get as far as she had? She might as well have tried to explain colours to a blind man.

The Imperial Court treated the old veteran standing near the empty throne with more respect. Even without the oversized scimitar strapped to his back, none of them would've dared jostle him if he'd stood up here now. Their barbs and jabs would've struggled to break his stance as he stood upon the bare flagstones.

A pointed cough roused her from her brooding, and she turned to the blond figure beside her.

"Did you want something?" She said.

The man eyed her for a moment before flicking his hair from his eyes and replying. "What's wrong? Problem?"

"What? No, it's nothing."

"Then why are you staring at the throne? Or is it the Champion?"

"Vandel?" She gestured towards the dais. "No. I was just thinking."

"But why the dirty look? Spotted something we should check out?"

She held back a laugh. "What's your name, Shadow?"

"Zecht," he gave her a half nod before leaning on the railing beside her to look down upon the hall. "And you're Fitz, right?"

She grimaced. "I prefer Heizl."

"Fine. Why the look?"

"Oh, that." The mage hesitated. Speaking her mind had landed her in trouble before. "I was just thinking about the Champion," she considered each word before it left her mouth. "It's weird, right? Having one at all, I mean. He's just one guy. Sure, he can swing a sword, but even the youngest student at the Spire can twist the world around them."

"'Cause no one trusts mages?" Zecht asked without turning.

"Still," Heizl bit the inside of her cheek in frustration but continued. "It could be an honorary position. Throw the title to some noble's brat and win their loyalty. Have a tournament and a party, and give the people some entertainment to latch onto. Instead, Uncle has Vandel, a real soldier, in the role. You'd think he could find a better use for someone who knows one end of a sword from the other."

"Who cares?" Zecht shrugged. "Doesn't change our job."

"And that scimitar," she went on. "It looks older than he is. And he already carries good steel – why the extra blade?"

"You could always go and ask him."

"No thanks," Heizl shook her head, tied-back hair snaking over her shoulders as she laughed. "He creeps me out."

Zecht snorted, and she found herself smiling. It felt good to have an actual human interaction with a Shadow. Too many of her past keepers had lacked a sense of humour. She understood, even if she didn't want to admit it. Few found it easy to relax when working with someone who might turn them inside out on a whim. Maybe this one wouldn't be so bad.

Below, other Shadows stood out in their stiff formal uniforms. The man at her side wore his like a child in secondhand clothing. It didn't surprise her all that much. Their type didn't often stand on display like this.

More noticeable, to her at least, stood the handful of lesser mages scattered around the room. Most kept to the walls, watching over the crowd, while a few mingled, drinking sparingly. Their Shadows stayed close, tracking their charges as much as they eyed the gathered nobles.

None of them impressed Heizl much. A troupe of circus magicians with their sleight of hand would serve just as well.

"Hey," Zecht nudged her.

"What?" She brushed his arm away, slowly realising that he'd said something. One's thoughts could prove too loud.

"I asked if you'd spotted anything."

"Huh? Oh, right. Nothing you'd care about. Normal background-level magic, mostly. No one's up to anything they shouldn't be. At least, no more than you'd expect from a bunch of stuck-up, self-obsessed, narcissists all hungry for attention."

The Shadow answered slowly, as if choosing each word with care. "We're not meant to talk about the Imperial Court that way."

"These bastards? I shouldn't worry."

"Bastards? I'm pretty sure the only bastard around here is–"

Instinct rising, Heizl failed to control herself fully. She could've dropped within herself to twist his threads and slow his thoughts to a crawl. She might've drawn the attention of those that surrounded them to his imperfections, and ensured no one would ever take him seriously. She could've just hit him.

Instead, Heizl reached out and grasped him by the jaw, thumb one side and fingers the other. In her grip, she could feel the smug grin upon his face. She'd have liked nothing better than to tear it off.

He must've seen it coming. Shadows were trained beyond the level of the Imperial Guard. They looked out for things like this. Stopping a mage like her – untested in actual combat – would've been easy.

No, he didn't see her as a threat, and so hadn't reacted. That was almost worse than his insult.

She released him, stepping away. "Come on, I wanna go down below."

"We're fine up here."

"Don't be dull." With some effort, she wrapped her tone in civility. "We've got Shadows in every corner, and guardsmen at every door. Nobody needs us up here, so let's go somewhere more interesting." As slow as she could, she held out both empty hands. "I'll behave, I promise."

"Fine." The blond man let out a frustrated breath through his nose. "We won't get in so much trouble if we take the side stairs." He waved to one side. "Less likely to be spotted that way."

"Oh, I know. I know all the good hiding spots. Nice to know you've checked the layout though." Heizl's smiled reached her eyes as she gestured towards the stairs. "After me?"

She'd made it a few steps before Zecht called out. "'Ere, don't forget this!"

Spinning on one heel, she eyed the copper rod that he now held out to her. She hesitated, smile fading.

Few would imagine any of the Spire's members forgetting their focus. It wasn't that they couldn't channel their magicks without whatever object they'd practised with, but that it was safer. Like a filter or a shield, they protected the flesh when drawing that bloody chaos through themselves to shape to their bidding.

Heizl had never had any luck with that though. Few in the Empire had the talent to join the Spire, and, it seemed, few of them strayed from that same style of sanguine-magic so common in the island nations to the south. Sometimes she wondered what it'd be like to be the same as the others. Those regrets often faded when reminded of the strict limits that her colleagues worked under. Prescribed gestures and techniques never failed to bore her.

Rubbing the back of her neck with one hand, she snatched the rod from Zecht with the other. "Thanks. Now, come on."

Without another look, she wove through the clusters of guests sharing the balcony with them. Disapproving faces turned her way, but she ignored them. It wasn't like their opinions mattered.

Down the narrow stone stairs, reaching out to brush the soft drapes and tapestries that hung upon its stone walls, Heizl soon reached the Great Hall's main floor.

Some trick of architecture had muted the sounds up above, but here they struck her full force. She hadn't realised how loud it was. Dancing couples laughed and boisterous youths sang as their elders whispered and schemed. The noise assaulted her, drowning out thoughts.

Pausing for the briefest moment for Zecht to catch up, Heizl pushed onwards. As she passed tables filled with rich food and richer guests, her belly grumbled insistently enough to drown out the celebrations. If anyone heard, they didn't care enough to turn towards her.

One foot before the other, she took in the room. It felt so different down here. Subtler yet more honest. More alive, but more desperate.

Growing used to the crowd, individuals drew her eye. More than just the Imperial nobility had received invites it would seem. Foreign dignitaries in their cultural dress moved from one group to the next, forging agreements and securing alliances. Staff, dressed in simple green and blue doublets, carried cups and platters the length and breadth of the hall. Officers in polished breastplates struggled to fit in, while the merchant class curried favour with whatever they had left after buying entry.

All had their own motives, but few ignored the excuse to indulge themselves. It wasn't every day that they'd celebrate the Crown Prince joining their number. If she wasn't technically on duty, she'd have counted herself among them.

Heizl hesitated at one such group. They spoke in raised voices to be heard over the other guests. She made out few of their words though. Instead, she eyed the woman at the centre who the rest of the circle watched.

Dark, braided hair, and an elegant, gold-hemmed dress worth more than some towns. It took a moment for Heizl to realise that she didn't know the woman. She'd seemed so familiar.

As she made eye contact, catching her watching for too long, Heizl gave a sly smile of acknowledgement. No, she hadn't met this person before, though she didn't mind the thought of getting better acquainted. A foreigner, probably, now that she'd looked closer. Maybe a few years her senior, but still young. Plain and serious, like so many non-Imperials there tonight, but with an exotic slant to her features.

There were more non-Imperials here tonight than usual. Few enough sent more than a token representative at the best of times. The Empire's approach to diplomacy hadn't always been appreciated by other nations. Curiosity had got the better of many of them now. Uniforms and cultural dress from a dozen city-states, lands, and factions dotted the crowd.

She'd expected a more obvious contingent from Seorsa, their nearest neighbour, but rumours of recent conflict hadn't escaped her.

Composing herself, Heizl threw the woman a sly wink and a grin, before moving on. Despite what she'd told Zecht, and despite her baser urges, she had other motives for walking the floor. Fun and flirting would wait. Family beckoned.

She found him only a stone's throw from the throne, back pressed to the stone wall of an alcove, gaze fixed on the ceiling in some infantile attempt to avoid eye contact.

In spite of everything, he looked as uncomfortable in his finely-tailored clothes as Zecht did in his uniform. Gold thread, polished silver, and expensive blue fabric couldn't hide the man's unease.

With a familiar nod to the pair of attendants forming a wall between him and the rest of the room, Heizl slid in alongside him. "You can't hide back here forever. Your guests might think it's rude."

"Heizl?" Startled, the man flinched as he looked at her with wide, brown eyes. "How'd you find me?"

She smiled broadly. "I'm pretty sure most people know where you are, Thaun."

"They do? I'm surprised they haven't ambushed me yet." He said, his brow furrowed.

"They're probably worried one of your friends is going to tear their arms off," she pointed with a thumb over one shoulder. Behind her, Zecht had joined Thaun's attendants, his quiet greeting eliciting a scowl from a redheaded man in a similar uniform.

"They wouldn't do that," a matching smile bloomed on Thaun's face as he followed her gesture. "Well, not to all of them, anyway."

"I know that," said Heizl. "And you know that." She awkwardly draped an arm over his shoulders and waved towards those that filled the hall. A few hopeful faces turned their way. "But I'm not sure they do."

With a faint smile, he shrugged his way out to stand alongside her. "I'd wondered when you'd turn up. Where've you been?"

"Some of us have to work for a living."

He frowned. "What? You're on duty?"

"That's right. I guess our dear Uncle couldn't show weakness by inviting his bastard niece along." She waved dismissively at nothing in particular. "I wouldn't want to spoil your party."

"That's unfair. You know it's not that simple."

"Yeah, well, maybe," she admitted. "We both know that I've got as much royal blood in my veins as you do."

Thaun laughed, though bitterness tainted the sound. "You are welcome to deal with all this. Void knows, you'd do a better job than I do."

"I think there'd be a lot of unhappy people around if I were in your shoes," Heizl put one hand to her chin in exaggerated thought. "I don't think it'd bother me that much though."

For a moment everything felt normal. The looks of disapproving nobles didn't reach her. The Hall's revelry fell short. Her own frustrations – so many people and circumstances beyond her control – faded to a dull ebb. Family and friends could do that. Shared experiences, lessons, and trials swam beneath the surface, tantalisingly within reach.

As Thaun spoke, the peace didn't last. "How're you doing?"

Heizl turned away. "Oh, you know me. Just the usual stuff."

"*Which* usual stuff? Your scathe? Or the Spire?"

"They're the same thing, Thaun."

"Not all scathed people do magic, Heizl," he replied, failing to hide the criticism in his tone.

They'd had the conversation a dozen times before. The only person she'd argued with about it as much as her cousin was their Uncle, the Emperor. "Look, I don't want to talk about it. Not right now." She looked back at him. "Come on, let's go get a drink."

"I don't know if I've got my breath back yet."

"You'll be fine," she looped her arm through his, and began guiding him back towards the room's centre. "Together, we can make the most of this. Most people aren't going to grovel before you with me around, and I might catch a few people's eye. It'll be fun." She thought for a moment. "Probably."

Thaun didn't object, but she could feel his discomfort coming off in waves. The stilted walk, the tense stance – it didn't take a mage to tell he felt overwhelmed. Many wouldn't notice, too caught up in their own narrow lives, but enough spoke about his unsuitability for the responsibilities thrust upon him.

Skirting the couples pirouetting at the Hall's centre, the pair walked. Space appeared before them as guests parted, offering sycophantic smiles and excessive bows. More than once, Heizl felt her cousin stiffen as one noble or another started picking their way through the crowd towards him. Falling within and seeing those glowing orbs and lights, of every soul and bond between them, it wasn't so difficult to flick their attention away.

In their wake, Zecht eyed the throne, and followed after them a pace behind Thaun's own attendants. The pair of them had guarded and guided him for years. As much friends as they were bodyguards. They'd grown to accept Heizl, but she wouldn't describe it as a close relationship. Associates, maybe, or even just colleagues. That stung, though she'd never admitted it.

Reaching a long table near one wall, they slowed. Guests seated on long benches shuffled aside, making space for their Crown Prince. None would consider denying him space there, but still some hesitated. Staying seated would be overtly rude, but moving too much meant sacrificing any opportunity to parade before their future ruler.

Heizl had to force open a space for herself opposite him with her elbows. Few would risk outright insulting a mage by refusing, as much as they might've liked to. The risk, no matter how small, of being set ablaze or turned into a rat was too great. It didn't even matter that Heizl didn't know how to do either of those things. Most people didn't appreciate her subtlety.

"See?" She said, watching one of Thaun's guards move to stand behind him. Standing half a pace from his elbow, the stern, mail-clad woman cast an eye over the crowd. The other, as well as Zecht, found places further out but still close by. Their quiet words and hard gazes cleared a small space around the Crown Prince, though the hungry expressions upon many guests' faces revealed the mob's reluctance. "That wasn't so bad, was it?"

"I guess," said Thaun as he nodded in thanks to the staff who placed a plate of steaming food down in front of him. "Did you have to, you know, push anyone away?"

"A couple," she said, claiming an unattended cup of wine from the centre of the table. "Just the usual types. Governor Strahl, and a guy who I think was from the Guild."

"Thanks."

"It's fine. You'll have to deal with them sooner or later, but I figured it'd be easier after a drink." She eyed him, a couple of years older than her but still pushing the food around his plate like a distracted child. "Are you alright? What's on your mind?"

"Nothing, I'm good."

Lowering her voice, Heizl leant in across the table. "You answered that a bit too quickly."

"You don't want to talk about your scathe or your career, and I don't want to talk about this. Can we just drop it?"

"I'm trying to help, Thaun. Have you had, y'know, another episode?"

"Not a bad one, no," he replied, his gaze lingering downwards upon his meal as he hid his expression.

Trying a different approach, she cocked a smile. "Well, if it gets that rough again, may I kindly suggest that you don't defenestrate yourself?"

"That happened once."

"Once would've been enough." She regretted the words as soon as they left her mouth. Opposite her, Thaun shrank before her eyes. Shoulders slumped, head bowed further, he said nothing.

The family had managed to keep that one mostly hidden. No small feat, with suspicious and ambitious nobles always trying to get one up on their competition. She should probably make an offering to one of the gods in thanks for that. Hein or Zehran, probably, not that it really mattered.

Only a trusted few knew of that incident a few years past. Whether a curse, fever, or something else, they'd nearly lost him. None of them, even with all the resources that the Throne and the Spire could throw at it, knew what had caused the Crown Prince's sudden suicidal intentions. Whispers of assassins and poisons still haunted their family, even with the Civil War long gone.

"Sorry." Heizl cleared her throat, her mind racing as she sought a distraction.

It presented itself from behind a moment later. "Sir?" Heizl flinched at the voice that came from close behind her. She hadn't heard anyone get close. Thaun's Shadow – a lean, uniformed man, with red hair so short he might as well have been bald and a bubbling intensity behind his eyes – spoke in a low tone. "Master Acquiel has requested to join you."

Thaun looked up, jaw clenched and eyes red with restrained emotion. The moment stretched as he composed himself. On either side, a few of the other guests whispered as they watched the Crown Prince struggle.

Unable to bear it any longer, Heizl gently prompted her cousin. "That sounds good, right? Better him than most of 'em."

Another dozen heartbeats passed, and she thought he'd refuse. Thaun shocked her with his answer. "Thanks, Sigren. That's fine."

The Shadow glanced to Heizl before nodding and disappearing behind her. A moment later, another figure joined them.

Dressed in almost modest clothes compared to many of the other partygoers, the mere contrast made him stand out. Though conservatively cut, his red and blue clothes, with their feather motif, likely cost as much as a labourer made in a year. Shining jewellery hung at his wrists and neck, bearing the Imperial Church's split circle symbol. Long, dark hair finished the carefully-curated look, filling the air with the faint aroma of mint.

"Toland," Thaun smiled, much of the tension draining from his expression as he stood to greet the young noble. "It's good to see you."

He bowed, straightening as he adjusted his shirt in an effort to avoid any unsightly creases. "May I join you, Your Highness?"

"You've asked that once already."

"Perhaps," he said, his pure blue eyes twinkling. "Such rituals have their place though. Gods forbid your guests forget whose party this is."

Heizl rolled her eyes as Toland sat down. She couldn't help but notice that those nearest to him made space on the bench more readily than they did for her.

"Please excuse my interruption, Miss Fitzerin." He grinned, and she couldn't help but feel one corner of her mouth tug upwards in response. "It was a difficult choice, but one of your colleagues has monopolised many of the serving staff. I saw an opportunity to stop my appetite from embarrassing me."

"It's fine. Pass me some of that wine and I can probably forgive you."

Reaching out, other guests leant out of his way as he snatched up a clay jug from further down the table. The noble didn't say anything as, rather than handing her the vessel, he poured into the almost-empty cup before her. Bowing his head to her once, she nodded in answer. For all her contempt of the Imperial Court, she struggled to dislike them all.

He turned towards Thaun. "A lot of people had wondered how long it'd be until you officially joined us."

"They did?" he replied, the slightest hint of certainty forming beneath his words.

"So I'm told," Toland sipped his own wine. "I can't think about them all though. I've always thought it best to care about as many as you can, not as many as others think you should."

"...Uh huh."

"Are you, well, Your Highness?" He continued as if unaware of the confused effect his comment had caused.

"I'm good. Just a lot to get used to. It all feels so sudden."

Heizl couldn't help but chuckle. "Really? You were born to sit on the Throne. Pretty sure this has been coming for a while now. You'd probably have both ascended to it and then fallen off by now if the court hadn't made Uncle step in."

"Yeah, I know."

"I think Heizl's trying to say you've had the best tutors and opportunities," said Toland. "You'll do wonderfully."

Thaun frowned. "Thanks, I guess."

"I'm sure," he added, casting a sidelong glance towards Heizl. "Are you both well?"

"You know me," she said with a smile. "If I'm at a party, I'm most definitely well."

"Not working?"

"Only technically," she took a mouthful of her own wine. Food would serve her body better, but didn't help her tolerate the nobility in the same way.

"And you, Thaun?"

"I'm not sure if this whole thing," he gestured around, "Or coming through the Nexus has upset my stomach even more. I'm just great."

"I understand. I arrived that way myself just this morning. I'm not sure I'll ever get used to it." Toland smiled reassuringly. "It's warmer here than Tarnac at least. Probably the other places on your recent tour too, for that matter."

"Maybe," Thaun admitted, lowering his voice. "I think I'd rather be out there still though. People outside the Capital don't expect as much of you. At least not the same things, at least."

Pursing his lips, Toland let the conversation lull into silence. Noise filled the gap with song, music, and arguments weaving together into a seamless mass.

Heizl had never much liked sitting with her back to the room. Even removed from the line of succession as her illegitimacy made her, the risk of an ambitious knife remained. She could handle that uncertainty better than Thaun though, and so it wasn't the first time she'd tolerated it.

Making the most of the moment, she let her consciousness fall back within herself. She should probably at least pretend to work, anyway.

The world bloomed into colour once more, souls and sentiments glowing in a hue that only she could see. Those she knew – Zecht, her cousin's attendants, a handful of others – shone more brightly than others with their familiarity. Likewise, as she surveyed the room with her sorcerous eye, some bonds appeared brighter than others.

With some effort, she might be able to read some of those surface beliefs, but emotion came much more easily. Shades of feelings flowed from one to the next, as lust twisted into jealousy and indifference grew into the typical Imperial self-centredness.

None of the shifting threads that reached towards her flared with anything particularly concerning. A few hints of jealousy at her proximity to two such influential individuals, a whiff of prejudice, but nothing out of the ordinary.

Toland's voice alongside her pulled Heizl back to the physical hall. "I think many of your guests were hoping to see your Uncle here."

"He's got a meeting." Thaun said, returning to pushing his food around the plate. "Just him, Frida, and Hastigr. Maybe a governor or two afterwards. He'll be here soon though." He looked up to the noble sitting alongside Heizl. "How about you? I was expecting your father to be here. How come it's just you here?"

"Why are any of us here, Your Highness?" Toland left the words hanging in the air for a heartbeat. "In the service of the gods." He smiled earnestly. "I doubt that was the answer you hoped for, though. Father sends his apologies, but he was unable to attend. Illness dictates he remains at home."

"Well, if it helps," Thaun forced a lopsided smile, "I don't much want to be here either."

"Such is the burden of leadership," Toland rose and offered an almost imperceptible bow. "Now, if I might be excused, such burdens beckon. I'd hoped for more opportunities to share a drink with old friends, but Father tasked me with other, less enjoyable duties."

"It's fine, Toland, really. Go and do whatever it is you need to."

"Y'know," Heizl said, half over one shoulder as he started to move away. "You're not like the other nobles, are you? You actually mean some of what you say."

"Miss Fitzerin, you have no idea." With those words, his not-quite-insufferable smile faded into the crowd along with the rest of him.

Heizl's gaze lingered on where he'd stood for a moment, eyes narrowing as she glanced from one noble to another.

"I think I should go too," she said after a moment, turning back to her cousin.

"You're not going to stick around for moral support?"

"You know me," she stood. "I only really do immoral support. I won't be far away."

"Said like that, it sounds more like a threat than a promise."

"Someone's got to get you used to life here."

"When I'm in charge, I'm going to get you assigned somewhere far, far away from here."

"Nowhere far enough. You'd have to cross half the world to get away from me."

"You're probably right," Thaun shrugged. "Go on, you wouldn't want to keep anyone waiting."

"Thanks, Your Highness." Heizl smiled and walked away.

Tooth and Nail – Chapter Two

'While the Konreig line gained their throne through blood and gold, they held it with tooth and nail.'

An Alternative History of the
Empire, Myron Paluch (422 I.Y.)

23rd day of Indern, 406th Imperial Year
17th Year of Emperor Rufenrich Konreig's Reign

Dry bitterness coated the inside of his lips as garnet wine lingered upon his tongue. Drawing the mouthful through his teeth one more time, Thaun swallowed, feeling its warmth descend into his belly.

It did little to settle his churning stomach. The half-empty plate before him hadn't done much better.

Heizl's interruption had helped for a while, but she'd gone now too. She'd return sooner or later, but that knowledge offered scant relief. It'd never been her responsibility to care for his mood, but he appreciated her efforts nonetheless. Sometimes just her presence, that of someone he knew like a sister, calmed the visceral emotions churning beneath the surface.

She claimed that, with her sorcery, she could see that chaos. Thaun didn't really understand her magic, or that of anyone else, but he believed her.

Their uncle had called her, along with several of the Spire's more senior members, on that one fateful night some years ago. None of them, not even their most experienced healer, had a good explanation for what had happened.

Most people understood a physical injury. A wracking cough or bruised flesh made sense to them. Visible symptoms fitted into their lives as cleanly as comforts and simple answers. Thaun could count on one hand how many people he believed could accept the thought of a pain that they couldn't see.

He'd grown used to that blindness.

Dull melancholy and unbidden worries had accompanied him as long as he could remember. He wished he could say that they'd hounded him less before that dreadful night years before. They'd just hidden within until then, revealing themselves to those closest in sweat, panic, and confusion.

He still got a hint of that moment sometimes. Like a waking dream, or a memory beyond his grasp, it haunted him. It hung just out of reach, a figure at the corner of his vision, a name not quite upon his lips, an empty space beside him upon waking.

"Thaun?" a woman's familiar voice, breathy and husky, cut through the murmur, drawing his thoughts outwards from their dysfunctional spiral. "You've gone quiet. Do you need a break before His Majesty gets here?"

Noise assaulted him from all sides. His senses strained to hear every conversation at once. Whispers of his own name made a poor reward for his efforts. Stares and furtive glances shot his way

He'd have rather remained ignorant.

His hands balled into fists beneath the table, knuckles white with tension. People had warned him that this day would come. The weight of the Imperial Court, and his duties to it, had always loomed over him. Knowing that inevitability didn't make it any easier.

Breathing in a lungful of warm air, he found a wan smile from somewhere inside. "I'm fine, Lena, really."

"Good answer, sir," Sigren appeared almost from nowhere, the Shadow, bald before his time, stepping to the other side of the table. "But will you still say that after mingling with your guests for a bell?"

Thaun snorted a laugh. "Maybe if I ask nicely they'll let me mingle in the training yard instead?"

"Most of them know better than that by now," the Shadow admitted.

"I think what Sigren means to say," Lena interjected with a stern look. "Is that there are better ways to work out your feelings." When the Shadow didn't add anything, she continued. "You can talk to us. Or you could try a priest? I knew someone who got a lot out of the Church."

"I dunno." Thaun turned away. "I'm busy enough as it is."

Sigren cleared his throat with a noise that could've been mistaken for a growl. "Come on. Enough excuses. People will start to talk if you spend the whole evening avoiding all the Empire's big names." He glanced over one shoulder. "I can only keep Governor Strahl from barging in for so long. Say what you like about your cousin's latest Shadow, but the extra pair of hands had its uses."

Thaun took a moment, bracing himself, hands still in fists. Standing, he gave a single nod, not trusting himself to say anything more. His attendants shared a knowing look, before Sigren peeled away.

"You're sure you're alright?"

"It's fine." Despite his words, Thaun shook his head. If Lena noticed, she didn't say anything.

At some silent signal, the ring of nobles constricted like a noose tightening. Painted faces filled his vision as the Empire's rich and powerful crowded around him. As sure as any hangman's rope, air caught in his throat. Pressure built through the back of Thaun's jaw as he fought the urge to grind his teeth. Billowing darkness threatened the edge of his vision as all too familiar sensations rose within him.

Greedy smiles flashed his way, but none approached immediately. The unspoken rules of such gatherings bound his guests as much as they did Thaun. Men and women made political calculations, assessing who they might risk offending to reach the Crown Prince first.

Beyond his entry to the Imperial Court, other agreements might be forged tonight. Opportunities would be seized, grudges formed, and vengeance wrought, all in the most socially acceptable of ways. The nobility remembered the more literal backstabbing of the Civil War all too well.

Their self-centred scheming passed in the blink of an eye. A stout man's arrival shattered any further weighing up of chance or consequence. Lesser nobles shrank away, polite smiles hiding bitter resentment. He bowed low, expensive shirt, trimmed in gold, almost brushing the floor as he struggled to rise gracefully again.

"Your Highness!" At his booming voice, more heads turned their way. Others flinched back. A dark, tangled beard, flecked with bronze and silver, shook as he straightened. "I hear that I have you to thank for returning my property from those Void-damned Fjujan devils!"

Thaun braced himself, dragging the same brittle smile back into place. "Governor Strahl."

"Please, call me Dasimir." Nearby crockery all but rattled at his voice. "I'm sure the whole Court resonates with your heroics."

Thaun kept his voice low in the vain hope that the Governor might follow his lead. "You should probably thank the Second. I didn't really do anything."

"Nonsense, Your Highness. Your presence alone must've driven the legion to new heights! What else could they do when accompanied by such an acclaimed duelist?"

"I don't think I drew my sword. I definitely didn't see any actual combat."

"You may not have drawn steel, but such modesty cannot deny your contributions."

"Thanks," he managed. Thaun looked around, desperate to escape from Strahl's attention. Nothing presented itself. Lesser nobles lingered, close enough to eavesdrop and to be seen. Lena remained a pace behind him, while Sigren stood further away, sharing curt words with another Shadow. Occasionally the mob of guests parted, and he caught a glimpse of Toland laughing, now with his own ring of sycophants that Thaun was occupied with. He saw no sign of Heizl.

Struggling for something to say, and keen to not offend, Thaun pulled at wisps of polite conversation. "Kragiv-Stal is beautiful at this time of year."

"Your Highness is too kind." Dasimir looked as if he'd place an arm around Thaun's shoulders, but at a harsh glance from Lena he thought better of it. Instead, he gestured with one hand, and guided Thaun to walk alongside him. Other guests moved out of their way. "My fair province pales in comparison with my daughters' charms. I do hope that you'll spend some time with my Jilia while we are in your most majestic city. Have you seen her since we arrived?"

"Jilia? No, we haven't spoken recently," he felt an awkward knot form in his gut at the Governor's subtext.

"A pity. I learned that she sends letters to the capital regularly, though the girl thinks she can hide it. I'd hoped that they might find their way here, to the Palace?"

Thaun held back a grimace. "I don't know anything about that, I'm afraid. We haven't talked since she came here for schooling."

"A great pity," he repeated as the enthusiasm in his tone dwindled. "It was my hope that she'd contacted you, perhaps to arrange a meeting..." The Governor trailed off, the strength leaving his voice. "Jilia does as much for

Kragiv-Stal as I do. I'd left her to her own desires out of the faith that she would make good choices. In light of this, perhaps I shall investigate who she writes to."

Realising that Strahl had forgotten about him, at least for the moment, Thaun clamped his mouth shut. He'd not seen the Governor's daughter in years, not since she'd spent a summer at the Palace. His uncle and her father had claimed that the tutors were better here, but anyone could see through their excuses.

The Empire's governors were a loyal enough bunch, but bonds could always be stronger. Even the closest of friends would act in self-interest under the right circumstances. Reminding their supporters of the potential rewards for their fealty could only be a good thing.

Thaun knew all this. His uncle's disappointment had hurt, even as hope had kindled for so many noble parents with unwed daughters. Behind closed doors, the Emperor had spoken with his Governor at length. For a time, fears of quarrels with the highland region of Kragiv-Stal had circulated among the Court.

Many had expected the Emperor to force the issue on his heir. Any other ruler might have. To this day, Thaun didn't know why his uncle hadn't. He'd wondered, as had much of the Court. Familial respect, pragmatic politics, even crude spite. None of those potential answers satisfied him.

He knew one thing though. Jilia was beautiful, smart, and funny. More than a few people thought him a fool for not doing anything. Sometimes he agreed with them – but that didn't change anything. As soon as Heizl had expressed an interest in the other woman, Thaun had backed off. Even with the disapproval of Spire, Court, and Church, he wouldn't do that to his cousin. A pariah in more ways than one, she had enough to deal with without him getting in the way.

He could understand his thoughts of potential betrayal towards Heizl. People navigated such interactions – weighing up personal gain against that of those they cared for – all the time. If it came to it, he could explain it to someone else, though he didn't relish the idea. More than that though, he could neither shake the feeling of betrayal, nor justify it, when his mind wandered to that missing shape of a memory.

How else could you describe it but as ridiculous? Loyalty to someone he couldn't describe. Staying faithful to someone he couldn't name. Faithful to someone who might not even exist.

A subtle tap upon his shoulder shook Thaun from his thoughts. Recoiling away, he composed himself as he saw Lena standing beside him. Following her gesture, he looked across the hall, past Dasimir. The governor had kept speaking, but even he'd noticed the room's tone change.

Guardsmen, resplendent in their blue uniforms, straightened to attention. Men and women ran hands through their hair or adjusted their clothes. A space formed around the hall's main entrance as members of the Royal Guard took up position to either side. Music quieted as an impatient hush fell upon the room.

His hand, never having quite uncurled, clenched tight into a fist. A second later, and Thaun hissed with pain.

He looked down, seeing blood welling in four short cuts in the palm of his hand, a perfect match to his nails. Fingers refused to straighten fully, his tendons drawn as tight as bowstrings.

"What's–" Lena whispered, cutting herself off as she saw the trickle of red running to fill the lines of his hand. "You're hurt. What happened?"

"It's nothing," Thaun mumbled back, snapping his fist closed again. "Don't worry about it."

"Thaun, you're *bleeding*."

"It was just my nails. It's fine. I should've just cut them better."

"What's wrong?" Sigren appeared alongside them as if he'd always stood there.

As she took Thaun's hand in hers, Lena cast an eye between them. "He's hurt himself."

"Great," said the Shadow, voice flat.

"It's only minor. I can heal it."

"Just because you can, doesn't mean you should." He grabbed her by the wrist, for a second joining the three of them in close.

Thaun cleared his throat, holding himself back from trying to break Lena's grip. "You don't have to worry about me."

"I'm not worrying, sir, about you or otherwise," Sigren growled. "Respectfully, I'm not here for you. I'm here for Lena. If she heals you, no matter how small, she might not have the essence to heal someone when she really needs to."

"Sigren, respectfully," Lena said back, voice level and calm, but with a firmness behind it. "It's not your decision."

"You know the risks."

"I do," she replied, pulling free a small notebook and flicking through its pages. "And I can do the numbers too."

"What if you overdo it?"

"Unlikely. It's not like I'm without a focus," releasing Thaun's hand with her other, she patted the silver-inlaid axe hanging from her belt. "Chances of collateral damage are pretty slim."

Sigren didn't say anything, though he visibly clenched his jaw, temples bunching. Lena too stayed quiet, sliding the pad back into a pocket and pulling her axe out.

As she took hold of Thaun's hand in hers, she closed her eyes, and he could feel her magic work.

She'd healed him a handful of times before. The Empire had a few healers, but none of them could compete with Lena's family, or so he'd heard. Her grandmother had sat on the Spire's council as a Highmage for years. Most mages struggled to do more than seal a bruise, their talents lying in more overt schools. In spite of all that, the sensation still amazed him.

A gentle warmth flowed from her into him, enveloping his arm up to his elbow. Strength burgeoned from somewhere within, vitality flooding his flesh. Like a tear in reverse, skin stretched as it knitted itself back together.

"Thanks, Lena," Thaun murmured, inspecting his hand. Drying blood flaked away from fresh, soft skin. He straightened his fingers, the tightness now a distant memory.

"Don't worry about it," she said, sliding her axe back into its loop, her face losing a hint of colour, though she didn't waver. "I'm a Spire legacy. There're enough similarities between my circling vultures and yours. I know what it's like showing weakness."

"Nice to know I'm not the only one they salivate over."

"At least yours aren't likely to try and get you tried as a radical if you don't smile at them the right way."

Caught up with his friends, Thaun had pushed the room's swelling anticipation to the back of his mind. The blast of several horns brought him back to the present. He turned back towards the tall doors furthest from the Throne's dais.

More guardsmen appeared from the corridor beyond to form a line to either side. In unison, the azure soldiers faced inwards, their gauntlets rising to shields in salute.

Thaun shifted his weight from one foot to the other, wiping sweaty palms clean on his blue doublet. Only one man warranted such an escort, and they all knew it.

Two men and a woman entered, and the surrounding voices fell silent. Half a dozen Shadows, dressed in dark hues and bearing their clenched-star sigil, preceded them, fanning out to move deeper into the room. Another trio of Royal Guardsmen brought up the rear. The Emperor took no risks with his family's safety.

Most expected a charismatic or calculating figure when picturing their ruler. Thaun's uncle couldn't be described as either of these things. Even with every eye on him, he seemed to blend in with the crowd – his clothes a subdued set of greens and blues, and his gait nondescript. Outside of the Court, few would link this average looking man to the regal profile on their coins, even with the simple crown upon his brow.

Behind the Emperor, Thaun recognised the Imperial Shadowmaster, Frida, in her black dress. A younger man trailed his uncle, wearing plain white clothes that didn't quite disguise his weight, and elbow-length silk gloves. The faint smell of herbs, like overdone cooking or a cutter's ointment, filled his nostrils. Shadows, already deep within the room, cut through the crowd on either side, matching pace with the man like predators stalking prey.

The Emperor, Rufenrich – the first of his name – walked in a straight line towards his golden throne. He acknowledged a handful of those he passed, a subtle nod or a quiet word, but otherwise ignored the attention upon him. As he reached the bottom of the stone steps, his eyes – the same brown as Thaun's – turned to his nephew, and a weary smile formed beneath his thin beard.

He stepped onto the dais, circled the table, and clasped Thaun's hands before pulling him into a close embrace. Their guests resumed their murmuring again as he leant in to whisper in his ear.

"You're supposed to meet me halfway when I enter," said the Emperor.

"Sorry," Thaun mumbled, breaking free of the hug.

"Well, at least you're talking to me now," he looked him up and down. "You looked like you might hit me last time."

Shuffling his feet, he looked away. "Sorry, uncle."

"You don't have to be sorry," Rufenrich sighed as he lay a reassuring hand on his shoulder. "We'll talk about it later."

Thaun averted his gaze. At the edge of his vision, Lena and Sigren stood at rigid attention.

His uncle continued. "In fact, there's a lot we should talk about... But none of that matters right now. How'd it go without me?"

"I survived."

"How many of them tried to corner you?" Noticing Dasimir nearby, Rufenrich smiled, then turned away – no invitation offered.

"A couple," he finally looked his uncle in the eye. "Honestly, I might've spent most of the night hiding in a corner. Not that it helped much."

"You can't hide forever, my boy," the Emperor smiled, lines forming around his eyes. "Your father was the same." A tinge of sadness crossed his features. "You remind me of him more and more."

"Thanks..."

"Looking like that doesn't help." He reached out to run a hand through his nephew's cropped hair, but Thaun flinched out of reach. "Someone suggested it to him too, to help craft the 'warrior-prince' image."

"It helps keep you cool when you wear a helmet..."

"I wouldn't know – I haven't worn one in years – but I'll take your word for it. You'll have to work out how you'll cut it when you wear a crown someday."

"Do you have to remind me?"

"Yes, I do, but that'll wait until later too. For now, this is your party, you should be having fun."

"Uncle, you know I don't want to be here."

The Emperor spoke under his breath. "If I'm honest, there are places I'd rather be too... but I'm not going to be in charge forever, and you've put off getting involved for long enough."

"I know. You've told me before."

"At least pretend you're enjoying yourself?" He cocked his head. "It'll all go much more quickly if you do. You'll have fewer awkward questions to answer, too."

"Fine," said Thaun, defeated. "What do I do?"

"Smile," said the older man. "Mingle with your guests." He raised his voice, until others could hear him too. "I wanted you to meet one in particular, someone I invited especially."

"Is this another political marriage? Do we have to do this now, in front of everyone?"

Head tilted back, Rufenrich burst out laughing. "My boy, I'm fairly sure that he's not your type."

Thaun felt his face heat as he blushed.

"I've invited the Thala's Patriarch. Renyar's running late, but he'll be here soon."

"That's a long way to come for some wine. What've you called him for?"

"It's not so far, with Hastigr's improvements to the Nexus." He shook his head. "Besides, Renyar is capable in his own right. He's told me about his efforts at building his own Nexus. The mages there make the Spire look like they struggle with parlour tricks."

"He's here for you to steal some mages from him? Are we really that desperate?"

"The Spire isn't in such dire condition just yet, even compared to Seorsa. No he's..." for a second, his eyes grew distant and his brow furrowed as he struggled for words. "Well, dangerous, frankly, but fascinating, and, depending on how things go, he might be a valuable ally."

"Depending on how *what* goes?"

"I have a proposition for him, but we can talk after. Heizl too. Have you seen her?"

"Earlier, yes. She said she was only here as security."

At his nephew's expression the Emperor raised a hand to cut him off. "No, don't start this again. Her ambitions make the Court nervous. When you're strong enough to deal with their bickering and her drive like I've done, then we can have this conversation. Until then, this lets her attend without complicating matters."

Frida appeared at the Emperor's side, a light hand resting on his arm to draw his attention. Unlike her subordinates, the Shadowmaster wore a modest black dress, eschewing a formal uniform. "Rufenrich?" Her sharp, hard voice cut through Thaun like nails on a chalkboard as she addressed him. "Sorry to interrupt, Your Highness." Without waiting for a response, she turned back. "Governor Strahl is anxious for an audience. He's heard rumours of Seorsa's recent movements. It might be prudent to speak with him." She glanced towards Thaun. "Perhaps you should discuss arrangements."

"You're probably right." His uncle smiled at the woman, his eyes lingering before looking back to Thaun. "Try to enjoy yourself?"

A wry smile seeped into his features. "I'm not making any promises."

"Well, that sounds more like you." Rufenrich shrugged. "I'm serious though. Joining the Court doesn't have to be a chore. Have some fun, even if that means spending time with just your friends," he glanced over the Thaun's attendants – Shadow and Spire mage both – before turning away. "And, if you see Heizl again, tell her I want to talk with her later, too."

He sighed. "I will."

"Good. It shouldn't have been that hard to make you enjoy yourself." He clapped him on the shoulder and began to walk away.

"I meant I'd tell Heizl..."

"I know." He smirked over one shoulder. "I'm just having a little fun, like you should."

Thaun snorted in frustration as he watched his uncle walk away, Shadowmaster at his side. The last person with the Emperor, man in white, paused. Dawning recognition – the bald scalp, the burn scars, the expensive gloves with multiple jewelled rings on the outside – rushed through Thaun's mind as he saw the glowing smile. Out of sight behind him, both Sigren and Lena straightened at the man's approach.

"Your Highness," like smoke twisting in the summer air, his thin lips curled into a dry smile. "Please give my warmest regards to your cousin."

"It's... Korten, right? Highmage? Shouldn't you have some Shadows with you?"

"They're around." He nodded distractedly as his eyes wandered to the half-full table. "Could you send Heizl my condolences? Fitz didn't keep it a secret how much she burned for–"

"Don't call her that." Stone dropped into his voice. The heads of several of those closest whipped around at the tone.

Korten blinked several times before responding. "Sorry, no offence meant. I was just saying that everyone knows she's got aspirations. She's a decent mage, if an unorthodox one. I guess she just wasn't ready for a promotion."

Thaun clenched his teeth and forced his fists open. A quiet, seething voice mocked his restraint – that he wouldn't strike a mage just for what he *might* do in return. Another voice, no less his own, asked if it was the mage's power he feared, or the expectations laid on him.

He swallowed those thoughts. "It's fine. I'll let her know you asked after her." He broke eye contact. "Aren't you meant to be guarding Uncle Rufenrich?"

"There are enough other mages and Shadows here. It's not like I've had to actually worry about security while on duty. I'm just here for the free meal. This food is so much better than at the Spire."

"I think you might be a little late for dinner."

"Shouldn't worry; there are plenty of servants around. I'll light a fire under one of them, get them to cook something up." Korten looked around, his gaze following a tray of steaming sweetmeats as it crossed the room before he whipped back around to face Thaun. "Your Grace, may I be excused?"

"May you... That's fine," Thaun shrugged, struggling for something to say. "Enjoy yourself?"

"The servers and I will get on like a house on fire." The mage smiled, gave the most cursory of bows, and disappeared in the direction of the nearest servant. Thaun watched as the younger man cornered one, talking through mouthfuls as he described his needs to the staff.

As Thaun stepped away from the crowd, a blunt jolt of pain lanced through his foot. He barely stumbled – years of blade drills made sure of that – but the shock still left him blinking.

Taking half a step away from the centre of the room, an unyielding pain struck his foot, lancing up his shin. Years of repetitive footwork, blade in hand, served Thaun well as he steadied himself.

He glanced down, uncaring for the scuff upon his soft shoe's toe. Inside their supple leather, he curled his stubbed toes, feeling the pain reside to a background ache. Instead, jaw bunching, his gaze settled upon the hall's stone floor.

One of its square stones protruded a fraction of an inch. Since its construction generations before, the Palace had experienced countless repairs, extensions, and additions. Scars remained upon the masonry, stark reminders of the Civil War. Lying so close to the river, subsidence wasn't unheard of either.

Still, someone should've noticed sooner. The slightest sign of imperfection could plant seeds of doubt in the minds of ambitious nobles and opportunistic guests.

Looking around, no one seemed to have noticed his stumble, not even Lena and Sigren, standing close but facing the crowd. He started to crouch down, to look more closely.

"Can you believe it? Korten gets invited and I'm the bastard." Heizl's voice whispered in his ear – smug, amused, and full of food. He whipped a glance around, flagstone forgotten, expecting to see his cousin mere inches from his side, but found no one there. "Relax, you're going to make a scene. I'm over with the rest of your oh-so-important guests."

"Can you hear me?" Thaun muttered under his breath as he sought the disembodied voice.

"Well enough." Her smug grin came through loud and clear, even without her in front of him. "Having fun over there?"

"I'd rather be training," he drawled. "This is about as much fun as being hit with a practice sword."

"How would you know? It's not like anyone would lay a finger on you," she said, apparently around a mouthful of something.

"You know what I mean," Thaun sighed, drawing a quizzical look from Sigren. "What are you doing here?"

"I've been enjoying the company of a charming Seorsan. Such an interesting language to wrap your tongue around…"

"Should you be flirting right now? You'll get in trouble if anyone notices."

"Oh, you're no fun when you get like this. Don't be such a prude." Over the crowd, Thaun thought he heard a feminine giggle. "So, ready to get out of here?"

"With all these eyes on me? I don't think that's likely."

"Shows what you know."

Lena's hand resting on his shoulder made Thaun look up. "Are you okay? You're mumbling to yourself. People might talk."

He shook his head. "I'm fine."

"You're sure?" The healer's eyes narrowed as she inspected him.

"Certain." Thaun's own eyes grew wide as he tried to reassure his friend. He gestured to the nearby guests as they began gathering to approach him once more. "I just need a little space. Can you stall them?"

"If it'll help," replied Lena. "Sigren?" With the Shadow only objecting for a moment, the pair exchanged quiet words. A second later, and they both moved a short distance away, each heading to intercept a different petitioner.

Thaun watched for a moment, a knot of guilt forming in his stomach at the lie he'd just told his friends.

"Pretty slick," Heizl's voice whispered to him again. "Are you sure you're not up to Court life?"

"Everybody lies, okay?" He growled. "What did you have in mind?"

"Well, now that you've so effortlessly removed your watchers, I'm guessing you probably want to get away from all this attention?"

"If only..."

"Easy enough, so long as you don't mind me borrowing some of it for a while?"

Thaun paused, his brows furrowing. "I don't understand."

"With all the time you spend playing with your sword, I'd've thought you'd work it out. Most people can only focus one way at a time. Doesn't matter if it's in a training yard or this nest of vipers."

"Is that such a good idea?"

"It'll be for a few minutes, tops. I've eaten already, so what else is there to hang around for? It's not like I need to hold back for anything else tonight. My natural charm seems to be more useful than my magic right now."

"...Fine, what do I do?"

Tooth and Nail – Chapter Three

> *"The Imperial fears their greatest weapon. They shun and neglect those burdened with the divine spark, shackling them to thieves and murderers in the name of safety. Ignorant merchants lead their people, blind to the world. How they have found success, beneath duplicitous gods and disarmed amongst foreign realms, remains a mystery."*
>
> Jalor's first letter,
Jalor of Thala (398 I.Y.)

23rd day of Indern, 406th Imperial Year
17th Year of Emperor Rufenrich Konreig's Reign

Heizl smiled, one corner of her mouth twisting upwards as she watched the room's currents. Drunken lordlings slurred and laughed at one another's arrogant boasts and simple-minded jokes. Servants forced blank expressions upon their faces as they wove between the boisterous young men. Such ignorant youth would someday make up the Imperial Court. The mage's smirk faded. Those boys would be recognised a hundred times over before her.

Older nobles, tempered by experience, spoke in twos and threes. With rare exception, they held cups of strong wine, but few did more than wet their lips, hiding their sobriety from rivals and friends alike. Heizl strained her hearing towards the nearest group, struggling to pick up on the subject of their conversation. Trade, territory, and politics, no doubt. Foreign representatives

– Seorsan, Thalan, even the odd Tszerrichan – approached such groups with their petitions. It'd be a simple thing to reach out and twist their emotions, though Heizl saw no reason to waste her strength upon them.

Standing at the centre of a ring of his subjects, Thaun stood alone at the room's edge, his back towards the golden throne. Heizl watched as some of the nobles pursued the Emperor, leaving a handful to vie for her cousin's reluctant attention.

Frida trailed behind their uncle, interacting little with the swarming nobility. Upon the floor, Korten devoured any food that came within reach. Heizl recognised several individuals of note – Toland and Dasimir Strahl, among others – as they mingled. Under normal circumstances, such individuals would've drawn their own lines of admirers, but the guests had only one goal in mind tonight.

Copper rod in one hand, the arcane focus they all expected her to carry, she absentmindedly waved away an approaching servant with the other. Heizl dipped inside her own mind, before reaching out. Something, like a bright light at the corner of her vision, pulled at her. She'd first noticed it weeks before, and at the time it had fascinated her. The way it drew in all around it, souls' strands flickering as if in a current, mesmerised her. Though she made no habit of spending time with her colleagues at the Spire, those that she'd crossed paths with seemed ignorant of the phenomena. She should've asked her mentor about it.

Heizl shook her head. She could afford to get distracted later.

The thread between her and Thaun remained strong as ever, still ringing with her recent communication. Those closest, as well as the handful of Shadows scattered throughout the room, spared the mage a cautious thought, but few others looked her way. Even Zecht felt preoccupied by the extravagant sights before them.

Compared to the meagre handful of strands linked to her, the multitude that stretched towards her cousin challenged her senses. Heizl gave the most cursory of inspections to Thaun's tangle of strings – the interwoven professionalism and friendship of Lena and Sigren, and the sharp wires that extended out from Frida – before settling in close to the soul upon which they met.

"Ready?" She sent the message running down their shared thread, its silvery length humming with the sound.

"I think so," Thaun whispered back, though the words came through as clear as if he sat alongside her.

"You won't have long. Where do you wanna meet?"

"I don't know. Somewhere in the garden?"

"I never knew you enjoyed stargazing, even with the Comet due. I'll find you."

"Are you *really* sure about this?"

The length of the hall away, Heizl smiled. "What's the worst that could happen?"

"You get another Shadow assigned?"

"And you'll just get a slap on the wrist. So, when I tell you, move quickly, alright?"

"I don't know..." Uncertainty hung from Thaun's whisper. "Maybe I should just stay here and put up with all this."

"Oh, come on!" Heizl snorted. "You're not enjoying yourself here, and I can have fun wherever we go."

"But what if you hurt someone? Or you exhaust yourself?"

"What else am I going to do with myself tonight? It's only a little taxing, and it means we can catch up properly. I'll sleep in and eat well tomorrow, and I'll be fine."

"You might be right..."

"Of course I am." Heizl took a deep breath. "Now, stop arguing, and hold on."

As she ran arcane fingers over Thaun's branching strings, each thread sang at her touch. For a second, she wondered if musicians felt like this, their every caress altering the minds of those around them. Casting the thought aside, she moved along the strands and glanced at her cousin's soul. They met in a single knot, a hundred channels funnelling into one tangled mess of intrigue.

As if crouching to inspect them, Heizl leant in. Reaching past the incandescence, more details grew clear. Ambitions, envy, and lust – every primal, human instinct flowed like driftwood down a river. Like such a stream, they moved in one direction, each gravitating towards Thaun with rare exception.

She pulled on the mass of bright strands, their fibres growing taut like thread on a spinning wheel, and a handful of the more sober individuals around her changed, their moods drawing close to the surface. Easing in as close as she dared, her own writhing emotions a meagre reflection of those before her, she gripped the knot. At the contact, the sensations before her pulsed and grew. Every primal urge washed over her, threatening to consume her identity, even rising to overwhelm her sense of self.

Muscles – crude, mundane matter – tensed as she suppressed a growl and gritted her teeth. With a wrenching motion, she tightened her grip. For a brief second, a handful of souls, Sigren and Lena among them, resisted. She tugged, and they too came free.

Sliding into place among them, her own threads weaving over and under those that had reached towards Thaun, Heizl forced tranquillity upon herself. One by one, she found strands that she held in common with her cousin. Pulling them closer, slender tendrils reached out from her being, stubborn will wrestling the stolen knot like a thief ambushing their victim.

The room's tone changed once more, emotions coming under control and conversation returning to normal.

Blood pounded in her ears as she kept the tangled minds bound to her. The mage's muscles strained, a crude reflection of the arcane forces upon her.

"Get on with it," she whispered through clenched teeth, unsure if Thaun had heard her.

Had anyone looked then, they might have seen her skin pale, her breathing quicken, or her shoulders tremble. If not for the veil of hair and her raised collar, they might've noticed the patch of dry, grey skin upon her neck spread. Instead, those closest – including a pretty Seorsan woman who'd proven open to Heizl's advances despite rising political tensions – only cared for their own business. Such self-centeredness didn't last.

Heizl opened one eye just as admiring faces started turning her way. Powerful nobles and ambitious individuals faced her, eager humanity flowing towards her like the turning tide. Even Toland, the centre of his table's attention, stole furtive glances her way. She closed her eyes again.

In her ethereal grip, their attention squirmed and bucked as they resisted her unnatural hold. Her face twisted into a scowl, a trickle of sweat beading upon pale skin.

As she released an anxious breath, she relinquished the room's attention. Chin dipping onto her chest, Heizl took several deep lungfuls of sweet air. She slipped back to her body, the taut aches of physical exhaustion setting in. The sensation of blood rushing through her veins returned to her, and bright hues swirled before her eyes.

Looking up, she blinked several times, before focusing on the man looming over her.

"You're not..." Dasimir frowned down at her, untamed brows furrowed. He flicked his gaze to those nearest before returning to Heizl. "Did you do something to me, girl?"

Heizl hid a yawn behind a raised hand and scratched at the back of her neck. "I didn't do anything, governor."

Rage smouldered in his eyes. "What did you do?"

"I'm hoping–" She stood, steadying herself on the wooden table. "–that I made a good impression." Heizl held out a hand, smiling.

"It takes more than a firm hand and a grin to impress me, Fitz."

Even drained, Heizl's features didn't betray her emotions. With a sneer, Dasimir turned his broad back and made to walk away. The mage's whisper snuck out louder than she'd meant. "It impresses your daughter just fine."

Spinning, the governor seized a handful of her shirt front, bodily pulling her away from the table. A low growl escaped his throat. "If I ever find out you've gone near Jilia again, I'll kill you myself, Shadows be damned."

"Governor?" Heizl held his wrist, but Dasimir's grip only tightened. "You're making a scene."

"Every man, woman, and child here would thank me for putting down a bastard mage like you."

"Maybe." she cleared her throat and lowered her voice. "But a member of the Royal Family just disappeared. No, don't look around. How do you think it'd look if, at the same time, you're seen pummeling his cousin?"

"I–" Dasimir started, his hold weakening.

"Didn't think it through? I can tell. Jilia would've, I think." For all her weariness – affecting so many at once took its toll – a smile still crept back across her face. "Governor? May I make a suggestion?"

"I swear, girl, someday–"

"Just clap me on the shoulder, smile, and walk away. Your career – Voids damn it – your legacy will thank you for it."

For a moment, Dasimir readjusted his grip as he considered. Eventually, he took a deep breath and released her. Heizl nearly collapsed as her weight settled back onto her own feet. The governor took her hand in a surprisingly deft motion, and planted a gentle kiss upon her knuckles. A wolfish smile curled behind his beard.

"I look forward to seeing you again soon, *Your Highness.*"

"Until next time," Heizl flashed her own humourless grin, and watched as Dasimir walked away, the crowd parting around him. She'd have avoided him herself, if she could.

Still weary, she braced a hand on the table to steady herself. The moment of weakness passed, and she straightened.

Around her, Heizl listened to the crowd's rising mob mentality. Not the shift in attention that her sorcerous meddling had caused, but a swelling unease, as of waters rising around a monstrous benthos before it breached the surface. By now, people's thoughts would be returning to their normal paths. Drunk or not, they'd soon suspect someone had manipulated them.

Heizl edged through those gathered close around her, and made for the glass doors leading from the hall. Halfway there, murmurs of confusion rose as she caught movement across the room. The Shadowmaster whispered something into Rufenrich's ear. Shocked expressions crossed their faces before both set their jaws in stony resolve.

Shadows left their posts, responding to Frida's subtle hand gestures. Heizl watched as Zecht joined them from his own hiding spot. Each of the men, trained to protect mage from Imperials and Empire from mage, moved unseen among the Court. Only someone of the Spire, used to their ways, might notice their change of behaviour. Others stood a better chance of spotting Lena as she, accompanied by Sigren, peeled away to seek Thaun less inconspicuously.

Heizl kept walking, smiling at a Royal Guardsman and gesturing to her copper focus. Others would soon realise that the Crown Prince had disappeared, and then security would swarm beyond the actions of a few Shadows. For now, as she stepped into the balmy evening, regret stirred – but only briefly. There were worse crimes than kindness.

Behind her, the hall's sounds changed. The subtle murmur of low conversation and distant music replaced the drunken revelry's drone. No one out here missed Thaun's presence yet. If it stayed that way, she might still salvage the evening.

Heizl waved, and a servant bearing several bottles changed direction towards her. Relieving the man of two, she looked around. Younger guests sat in small groups upon the terrace. Lanterns, their crystal imported from Seorsa before the island nation had closed its ports, cast faint shadows. Couples, out from under the watchful eyes of chaperones, shared quiet words beneath an amber sky.

The mage smiled. If she hadn't agreed to help her cousin, she might've done the same. Instead, she looked beyond the stone terrace, where immaculate lawns, pruned hedgerows, and bright flowers opened out into the Royal Gardens.

A hundred paces distant, the Palace's outer wall loomed over all but the tallest manicured tree. She didn't remember the Civil War, when her family had fled their Capital, but its scars lingered. Invisible in the dying light, patches of the ramparts still bore gouges. Engineers had replaced several lengths after they'd become unstable from repeated assault by loyalist battalions and siege weaponry, but signs of their work remained.

Above the walls, the first of the night's stars bloomed against the dying light. A blanket of grey clouds whispered in from the south, smothering them one by one. Through the rolling shapes, a gap formed, revealing the lights behind it. Though she saw a few flickers of constellations, something else distracted her.

A few weeks before, nobles had attended countless gatherings to watch the Comet. Heizl had even attended a couple herself, not that she'd spent much time stargazing. The rich and privileged had turned the whole phenomenon into another excuse to dance and drink. She rarely had difficulty entering such events, but she'd rarely felt truly welcome in such company.

The Comet had other groups' attention too. Scholars across the Empire pointed telescopes skywards to track its trajectory, predicting when it would next return. Mages plied their magicks, exploring the celestial body's effects upon the arcanosphere. Priests of all faiths consulted texts and meditated in prayer, seeking some omen or sign in its passage.

Heizl herself didn't care in quite the same way as everyone else. Sure, she appreciated a good light show as much as anyone, but she'd found something else of value in the Comet's appearance. With most of her colleagues at the Spire obsessing over the Comet's passage, she was bound to find an opportunity to impress the Highmages with something more practical. Already, without their distractions, magic felt easier, like running downhill.

She hesitated, the air thick with the unseen swirls of sorcery. More than just the usual hum of background magic she'd grown accustomed to, or even the aftereffects of her own machinations. Alone outside, without Zecht to guard her back, Heizl raised her copper focus in a clumsy, one-handed, grip.

As a dry, acrid smell touched her senses, she recognised its source. The familiar voice that followed – deep and gravelly – only partly reassured her. "I thought I might find you here."

Heizl breathed a little easier as she took in the man stepping from dissipating darkness a short distance away. In a baggy, ill-fitting robe, he leant upon a silver-tipped cane, hands lost within deep sleeves. The scent of mothballs filled the air.

"Hastigr." She lowered her makeshift club. "You were quick. Keeping an eye on me?"

"Hardly." The old mage grunted a derisive laugh. "You interrupted my meditations. Sheltz's Comet has visited before, and will again, but it should not be ignored. Opportunities to study such distortions aren't common." He straightened slightly. "Mere coincidence that I quested in this direction when I sensed your activities. Had I known it was your usual irresponsible antics, I might not have responded so quickly."

"Oh." Heizl shuffled her feet. "You didn't know I was here?"

"Still such a fragile ego?" Hastigr smirked and turned to look out across the terrace to the shadowy undergrowth beyond. "I knew you were here, Heizl. I couldn't have arrived so quickly if you hadn't been."

"Huh?" She followed his gaze, but saw nothing new. "I don't understand."

"You will. But not tonight."

"Voids, I'd forgotten how annoying you are. Shouldn't you be working? Or bothering someone else? I'm not exactly your student anymore."

He smiled, staring outwards at nothing in particular. "The bond between a master and apprentice is not so easily discarded."

"Seriously though. Won't someone notice if the Nexus isn't running?"

"Hmm? Oh, there are no more appointments tonight. Besides, I anchored a glamour there for my Shadows. It helps when they feel that their contribution is a necessary one."

"And how do I know this isn't some illusion? You've done it to me before." Not entirely paying attention to him, Heizl glanced back over one shoulder. No one else on the terrace looked in their direction. Despite their cultural fear of magic, few Imperials could resist gawking when witnessing a mage at work. At the sight of a Highmage appearing among them, stares should've turned their way, but she'd long grown used to strange reactions to Hastigr's presence.

"I take my duties very seriously, thank you." From anyone else, the tone might've hinted at humour.

"So, now what? Going to tell me off for sneaking out? Send me back to my Shadow?"

His voice dropped to a murmur. "I can't imagine it took much to slip away from him."

"Oh yeah? And why's that?"

"He didn't sign up expecting to be paired with you. I suspect his attention was already elsewhere."

"What's that supposed to mean?"

"Just that you're not the only one with family loyalties, Heizl. He, too, would rather spend his time with kin than working."

Heizl kept her mind from straying. She didn't know what thoughts the Highmage might sense from her. Even the gentlest probe towards her would likely notice the control she now exerted, but she'd rather that than the alternative. Secrets, once loose, didn't return easily to their hiding places. Even edging close to those that she held dearest like she did now – about a brother, a parent, and a promise – presented an uncomfortable level of risk.

With some effort, she returned to the subject at hand. "You're sure? I don't remember Zecht saying anything about his family."

"A sister, specifically. She learns within the Spire." Hunched neck straightening and weight upon his cane, Hastigr turned his gaze skywards to stare up at the stars. "Well-behaved, and mildly promising. When your Shadow was fortunate enough to find a patron to fund his commission, I suspect he'd envisioned a partner that he shared kinship with. Not you."

Narrowing her eyes upon him, she stayed quiet. Mages weren't so different from the Courts. The weak gravitated towards the powerful in the hope of recognition and advancement. Men and women sought greater responsibilities in the hope of gaining greater importance.

Few flocked to the man beside her though. Even Korten, insufferable and brash, had more petitioners than Hastigr. She'd heard the whispers, of course. Dwindling sanity, strange appearances, and unfounded claims. Only the most desperate wouldn't have their doubts when approaching the elderly Highmage.

Still, the Emperor tolerated him. More than just tolerated, in fact. The Empire didn't have another mage like him. No one else could run the Nexus, not without a massive investment of personnel and stockpiled essence. Without it, they'd be forced to rely on the old methods of communication, with messages taking days to cross from one city to the next.

"You can ask me now," he said, startling Heizl from her thoughts.

"Ask you what?"

"How I travelled so quickly."

"I don't remember asking."

"You didn't." Hastigr eyed her sidelong, a faint smile rising. "But you were curious."

"I guess." She cocked her head. "Fine. How'd you get here?"

Satisfied at some small victory, his smile broadened. "There are paths and beacons beyond the Nexus, Heizl." He reached into the folds of his robe, jewellery gently chiming, before revealing a wrinkled hand with thumb and forefinger pressed tight together.

"Right, you magicked yourself here. I've seen you pull that trick before."

"Don't be impudent."

Heizl rolled her eyes, but half-closed them as she fell within herself and reached outwards. The Highmage blazed mere feet from her, a burning thread bridging the two of them. It glowed like a chain fresh from the forge, each link a different experience or bond. His soul swirled and danced, a handful of colours twisting together but never mixing.

Pushing aside his luminous form, Heizl dug deeper. Weariness grew, but she pressed on.

Living souls shone, their lights flickering and shifting as their emotions flared and changed. The inanimate proved more challenging. They cast no light of their own, instead forming dim shapes, poorly reflecting all that surrounded them. If not for the coruscating fire thrown outwards by Hastigr, she might not have sensed what he held.

"A hair? You got here by hair?"

"I came here by *your* hair." He chastised. "Pay attention. Find its threads."

"Because that's so easy," she drawled, but nonetheless fell more fully into the web before her.

Sorcerous senses focused upon the slender shape in his hand, a silhouette of flickering shadow against soullight. The hair faded in and out of her vision, reluctant to be spotted.

She understood what he wanted her to see only moments before running out of patience. Too small to catch the light, and casting none of its own, she'd have missed it under other circumstances. Beneath spectral fingertips, she felt the hair's own thread. Not the tangled web of a person, but the singular, gossamer-thin connection to where it had come. The bond linked it to her still.

As if from a great distance, she heard Hastigr's voice. "All things are connected."

"Fascinating, really." Blinking, she relinquished her arcane sight, eyes adjusting to the lamplight of the terrace once more. "I don't get why it's so important though."

"Some bonds are harder to see," Hastigr continued as if not having heard her. "Cause and effect. Chance. Time."

"Look, I'm getting a headache. If you wanted to show me this, you could've called for me at any time."

"'There's more you can do, when you learn," he said. "Watch."

"Unless this is going to–" She never finished her sentence. Though Heizl didn't see what the Highmage did, she felt its effects.

The breath caught in her lungs. Muscles strained against an unseen cage. Blood pounded in her ears as panic rose.

Alongside her, Hastigr stood still, eyes half-closed and fist clenched. At his wrist, silver charms trembled. The night air – already cool – chilled further.

As swift as control had left, it returned. Like a puppet with cut strings, Heizl sagged.

She glowered. "Really?"

"You'll appreciate it someday," he said.

"No apology?" she spat. "Do I get to be a jackass when I'm a Highmage?"

"You still desire that?"

She straightened. "Did you want something, Hastigr? Or have you just missed tormenting me in the name of education?"

"Like I said, this isn't all about your delicate ego." He stood, one hand still on the parapet to steady himself. "I should go."

"Just like that?"

"You should be glad, Heizl. In my absence, you'll have the freedom to weave whatever magicks you wish. I won't interfere tonight."

"Fine. Go." She turned towards the dark gardens beyond, hiding the hard expression growing upon her face.

She could almost hear his wry smile. "You've got potential, child. More than many. Don't squander your gifts."

Before she could speak, let alone turn towards her one-time mentor, Heizl felt a wave of pressure roll over her like air before a storm. A stale smell, like dry ash, filled the air. For a moment, a handful of the nobles out on the terrace glanced her way. Whether they saw a mage, a servant, or another guest, they soon returned to their own conversations, uninterested in whatever disturbance had caught their attention.

Heizl shook her head and glanced around, scratching at the back of her neck. She hadn't come out here to enjoy the view, nor to reunite with an old teacher. She thought of the last few times she'd visited the garden. A stray memory rose in her mind, and, in an instant, she knew where she'd find Thaun.

Her pilfered bottles in one hand and useless focus in the other, she strode across the terrace, avoiding the guests, and along a winding path. Gravel crunched beneath her soft shoes, rounded edges pressing through the thin soles to rub against her feet. Low borders of blooming plants and shrubs gave way to arching fruit trees that shivered in the breeze over her head.

Gravel and stone faded into verdant grass and shadows deepened all around her. Several twists and turns in, and statues loomed out from the undergrowth. Rulers, heroes, and dragonslayers the lot of them. Poor company for a bastard and a mage like her. Thin flowers hung from the crowns of many, and the soft scent of autumn roses filled the air.

The path opened out into a small square of manicured grass. A circular, stone bench surrounded a tall, well-pruned tree at the centre, while flowers grew within its shadow. As children, they'd used it for various games when away from supervising eyes – hide and seek, king of the hill, let's pretend – yet Heizl hadn't visited it in years. Nostalgia trickled inwards, but she pushed it aside as she looked to the two figures perched on opposite sides of the stone ring.

Thaun sat with elbows on knees and his chin in his hands. He stared unseeing into the middle distance, eyes glazed and unfocused. His face held a flat expression, as if a neutral look was better than how he truly felt. Heizl had seen the same bearing in him a dozen times, most often when her cousin's entourage had called for her to try and break Thaun out of another melancholic episode. Such expressions seemed less common of late, but she suspected that Thaun had simply grown better at hiding them.

A quarter turn around the circle, a breathtaking woman, a little younger than Heizl, perched with feet together and skirts wrapped around her legs. Upon seeing her, any thoughts of her cousin's depression left her. Auburn hair tumbled down the woman's back and over smooth shoulders in loose curls, hiding the gold and bronze trim of her green dress. She stared at an unseen point off to one side, her face as composed as the statues around them. The maiden couldn't have failed to see either of them. If she'd discussed anything with Thaun, their conversation had already died.

Weariness forgotten, the mage felt something primal rise inside her. She struggled to find words for the emotion that came with it. Confusion, despair, hope, desire – none of them accurately described the feelings welling up within her. Her mere sight drove barbs into Heizl's soul, but she couldn't bring herself to look away.

Had she opened her sorcery to see the tangle of bonds between the three there among the roses, she might have seen the mismatched feelings among each of them. She might have seen her cousin's regret, or the other woman's confused emotions. Heizl might've found shared childhood memories, or broken hearts.

Instead, she smiled.

Honeyed words had always rested well within Heizl's reach. Whether cutting or charming, she'd long borne the talent for them. Faced with the young lady before her, silence filled her mouth.

The woman looked up, recognition forming on her calm face. Wide eyes blinking rapidly, she smiled. "Hello, Heizl." Around the bench from her, Thaun faced the mage.

Heizl paused, staring back. Even in the dim light, the woman's blue-green eyes burned through her. Behind Heizl, the feasting and festivities continued unabated.

Her various intimate conquests flashed through her mind. Soldiers and entertainers. Nobles and commonfolk. She'd charmed each and every one of them. Sometimes several at once. It amazed her how a simple approach – just the right amount of confidence, a touch of flattery, or appealing to their seemingly universal desire for the forbidden – opened so many doors. Despite every experience behind her, she struggled to speak.

"Heizl?" the woman repeated.

She shook her head, before drawing out a smile to wear. "Jilia…" In three long strides she stood by her. Jilia proffered a porcelain-like hand, which, after a moment of hesitation, Heizl took and helped her to her feet.

"Didn't you read my letters? I said I'd be here," said Jilia.

"I've been away," she shook her head. "Spire business. I've not had much time for reading." Heizl looked away, unable to hold her gaze for long. "Sorry," she murmured, glancing at Thaun before shifting her attention back.

"It's fine. The Spire must be as complicated as the Courts. I know you can't always get away."

"I would if I could," she took a deep breath. "I'm not sure I was expecting to see you here."

"Heizl?" Thaun interrupted, rubbing at his face as he squinted at them. "Did anyone see us leave?"

She didn't take her eyes from Jilia as she turned towards her cousin. "No, but they'll all be looking for you by now."

"Are we going to be in trouble?"

"Probably a little." She shrugged, a smile growing as she looked at Jilia. "But it'll give the Court something to talk about."

"I believe they have a different subject in mind," the noblewoman smiled and eyed Thaun. A girl's voice at the back of Heizl's mind shouted to make Jilia look back her way, though she gritted her teeth and ignored its pleas.

"Probably the same they he always have," said Heizl. "Family, legacy, stability. That sort of thing."

"I guess." Thaun continued pacing.

Jilia cleared her throat, drawing their attention. "So, Thaun told me you were making a distraction so he could sneak out. What did you have in mind after your disappearing act?"

"I don't mind," said Thaun. "It's just nice to be somewhere less stifling."

"I've a suggestion." Heizl raised her stolen wine. "Thirsty?"

"We don't have any glasses," objected Jilia.

Heizl smiled. "I'm sure we'll survive." She handed one to her and raised the other to her lips. For a split second she felt Jilia's light touch as she took the drink from her. A bolt of lightning shot up her arm at the contact. She looked away.

She'd never quite known where she stood with Jilia. For every flaw that the Courts saw in Heizl, they found a virtue in the young woman. A noble heritage rather than her own questionable parentage; a traditionally feminine aristocrat while she ate, drank, and twisted souls. If not for spending several years together as small children, protected from the horrors of civil war while their houses battled together, she couldn't imagine them sharing much common ground.

It felt wrong to be grateful for a conflict that killed thousands. If not for the Kuhlner family's attempt to seize the Throne, then she might never have gained one of her most valued relationships. She just wished that her sorcery gave her the wisdom to understand just what that relationship was.

The three of them had spent months at a time together as youths, before the Spire had taken Heizl in. Lessons, Court functions, festivals, all of them at one another's sides. She hadn't realised at the time that it had all been a dance to arrange a betrothal between Jilia and Thaun. It had sent painful tremors through her own fledgeling feelings back then. She'd never found the courage to ask why it hadn't worked out.

"Should you be drinking?" asked Thaun. "Aren't you tired after... after whatever it was you did back there?"

She held up a hand, taking several more swallows before lowering the bottle and speaking. "It's nothing some good wine and better company won't fix. Don't worry about it."

"Sounds like an excuse to drink," Thaun held out an open hand. "But, in that case, I might as well join you."

Heizl took another swig then handed her cousin the bottle. She waited until Thaun lifted it to his mouth, keeping him quiet, before Heizl faced Jilia. "How long are you in Reiget City for?"

"As long as it takes for Father and the Emperor to fall out again. Or for them to find some compromise." She smiled as she ran an absentminded finger around the rim of the clay vessel. "He said it might take some time. I believe him."

Heizl stifled a grimace at the obvious implications of such meetings. "Well, it's nice to have you around again. How long has it been?"

"Since I was here in the gardens? Or since we were all without chaperones?" Mischief and nostalgia tugged at her eyes. "Probably when Father suggested marriage the last time."

"That reminds me," Thaun raised a hand, drawing their attention. "You two keep in touch by letters, right? I think the Governor thought you were writing to me." Heizl and Jilia glanced at each other. "He's going to look into it."

"What's so bad about that?" the noble asked with faux innocence. "They're just letters."

"He was pretty disappointed I hadn't spoken to you recently," Thaun ventured, glancing sidelong at his cousin. "I don't think he liked the idea of his daughter speaking to a…" He looked away.

"To what?" said Heizl. "A bastard? A woman?"

"I was going to say a mage." Thaun winced, averting his eyes.

"Oh. Well, he probably dislikes that too."

"Sorry about that," said Jilia. "He doesn't care much for the Spire."

"Not many do," Heizl sighed.

"You should have heard him when he went through the Nexus."

"Thaun's worse." She gestured towards him. "He threw up last time."

"I don't like travelling, alright?" Thaun threw up both hands, a drop of wine escaping the open bottle. "There's the smell, and I get all dizzy…"

A flash of light and a loud, cracking sound hid Heizl's response. The three of them turned towards the noise, eyes tracking upwards. Against the darkening sky, a second firework went off, burning a web-like pattern into their retinas.

Several more erupted against the cloudy backdrop in rapid succession. For that moment, their bright bursts drowned out the cerulean light of Sheltz's Comet. Beyond their peaceful circle of trees, other watchers clustered upon the terrace, faces tilted skywards.

More fireworks followed them into the air, launching from somewhere on the other side of the Palace. The Empire's citizens, down below in the sprawling city, looked up to see the coruscating colours. Mages watched from the gilded cages of the Spire, while Shadows – stalking targets from the rooftops, or training beyond the Capital's walls at their Forge – fled from the bursts of light.

"I've not seen fireworks recently," muttered Thaun to no one in particular.

"My father imported some from Daqin to celebrate defeating Fjujhost," said Jilia, distractedly. "That was months ago though. I don't think he's decided to use... them... yet..."

The sounds of guests swelled, their muted conversations picking up in excitement. Even the powerful and wealthy turned into children before a series of pretty lights.

Heizl looked away, eyeing Jilia instead. The noble remained staring skywards, the occasional flood of light illuminating the smooth lines of her face. A wondrous smile tugged at her full lips. For all the expenses involved in importing the scores of fireworks, she found herself unable to stop watching the woman at her side. She lost track of how long she stared at her.

A louder explosion cut through her, reverberating down to her bones. Heizl looked away from Jilia, and turned towards the display. No star-shaped clouds of smoke, no flash of light to accompany a larger rocket. She felt a pang of disappointment that she'd missed part of the show's finale.

Something tugged at her senses, and she felt the faint pull of her magic, like a dog pulling on its leash. Her two companions continued watching the fireworks, as she turned back and forth between them, searching for the subtle disturbance around her.

Another dozen heartbeats and she might have projected herself outwards, burning the wine in her belly to search for its source. Instead, over the vintage's heady sensation, a familiar, acrid, aroma joined the smell of blossom. Smoke.

On either side of her, Jilia and Thaun turned their gazes from the sky. As they glanced at each other, and Heizl opened her mouth to speak, a distant scream broke the night.

As one, the trio turned back towards the Great Hall, just as another flash of light washed over them. A shockwave followed, washing over both bastard and noble. More cries of alarm broke the growing night, interspersed by the unmistakable sounds of breaking glass.

Tooth and Nail – Chapter Four

"...it was perhaps Ulora's grand plan that the Daericani, a blight sent to punish us for our straying, should unite the people in alliance. That Conglomerate of roving bands and squabbling fiefdoms would one day give birth to the Urlanst Empire."

The Trade Guild's Guide to the Empire,
Filip Daylen (403 I.Y.)

23rd day of Indern, 406th Imperial Year
17th Year of Emperor Rufenrich Konreig's Reign

"Thaun, get somewhere safe, and stay there!" Heizl raised her voice over the panicked cries that followed the explosion. She pushed him away from the source of the smoke, distant light throwing one half of her face into shadow. "I'll find Uncle."

Nausea rising in his chest, Thaun looked back across the green lawn. His legs touched against the stone bench. Shaking his head, he grabbed Heizl's wrist. "You can't go. That was an explosion!"

"No, *you* can't go." She broke free of the grip. "Magic caused that explosion. I'm here as security. I have to try and help."

"But you're not the only mage on duty! There are Shadows, Highmages, and..." Thaun trailed off, his breathing shallow and rapid. His head spun.

"You can't go in. If you do, too many people will run in after you. It wouldn't be fair." Heizl lowered her voice. "Besides, what would you do?" At his cousin's blunt words, Thaun's helplessness settled in around his panic like a damp blanket. "If I go in there, no one else will risk themselves for me, and I might just make a difference."

He bowed his head and averted his gaze. Several feet away, Jilia stepped alongside Heizl, and laid a hand on her arm. Thaun watched as the mage's chest swelled at the contact.

"My father was in there..." Tears welled in the noble's eyes.

"Don't worry, I'll find him, I promise."

"I'm not sure this is such a good idea," said Thaun.

"Maybe Heizl's right," she replied, hand still resting near her elbow. "We're wasting time. What else can we do? You don't even have a sword. Heizl at least has her magic."

"I..." he stammered, looking from mage to noble and back again. Thaun sighed. "Be careful in there?"

"I'll be fine." Heizl placed a hand on Jilia's. "Look after Thaun for me." Patting her fingers again, she shifted her grip on her copper rod and jogged away. As she disappeared from sight beyond the rose arches, she tossed an empty bottle away over one shoulder. The gentle scent of blooming flowers gave way to the stench of smoke.

After a moment, distant cries still rising into the night, Jilia turned to Thaun. "Will she be okay?"

"She..." Thaun flinched at the distant sound of breaking glass. His cousin had told him stories of her exploits with the Spire. It didn't take a genius to realise that she'd embellished such tales, but, despite that, Thaun had confidence in her abilities. Still, seeing his closest friend running towards the sounds of chaos sent an ache through his soul. Thaun stuck out his chin. "Heizl's the best. She's smart enough to run from anything she can't handle. She'll be fine."

"I've not seen much magic..." she whispered as if far away.

"You've not used the Nexus?" Thaun didn't turn from the Great Hall.

"I–" A man's shocked cry interrupted her. "What do you think Heizl'll try to do?"

The distinct sound of metal on metal cut through the night a dozen times in rapid succession. At the last, punctuated by a man's death cry, the gardens fell into eerie silence.

Thaun grimaced. "I don't know."

He strained his ears for any change. The guests' shrieks and the rumble of collapsing masonry blended into a jagged wall of noise. He'd witnessed the lead up to battle while touring the Empire – the drum of marching in step, the bass drone of warsongs – but this felt different. While the Imperial Guard's cacophony had carried an undertone of order and control, he only knew one word for what he heard now. Chaos.

A high pitched whimper at his side pulled his attention to the woman standing with him. "Father's still in there," she whispered, turning her gaze away from the Hall.

Thaun didn't respond for a moment. With his heart in his throat, he struggled for words. "There were guardsmen, and he had his own men, right? I'm sure he's fine."

"We weren't allowed to bring many of our own attendants in with us."

He couldn't stomach the expression upon her face, and the way it echoed how he felt. "Heizl's in there. She'll find him."

"But she'll be looking for the Emperor – everyone will!" she wailed.

"Uncle Rufenrich had people with him. A Highmage, the Shadowmaster, Royal Guard..." Thaun paused at another clash of steel.

"Thaun?" she murmured. "I'm scared."

He swallowed. "Yeah. Me too."

"What do you think happened?" She swallowed and looked at him. Tears welled in her big, blue-green eyes as her chin tilted forwards and her lips quivered.

"Maybe a firework went off by accident." Even as the words left his mouth, he knew them as false.

He took a deep breath, vivid imagination flooding with death and destruction. If an accident had caused all this, people might be hurt, people he cared for. Few could match Sigren or Lena in their own disciplines, but a falling chunk of stone didn't care for the skill of the person beneath it. They'd be looking for him among rubble and flames. He had to let them know he was safe, so they could get out, so they could save themselves.

And what about the Emperor? If something happened to his uncle, the Court would look to him for leadership. The thought of navigating the Empire's nobility had daunted him enough when he could count on his family to help guide him, but doing it alone... He choked back a pitiful sob.

Jilia's quiet voice broke him from his private, self-destructive cycle. "We have to do something."

"Like what?" He shook his head, his own tears starting to form.

"All the sounds are coming from the Hall," she sniffed. "We should go around the side, to one of the gates. Someone there will be able to help us. A guard, or a Shadow, or someone." Wiping her face with a handkerchief, Jilia composed herself. "Or maybe into the city. Father has the best soldiers money can buy at his estate. It'll be safe there."

"That's a good idea." Thaun clenched his fists, his muscles trembling. "You should go for help."

"Thaun," she wrapped both hands around his forearm, tugging him towards her. "We should *both* go. It'll be safer away from here."

He shook his head and looked away to hide his anxious tears. Living alone, without his cousin or uncle, would be as painful as any death. "I can't leave Heizl in there."

"Don't be stupid!" she cried. "Now isn't the time for ill-conceived heroics. Soldiers or Shadows will deal with it. You don't even have a sword!"

"It's not about heroics." He spat the word as he broke free of her grasp. "I can't leave my family."

"Thaun…" her shouts faded to a plea. "Please, don't go in there."

"Jilia, go find help." He turned away, moist trails running down his cheeks. "I'll look for your father, too."

Not trusting himself to speak further, and fearing that she might talk him out of chasing after Heizl, Thaun broke into a panicked sprint. He didn't know a single person who'd tell him that this would end well.

A couple of slender branches, missed by their army of gardeners, clawed at his arms as he ran. The sounds of fighting grew louder as he sprinted down the verdant paths. Half-forgotten memories of the grounds' layout flashed before his eyes, and it didn't take him long before he trod once more on gravel instead of grass. Underfoot, shards of glass glistened among the stones in violent imitation of the flickering stars high above.

He'd never experienced anything like this, not so close to home at least. As a child, his uncle had spared him from the civil war by sending him far to the south. In spite of that, he'd heard rumours of the conflict as noble had fought noble in the name of Konreig or Kuhlner. Even his most vivid imaginings fell short of the madness before him.

That conflict had passed more than a decade ago, but stray rumours still reached the Court of rebel sympathisers and surviving usurpers. Could they have done this? Or what of the Empire's other rebel groups? Fjujhost's revolution in the west, Rigar's Stricken in the north. The mixed gossip of a Seorsan fleet gathering didn't help matters.

Was the Court always like this? Never knowing their true enemy? Men and women's words not matching their intentions? Thaun shook the thoughts away. A moment later he stood at the terrace's edge.

Dark, caustic smoke plumed from the Great Hall's shattered windows, twisting to join the thin clouds and Sheltz's pulsing Comet overhead. Many of the guests had already fled, trampling the nearest flower beds in their haste to flee. Those unable to run further lay upon stone or grass nearby, tending to their wounds with whatever they had at hand. Burns and soot-stains covered those closest, while others bore bruises and grazes gifted by falling stonework. The sounds of fighting continued beyond the doors' shattered remains.

Somewhere within, a clear voice barked commands as someone attempted to restore order. Thaun flinched as they fell silent. Fewer men and women pushed through the doorway now.

Acrid bile rose in his stomach, burning within his chest. Still, he forced himself to move towards the Hall. Few looked Thaun's way as he mounted the steps, not recognising him from the depths of their own pain. Survivors instead nursed their wounds, uninterested in a foolish man heading towards obvious danger.

As he walked, he searched. Hoping the young woman tending to the wounded might be Lena. Wishing he'd find his uncle directing rescue efforts. Longing to see Heizl among those taking refuge on the terrace.

In spite of the images that formed behind his vision, he still found no sign of any of them. His heart sank, the sickness in his stomach intensifying.

At the door, Thaun pressed his back to the stone. Despite the deepening evening, the wall still held some of the day's warmth. For a moment, his thoughts flashed to Jilia. She always seemed to know what to do within the Court. He knew few who could match her wit and cunning. Had she found somewhere safe? Or help? He had to trust that she had. His chest rose and fell in rapid succession, his heart a quicker rhythm still within him, like the growing intensity of shifting earth.

Peering around the door, another wave of nausea washed over him at the sight within, and he forgot about the noblewoman.

Through the obscuring smoke, dozens of bodies lay motionless, their skin dark and burnt, or red with flesh cracked open from the magicks released. Half of one massive table lay in a charred heap, amber flames licking up around the twisted wood. Tapestries lay in smouldering heaps.

Coughing, Thaun scanned the room, once more looking for any sign of his family. Broken movement through the smoke pulled at him, but he saw no sign of anyone that he knew. His muscles tensed, and he continued searching like a man possessed. A woman's face rose before his eyes, but he had no memory of them. She bore no resemblance to Heizl, Jilia, Lena, or even Frida. No words came to describe her, and he saw no sign of her among the bodies either. Still, he knew her, and had done for a long time, but didn't know where from.

As he watched, sound and light interrupted his thoughts. A slender stream of golden fire roared from the dais and across the hall. He clenched his eyes shut at the sudden brightness. Amber poured through his closed eyelids. As he opened them again, Thaun caught a subdued flash of green.

The flickering flames died, and he eyed the throne. Korten commanded the steps, arms spread out to either side. His once immaculate white clothes streamed with dark smoke, several patches burnt through to reveal reddening skin beneath. Coruscating fire, the same golden hue as the throne he stood before, enveloped his ring-covered hands, dripping like liquid to crackle and pool at his feet.

With a pained, bestial roar, the mage clapped his hands together. Another tongue of golden fire reached out from him, straight as an arrow. Smoke billowed from its path, revealing the room's centre. A growing shell of emerald pulsed outwards from a new figure, meeting the incandescent blast between the two. The resulting shockwave pushed Thaun back a step, picking up the dust around him and driving the sting of smoke through his nostrils.

Daring to peer back around, he inspected the second figure for the first time. Standing with weight on his back foot, the stranger stared at the Highmage through piercing grey eyes. A flow of hot air from the broken windows plucked at the coarse mantle hanging from his shoulders. He lowered his free hand from where he'd held it out before him. His other held a slightly curved sword, its notched, steel length a practical contrast to the elegant black and bronze scabbard at his hip. A handful of shallow wounds criss-crossed his body, slicing through pale linen and flesh alike. Fine links of unbroken chainmail glistened beneath the torn, scorched cloth.

As the interloper opened his mouth to speak, Korten launched another orb of fire through the air. It flew past stunned guardsmen and burning furniture, before reaching his target. Flames wrapped around the stranger in a rolling inferno, consuming him for a dozen heartbeats, before another flash of green light blinded Thaun. Upon the shell of emerald, the Highmage's attack petered out as it found nothing to sustain it.

"Renyar, you sandspitting Fitz-bastard, I'm just warming up!" shouted Korten. More flame spewed from his fingertips, forcing the stranger back several paces despite the green-tinted, defensive wards he wove around him.

Tearing his gaze from the Highmage's fiery barrage, Thaun looked around the rest of the room. In the stranger's wake lay a trail of bodies, reaching from one end of the hall to where he now stood. Many had worn the blue uniform of the Royal Guard. Despite the smoke-induced tears welling in his eyes, he could make out the surgical cuts made around their armour – base of the neck, under the arm, beneath the chin. Thaun felt sick, and not just from the heat.

Others in the same sapphire uniform stood scattered through the hall, swords still sheathed or hanging limp in their twitching hands. Few bore any obvious injury, though each carried the same blank, weary expression upon their faces. Their unnatural stillness turned Thaun's stomach.

Behind the stranger – Renyar? – a dark form lay beneath a collapsed beam, moving in fits and starts. Another man, dressed in a burnt robe and with a heavy pendant around his neck struggled to lift the debris from the downed Shadow.

The now familiar sound of screeching steel, punctuated by grunts and cries, echoed from beyond the Hall's entrance. More than one attacker had invaded Thaun's home. Frida had handpicked the Shadows and Royal Guardsmen assigned to their security, the best of the best. In spite of their skill and prestige, the soldiery lay in unmoving heaps. He saw no sign of any of the Empire's agents anywhere.

A sombre realisation fought for clarity among the maelstrom of his mind. As soon as he had sneaked out, the Shadowmaster would have tightened their security. How many more might have died if this stranger had had the element of surprise?

At a change in the timbre of Korten's assault, Thaun squinted through the smoke towards the room's centre again. Leaning upon an upturned table halfway up the dais, flames streamed from the Highmage's outstretched hand. Where before they'd hammered upon Renyar's green wards, fire now struck something else.

Whether arriving via sorcery, or obscured by flames, he didn't see a second figure intercept the assault. A battered shield raised before her, the flames struck the bronze and simply disappeared. Loose clothing of the same cut but a darker hue hid the woman's muscular curves, while a hood concealed all but a few strands of raven hair. Behind her, Renyar straightened and adjusted his grip upon his curved longsword.

The Highmage's face twisted, rage burning in his eyes at the interruption. His pale lips curled into a snarl, and yet another ball of rolling flame left Korten's hand. She didn't move, the arcing magic curving sharply through the smoky air until it met her raised shield, disappearing in the same way as before.

It took a moment for Thaun to realise that the sounds of fighting from the passageway had halted with the woman's appearance.

"Imperial." Renyar's heavily accented voice cut across the room clear as day. Thaun couldn't help but look at him as he spoke. "Stand aside, and let us pass. My quarrel isn't with you."

"Your silver tongue won't work on me, you murdering son of a bitch!" Korten raised an arm and flames filled the space between his fingers.

Renyar lifted his free hand to wipe sweat from his brow, before gesturing towards the Highmage. "Elhin?" The woman at his side nodded once, and shifted her weight onto the balls of her feet. She flicked her wrist, and Thaun found his gaze drawn to her sword arm. Attention fixed on the strange shield and Renyar's hypnotic words, he'd paid little attention to the weapon.

Now, he noticed for the first time how the short, iron blade erupted into darkness. Like a sable reflection of the flames surrounding them, it flickered and spat with twisted energy.

Her sudden movement, faster than he thought possible, sent her hurtling forwards at a sprint. She leapt the steps in two long bounds, landing before the Highmage with sword high.

The woman swung.

From the doorway onto the terrace, Thaun didn't see where Korten's Shadow had come from, but the man, clad in dark leathers, appeared between mage and assassin. His own blade met hers, angled to deflect the blow.

Leaning into the swing, her blackened sword struck polished steel. Darkness exploded outwards like shards of glass. Even across the room, Thaun flinched back as another shockwave struck him. At point-blank range, the Shadow flew backwards, hitting the ground hard enough that he bounced. To the agent's credit, he rolled, keeping his grip on the long dagger in his hand.

Rising unsteadily, blood streaming from his mouth, the Shadow wiped his lips and advanced. The woman, sword and shield both raised, met him, ignoring the Highmage. Their rapid exchange proved too fast to follow through the intervening smoke, but Thaun couldn't miss the gush of red from the Shadow's neck when he couldn't match her deadly pace.

Down among the upturned benches, Renyar cocked his head before stalking towards the dais once more.

Relief flashed over Thaun as the interloper paused and turned around. A moment later, he heard what had drawn the stranger's attention. The rustle of chainmail, the steady drum of boots.

Imperial Guardsmen, blue and green surcoats over their armour, appeared from the hallway. Shields raised in an ordered wall, each in the colours of the First Army, they maintained formation as they wheeled to face the would-be assassins. A second row followed, shields slung over their backs and crossbows raised. Thaun watched, fear forgotten, as the squad took up a defensive position.

Short, stubby bolts leapt from grooves. One buried itself up to its leather fletching in the dry boards of the upturned table, while another flew a hand's breadth past Korten's face. The rest sped towards Renyar or the woman.

Two struck the bronze surface of the woman's shield, before dropping motionless to the floor – not ricocheting away as they should – while a third bounced from her raised, black-wreathed blade and a fourth found its way past to draw blood on her upper arm. Renyar's pearlescent green shield rang with each impact like a falling bell. Bolts scattered to the room's dark corners, with one narrowly missing an enchanted guard.

As the guardsmen crouched to reload, the would-be assassin drew a deep breath. His lips curled into a snarl. A heartbeat later, and Renyar regained his composure. Like oil spreading over water, determination found its footing once more.

"Guardsmen!" His accented voice echoed between the hall's walls. "Halt!"

Thaun arched an eyebrow as his mouth hung open. One by one, some trembling before succumbing to Renyar's command, each Imperial slowed before stopping. A handful of weapons clattered to the floor, as others straightened and stared vacantly at the unknown man that they had assaulted only seconds before.

Veins of visceral horror wove between his flush of relief, and realisation dawned. Thaun looked to the handful of mesmerised Royal Guardsmen already standing around the room. Only their uniforms separated them from the enchanted reinforcements.

His neck aching from flicking back and forth, and his mind racing as he struggled to take it all in, Thaun watched as dark fumes, black as night and thick as death, breathed from every fire. As unnatural vapours filled the hall, denser than any mundane flame might produce, Thaun spotted Korten standing with his back to the dais' single exit, both hands raised. As the smoke thickened, the Highmage squeezed through the narrow doorway and disappeared.

Blinking, his eyes stinging almost as soon as the smoke enveloped him, Thaun leant back into the garden, gulping down clean air. Some of the nobles had fled further, the violence giving them the strength to push beyond their injuries. Others, who had writhed and moaned in pain moments before, lay still as the grave.

Taking another deep breath of evening air, Thaun clenched his fists. Dozens lay dead, dying, or dazed around him. Reinforcements had proven ineffective. And he still didn't know where Heizl was, nor their uncle. He had to find them.

Thaun ran into the Great Hall.

He stumbled within a bare handful of steps, his foot catching on an upturned chair that sent him sprawling to the floor. As skin and fabric tore, and blood welled to the surface, he punched the warm stone, and pushed himself back to his feet. All sense of direction lost in the thickening smoke, he chose a way at random, and limped forwards with arms out before him like a blind man without his stick.

Eyes clenched shut against the fumes and chest wracked by the smoke, the back of one outstretched hand brushed something solid. Warm chainmail and singed cloth yielded beneath his touch. Opening his eyes to a slit, tears filling the gap and blurring his vision, he looked up to see the vacant stare of the guardsman that he'd stumbled into. Glimpsing a copper charm of concentric circles hanging over the man's uniform, vague familiarity reached up from the back of his mind. This soldier might've guarded his family a dozen times over.

"Come on!" Grasping his shoulders, Thaun shook him. Steel links rustled. "We're under attack!" No response. "You have to do something!"

Some of his weight resting upon the unresponsive man, he looked around. Smoke still obscured the Hall, and with his fall he didn't know how to begin orientating himself. Sounds of screeching steel erupted again as if on all sides. The fresh roar of flames came from further within.

He had no idea where the two strangers had appeared from. Such figures would have stood out among the nobility, so they couldn't have entered with the other guests. With the destruction they'd wrought, he couldn't imagine anyone he knew helping them sneak in. Chances were, he reflected, they'd come here for more than the unfocused, wholesale slaughter that they'd committed so far.

Thaun felt like crying, and not just from the smoke. Instead, against all urges, he shook the guard again, harder this time. "Do *something!*"

A half-limp head fell to one side, looking at him with blank eyes. Sticky drool trickled down from the man's lips.

From somewhere behind him, he heard Renyar's heavily accented voice above the sounds of fighting. "Tell me where the Emperor is, and then get out of my way."

If anyone responded to his brazen command, Thaun didn't hear them. At least he knew why they'd arrived now. Even with their added security, any assassin would appreciate the value of knowing where and when their target would be.

Gritting his teeth, he looked down. Thaun hesitated. No one would blame him for fleeing, for letting trained professionals deal with the threat. The Palace itself, let alone the city beyond, held a hundred souls more suited to this fight. It wasn't their family at risk though.

With fear in his eyes, but determination in mind, he reached out and drew the guardsman's longsword.

Tooth and Nail – Chapter Five

> *"Not since the primal chaos at the dawn of Creation had the world witnessed such fires. The heartless dragon fell upon the ancient nation, ruination in his shadow. Death throes gouged valleys, convulsing wings flattened cities, and his dying breath scoured the land clean."*
>
> The Fall of Urathear,
> Lairz Larren Zarrek of Low House
> Zarrek (373 I.Y.)

23rd day of Indern, 406th Imperial Year
17th Year of Emperor Rufenrich Konreig's Reign

"Renyar, you sandspitting Fitz-bastard, I'm just warming up!"

Heizl ducked away from the fierce gout of flame that crossed the room. Sweat beaded upon her red skin. Hot, dry air scratched at the insides of her throat. Streaks of soot and grime covered her.

She pushed away the strands reaching towards her, all but unnoticed by both Imperial and Thalan as her scathe writhed. A stray blast would put a swift end to her regardless of Korten's aim.

Heizl risked a glance from her broken cover. The Highmage held himself back, unwilling to unleash everything he had. She'd seen enough in their training to know the frightening limits of her insufferable colleague's destructive potential. The structural integrity of the Great Hall vouched for his reluctance to fully engage the would-be assassin. She'd seen stone melt under his sorcerous assault once before, during one particularly chaotic practice session. If she could help it, she'd never see it again, either. Say what you want about his gluttonous, arrogant, grating personality, but Korten knew how to bring the house down.

Dipping inside her own reserves, Heizl skittered away again from the threads groping towards her. Unseen fingers dug into her belly, the growing emptiness within her clenching down as if seeking to draw power from her own flesh. Next time, she swore, she'd think twice before influencing the minds of a room full of nobles for the sake of a few drinks with family. Right now, even fine wine in Jilia's lovely company didn't outweigh her current condition. At least, out in the gardens, the initial blast hadn't caught them.

Heizl reached out to the few conscious bystanders remaining in the ruined room, stroking their own strands in an attempt to calm them. She didn't need any more panic right now. When she touched upon the minds of those still standing – Royal Guard, almost to the man – it unsettled her, like looking upon the art of a madman. Every thread of their disarrayed web wove into a single, tranquil braid reaching towards Renyar. She'd never seen anything like it.

The Emperor had fled from the room as she'd entered, pushed through the small, half-hidden door behind the throne by Frida. She admired Korten's attempts at rearguard action, but the mage fought the tide about as well as an actual fire would. Renyar had made several more inexorable steps even during that brief glimpse. Heizl couldn't leave yet, not until she knew her uncle had reached safety.

The roaring flame's timbre dropped, the deep noise fading to a low growl. Peering over the table's remains, she saw the green sphere wink out around the foreigner, as another figure stood between him and the Highmage. Another bolt of golden fire whipped towards the hooded woman, only for her raised shield to swallow the attack. Heizl stared at the pandemonium before her.

"Imperial," smooth and dry like snakeskin, she heard Renyar's accented speech as clearly as if she stood alongside him. Heizl blinked several times, before shaking her head, pushing away the mesmerising voice. "Stand aside, and let me pass. My quarrel is not with you." The words pulled at her muscles, urging her to stand. She clawed at the floor beneath her, fingers tracking lines through the soot as she resisted the Thalan's command.

The spell lifted as Korten growled back, the tentative grip upon her shattering. "Your silver tongue won't work on me, you murdering son of a bitch!"

Past her own lingering fascination, Heizl threw aside her caution to peer from her cover.

As a thick plume of smoke rose before her, hiding the swordwoman's swift movement, Heizl caught a glimpse of something she didn't understand. Darkness flowed over the hooded woman's blade like captive midnight. She felt more than saw the resulting explosion. The floor shuddered as cool air blew over her, tussling and tangling her sweat-slick hair.

Though she only caught glimpses of the Shadow's desperate defence against the assassin, Heizl felt the man's death. She didn't know Korten's attendant, just another person assigned to control a mage. His strands reached out nonetheless, the bond towards the Highmage brighter than many.

It snapped, then, like rigging torn apart in a storm. Frayed, dead ends whipped around as if to strike her. Weak already, she backed away, consciously retreating again from the room's other snaking threads. The thought of either assassin looking her way fed fear into her belly like a blade through flesh.

Still sensing the room, she caught the guardsmen's approach a moment before they entered the hall. As the two attackers wheeled to face the uniformed line, Heizl felt the interlopers' attention drawn away of their own accord. Distracted by this new threat, flicking their threads from finding her came as easily as batting aside flies.

The distraction didn't last long. Bolts lanced through the smoky air. Metal ricocheted from viridescent walls and wood splintered against stone. As black fire licked along steel, men succumbed to the accented commands of their target. Heizl shook her head – if she had power like that, the rest of the Capital wouldn't be able to dismiss her. They wouldn't get to ignore this Renyar, either.

Smoke, more than the smouldering wood could ever produce naturally, filled the room. Heizl sank down, muffling her wracking coughs in the crook of one arm. Caustic darkness engulfed everything, blinding Imperial and assassin alike. She sensed Korten channelling his will into the existing flames, drawing the billowing vapours out.

She started to sigh, but even that burned in throat. The Highmage had failed to stop either assassin in direct confrontation, merely slowing them.

Perhaps he'd exhausted the supply of sanguine essence stored in his rings, or miscalculated his reserves, and now spent his own blood where it flowed in his veins. Whether the clouds of smoke disorientated them or not, Heizl knew few options remained to her. She lacked training as a battlemage, and the Spire had made their priorities abundantly clear when they'd promoted Korten over her.

Against foes like these, she wished almost as much as they did that her talents lay in a more obvious place.

Crawling on hands and knees, she inched towards the Great Hall's entrance and the clearer air near it, hoping to escape before events worsened. Rivulets appeared upon her grimy skin as sweat soaked into her once fine clothes. Only a small, grey patch at the back of her neck remained cool and dry despite the flames. Between sore fingers, her copper focus all but burned, but she didn't let go despite how little it did for her. Eyes clenched shut against the smoke, smouldering splinters dug into her soft palms. Unable to drag herself further, she opened thin slits, and peered through the coiling fumes. The tall door, its edges burnt and smoothed with sorcerous fire, loomed through the shadows only a few feet to her left.

Stumbling straight, leaning on her rod to clamber upright, she glanced behind her as she fled.

Through some cosmic coincidence or will of the gods, the smoke cleared. A distorted path opened between her and Renyar like a crowd parting between star-crossed lovers. She watched him advance upon the throne. Something, some subtle tug upon her web, made her pause.

From the dark smoke, a figure appeared, sword raised. His controlled swing connected with the back of Renyar's head. Blood welled up as the Thalan staggered, one hand coming up as he stumbled away. Too slow, as the blade whipped upwards in a diagonal slash, Imperial steel dragging over iron links and pale cloth.

Such a strike should have finished things there and then. Even a greathelm would've rang an audible toll beneath the impact. Though reeling, Renyar remained standing.

The inferno made the Hall feel like the inside of an oven, but still a ghostly chill descended upon Heizl as she recognised the swordsman.

Thaun.

Expertly, a dozen years of courtyard practice directing his muscles, her cousin followed up on his assault. One masterful blow flowing into the next, the sword in his hand danced, raining metallic thunder down upon the assassin. Renyar's armour took the brunt of several hits, his own blade deflecting more, but blood bloomed from a half-dozen more places to stain his clothes.

At some break in his rhythm, Thaun hopped backwards, resetting his stance to appraise his foe.

In that frozen moment of time, Heizl understood. Her cousin had only ever trained. She didn't think he'd drawn a weapon in anger before. Working to improve alongside a friend or teacher, he'd often turned the flat of the blade to prevent serious injury. In a practice bout, scores would be marked after such a decisive combination of cuts and thrusts, ready for the next round.

The rules of real combat worked differently.

Coughing back the smoke, he appeared to realise this at the same time. Thaun lunged back in, forcing Renyar back a step. The Thalan's own blade moved more quickly this time, fending away the sword tip as he recovered.

Stemming the flow of blood from his head with one hand, Renyar fought defensively with the other. Sluggish, as if limping from an injury, several more attacks crept through, but none so serious as before.

"Imperial, stop your–" Renyar never finished his command. Thaun stepped in close and drove his sword's crossguard up beneath his bottom rib, forcing the air from his lungs.

Across the hall, vision obscured by smoke, lungs burning, Heizl couldn't tell if her cousin had done it on purpose or not. Did he understand the unnatural commands that this outsider had placed upon those that had stood in his way? It didn't really matter. Either way, it had bought another second.

It wasn't enough.

Against any other foe, Thaun might've emerged victorious. Such an outcome would've impressed anyone who'd heard it, securing a reputation among the Court. Instead, he continued attacking a foe that refused to fall.

Weary and suffering from the heat and smoke, Heizl realised too late that Renyar had yet to lash out. He'd only defended himself, rarely attempting his own counterattack. He'd not drawn upon his emerald wards despite the advantage that they'd provide.

Heizl's warning shout came too late. Thaun lunged, his body weight shifting him out from Renyar's thrust even as he turned the blade to cut across his opponent's chest, using the edge this time.

Green light flared. Dancing flames reflected like upon stained glass, casting strange shadows. A translucent surface shimmered before Renyar, a jagged fissure forming beneath the blow.

As her cousin moved to draw back, a second ward formed along the blade. Another followed, then another, each pressing in on the sword and the hands gripping it, trapping Thaun.

Across the room, Heizl watched, ice running through her veins, as Renyar leant to look along the blade's length. Silver eyes met brown, and the foreigner smiled.

"Stay there, Crown Prince," commanded the Thalan. Still gripping his sword, Thaun stopped struggling to free himself. Hands on the hilt and his body calm behind it, he fell still at the order. "We haven't met yet, have we?"

The chill in Heizl's veins spread to her flesh, her body freezing as she watched.

Still clutching his head, Renyar whispered a few words, the foreign speech falling from his mouth smooth as honey, before he spoke, once more in Imperial. "I'd hoped to have a word with His Majesty, but you present another option. Maybe our visit won't be a waste after all."

If their attacker said anything else, Heizl didn't catch it. As naturally as another woman might fight or flee, she fell within herself. Blind to the choking smoke and numb to the warmth of dying flames, she sprinted along her web towards the assassin's radiant threads. A hundred times in the past she'd found the strands of a friend or a foe, and slipped in as subtle as a spider to draw their attention wherever she willed.

The time for an understated approach had passed, if it had ever existed at all. Pushing attention and twisting focus had achieved little. Most wouldn't even notice her subtle attempt at stalling them. Her body trembling and her skin slick with sweat, Heizl wrapped ethereal fingers around the silken chains stretching from Renyar to Thaun. She tugged. Each thread protested at the treatment, resisting her rough pull. After a moment, like barbed thorns tearing free from tender flesh, they came loose.

Knuckles white, she held the threads to her heart.

Just like before, eyes turned towards her. For once, Heizl didn't relish the attention. Recognition from the Spire and the Court wasn't worth staring down such danger.

Staggering upright, she reached out with one hand to lean against the broken wooden doorway. Bronze hinges creaked beneath her weight. Eyes creeping open, she held the threads tight, feeling them slip, inch by inch, through her fingers as they returned to their prior paths. The last one falling away, Heizl looked up, squinting through the swirling smoke and sparkling lights that had appeared across her vision. Upon her neck, her raw skin crawled as her scathe spread.

Renyar cocked his head to one side, emerald shells still locking Thaun's swordarm in place. The Thalan blinked as he considered her.

"I," Heizl sighed. "I regret this immediately."

"Who in the Void are you?"

Renyar received no answer beyond the timely shattering of a glass decanter against his back. Shards of glass sparkled through the air as the spirits within, aged and amber, flashed into short lived flames.

He spun, turning towards the latest assailant as Lena arrived, shield raised and charging. The wooden surface barrelled into him like a battering ram, driving him up and backwards. Her axe followed in its wake, but met only air as he dodged back further.

Another figure stepped from the smoke at an angle from him, swinging downwards with half a broken chair, the wood still alight. As bright wards flashed between them, intercepting the club, sparks and cinders burst outwards, showering both Renyar and the attacker.

Improvised weapon shook from his hands, Toland fell back, letting Lena pass. He wiped his face clear, coughing hard enough to shake tears from his eyes. Behind him, his red and blue cloak swirled and billowed in the roiling air.

Seeing her partner under attack, the woman upon the dais hesitated, glancing between Renyar and the small door behind the throne. As if coming to a decision, she turned and started jogging back to help.

She didn't get far. A crossbow bolt struck her in the upper arm. Blood fountained as the quarrel passed straight through flesh. The woman cried out in pain, almost dropping her sword as she pressed a fist to the wound, her bronze shield hung a little lower than it had before. She turned, face looking more irritated than hurt, staring down Sigren as he crouched to reload.

Each step towards the Shadow heavy with the promise of further violence, Zecht cut the swordswoman short. A knife flew across her path, missing by a handspan. A second thrown blade bounced from her own weapon to ricochet away. As she engaged him, she ducked Sigren's next shot. Her own blood joined that of those she'd killed, as her movement grew sluggish and predictable from her injuries. Unable to raise her shield, her sword sang as she deflected knife thrusts, though neither seemed willing to commit fully.

Under calmer circumstances, Heizl might've appreciated their display. Two skilled combatants in the prime of life moving as if in a choreographed dance. Though blood streamed – first from the woman's arm and then from a dozen superficial wounds across both bodies – it merely slowed them to a pace that Heizl could follow. Had Sigren's shot connected with bone, it might've been different, but some blend of adrenaline and training kept the assassin moving even with a hole in her arm.

Despite their ambush, Zecht swiftly lost ground as the heavier weapon proved more deadly than his own. Even with Sigren firing a third time, his powerful crossbow bucking with the shot, she didn't slow. The bolt grazed her thigh before digging into an upturned table across the room.

Upon the floor, Lena and Toland pressed their attack harder. The noble had found a charred spear from somewhere, thrusting at Renyar as he fought to keep his distance. Dressed in expensive clothes and lacking armour, Heizl could hardly blame him.

Renyar's chainmail, expertly crafted and proof against cuts and blades, would've done little beneath Lena's axe swings. He didn't need it though. With each breath he recovered further as he batted aside attacks and dodged past steel. The flow of blood slowed to a trickle, leaving his dark hair matted and lank. He straightened, blocks and parries growing more certain as he gave up less and less ground.

Through blinding smoke and chaos, Heizl thought she caught the Thalan open his mouth to speak. After the single blink of an eye, his expression changed, lips twisting in cruel pleasure as he closed it once more, some silent decision made.

A dozen swings later, and he found the offence. Between spear and axe, his blade licked outwards. It took only a few attempts before its razor-sharp tip found its mark.

Slivers of wood spiralled from the spear shaft. Shreds of Lena's surcoat joined ash upon the floor. Blue and green paint upon her shield flaked off under repeated impact. Imperial blood flowed.

Across the room, Heizl saw as much of the melee through her weaving sorcery as she did by her mundane sight. A dozen shades, the colour of pain, coated every soul and strand. Here and there, like flames through dirty glass, the light of their emotions shone through. Angry, confused, and desperate, tempers flared.

Heizl smiled faintly. Chaos, almost too much to keep track of. Not so different from the turmoil in most human souls.

She seized upon Renyar's threads once more. Caught up in with more immediate threats, Heizl required only the slightest touch. Had she needed any more, she might've collapsed at even that effort.

Attention disrupted, Renyar's fight grew more frantic. Heizl didn't know quite what he'd feel. Flickers at the corner of his vision, discordant tones filling his ears, she didn't really care so long as it worked. By his grunts of pain – Toland slamming the spear butt into his leg – it seemed effective enough.

Emerald wards, their hues rippling in the firelight, burst into being on either side of Renyar. Steel screeched across their unyielding surface.

As the Thalan drew upon another ward, fending off Lena's steady assault, the flickering shells trapping Thaun faded. Still dazed, he stumbled, sword clattering to the floor. Toland caught him before he entirely lost his feet pulling an arm over his own shoulder as he steadied the Prince.

Heizl fell to the floor, relinquishing her astral grip on the assassins' threads. Relief flooded her senses as she saw the noble guide Thaun towards the terrace doors. Though it felt like a bell had passed, she likely hadn't been in the hall for more than a few minutes.

Upon the dais, the two Shadows continued their fight with the swordswoman. Where noble couples had once danced, Lena now beat upon Renyar's arcane shields like a drummer keeping rhythm. His occasional muted laugh broke through the flames and violence.

Limping away, Toland glanced at Heizl once, before snapping back in recognition. Arm under Thaun's shoulders, he shifted direction and cut towards her.

"Heizl! Take him!" he shouted. Beneath dark, matted hair, his face glowed red with heat and exertion, a stark contrast to the paleness of Heizl's.

"Toland?!" She exclaimed. The young nobleman's clothes had suffered since she'd spotted him across the Hall earlier in the evening. Burns and tears criss-crossed his shirt, and blood stained what was left of one sleeve. "What are you still doing here?"

He grinned, hints of shock or mania tugging at his too-wide eyes. "Divine intervention, I guess."

"I won't lie, I don't think we've really got time for witty banter."

"Right." He dropped into the cover of an upturned table a few feet away. "What's the plan?"

"Damned if I know. Did you see what happened?"

"I think they magicked in, like the Nexus. I didn't see it though."

Heizl closed her eyes against the smoke, joining him behind the table. "Did uncle make it out?"

"Probably? He's not here now."

"Then we need to get Thaun out of here."

"Gods forgive, I don't think he's going far without us."

"Then we go as well."

"And leave everyone else?"

Heizl grimaced. Toland was right. They couldn't save them all. If they fled with Thaun, they'd be leaving who knew how many motionless, enthralled men and women to the flames and smoke. If they tried to drive Renyar and his partner off, they had no guarantee of success. If they fought the flames, the assassins would be free to do as they pleased.

She looked down at her cousin. Red flesh covered in grime, he didn't look back. No visible wound had laid him low. Flickering eyelids cast hints of dilated pupils, eyes blind to the world.

Through arcane senses, she could sense the bond linking him now to Renyar. Pulsing and flowing from the Thalan, it overpowered Thaun's own twinkling light. So many others in the room felt the same. Magic, whether her own subtle twistings or the more predictable enchantments of her colleagues at the Spire, could do strange things like this. She'd rarely seen its control so absolute. Body, mind, heart, and soul – it didn't matter which, Renyar's command held them all.

Heizl's magic had always served her better manipulating thoughts and feelings than it had in direct confrontation. She was the wrong sort of mage to unravel such eldritch mastery.

She wasn't the only mage present though.

"Toland, we need Lena," she said.

"Pretty sure she's busy!"

"We still need her. With her helping, I might be able to, I don't know, break whatever's been done to Thaun. And everyone else too, maybe."

Still cradling Thaun between them, Toland stared at Heizl. "Are you sure?"

"Not as much as I'd like. Got a better idea?"

"If only." He shuffled sideways, moving out from under Thaun's weight as gently as possible. "If this is our best chance at saving the most people..." Toland coughed. "I'll distract Renyar, you get her and do your thing."

"Right."

"Oh, and Heizl? Promise me one thing?" Rising into a crouch, he threw her a weak smirk. "Get it done quick? I don't want to face that guy any longer than I have to. Not armed like this, anyway."

She nodded once, clutching her cousin as she fell back within herself. All but spent, the urge to simply drop unconscious tugged at her. Heizl didn't see Toland as he rushed back in, scooping up the same sword that Thaun had dropped moments before. She sensed him though, and that was enough to realise that their half-formed plan wouldn't work.

Renyar's magic rolled like a storm around him. A swirling sphere formed and dissipated, each time blocking one of Lena's swings. His sword moved only now to lash out in between his wards, unneeded in his defence.

Near the throne, the black-clad woman fought black clad Shadows. Ribbons of dark cloth fluttered from all three fighters, like trailing smoke, where they'd moved too slowly. Sigren appeared the worst off, but even he'd managed to avoid any serious wounds so far.

Feeling along her tentative thread towards Lena, Heizl's hopes faded as Renyar's voice reached her ears. His patience had come to an end. Any thoughts of calling the healer back to her slammed straight into that hard, unyielding tone.

"Enough! Halt!"

None obeyed willingly. Zecht stopped first, slowing and then standing still almost instantly. A knife dropped from a limp hand. Sigren lasted a heartbeat longer, fighting as if moving through tar. The swordswoman casually stepped out of the way before bringing the pommel of her blade down upon him. The Shadow crumpled.

Toland, only halfway back into the fray, stumbled as the sorcery took hold of him. He skidded to a halt.

Within the melee, Lena lasted longest as the command sank in. Will hardened by years of training, even she succumbed eventually. Shield still in a loose grip, but now hanging at her side, she swayed slightly as her silvered axe slipped from her fingers. The focus clattered to the flagstones.

Gripping the wound in her arm, the cowled woman limped towards Renyar as his green barrier faded. Smooth, foreign words passed between the two, and he shrugged once before gesturing towards the Throne. She nodded in understanding.

"Crown Prince? Where are you?" the Thalan called as he looked around. In Heizl's arms, Thaun stirred. "Come to me."

Her cousin pushed once, fighting to rise from her weary embrace. Overwhelming panic welling up within her like a fountain, Heizl pulled back from Lena's thread, any attempt at speaking to the other mage forgotten. Instead, she found the flawless, braided strand linking Thaun to Renyar again. With no energy to fuel her magic, she drew upon her body's mundane strength. If she survived, she might regret the side effects, but at least she'd be alive.

She struck the strand binding Thaun to Renyar, like a ram slamming against a castle gate. It reverberated, but held. Steadying herself, darkness formed at the edge of both her mundane and magical vision from the exertion. Heizl lashed out again, willing the link to break. It shook, humming like a violin string, but held.

Chest and shoulders slumping forwards, her grip on Thaun faltered, and her cousin rose.

She struck a third time, the strike glancing off in her unaimed frenzy. For a second, Thaun paused. He continued a heartbeat later as if nothing had happened.

Heavy footsteps joined the royal's, like falling stones striking the ground. The Void beckoned seductively as Heizl slipped forwards, the warm stonework breaking her fall. At the impact of her skull on stone, sunlight flashed inside her head, and her vision swam. As pained lights filled her sight and her eyes blurred, she could only listen to what followed.

The footfalls drew closer. Metal over wood, the sound of a drawn sword drowned out the lingering crackle of dying flames.

"Imperial, stop," Renyar's voice sounded far away as it lost his stoic calm. "Halt!" Soft brushing footsteps, and the woman's rushed foreign speech followed.

A new voice drove through Heizl's pain to reach her ears, shaking her soul. Though vaguely familiar, she couldn't place the man's strange accent. Hard and old as stone, sure as a keen blade, and unerring as an arrow in flight. Unease rose in her stomach. "One Fang, a Claw, two Scales, a Wing, Bone, and Heart." The footsteps stopped. "Yield the Tongue."

"Who are you?" the Thalan's words trembled.

"If you don't know me already," the new voice growled. "It won't matter."

If either assassin answered, Heizl didn't hear them over the sudden exchange as steel met steel. The noises blended into a single screech, interrupted by a *thud* and the wracking cough of wind knocked from lungs.

"I thought I knew all of the First Generation," came the new voice as the heavy footsteps resumed. "You aren't one of mine. Which of my brothers spawned you?"

"Kwen was my grandfather," Renyar answered slowly, his own footfalls joining the newcomer's.

"Second Generation? Impressive then, even with a Fragment."

"What of you?" The Thalan ignored the stranger's comment. Heizl might have shaken her head in confusion if she'd had the strength. "Who was your sire? Are you of Body?"

"Not one of Body's, no," he laughed. His deep laughter continued behind the next exchange of blows. They didn't last so long this time, ending with Renyar crying out in pain.

"Not one of..." In spite of not applying herself when it came to learning other languages, Heizl recognised the sound of swearing regardless of its tongue.

"I won't ask a second time," offered the newcomer.

For the first time since crossing paths with him, Heizl heard Renyar's voice waver. "It's not that simple."

"Simple as a sword, complicated as family. Either way."

The foreigner made no response. Heizl's ears popped as pressure washed over her. A sulphurous smell joined the smoke seeping into her nostrils. The hair on her arms rose and fell, and faint nausea tugged at her gut. Despite her time in Hastigr's company, Heizl had never adjusted to the alien sensation that came with such magical travel.

A moment later, and even the faint crackle of flame faded as Heizl tumbled into blissful unconsciousness.

Tooth and Nail – Chapter Six

> *"Who could tell how many of the divine fell to the wayside in payment for hard fought victory. Its dominion in ruins, they turned to the defeated abomination. Only one punishment fitted its crimes, but neither sword, strength, nor sorcery could slay it. Their foe's undying nature revealed to them, it was the Collector that suggested the survivors make it like itself – one soul over many bodies."*
>
> A Treatise on the Shattering of Imes, Dwysil (359 I.Y.)

23rd day of Indern, 406th Imperial Year
17th Year of Emperor Rufenrich Konreig's Reign

The guardsman saluted, steel gauntlet touching blue surcoat. Thaun returned the gesture, ignoring the throbbing in his skull, and stepped past. Placing both hands on the heavy, wooden door, he paused and sighed. Bowing forwards, his forehead touched the cool, oaken panels.

It felt like a blur. He remembered taking a sword from an unresponsive guardsman, and charging a stranger. The sounds of chaos, the stench of smoke; pieces rose within his memory like scum floating to the surface of a still pool. Everything that came after seemed distant and indistinct, like recalling a half-forgotten dream. He wheezed, still tasting the flames.

"Thaun?" Lena whispered behind him. The mage adjusted the straps on a borrowed breastplate, her axe hanging from a new leather harness. Bruises and red marks marred much of her visible skin, yellowing and half-healed.

Sigren shouldered past the healer. "We're gonna be late." Like his charge, the Shadow had changed from his torn clothes. At his belt hung a replenished quiver, while he held his crossbow tight against his chest. If not for the haunted vigilance in his eyes and a single shallow cut across his forehead, he might've passed as unharmed. Any other wounds – magically healed or not – hid beneath leather and cloth.

"It's better we turn up late and in one piece than falling apart in there," assured Lena. "We're all shaken right now. Even you, Sigren. They'll understand."

"You think the Shadowmaster will *understand* if we're not here when we're told to be?" He seethed. "We need to pull ourselves together."

Thaun looked away. Even compared to their usual bickering, things felt off. Layers of fear, pain, and exhaustion all but hid the deep bond of friendship that they all shared. It reassured him a little that the evening's events had affected more than just him. "I'll be fine." He lifted his head and looked at each of them in turn. "Come on, I should..." He trailed off as footsteps approached from behind. Turning, he noticed the way Lena stepped out, putting herself between him and whoever walked down the passageway towards them. Thaun pressed his lips into a thin, white line.

A tall soldier descended the stone steps. Thaun recognised him before the veteran said a word. The Imperial Champion, Vandel. He stopped several feet beyond Lena's reach, and eyed each attendant in turn before turning to the Royal.

"Hear you two landed a hit on Renyar," he grunted, raising his chin towards Lena before looking down on Thaun. "Guy's got a reputation for handling steel. Probably lucky, but still." He shrugged, huge scimitar upon his back bobbing with the movement, before looking away, disinterested.

"Uh, thanks," muttered Thaun. Lena said nothing. He'd met the Champion a dozen times before, during one function or the next, and had seen him in action while touring the Empire. Despite all that, he couldn't remember having heard so many words from him before. "I've been practising." Vandel stayed quiet.

Under the veteran's silent, grey-eyed regard, he felt his legs tremble. As the silence lengthened, Thaun turned away, unable to hold the gaze any longer. "I should be going. Uncle will wonder where I am."

"Indeed," the Champion nodded. "Until next time, Crown Prince." Vandel faced back up the corridor, ignoring the Royal's presence as he took up guard duty.

Thaun considered him for a moment. For all his objections, most in the Palace would've saluted, bowed, or something. Yet the old veteran didn't. Anyone else might've asked why, but all he'd only ever felt gratitude.

With a shrug to his companions, Thaun turned to the door behind him, and pushed.

Frida's hard stare met him like a spear wall. Averting his gaze, he reached out to lean against the wooden doorframe.

After a moment, she spoke. "Your Highness, your entourage can wait outside."

"Shadowmaster." Crossbow balanced in one hand, Sigren saluted, only lowering his fist when Frida returned the gesture. With the briefest of glances towards Thaun, he moved to join the nearby guardsmen.

"Shadow, there are reports waiting for you in your quarters. Familiarise yourself with them." She looked at Lena, who hesitated. "Mage, dismissed."

"Ma'am," stammered Lena, "Respectfully, with the incident tonight, I feel that—"

"Feelings, mage, don't factor into the matter," her sharp voice cut across the healer's like a razor through taut thread. "The cutters upstairs require your assistance."

The mage paused before trying again. "I know more spells than just healing, ma'am."

Frida didn't dignify her with a response, instead turning to Thaun. "Your Highness, if you please?"

Thaun rubbed his eyes, "Lena, it'll be fine. If it's not safe here, where is?"

"You're going to be in the same enclosed space as the Emperor," whispered the healer. "Less than an hour ago, a foreign power tried to murder him, and successfully killed dozens. Nowhere's particularly safe right now."

"Miss Ortharn," Frida's tone dropped to a cold growl, "It's been a difficult night for many of us, and your efforts this evening are recognised. I suggest that you recover your strength." Lena opened her mouth to speak, but stopped as the Shadowmaster turned to Thaun. "Your Highness, this way, please."

Thaun gave the healer a weak smile and walked through the door. Behind him, Lena sagged onto a nearby bench, deflated.

As the door shut behind Thaun, Rufenrich appeared and wrapped him in a desperate embrace. He sagged towards him, drawing comfort and familiarity from the contact. Smoke filled Thaun's nostrils as he drew a deep breath. Neither man spoke.

After a long moment, the Emperor stepped back, one arm still outstretched to clasp his nephew's shoulder. "You're not hurt?"

"I..." Thaun couldn't bear the fear in the older man's gaze for long. He glanced away, peering over his uncle's shoulders at the rest of the room.

A broad desk of Noldanian hardwood dominated the windowless room. Dozens of books and a hundred sheets of parchment littered its dark, waxed surface. Here and there, a handful of scattered knickknacks held down the assorted piles – an old pair of hide gloves, a dagger of some pale metal, a silver seal with its wax – but no seat stood alongside the table.

Tall shelves lined all four walls. Books, many with loose leafs protruding, filled every shelf. Leather- or cloth-bound, with fresh ink or faded script, it'd take a lifetime to read them all.

Several low chairs huddled at the centre of the room, grooves in the carpet's deep fibres revealing where they'd rested before. In one corner, another matching seat lay unmoved. A familiar figure sprawled in one, head resting on a clenched fist and eyes hooded. Thaun's lips curled into a weary smile upon seeing Heizl there. He'd expected his cousin to be giddy as a schoolchild at being invited into a meeting of the Imperial inner circle, but he couldn't remember when he'd last seen her look so empty. The incident must've taken its toll. Her familiar rod, scratched and scorched almost beyond recognition, lay across her lap.

An older man studied one bookshelf while leaning on his cane, his hunched back to the room. Thaun hadn't spent much time with Highmage Hastigr, but the whole court recognised the man who made the Nexus possible.

He finally answered his uncle's question. "I'm fine. Just a little shaken up."

"Good," Rufenrich blew out a deep breath before raising his voice. "In that case, what in Vorsit's name were you thinking?!" Had the room's handful of occupants spoken among themselves at that moment, they might have fallen silent at their ruler's outburst. Instead, Heizl slowly looked up to stare at them, dazed. "You are *important*!" the Emperor's shout descended into a clenched teeth growl. "I heard what you did. Risking yourself like that... you could've got yourself killed!"

"I'm... I..." not for the last time, Thaun stammered. "I'm sorry."

The fearful rage faded from his uncle's eyes. "I know you are. I know." He shook his head. "You might prefer spending your time playing soldier, but that doesn't mean you can do it when something like this comes along. I thought I told you that Renyar was dangerous?"

"I know."

"What would your father say?" he continued. "Wading into chaos with a sword in hand was..." Rufenrich shook his head.

"Y'know, Uncle?" His cousin drawled from her seat. "You didn't seem this concerned for me."

"Heizl, you know as well as I do that your circumstances are different to Thaun's." He turned to his niece, "You're not such a valuable target. I don't *have* to worry about you the same way."

"Love y'too, uncle," she slurred, head still bowed.

"Oh, don't be like that. We all know that you're far from defenceless, and I'm told you did well tonight." With a glance to Thaun, the Emperor walked over to Heizl and placed a hand on her arm. "I'm proud of you."

Blinking like a drunk waking from sleep, Heizl squinted up at her uncle.

Frida coughed. "Rufenrich?" All turned towards her. "Time's short."

"Fine," the Emperor took a deep breath. "Thaun, Hastigr, sit, please. We've a lot to discuss."

The old mage turned and shuffled to the nearest padded chair, lowering himself into its soft cushions. As Rufenrich and Frida each found their seats, Thaun sat down alongside his cousin. He glanced at the empty seat outside the ring, the distinct feeling of something missing gnawing at his thoughts.

"Your Highnesses, Highmage, Miss Fitzerin." The Shadowmaster turned to each of them in turn. "You know why we're here."

"'Cause some foreign bastard crashed our party?" Heizl slurred.

"This is serious," Frida snapped. "At the feast tonight, the Thalan Patriarch, Renyar, attempted to assassinate the Emperor. If not for the intervention of the

Spire, and the Imperial Champion, we would be holding a different meeting right now."

Thaun raised a hand. "Champion? I didn't see him there."

"He arrived after you fell to Renyar's magic, Your Highness," said the Shadowmaster. "At his arrival, both Thalans retreated."

"I don't understand." Thaun shook his head. "Renyar and that woman with him didn't seem the type to run when threatened with a sword. I mean, I tried..." For a moment, no one uttered a word. He saw Frida eye first Hastigr and then Rufenrich, her expression unreadable.

The Emperor shrugged. "Renyar lost the element of surprise. After I escaped, he probably fell back to cut his losses."

"That seems..." Thaun closed his eyes as he processed his uncle's words. "That doesn't sound right."

"Thaun, your safety means more to me than Renyar's motives for fleeing." Rufenrich reached out to pat his hand.

"I suppose." He opened them again. "How did he get in in the first place? He was invited to the feast, right?"

"He was," said Frida. "However he didn't arrive with the other guests. My Shadows have since discovered a beacon hidden in the Great Hall, as well as the body of a missing guardsman."

"A beacon? Like–"

"My Nexus, yes," Hastigr interrupted. "But all of my beacons are accounted for. Renyar travelled here under his own power."

"It's since been neutralised," Frida continued, fists clenched at the interruptions. "However it raises unfortunate implications. Renyar has a skilled agent within the Capital, and may have his own network within our borders." Thaun paused, thinking of the many faces he'd seen through the Palace. A hundred nobles, merchants, servants, soldiers... He couldn't grasp the long list of suspects. "I've dispatched Shadows to investigate the guests present tonight. The garrison and the City Watch have likewise been informed of the situation."

"You think someone at the party helped him get in?" asked Thaun. His hearing dulled as anxiety pounded in his ears.

"Thaun," said Rufenrich. "You don't remember the Civil War, but many do. A lot of families lost power when the Kuhlners' rebellion failed. Our Empire isn't as stable as we'd like people to believe."

"Uncle…"

"I'm taking steps, but you need to help, understand? Just pay attention to Frida."

"Thank you, Rufenrich," said the Shadowmaster. "My men have started questioning tonight's guests." Beside him, Thaun saw Heizl straighten in her seat. "We've cleared some to leave. Young Lord Acquiel recently left via the Nexus, and Governor Strahl remains within the city, at his estate. He's made contact with several local mercenary groups to bolster his own, already considerable, house guard." Something cold burned in Frida's eyes. "I'll be sure to speak with him about his intentions."

"And Jilia?" Heizl blurted out. All eyes turned towards her, and faint colour rose in her pale cheeks.

"Judging by the runners intercepted so far, she's arranging contracts personally, Miss Fitzerin," Frida's voice came through emotionless, as flat as calm water.

Rufenrich cleared his throat. "I'll speak to Dasimir, he can't be behind this attempt. He's more interested in putting a grandchild on the throne than sitting on it himself."

"Uncle? I want answers as much as anyone, and I get that it's important I learn what's going on if you're going to…" Thaun cleared his throat. "But shouldn't we wait until we know more before deciding anything?"

"We know enough," reassured Rufenrich. The two cousins shared curious looks, each raising a single eyebrow in reflection of one another.

Heizl spoke first. "There's more going on here than a failed assassination, isn't there?"

"Much more," the Emperor sighed. "We'll explain it all, sooner or later, I promise."

"Uncle, what's going on?"

Rufenrich forced a smile. "Do you know who Renyar is?"

"A green, sand-spitting son of a bitch?" Heizl slurred.

"Heizl!" At their uncle's paternal outburst, Thaun smiled for a moment, the expression rising from his weariness.

"Sorry," Heizl bowed her head, hiding her smirk.

"You mentioned him earlier, right?" said Thaun, drawing attention away from the mage. "A Thalan noble or something."

"Good," said Rufenrich. "But there's more to him. Patriarch of Thala, master swordsman, powerful mage, and scion of a storied family."

"Too right he is," Heizl laughed, though her voice held little genuine mirth. "The way he shielded himself, fine, I've seen others use abjurations before, but the silver tongue? That wasn't normal."

"Thala's arcane history is somewhat longer than ours," he dismissed the question with a wave. "But we'll come to that."

"And that hooded woman of his?" asked Heizl. "Something wasn't right about her either."

"That would be Elhin," said Frida. "One of Renyar's senior lieutenants, or as good as. Drawn from their temple assassins, she's one of Thala's most dangerous fighters, despite no connection to the arcanosphere."

"So, she's not a mage, but she still did all that?" Heizl arched an eyebrow again. "What aren't you telling us?"

"Maybe I should explain," breathed Rufenrich. Both Hastigr and Frida turned towards him, but neither spoke as he raised an open hand. "No, if we're involving them, they deserve to know."

After a moment of tense silence, Frida ventured her opinion. "Now might not be the most opportune time."

"If we don't tell them now, when will we?" Rufenrich snapped. He turned back to his family, and so didn't see the hurt look appear in her eyes. A shocked moment passed, and cold, implacable control descended once more. "Thaun, Heizl, just sit and listen. I know how hard you find it, but no interruptions, please?"

Thaun looked to Heizl for support. His stomach rolled, nerves fraying and pulling tight. The Court's usual complications made him sick at the best of times, and now they stood at a precipice. He hated to admit it but he agreed with Heizl; something felt wrong. The two had spent enough time together that he could guess some of what she thought. They nodded to one another.

"Thank you," said the Emperor. "I'm no historian, but I'll try to explain.

"Before our Empire, before even the Conglomerate, there was an Empire in what's now Thala. Ruled by..." He hesitated. "The shattered remains of a god. It was an amazing place, apparently, more than what we have now even with centuries of advancements. It wasn't to last though, as all its accomplishments and riches drew attention from *outside*."

"Outside?" asked Thaun.

"I knew it wouldn't take long before one of you interrupted me." A regal eyebrow quivered, his tone weary. "Yes, outside. Beyond even the infinite Voids bordering our mundane world. As far from what you know as the sky is from the land. What it was out there that sensed their power, nobody knows, but we call it Urathear."

"This feels familiar," muttered Heizl to no one in particular, eyes closed once more.

"That's because you've heard it told before. The church, the Spire, every cult, temple, and madman has their own version of the story. Urathear, the first dragon, destroyed all that it saw. Where its shadow reached, stone burned and flesh boiled. Until Thala. The shattered god there confronted it, and tricked it. While three Aspects of their god faced the beast, the last made his way to its Heart, and... Hastigr?"

"You're doing remarkably well," reassured the Highmage. "But 'outside' is something understated, I prefer–"

"Will it suffice?"

"It's important to be accurate," Hastigr crossed his arms over his chest. "Though perhaps it's best not to complicate matters."

"Well, that Aspect bound himself to the dragon's Horn, and took the Heart outside again. A single one of the Voids, each of them infinite. Mages have sought the legend's truth, but without a path to guide them to the Heart, they searched in vain."

Thaun's mouth fell open at his uncle's words. Other worlds – he wasn't prepared for this sort of talk. Heizl, or anyone else from the Spire, might have the words for it, but he didn't know *how* to even think about such things.

"Without its Heart, Urathear fell apart. Fragments rained down, destroying that ancient imperium and scarring the world until today. Those Fragments remain." Rufenrich took a deep breath. "We saw the destructive potential of two such pieces first-hand this evening."

Next to Thaun, Heizl stirred once more and opened her eyes. "Is that how they did what they did? Commanding people and shrugging off Korten?"

"Renyar's far from helpless without it, but yes," the Emperor nodded.

"What do history and legends have to do with tonight?" asked Thaun. Despite his query, a part of him suspected the answer already. Rufenrich didn't respond straight away, instead turning to his nephew. He opened and closed his mouth a few times as he struggled to find the words, eventually looking away.

Professional veneer secured over her features once more, Frida lay a hand on the Emperor's arm and spoke for him. "When Sheltz's Comet reaches its height, and the realms are at their closest, Renyar will summon the Heart of Urathear."

Thaun bit his lip. He considered himself to have a warmer attitude towards magic than most in the Empire – regular exposure to both Heizl and Lena had taught him that it wasn't an inherently evil thing. Still, talk of ancient gods and monsters turned his stomach.

The Imperial Church preached about the dark things that came before the Empire often enough. Despite his own disillusion with their teachings, he'd always suspected they held at least a grain of truth. Dragons and their kin had existed once at least; every historian recognised the part that the ancient Daericani had played in forging that first alliance.

A few ruins and artefacts of their culture still remained, not that Thaun'd spent any time out among them.

Heizl's voice pulled him back to the room. "And summoning it would be bad?"

"Almost certainly, based on tonight's events," replied the Shadowmaster. "The Heart of Urathear is a source of incredible power. It can destroy or sustain nations. In our enemies' hands, it'd spell disaster."

"I'm far too sober for all this," the young mage sank down into her chair. Under other circumstances, Thaun might've laughed at the dry understatement. Instead, he turned to their uncle.

"How do you know this?"

He shrugged. "Renyar told me."

"What?!" Thaun exclaimed.

"He might've approached me a few years ago under the pretence of stopping someone summoning the Heart," Rufenrich mumbled.

"And you just believed him?"

"It was during several positive and profitable negotiations – we had no reason not to trust him."

Frida chimed in. "We only recently began to suspect that Renyar isn't all that he seems. His attack tonight confirms our suspicions."

"That's why he attacked us? Because you learned that he was after this Heart?"

"He attempted to kill your uncle when we stood in opposition to his plans," she explained.

Thaun looked from Shadowmaster to Emperor and back again. His sporadic training had failed to prepare him for this sort of meeting. "So, now what?"

"Now..." Rufenrich glanced to Heizl. "Now we stop him."

"Stop Renyar? Two of them cut through a Highmage, dozens of guardsmen, and who knows what else like they were children. Who knows how many like her he'll return with?"

Frida nodded once. "Fighting on their terms proved costly. We have no intention of making the same mistake again."

Realisation dawned on him. "You've got a plan."

"We hurt Renyar tonight, but he hurt us just as badly. So long as he doesn't summon the Heart, we might not need to beat him." Rufenrich smiled.

Heizl sat up and leant in. "And how do we do that?"

"Can I trust you both?" he asked. "The fewer people who know all this, the less likely we are to have to stop anyone else from trying something similar. Renyar already has at least one mole in our ranks – we're not so foolish as to trust someone just because they're Imperial."

"You can trust me, uncle," said Heizl. Though her skin remained pale, her eyes shone at the sight of Rufenrich's answering smile. Mage and Emperor alike turned towards Thaun.

"This is another of those things where I don't have much of a choice, isn't it?"

"Thaun." Sadness tainted Rufenrich's smile. "Everything I do, everything I ask of you, is for your sake, and for the Empire."

"Uncle..."

"You can't stay here – losing both of us at once would destabilise the entire Empire. I can't send you off on another tour either, as Renyar's already shown he's willing to ignore our forces and attempt to attack us directly. Sending you away secretly is the only way to keep you safe."

"But, uncle–"

"Hiding you won't help – if you can't handle this, nothing I do will help you. I thought you might like it, being away, getting to make a difference. You've hardly kept it secret, all these years, how you hate being among the nobility. This way, you'll be with soldiers. They might still try their hands at flattery, but it won't be with a silver spoon in their mouths."

"Where am I going?"

"Hastigr?"

The old Highmage coughed before speaking, the motion jangling the metallic charms at his wrist. "Sorry I was just... my mind was elsewhere. The ritual to summon the Heart can only be performed at several locations where the veil between our realm and the Voids is at its thinnest." He paused, eyes flicking to Heizl. "The Daericani forced their way into your Empire at one such Juncture. The portal there is gone, but echoes of power linger. When Sheltz's Comet comes closest, those echoes grow stronger, until the right ritual can bridge the gap and reach the Heart."

"We believe that Renyar will attempt to control the Rift where the Daericani first appeared, so as to complete his plan," explained Frida. "A battalion – elements of both the First and the Second – is assembling to travel there, to fortify it."

"And I'm going with this group?" asked Thaun.

"You're going to *command* it," said Rufenrich. "Even if squatters have taken up residence there, you'll have more than enough men to force them out, probably without even drawing a sword. Highmage Korten will go with you as well, to advise on any appropriate matter, and to provide support. There's not an army in the known world that could displace you from a fortified position." He thought for a moment. "Not before the Comet's height, anyway. At least, not without exposing themselves to the rest of the Imperial Guard."

"Uncle, are you sure about this? I'm no commander."

"And neither am I, but the troops still swear an oath and follow my orders. It might give you a chance to learn how to be one."

Thaun looked away. He'd prefer to spend time with a sword in hand over a goblet, but he hadn't considered the gravity of it until now. All of his teachers had told him how well he fought, how naturally swordplay came to him, but the thought of putting it into practice left a sour taste in his mouth. Still, compared to sitting among the Imperial Court with a bullseye on his back, perhaps it was the lesser of two evils.

He looked back. "Okay. Fine. Where am I going?"

"You'll take the Nexus the day after tomorrow," said Rufenrich, pride tugging at the corners of his eyes. "Hastigr will send you to an outpost on the edge of the Daer Sea, where you'll meet your command. From there, you'll cross to Insel Drach, and local scouts will guide you to the site."

"Uncle?" Heizl raised a hand. "What about me? You had a task for me too? Am I going with Thaun?"

"I have a separate task for you," said Rufenrich. "Frida?"

She nodded. "Heizl, Hastigr will send you to the northern frontier to assist the Reiget Trade Guild."

"I'm going to babysit some merchants?" Thaun couldn't miss the disappointment in his cousin's words.

"It's a *cover*, Miss Fitzerin," Frida growled. "The Guild has suffered multiple setbacks in Norjhost, mostly in the form of raids by the native population. They suspect a large scale assault is imminent."

"Who'd have thought that people don't like outsiders trying to exploit their homelands?" Heizl drawled.

"Last chance, Heizl. Interrupt again, and I suspect Frida will correct your manners, not me." Rufenrich breathed an irritated sigh. "Understood?"

"Yeah, I understand," she winked at the Shadowmaster. "Sorry."

"If you're quite finished, what few reports we've had from surviving scouts suggest an unheard of level of coordination among the frontier tribes. The Norjans have a new warleader, someone uniting them into a single fighting force. They've destroyed several outlying tradeposts, and have besieged the last holding a beacon."

"Umm, Uncle?" Thaun recoiled as all eyes turned to him. "What has this got to do with Renyar? Is he attacking our borders? Spreading us thin?"

"Sound tactical thinking, Your Highness," for a second, he thought she might smile as she answered for their Emperor. "We haven't discounted Renyar recruiting from Fjujhost or other dissident groups, but we don't believe his plans are so direct. Highmage Hastigr?"

"Hmm?" The older man turned, a blank expression on his bearded face.

"Norjhost?"

"What about it?"

"Would you kindly explain what you know about Norjhost's environment?"

"Gladly," he came alive as he spoke, a series of bracelets at his wrists jingling as he moved. "There's more than one Source of magic, as Heizl demonstrates to us daily. Those of the Spire would find their sanguine magicks greatly diminished upon the peninsula due to the region's influence upon the arcanosphere. For that same reason, Renyar hopes to find something that will affect his Fragment."

"It'll make him *more* powerful?" Thaun's mouth dropped open as he recalled the Thalan's deflection of Korten's flames.

"Pretty sure that's the last thing we need," muttered Heizl.

"Heizl." Frida's hard stare accompanied her flat tone. The colour drained from his cousin's face. After a moment, the Shadowmaster turned to the Highmage. "Hastigr? Carry on."

"I met someone who wrote a book, once," the Highmage mused, eyes distant. "Thirty odd years ago, I think. Before your Civil War. He surmised, quite rightly, that the Fragments latch on to those who carry them. More than just their crude flesh and bone. Their body, mind, heart, and soul each fall prey. Bloodthirst. Lust for power. Desire." With each sentence his boney hand clenched tighter. "Hallucinations. False Promises. Urathear's claws dig deep." Hastigr sighed sharply. "Death offers the simplest escape." A smile flickered over his face. "But not the only one."

Thaun happened to glance at Heizl as she stared at the older mage. Rufenrich and Frida each wore a similar expectant expression. With no one filling the silence, he spoke.

"If we think Renyar wants to get rid of his... Fragment? Is that right? If he wants rid of it, why don't we just let him?"

"There's more to Heizl's mission," the Emperor spoke softly.

"This warlord," said Frida, "He has his own piece of Urathear. Another in Thala's hands would be disastrous, but if held by a loyal Imperial... well, Renyar wouldn't be so unbeatable."

Thaun arched an eyebrow "How do we know that?"

"Now," Rufenrich stood, not hearing the question. "We've other things to deal with, and you're both tired. It's been a trying day for all of us, and there are more of them ahead. You need to rest."

"Uncle, I have more questions," Heizl looked up at him.

"They'll have to wait. Right now, get some sleep. We'll have plenty to do soon enough."

Tooth and Nail – Chapter Seven

"Though the end of their line saw different circumstances, the first Konreig upon the Imperial throne heralded the decline of aristocratic power. No longer would lords raise their banners and travel to support liege and Empire. Instead, the Imperial Guard took charge of the fronts. No longer did merchants bicker amongst themselves over the price of grain. Instead, the Trade Guild regulated and controlled the goods running to and from the continent. No longer could hedge wizard, shaman, and shadow walker strike fear into the populace. Instead, the Spire rose over Reiget City, and with it the Shadows that would guard and guard against it."

Common Imperial History,
Introduction,
Archimand Märchen (408 I.Y.)

25th day of Indern, 406th Imperial Year
17th Year of Emperor Rufenrich Konreig's Reign

Beneath the flickering amber of a dozen covered lanterns, an ocean of level flagstones yielded to a raised coast of polished limestone. Jagged veins of calcite and smoothed fossils of long dead creatures broke the grey surface. Engraved beneath the loving hands of master craftsmen, the unbroken slab of ancient seabed revealed the reach of Imperial rule.

In the west, a length of cut diorite rose from the level floor, separating a huge, curving peninsula from the rest of the Empire. Beyond such a mountainous spine, Imperial control floundered, and the territory rose in open rebellion. Lesser ranges appeared elsewhere, casting dancing shadows over the seven provinces.

Hundreds of rivers ran across the map, each carved into the hard stone and filled in with cerulean quartz. A rare mineral, a byproduct of a single gold mine in northern Kragiv-Stal, its expense outstripped the map's mundane costs. Slender streams trickled into broader stretches, but all flowed towards the sea. Blue lines fought to carve their own path, but each ended in the same place – some things couldn't be fought.

Islands and sheets of raised jade broke the marbled plains marking the largest of the Empire's many woodlands. The wavering gold of the room's lights reflected on its smooth, verdant surface like an all-consuming forest fire. Every edge bore the scars of artisans' tools where green expanded unchecked or fell back beneath the axes of woodsmen. Imperials would exploit such resources wherever the opportunity arose, but the tree's roots dug deep.

Despite the expense of constructing such a piece of craftsmanship, the semi-precious stones and imported materials formed the least valuable thing in the room.

Slender, knee-high pedestals of carved, dark basalt arose in dozens of locations across the map. Minute bronze plaques hung from them, the name of each town engraved in a careful script. Each bore a strange burden upon a small velvet square. Sand-smoothed glass, foreign coins, and a dozen other myriad trinkets, no two were alike.

Across the Empire, in dozens of locked rooms, the partners of such beacons waited. Each year, a couple of Spire acolytes would show promise with such magicks, but all but the best of them could only handle a few pairs at a time. Of their Council, only a single elderly Highmage had the capacity to run such an array.

Heizl stood in the wide room's single doorway, taking in the familiar sight as she took the last bite of her sandwich. A dozen Shadows hugging the outer walls, the smells of sulphur and mothballs filling the air, and the faint twists of sorcery – to her they made up the room as much as Hastigr's kneeling shape near the map's heart. She was less accustomed to the presence of the room's other figures, or the clustered attendants and guards standing outside.

Even with the small crowd that had gathered, no one beyond the Highmage himself seemed willing to step onto the map's carved surface. The Empire's fear of magic ran deep. None spoke in more than a whisper, afraid perhaps of disturbing Hastigr's meditations, or worried about drawing the attention of anything outside of their own understanding. The young mage smiled to herself. She'd long learned that her mentor couldn't be so easily roused. Beyond the Spire, such superstitions served her well enough.

A pair of nervous porters placed a collection of bags and boxes before the Highmage – gear and belongings for the mundane legs of her and Thaun's journeys. No sooner had the men scurried clear, than darkness clawed up from the floor to envelope the equipment in an impenetrable sphere of rippling blackness. A circle of dust shuddered towards the orb, flakes disappearing within as it consumed the things closest to it. Though they'd seen it occur several times already as Hastigr ferried supplies and gear to both destinations, the room's low conversation ceased. Shadow, mage, and every other occupant stared at the brazen disregard for the world's natural laws.

A second passed, and the swirling ball tore itself apart like a whirlwind throwing out debris. Heizl coughed, hiding her amused smirk as one of the nearer Shadows flinched away in spite of their training. In the orb's wake, nothing but a faint musty smell lingered.

As Hastigr's godlike magicks faded, Heizl looked past the old man – his dark skin almost pale – to the opposite side of the Nexus. Her uncle stood with arms folded over his chest, his retinue clustered close. Korten leant against a wall, eyes shut, skin ashen, and with fresh bandages hiding the rings upon his fingers. Vandel for his part walked back and forth, head bowed while he whispered to himself. Only Frida watched the room.

Heizl's latest Shadow, a skeletal man with a long birthmark stretching up his neck, stood near the Emperor's group, awaiting his orders. Zecht waited a short distance behind her, alongside the Royal Guardsmen that had escorted them into the Spire's underbelly.

She still didn't know how she felt about the second man. Few mages merited two such attendants. In a backhanded way, she could take it as recognition of her abilities. The flipside of that coin though, of another man trying to control her, chafed. The dangers of their task demanded it.

Across the room, she caught a worried glance from Thaun where he stood with Lena. Her cousin had grown sullen since watching Sigren disappear from the room inside a swirling, black orb several minutes earlier. Heizl could hardly blame him. She'd never found journeying through the Nexus a pleasant experience either. Hastigr had taught her some of the theory, describing the way such travel skirted the Voids outside their world. The thought of being in multiple places at once, in a space with the wrong number of dimensions, stretched her own understanding, let alone that of someone without her training. Mortal man was ill-suited to such an unnatural environment.

With an exaggerated roll of her eyes, Heizl pushed off from the wall. Half the room's occupants looked to her as she walked straight towards her cousin, stepping over false mountains and rivers like one of the gods. Shock, fear, and a dozen other emotions appeared on the faces of those eyeing her, but she didn't return any of their mixed looks. She smiled. They'd have to get used to being in awe of her sooner or later, so she might as well start getting them accustomed to it.

"You can just walk straight across that?" Thaun pulled a puzzled face. "So why've we all been hugging the walls like that thing is made of lava?"

"A penchant for children's games?" She smirked as she clapped him on the shoulder. Off to one side, Zecht wore a similar smile to her. "The Nexus is... complicated, but it's not too likely to send you in opposite directions at once just for walking over it."

"Too likely?"

"Well, I mean, it might if you tripped over a beacon or something, but that hardly ever happens."

"So it has happened?"

"Oh, stop worrying." Heizl failed to give him a reassuring smile. "Ready to leave?"

Thaun looked away, his discomfort beneath their attendants' gazes plain upon his wincing face. Heizl waited patiently as she watched her cousin struggle for the right words. "When Uncle first told me that I was going to be joining the courts all I wanted was a way out. I'm not ready for that sort of responsibility." He shook his head as he sighed. "Going and sitting on an island in the middle of an army isn't what I had in mind."

"It's hardly an army. A battalion at most."

"That's not really my point..." Thaun shot her a sharp glance, evoking a wicked answering smile.

"Look on the bright side – it'll be quiet, and you'll be armed, so just think of how much practice you'll get. You might even have fun."

"Come on, we both know that, even if there's anyone there willing to swing at me properly, Uncle wouldn't let me do anything like that for real."

"Then how about the fact that you'll have your friends around, and the nearest noble should be miles away?" Heizl said, exasperated. "Or that you won't have some emerald Thalan snake trying to kill you?"

Her cousin looked away, and Heizl felt a fist clench around her heart. "...You don't know that."

"Thaun..." she tilted her head forwards as she whispered. "You don't have to be afraid."

"I'm not afraid!" Thaun snapped. "I just... I don't know." He trailed off again. "What about you? I bet you're glad to have a chance to show off to Uncle? And the Spire?"

"Well, yeah, I guess, but it's hardly going to be comfortable. I'd rather be in someone else's feather bed than sleeping out under the stars," Heizl shrugged. "I'm not even sure what I'm meant to do. This outpost is supposed to be under siege, but if that doesn't work out, how am I supposed to find some crusty warleader, let alone fight him? Me and two Shadows against one of these Fragments? You saw what Renyar did."

Thaun lay a hand on her shoulder. "Uncle wouldn't send you if he didn't think you'd do okay."

"What makes you so sure? I'm not Kor–"

"Heizl!" Rufenrich's voice cut across her protests as the Emperor crossed the room towards her. Behind him, Frida scowled, Korten smirked, and Vandel seemed absorbed in his own thoughts. "Are you quite finished?" said their uncle.

"I had a few more things to say, actually." Heizl smiled.

"You can save them for later," he snapped. "Thaun, you're next. Are you ready? Do you know what you're doing?"

"Are you sure I can't travel by land?" he replied, colour draining from his face.

"Certain. While the Comet still rises, time's on our side, but it won't be forever. We're acting while we can."

"I suppose..." Thaun's shoulders slumped. "Where do I go?"

Rufenrich smiled. "About a foot in front of me, so I can say goodbye properly." Heizl felt the corners of her lips twitch upwards at the clumsy sentiment. The Emperor reached out with both hands and dragged his nephew into an embrace. "You'll be fine. A handful of Royal Guard went through earlier, and a platoon of Second Army are waiting for you. And that's not counting the auxiliaries and the Trade Guild's own men. There won't be many safer places in our Empire."

"That's not what I'm worrying about," said Thaun.

The mage tapped her copper rod on her shoulder as she waited. She knew Rufenrich cared for her, but she'd never felt like their relationship matched up to that between her cousin and their uncle. Heizl'd always thought that green was her colour, but jealousy didn't suit her so well.

"Then what is it?" asked the Emperor. "Renyar doesn't know you're going there, he won't be able to hurt you."

"It's not that..."

"Uncle?" Heizl spoke up. Both men broke their hold on one another and turned towards her. "He's obviously nervous about the Nexus."

"Oh. That," Rufenrich shrugged. "I wouldn't put you through this if I didn't think it'd be good for you. It's perfectly safe, and some things can't be avoided, even by me. You know what you're doing?"

Thaun took a deep breath before speaking in a flat, well-rehearsed, tone. "Arrive at the crossing. Meet my command. Go to Insel Drach. Find and fortify...somewhere. Hold the Rift there until after the Comet passes."

"The Daericani site there, yes. Your scouts will know the way, but you forgot the most important part of your instructions though."

"I did?" Thaun frowned.

"Keep *safe*." At their uncle's words, Heizl couldn't help but smile. "You're under strict orders from your Emperor to be in one undamaged piece when I next see you."

"I'll be careful," he reassured.

"Good." Rufenrich turned to Heizl. "I imagine you two have your own goodbyes to make. I'll try not to interrupt."

"Thank you, Your Majesty," she had to control herself to keep her tone respectful. Heizl nodded and watched as he walked a short distance away. She turned back to Thaun, made awkward eye contact before breaking it again as she scratched at the back of her neck. The dry, grey skin there had spread since the night of the feast. A day's rest without casting had let it shrink again, but not as much as she'd have liked. "This has become awfully serious all of a sudden, hasn't it?"

"Seems that way. Are you going to be alright?"

"I'd like to say I've had worse... but I dunno," Heizl shrugged. "I'll survive."

"You're sure?"

"Not in the slightest," she smiled wryly. "Go on, you're going to be late."

"I'm in no hurry." Thaun smiled back. "I don't much like long goodbyes either, but between that and the Nexus..."

"I know," Heizl opened her arms wide, inviting him in for a hug. "Let's just get this over with."

Thaun stepped in, embracing his cousin and patting her on the back. "I'll see you when all this is over?"

"Maybe before, if you're unlucky," Heizl joked as she broke from her cousin's grasp. "Now, go stand over by that beacon. No, the rust-coloured one. Hastigr's ready."

"How do you know?"

"Oh, come on." Heizl laughed. "I carry the rod, I get followed by Shadows. It can't be that hard to work out that I'm a mage too."

"I guess not." He smiled, sharing a forced chuckle. Her cousin placed a hand on Heizl's shoulder and opened his mouth as if to speak. With a shake of his head, Thaun walked away to stand near the kneeling Highmage. Lena checked her axe before following him.

"Wait, Lena," Heizl murmured. The healer paused and eyed her from behind her cautiously. "Look after him for me?" A single nod and she moved to Thaun's side. A sly smile growing on her lips, the mage called after her. "Oh, and look after yourself too!" Lena rolled her eyes.

Both royal and mage stopped a couple of paces from Hastigr. Though she attempted to hide her emotions, Heizl could still sense the discomfort in Lena's stance at standing so close to her charge. Though the bastard remained silent, sympathy rose into her chest at the healer's position.

"What do we do now?" asked Thaun.

"Just keep your arms in tight," said Rufenrich, watching with tears welling in his brown eyes.

"I know, I've done this—"

Wisps of glistening darkness wrapped up from the floor around their feet to envelope the pair in a roiling black sphere. The air, already stale and thick from the room's many tentative occupants, grew bitter as the magic flared. Heizl ignored the sorcery — she was hardly a stranger to it. Instead, she watched the people around her.

Frida placed a hand on Rufenrich's shoulder, only to remove it when he shrugged her away. Behind them both, Vandel stood with his arms across his broad chest now, staring intently at Hastigr as if for the first time. A flickering hint of caution glimmered in his grey eyes like glittering stars.

Several Shadows and guardsmen reached towards their weapons, but none drew steel. Even having witnessed the phenomena before, their vigilance had dulled little.

A moment later, and Hastigr's magic tore itself apart. Knowing she'd see nothing, Heizl still looked to where it, and her cousin, had stood. Empty, foul-smelling space greeted her.

No one spoke until their Emperor broke the silence. "Heizl? A moment?"

She didn't respond straight away, still watching the spot where Thaun and Lena had stood. Her cousin knew how to spar with a sword, but he'd not fought a true opponent before the night of the feast. Heizl couldn't shake the feeling that, even surrounded by several hundred soldiers, Thaun might not be as safe as they all hoped. A dozen more heartbeats passed — a measured length of time, long enough to show her independence but not so great as to cause true offence — before she turned and walked towards her uncle.

"You're next," said Rufenrich. "Are you ready?"

"Of course," Heizl grinned.

"You know what you're doing? This is important."

"I'm going to get me a piece of dragon," she shrugged. "Seriously, if there's anything I've missed, Zecht or... or the other one will be more than happy to correct me."

"Zecht?" The Emperor arched a regal eyebrow.

"Oh, right. One of my Shadows," Heizl looked around, finding the blond man a short distance away. "That guy."

"This is *your* mission, Heizl," said Rufenrich. "Theirs is just to keep you safe, and to be subtle about it. If I didn't think that this would be dangerous, I'd have considered sending you by yourself so fewer people knew what was happening."

"I know, I know," she sighed. "Wait, you'd send me solo? Sorry, not the point. I'll get it done, I promise."

"Will you promise me you'll take it seriously too? And that you'll be careful about it?"

"What's the worst that could happen?"

The Emperor lowered his voice, bowing in close. "Heizl, you're going beyond our borders to find and face someone who we're almost certain has a Fragment of a dead god. The worst that could happen is *bad*."

"Uncle." She took a deep breath. "You understand, right, that humour is how I'm trying to deal with all this?"

"You didn't want to make Thaun panic, I know." Her uncle nodded. "But he's not here now to benefit from your bravado, and I don't want you to underestimate what's ahead of you."

"You've already told me that this is a chance to prove myself to you, the Spire, your Court – what other motivation do you think I need?"

"I'm serious. If you'd become Highmage before, people would've talked about nepotism and politics. If you succeed in this, no one will argue that you earned it. That way you can support Thaun best when he's in charge." Rufenrich's mouth tightened. "Just don't get yourself killed trying. Your mother wouldn't have wanted that."

"No, she probably wouldn't." She grimaced at a memory rising unbidden. What would her mother have said now, if she knew everything that Heizl had done since? Extorted promises, hidden family, and unspoken fears. A dozen secrets kept from anyone. "Anything else? Or can I get in position? Hastigr's ready again."

"...I suppose not," he looked crestfallen, but stepped forward and wrapped his arms around his niece. "I'll see you when you get back."

"Yes, sir." Heizl smiled, and broke away. Turning her back, she walked to stand before her kneeling mentor, stepping around the strange collection of scattered trinkets before him. Open books of maps and equations, plates of half-eaten food, and heaps of mismatched jewellery storing the essence of a dozen lesser mages – she didn't dare risk disturbing any of them.

Zecht stepped alongside her, arms crossed over his chest. For a moment, she considered a sharp word to her companion, something to make the man question the safety of travelling through the Nexus. Instead, Heizl half-closed her eyes and probed out towards Hastigr.

The Highmage shone. His usual threads, linking him to Shadows, Emperor, and Heizl herself, seemed dim in comparison to their usual splendour. A second web, binding him to the pedestals and the objects borne upon them, flowed out from him now. Every beacon glimmered with prismatic hues, but one in particular, a chunk of polished seal ivory in the north of the map, glowed greater than the others.

A faded line, broken and indistinct, reached from it and out of the room, into the great Outside. Heizl had the barest sense of it continuing in a way beyond her senses, though she had no way of knowing where it led. Heizl moved away from it, uneasy at seeing her own path through the Nexus too closely. In such things, ignorance was bliss.

Finding her bond to Hastigr, she considered twisting it, of sending some emotion or thought to her mentor. Risking something that could actually distract the Highmage from his task seemed a bad idea. Like the rest of her family, she wasn't too fond of goodbyes anyway.

Zecht's low voice in her ear pulled her back to the physical world. "Have you done this before?"

"Done what?" asked Heizl, feeling a shiver travel up her spine. Had the room grown colder?

"Travelled like this?"

"Oh, sure, plenty," she replied.

"Does it hurt?" the Shadow whispered.

"That depends. What did you have for breakfast?"

"What does that matter?" The young man frowned.

Zecht never learned the answer, as darkness flickered around their feet. Heizl drew in a deep breath of relatively fresh air, and the light disappeared. At her side, she heard the Shadow's shocked gasp.

Her lungs tingled, burning as she held her breath, though it was better than the alternative. The Shadow coughed, and she heard him hawking up spit only for it to sizzle away within the Void like water sprinkled on flames.

As the ground beneath her feet lurched, Heizl stumbled but maintained her footing. Her stomach rolled at the movement, acid clawing to climb up her throat. Purples and greens swirled behind her vision and her ears popped as unnatural pressures closed in around her. The hairs rose along her arms while sweat soaked her skin. Her scathe, hidden by long hair, tingled faintly.

Heizl's senses didn't seem to work properly when travelling through the Nexus. She'd never found a satisfactory answer as to whether or not others saw it in quite the same way though. It reminded her of using her own sorcery, except threads didn't cross her vision like spiderwebs. Instead, a single dull grey path lay at her feet like a road among the starry darkness, guiding her along it. The journey felt timeless, and it never seemed like she walked, but she always reached her destination.

The black around her, like some long dead sky, flickered and twisted beneath her gaze. Against the fluctuating background, an orb of light pulsed and roared. Blue, green, grey, and purple, each colour rolling one into the next. She'd seen it before, but never so big or so loud. A second later, and her path took the glowing ball beyond her sight.

Another moment and flickering lantern light flooded her vision once more. Lowering herself to one knee, Heizl clamped her eyes shut as she reorientated herself. A short distance away, she heard Zecht's guttural retching as he threw up his stomach's contents.

All things considered, it sounded like the Shadow had done better than she'd expected. The last time Heizl had travelled with someone through the Nexus for their first time, the other man had cried for his mother like a child.

Opening her eyes and drawing in cool, fresh air, Heizl looked up at the noise of hurried footsteps. She found herself in a small, otherwise empty room.

Behind her, the beacon, a second piece of polished ivory, rested on a small cushion. In a ring around them, a dozen pieces of old jewellery and partially eaten food tumbled to the floor as the Void lost its grip upon the detritus. Weak light flickered through the smoke-stained glass of a lantern hanging from a beam, illuminating the room's single reinforced door.

A scrabbling of metal on the far side of the barrier drew her gaze as the door opened. In the doorway, a short, balding man appeared.

"You're from the Spire?" the stranger growled.

"I guess I am at that." Heizl straightened, a proud smile tugging at her lips.

"How long until the others get here?" he asked, craning to look behind the pair.

"Others?" Heizl took half a step back, careful to give the still vomiting Zecht a wide berth. "I've another Shadow coming through soon with our supplies."

"No more of your kind?"

"Just me." She eyed the man before her, taking in the battered armour, and the scattered injuries. "Were you expecting anyone else?"

The man lowered his voice, breaking eye contact. "Expecting? No. Praying and hoping, perhaps..."

Alongside her, Zecht rose unsteadily to his feet, wiping his mouth clean. "What's going on here?" he demanded.

"Are you the Shadow?"

"That's right." He stuck out his chin.

"Come on then." He looked between the two of them. "There's no time to lose."

Tooth and Nail – Chapter Eight

"Prior to the Daericani's violent arrival, countless warring fiefdoms called the Imperial continent home. Their borders shifted as banners rose and fell. Until they met these alien people, they cared only for their disputes with one another. The first meeting of worlds is lost to time, but the wars that followed, seeing man set against dragon, scars the Empire to this day."

An introductory letter,
Myron Paluch (397 I.Y.)

26th day of Indern, 406th Imperial Year
17th Year of Emperor Rufenrich Konreig's Reign

"There's no way I'm going to remember all these names," Thaun murmured.

"You don't have to," replied Sigren. "Read the context clues. Use the chain of command. Keep track of your officers and they'll handle the rest. Do that and you'll be fine."

Thaun surveyed their assembled ranks. One battalion from the Second Imperial Guard. A half-strength battalion taken from the First, mauled from their time supporting the Vigil in the northeast. A single squad of their family's Royal Guard. Almost a hundred soldiers from the local garrison.

Some eight hundred men and women all told, not counting camp followers, ships' crews, and the odd member of the Trade Guild. His army.

Thaun blew out a sharp breath. How had things reached this point? A month ago he'd toured legions and estates. A week ago he'd moaned to his family about his situation in, even he had to admit, an adolescent manner. Now, he sat astride an indifferent horse, almost a thousand faces before him. None of them expected much from an untested royal. Any mistake would get back to his uncle. Some legacy that'd be. What he wouldn't do to be a thousand miles away.

To his left, Korten lounged in a folding chair that creaked beneath his weight, a cup of strong wine nestled between gloved fingers. At first glance, only the perfumed smell of lotions hinted at his recent defence of the Emperor, though his flesh bore a raised, reddish colour of half-healed burns.

The Highmage's Shadows stood nearby, their black uniforms a sharp contrast to his white clothes. They formed a loose triangle, while a handful of servants scurried to and fro between them, fulfilling Korten's demands.

Beyond them, the Crossing's angular shape loomed. Its small keep still showed the old stone of the original fort, built back during the early Empire, while its outer walls revealed more modern additions. Multiple materials made up the construction – different stones, dense wood, and even metal sheets – while steel nets hung from brackets an armspan out from the wall and copper rods rose into the air. Out of sight behind ramparts, buckets of water, sand, and oils awaited hands trained in their use. During its centuries long existence, the Empire had developed many mundane methods to stall the mages that it feared so much.

Lena conversed with an irate officer and a Trade Guild shareholder a short distance away while Sigren wobbled uneasily on his own mount alongside Thaun. Overhead, gossamer clouds whispered by, blown in from the sea. On a clearer day they might've spied Insel Drach's shore from where they stood, but a faint mist rose above the water.

Thaun tilted his head. "I feel sick."

Instinctive annoyance flashed across the Shadow's face, before control rose around it once more. When he spoke, he almost sounded sympathetic. "You're not trying to avoid the Court here. Every soldier down there probably feels sick too. You'll get over it."

"It's not that. I've not felt right since the Nexus."

"Oh." Sigren shrugged. "Yeah, me too, I guess."

Thaun turned, an amused smile blossoming upon his face. "Really? I didn't think anything fazed you?"

"Come on," he grinned. "Being a Shadow doesn't mean I'm any less human than you."

"You're sure?"

Sigren didn't answer, his gaze tracking past Thaun as Lena approached them.

"I don't know how much good that did," admitted the healer.

"Told you so," smirked Sigren.

Thaun looked between them. "What's going on?"

"Turns out the garrison commander doesn't much like the Spire." Lena shrugged. "Korten bullying him into loaning us half his troops hasn't helped matters."

"Trouble?" The Shadow glanced past to where an officer continued arguing with the shareholder.

"I doubt it. A lot of the locals are superstitious about the island, but their curiosity outweighs their worries. For now, at least."

"What about the guilders?" asked Sigren.

"Pretty irate. Complaining about losses and costs, mostly."

Thaun raised a hand. "Do we really need the extra troops? It's not like we're expecting any resistance. People might notice if there aren't squads helping the tax collectors. Not that they'll complain."

"It won't hurt to have a few extra swords, especially ones who might know the area."

"Maybe..." a reluctant nod. "And the shareholders? Do we need to do anything about them?"

"Just use their ships and supplies," said Sigren. "They'll charge the treasury enough that I shouldn't worry about them."

"I'm just... We're trying to avoid notice, right? A dozen transports are hardly subtle."

"It'll be fine," replied the Shadow. "We only need to keep things quiet until we can find these ruins and set up. After that, we can hold out against anyone that knows about us... Anyone who can get here before we can call for reinforcements, anyway."

"I guess it's too late for us to change the plan," Thaun murmured. "When do we board?"

"Pay attention, sir," chided Sigren. "The first elements have already started. Over there." He pointed. Several hundred paces off, standards and uniforms rippled in the favourable wind as soldiers and staff boarded the ships.

"Oh, I thought they were just... Never mind." Thaun lost track of the time he spent watching them embark. A handful of smaller transports rested at the Outpost's stone quays, while longboats ferried troops out to the larger vessels anchored offshore. At some unseen signal, boats sitting lower in the water, Lena guided his retinue down the gentle slope towards the last few unfilled ships.

Curved wooden boards rocked beneath Thaun's weight as he stepped down from the jetty into the longboat. Upon the wharf, an aide took their horses by the reins. Three of the four oarsmen eyed him – such labourers rarely crossed paths with the nobility, let alone royalty – while the fourth stared out across the freshwater sea.

The short journey, accompanied by Lena, Sigren, and a handful of the Royal Guard, led them to the largest anchored ship. Clambering up the lowered ladder, strong hands helped Thaun the last armspan onto its deck. Ignoring the clumsy flattery of the merchant in front of him, he looked around.

Guardsmen shed their armour's extra weight, keeping only their coloured surcoats – blue and green for the First, blue and yellow among the Second. Few from the Legions learned to swim, and so treated the open waters with caution. Several threw charms and offerings overboard to appease Modra or whichever of her children claimed the sea as their own. Crewmen scurried to and fro, shifting their supplies or securing ropes as they weathered the shouts of their red-faced captain at the ship's wheel.

The others followed him onto the deck a moment later, and soon herded Thaun to a cramped cabin at the ship's stern. A feather bed and a degree of privacy – more than anyone else on the ship would likely get on their short journey. Ignoring Lena's concerned questioning, he shooed the pair away as soon as he could.

Alone for the first time since leaving the Palace, Thaun peeled off his all-too-polished armour, stacking it in a loose pile, before lying down. Fingers interlinked beneath sweat-slicked hair, he stared up at the wooden ceiling and felt the transport sway beneath him. He'd never much liked sea travel, but he'd take it over the Nexus any day. It couldn't be any worse than fending off the Court.

Before Thaun could lose himself in the mire of his mind, dwelling on his multitude of worries, sleep overtook him. Images rose unbidden among his dreams, of assassins, armies, dead gods, and a face he knew but couldn't remember.

Thaun awoke with a start as someone touched his shoulder. Shadow greeted him as a patch of deeper darkness loomed over him. He let out a startled yelp and clawed at the hand pressing upon him. As his feet worked beneath him, pushing him into a seating position, the figure recoiled.

"Thaun, it's okay," Lena's reassuring words reached him, high with shock. "It's me. It's Lena. Relax."

"I..." He wiped at the cold sweat on his face, and glanced down at his soaked clothes. Fleeting dreams tumbled from his grasp. They felt so close, so important, yet the memories faded like shadows before the sun. "Sorry. It was just a nightmare. I'm fine."

"Are you sure? It's not another..?"

"I don't think so."

"Good." In the darkness, she nodded once. "You've been asleep for hours."

"Just resting up – it's been a stressful week." He couldn't make out his bodyguard's expression as she replied.

"I know. A lot's changed recently, but some things are still the same. We're all here for you."

Glad for the gloom hiding his own features, heat rose in his cheeks. "I know. Thanks, but I'll be fine."

She didn't respond for a moment, instead looking around the small room, anywhere but at Thaun. Eventually, she broke the silence. "Sigren says we'll make landfall soon."

"Already?"

"Sun'll be up shortly. You've slept the whole night through."

"I didn't think it'd be that quick."

"Everything went right," she shrugged. "Favourable winds, clear skies, no snags or delays... Vorsit's arguing on our behalf."

"Right." Thaun rubbed his face again. "I should get up. Do I have any clean clothes?"

"There's some by the door," she replied. Her voice cracked as she continued. "Do you need help with your armour?"

"I'll manage."

"Then I'll be outside."

As the door shut behind her, he scowled, more at himself than at his friend. For all his training, and for every opportunity his bloodline had granted him, he was useless. She wouldn't offer such help to Sigren or to a soldier. They could look after themselves, not like Thaun. Between that implicit condescension and the shameless flattery of the Court, he didn't know which felt worse.

He pushed those bitter thoughts away, scrabbling for perspective. His first instincts led to resentment and anger, but he didn't want that. That path had served him poorly before. The calm words in his mind now sounded all too much like his uncle.

Lena meant well. She did her duty. Admirably, too. Neither she nor Sigren had had orders to be his friends, but they did it anyway. Reluctantly sometimes, but still. The unspoken words implicit in that offer of assistance cut though regardless, no matter how much he clamped down upon them.

He'd probably hurt others in the same way before now, blind to the effect his words and deeds had on others. In his all-too-few grounded moments of clarity, he could sometimes see it. Thaun hated himself the most in those instances. Awareness of those consequences didn't heal them though. All he could do now was try to be better.

Thaun steeled himself. Stripping from his crumpled clothes, he pulled on a fresh set before starting on his armour. A wash would wait. After a few minutes, the bulk of the plates and mail distributed evenly across his shoulders and waist, he stepped out into the pre-dawn.

Amber hugged the east with the morning's approach, revealing Insel Drach's uneven shape. The land swelled at the island's centre, like some bloated monster. Here and there, sparse trees broke the silhouette like claws reaching skyward. A few covered lanterns swayed around the transport's deck, and other lights blinked off both sides, marking the vague shapes of their fleet.

Between dark clouds overhead, a hint of blue and green light filtered through the grey. Even hidden from sight, the Comet made its presence known. He couldn't help but feel like it would get an awful lot brighter before all this was over.

Thaun shielded his eyes as Sigren walked towards him. "Mind pointing that somewhere else?"

"Sorry." the Shadow lowered his lantern before leaning close. "The strap under your arm isn't on properly."

Thaun spoke through clenched teeth as he adjusted his armour. "Thanks."

A rare smile flickered on Sigren's face. "You don't mean that."

"What now?" Thaun stepped past him, ignoring his friend's comment, and leant against the ship's wale. Few of the crew spared him a second glance, busying themselves with their own tasks.

"There's only a small dock at this end of the island, apparently, so it'll take a while to get all your men onto dry land." Sigren stepped alongside him. "The plan's to regroup with the scouts, and march towards the ruins tomorrow."

"*My* men..." he shook his head.

The Shadow continued as if not having heard him. "The Spire sends someone here occasionally to report on the local arcanosphere. Other than that, I hear Insel gets a few seasonal fishermen and hunters, but not much else. There's not much of any value around here."

Hints of sunlight broke over the jagged horizon, catching high points in the rocky terrain. A maze of shadowy faults and fissures sprang to life. Clumps of hardy brush-like plants broke the dim surface.

Several pinpricks of yellow light huddled together near the shore – scouts, awaiting their arrival.

Something crept into Thaun's stomach. Like ice water, it settled in, low and heavy, drowning out all prior urges to berate himself. The familiar sense of veiled panic came with it, though his mind stayed clear.

"Something's wrong," Thaun whispered.

"What is it?" asked Sigren.

"How many scouts got sent ahead?"

"I'm not sure," admitted the Shadow. "A few dozen? Maybe a handful of squads. Why, what's wrong?"

"There aren't enough lights."

"I think you're right."

"What does that mean?" Thaun eyed the cluster of lanterns.

For a moment, the Shadow didn't reply. Sailors and soldiers hurried about behind them. Lena appeared at their side, her armour clanking. "They're not all here," Sigren mused. "Or they're lying low."

"This place is meant to be empty," said Thaun. "Why would they hide?"

His question met only the sounds of the ship and the sea. The sun continued its slow rise into the golden sky, drowning out the scouts' scant fires. As the first rowboat touched the water, the morning light reached the wooden dock. Thaun strained his eyes to watch uniformed shapes clamber onto the damp planks. They disappeared from sight within the shadow, as if Insel Drach consumed them body and soul.

Squads would move to form pickets and perimeters, securing their mustering area. Shovels would dig into the hard earth, clearing trenches and foxholes. The second wave of guardsmen would consist of skirmishers tasked with moving beyond the new camp's growing borders to patrol. Imperial doctrine and taxes hard at work.

Thaun wondered if men had ever performed such tasks here before. Though the decisive battles of the Union War centuries before had occurred in traditional Imperial territories, he recalled mention of heroes and rulers striking for draconic strongholds. A fraction of such historic figures found glory here, only fire and death instead.

The bulk of their soldiers had reached the shore by the time Lena suggested they make the crossing themselves. Preceded and followed by the Royal Guard, Thaun straightened as he stood on solid ground once more. Most of the guardsmen bustling round ignored him, preoccupied with their own orders, but a few recognised him. He frowned at their uncertain salutes, but returned them all the same.

Lena guided him uphill to the command tent. The Royal standard flew before it, green horse rearing in the cool breeze upon its blue field. Gold thread trimmed the fabric, glinting in the rising sunlight.

Ducking under the canvas – one hand resting on his slung crossbow – Sigren entered first, scanning the empty space for threats.

All that rested within was a heap of bare, unassembled furniture.

Sigren sucked in air through clenched teeth. "Somebody should've assembled this by now." He reached to push aside the tent flap again.

"Wait," Thaun called after him. The Shadow turned. "We can handle a few seats. We might as well make ourselves useful while we wait."

"Let us," Lena stepped forward, leaning down to place her helmet upon the ground. "You shouldn't have to do this sort of thing."

"Don't be stupid," Thaun couldn't help but smile. "Hand me a chair."

When Korten plodded into the tent half a bell later, his Shadows trailing, a very different scene greeted him. Thaun perched on a low stool, while his bodyguards argued over a map that they'd pinned to a flimsy-looking table. The Highmage bowed, and moved to occupy a canvas-backed chair. A silver flask appeared in his ring-bedecked hand, but he paused before it touched his lips. "Nice place you've set up here. Little chilly though."

"What're you doing here? Staff meeting can't be for another hour." Sigren crossed his arms over his chest, and leant back on the table's edge. His crossbow weighed down one curling corner a few inches from his hand.

"Thought you might want to strike while the iron's hot," he shrugged, and took a sip.

"We shouldn't rush into anything," said Thaun despite the low anxiety still nestled in his gut. Moving camp chairs had distracted him for a few moments, but now it took an effort to control himself. Choosing to descend into panic always came easily. "The captains are probably still organising the squads."

"You might be tempting fate, there," Korten smirked. "Shouldn't worry though – I lit a fire under a couple of your officers – they'll be here soon enough, and then we can deal with it."

Thaun opened his mouth to point out that he'd heard the Highmage use that pun before, back in the palace, but shut it again when expectant faces turned towards him. A second passed, and he realised they all waited for him to say something, whether to order the Highmage out, or to suffer Korten's subtle disrespect. "Umm, deal with what exactly? The briefing isn't due yet."

"You should be thanking me, really – even too old or too young, those extra swords from the crossing might come in handy. It's not like there was much else for them to do there anyway."

Sigren raised a hand, "Korten, slow down – start from the beginning."

"Sorry, I get fired up sometimes," the Highmage shrugged, and drew an apple out from a deep pocket. "One of your officers was dealing with the scouts. You sounded like you were having so much fun playing house, I had them gather in one of the other tents – figured you wouldn't want to be bothered with–"

"That's not your call to make." Sigren stared daggers.

"They said that too, until I worked my magic on them." The bald mage smirked.

The Shadow bunched his fists, but Thaun's reply cut short his harsh words.

"Korten. Highmage," he started, taking care over his words as he tried to ignore his discomfort. "With, uh, all due respect, I'm meant to be making those decisions." Even with the fat mage sat down, he felt a little intimidated by the destructive potential at the man's thick fingertips. As he realised that both Lena and Sigren had straightened as if readying for confrontation, Thaun couldn't help but feel silent gratitude towards them.

"Nice to see you're not entirely untempered, Y'Highness," he said around a mouthful of apple. "Knew it was in there somewhere. I'm just here to fan some life into that spark I saw when you stuck up for Fi–... for your cousin."

Thaun half-smiled, as Lena and Sigren relaxed. The twist in his gut faded only a little. "Fine. Next time though, do you want to just tell me that? It might be easier for both of us."

"As you command." Self-satisfaction warred with something resembling a good nature as the Highmage grinned. "Permission to round up the troops? Your officers' ears are probably burning by now."

The world flowed around Thaun as if through tar. In just a few short minutes, the tent filled. He stood almost mute as he watched soldiers whom he only vaguely recognised talk in hushed voices. Returning salutes and shallow greetings, he let instincts guide him. As much as he'd resented lessons in etiquette and behaviour, some of that training had sunk in.

Despite his desire to leave the weight of the Imperial Court behind, its burdens had followed him to Insel Drach.

A handful of uniformed officers soon waited patiently for their young commander, busying themselves with maps and papers. Against the canvas wall, a pair of muddy scouts stood at nervous attention. Within the tent, only they looked as nervous as him.

"Thaun?" Sigren whispered from the corner of his mouth.

"Huh?" He drew in a sharp breath through his nose, composing himself. "Right." He rose from his stool and looked to those with him. The captains turned, and the scouts stood straighter. Korten, still seated with his legs stretched out in front of him, gave an amused half-smile. "Men," Thaun raised his chin a fraction of an inch, and did his best to sound like he knew what he was doing. "I hear you've something to tell me?"

At first, none of the soldiers replied. It didn't surprise Thaun – surely his inexperience showed – but he couldn't help but feel disappointed at their lack of response. A torturous few seconds later, one man stepped forward. In an almost-clean surcoat of blue and yellow over his armour, and a shortsword at his hip, he looked every part the professional soldier.

"Your Highness," he inclined his head, but maintained eye contact, watching for Thaun's reaction. "Captain Halig, Second Army. We sent some scouts ahead, before departing the outpost." he glanced at the ragged pair of soldiers still standing at attention. "But some've failed to report in."

A heavy silence filled the room. Thaun slowly noticed eyes settling on him. "What's happened, colonel? Is it… " he paused, realising as he said it that he'd got the man's rank wrong. He pushed on regardless, doing his best not to chastise himself. "Are they dragons?"

Halig's face hardened. Behind his eyes, Thaun could almost see the officer's growing, measured response. "It's captain, sir. We've had no confirmed signs of Daericani activity on Insel Drach in years. Some of the troops report movements further inland though. By the time they were at the muster point, our transports were already underway."

"Movement?" Thaun glanced at Lena, but couldn't read her expression. He turned back. "What kind of movement?"

"…We're not sure, Your Highness. They don't fly any colours, and none of the scouts that have returned can offer a detailed report."

"So what *do* we know?" asked an exasperated Thaun.

"Whoever they are, they don't like being watched." It was Halig's turn to glance around the tent, lingering on the scouts. "They're dangerous enough that we've lost contact with some smaller units entirely. We suspect they've a radical mage among them, based on inspection of their ambush sites." The captain paused, settling on an unmoving point on the canvas wall rather than making eye contact. Perhaps Thaun wasn't the only one to feel anxious. "And so far they've stuck to one region, inland from here, and its approaches."

Korten raised a hand, drawing attention. "Let me have a go at what you're building up to."

Thaun couldn't help but notice the matching looks of resentment that grew upon his officers' faces. For a split second, Thaun wondered if he might share that prejudice towards the Spire if not for the likes of Heizl and Lena. Human nature feared the unknown. He suspected only a fraction of the Empire knew a single mage firsthand, whether by choice or circumstance.

"They're mostly that sort of way." Korten waved his raised arm ambiguously towards one wall of the tent. "You can sense it too, right, Lena?" The healer didn't respond, but the two muddied scouts failed to hide their knowing looks.

"Lucky guess," Halig crossed his arms over his chest. "Most of Insel Drach is to the east."

"But it's not too far, is it? A day's journey from here?" The Highmage took a bite from a pastry that Thaun hadn't noticed in his hand. "Maybe near an old ruin that you folks don't like visiting?"

The captain's expression hardened. With the Highmage's growing smugness all but palpable, and the officer's unease visible on his face, Thaun found himself speaking up. "Korten, what are you getting at?"

"Our destination, Your Highness. I can feel it from here, and your healer friend probably can too. It's like a migraine coming from the outside." The Highmage cocked his head. "A juncture between realms, a Rift where the Daericani first appeared. Someone's beaten us to it."

Thaun bit the inside of his cheek, distorting his face for a moment before catching himself. He doubted that such expressions would help with their opinion of him. If his luck held, they might be thinking about this development too, and so hadn't noticed.

His uncle's plan had failed. Part of it, at least. Holding the ruin wouldn't be so simple. He'd been foolish to think that it might be. Nothing ever felt like it went easily for him.

With a start, he realised that he'd fallen silent for too long. He had to say something.

"Is it Thala?" Thaun looked to the Highmage, but Halig answered first.

"It fits with what we know." A faint smile appeared on the captain's face at usurping the mage, though it didn't last.

"Then you know what we've gotta do." Korten leant forwards, elbows resting on his crumb-coated knees. "Even if it turns out it's nothing to do with Renyar, we're meant to hold that forsaken place, Your Highness." He faced Halig. "How quickly can you have your men mobilised?"

"With all due respect, Highmage." The soldier scowled, "What our men ready themselves for isn't something you have to worry about. You and I both take our orders from the same place." He turned reluctantly towards Thaun. "Just give the word, Your Highness."

Thaun took a deep breath, feeling the eyes on him. Their opinions shouldn't matter to him too much, he knew that, but he couldn't help but worry about what they thought. With the threat of some scheming sorcerer dragging a half-forgotten god into the world, he had other concerns than his reputation.

He'd come here to secure a tactical location. Just because someone – whether bandits, Daericani, or Thalans – held it already, that hadn't changed. If he didn't make a decision, then someone else would. What if they got it wrong? Was that better or worse than if he made the wrong choice himself?

Anxiety growled from the pit of his stomach. Whether the right choice, or simply a choice right now, no one would give the order on his behalf.

Thaun cleared his throat. "Captains, see to your men. We'll march as planned, but we'll keep the scouts in closer." He thought for a moment. "Until we're close to the target site. Send word, we'll form up on the approach, and arrive ready to face whoever we find there."

A flurry of salutes responded and, one by one, the officers filed from the tent. As the last one left, Thaun drooped, shoulders slumping as if deflated.

"Well done," Lena said, low enough that no one beyond the tent's canvas walls would be likely to hear.

"Thanks," said Thaun, dropping onto a camp chair and raising one hand to rub his face. "I didn't see much other choice."

"The march will give us some time," said Sigren, returning once more to their map of the island. "There'll be plenty of time to come up with a better plan."

"Got something in mind?" Lena asked as she stepped up alongside him.

"Nothing yet. Nothing good."

From where he sat, chin resting on steepled fingers, Thaun eyed the pair. Already, they thought two steps ahead of him. His mind raced as he tried to answer questions he couldn't quite form. For every solution he found, a dozen problems and 'what ifs' rose crowded around him.

Thaun swallowed. So much for staying out of trouble.

Tooth and Nail – Chapter Nine

"Had the recent civil war ended differently, the Empire might have become a very different place. Fjujhost's uprising unchecked by the Imperial Guard. Baras of Yrgol incited to attack civilians. A Vigil unfunded by the Throne. The nobility emboldened by one of their own crowned. Thank the gods that such an eventuality never came to pass."

Communique between the Uloric churches of the Konreig Empire and Seorsa (394 I.Y.)

26th day of Indern, 406th Imperial Year
17th Year of Emperor Rufenrich Konreig's Reign

"That shareholder could talk the ears off a saedura."

Zecht's voice washed over Heizl as if from a great distance. Barely aware of her flesh, her soul drifted back to the Outpost's dinghy basement. She'd long learned how to split her attention, conversing while still seeing the unseen. No point in wasting her strength though. Instead, conserving her energy, she felt the slow pull of her magic's natural current drawing her home.

Eyes still closed, she took a breath, feeling the thick air fill her lungs. As she blew out again, she processed her Shadow's words. The Spire only had a few saedura left, and she considered herself lucky to have avoided any close encounters with the monstrous creatures. One of Hastigr's former apprentices, a foreigner called Henlech, had developed them, drawing out the rare forest apes' primal aspects. Walking, breathing siege weapons, the old Empress had loved them. "Have they got ears?"

"Dunno, never seen one."

She blinked several times, trying and failing to work through the nonsensical exchange. "Did you want something?"

"No, not really." He shrugged. "It's dull up there. Those savages have left. That guilder is showing Termal around, seeing what we can scavenge."

"Native."

"What?"

Heizl rolled her eyes. "They're natives, not savages." She hesitated, mind sluggish and heavy. "Who's Termal?"

"Seriously? After how excited you got with two of us coming along?"

"Right. The Shadow." She looked away. "Of course I knew that. I can get a bit forgetful right after stretching myself."

"Whatever you say, Fitz." At Zecht's disbelieving grin, Heizl clenched a fist. "'Ere, talking about magic, got a light?" He raised a brown, hand-rolled cigarette that she hadn't noticed before.

She didn't answer straight away. One hand on the back of her neck – her scathe had yet to fully recover following the violent events at the Palace just a few nights ago – she turned to regard their single candle. She wondered at the tiny flame's threads, and how they might appear. No doubt it'd cast no arcane light itself, like her hair had in Hastigr's hand, but her thoughts lingered on that mote of heat and energy. The Highmage had hinted at influencing things other than simple thoughts, hadn't he?

Heizl shook her head. "I'm not that sort of mage. How don't you know that? Doesn't the Forge have files on people like me?"

Zecht shrugged in response and moved to pick up the candle. Holding the wick close to his mouth, the cigarette's end bloomed red as he breathed in. Smokey tendrils snaked out, obscuring half his face. After a moment he offered it to her.

"No, I'm alright, thanks." Cocking her head to one side, she narrowed her eyes. "How did someone like you become a Shadow? You're not as... you're not like the others that I've had before."

He glanced around the small room that they'd arrived in as if for the first time. "I do alright."

"Sure, I saw you fight in the Palace, but there are, like, aptitude tests too, right?"

"Yeah, but they were written by some Void-damned pencil pushers. All they show is how good you do paperwork."

"...You still had to pass them though."

Zecht turned towards her, a bright grin on his face. "Let's just say that my sponsor found an easier alternative."

"Of course." Heizl leant back, feeling the cold, panelled wall against her. "Bureaucracy and corruption hand in hand, the twin pillars of Imperial administration."

"What 'bout you, Fitz?" He took another drag of his cigarette. "I thought the first thing most mages learned was how to strike a light. Your uncle pull some strings to get you promoted or something?"

Unprompted, the muscles in her shoulders tightened. "I earned my position the hard way."

"Fine, then why can't you conjure a flame?"

"Magic's not that simple. How did you not learn this when... right, bribed through tests. Got it." Heizl drew a calming breath as she eyed her Shadow. Faint, amber light flickered across his features. "Most mages in the Empire are sanguine. They use up something special – essence – in their blood in very precise amounts to shape the arcanosphere into doing what they want."

"Yeah, I know that. Bloodburning."

"Close enough. Well, I don't. Occasionally a mage turns up at the Spire like me. Maybe as many as one in a hundred. We do things differently."

"Y'know what? I don't really care for the theory. What can you do?"

She blew a frustrated breath out through her nostrils as she held back from rolling her eyes. "Mostly, I change what people are thinking or feeling."

"Huh." The Shadow seemed to contemplate this for a moment. "I think I'd've preferred someone who could blow stuff up."

Heizl didn't reply, not trusting herself to remain civil. The temptation to make him imagine something in the passageway, anything to make him leave, held strong. A weariness hung on her like a hollowness in her soul. She'd probed outwards for too long. Stretching herself, both her body and her magicks, always left her tired. Sleep would have to wait though.

Still sitting on the cool ground, she dragged over the nearest of their travelling packs. Weak fingers fumbled with a strap before she pulled out a paper-wrapped bundle of rations. Too hungry to care what it was, Heizl began stuffing food into her mouth. She'd swallowed several times in rapid succession before its taste registered. Some kind of dried fruit in a glaze – the sticky remnants clung to its wrapping.

It took her only a few moments more before the paper lay empty, and she began licking her fingers clean.

"Huh," Zecht drawled as he stubbed out his cigarette. "For how much you always seem to eat, you're pretty small."

The mage glowered up at him. "You wouldn't say that if I was a man." She sighed. "Why don't you do something useful like take a nap? None of us have had enough sleep since getting here."

"Maybe later. What're you gonna do?"

Green eyes closed once again, Heizl didn't respond. She already gazed out at her web of interconnected thoughts and emotions, scarcely able to hear the Shadow's inane questions. Stretching her senses beyond her physical form felt preferable to listening to Zecht for any longer.

At the back of her neck, her skin crawled. A distant numbness seeped into her left shoulder as her scathe spread. Heizl did her best to ignore that sensation too.

Compared to the frenetic mass of minds she'd grown used to in Reiget City, the Norjan wilderness felt empty. Four human souls hung in the darkness, each with their tangle of conflicting thoughts and feelings. Her own, two Shadows assigned to work alongside her, and the single guilder that had neither fled nor succumbed to the locals' raids. She'd already inspected both the merchant stranger and her latest guardian at length, finding fear, confusion, anger, and impatience. All honest enough emotions, at least.

Beyond them, tiny sparks of lesser life flickered. Mice scurried through the Outpost's scorched remains, their simple minds seeking only safety and sustenance. A stray dog skulking beyond the broken palisade walls sniffed the air, wary of the smoke but seeking some long-gone owner. Flies, barely perceptible, wove through the air, flitting and flowing around her probing like at a waved hand.

As the light of souls caught on corners and walls, Heizl found a sense of the trade post's layout. Like ripples bouncing back from a pool's edge, their shape formed in her mind's eye. The faint outlines of burnt buildings and shattered lives flickered with unearthly illumination.

Collapsed roofs of thatch or wooden tile, shattered beams, and scattered belongings all hinted at the fight that had occurred here. A line of crates, sacks, and boxes ran the middle of the compound in a crude barricade. Broken arrowheads and splintered spear shafts littered the cold ground. The guilders had left before her arrival, those that had survived, but they'd fought to defend their home before retreating.

Far away from her projected senses, Heizl grunted. The Norjan natives had almost certainly thought they were just defending their home too.

She pushed outwards further. So far, she'd contented herself to inspect the almost lifeless spaces closest to them. It hadn't taken long to realise that no one but the four of them remained alive here. Instead, she'd hoped to see any unwelcome company coming their way. For a hundred paces out in each direction, she'd found nothing new for hours. They were alone out here at the edge of civilization.

Leaving the Outpost's faint shape behind her, Heizl swiftly lost track of distance or time. Few souls lit the darkness, fewer still casting enough threads to illuminate the inanimate things out here. She wondered for a moment if Hastigr might've known a way to see more clearly, but left the thought behind her – right now, it wouldn't make a difference.

A huddle of stars revealed themselves as a small herd of some kind of deer following a streambed. They scanned outwards for nighttime threats, though none reacted to Heizl's spectral presence. She moved further upstream, passing the soul of a single wolf stalking the beasts.

There was life here, but no sign of their Fragment-carrying warleader. These damn flies had probably driven him off. Heizl struggled to maintain her composure with them despite her body being far from the swarm that seemed to twist and follow her. The smallest things could drive anyone mad.

After a while, the mage drifted back towards her physical form. She'd spent too much time out here and could feel the weakness trickling into her own soul like water through cracks. Had she the strength, she'd have simply ridden a thread back to her body, but instead she felt the gentle draw back to the physical. It'd take longer, but at least she didn't have to strain to do it.

As the almost imperceptible outlines of the Outpost came back into view, a block of ice fell into her stomach. When she'd left, she'd seen four souls. Now, she sensed nine. Her own and Zecht's remained huddled in a cellar, while her Shadow – what had his name been? – and the guilder radiated fear as they hid among ruined walls up above. Not far from the pair, a handful of strangers picked their way through the rubble.

Even at this distance, she could see the ease with which they moved. Confident, satisfied, and with a low-lying anger, it didn't take Heizl long to realise that she looked upon native Norjans for the first time. No new bonds reached towards the other Imperials, though her new Shadow watched them with a cold, calculating intensity.

None of this worried Heizl quite so much as the final soul that had come. It approached the group of natives like a raging inferno bearing down on candles. Physical objects glowed as if under the midday sun wherever it passed. For a moment, a sickly warmth washed over her. Had she stayed close, she'd have seen a soul like that approaching long before it arrived.

Heizl abandoned her slow return, drawing on what strength remained in her flesh to drag herself back to the dark basement. She returned panting, falling forwards onto outstretched hands.

"What is it?" Zecht asked, brow furrowed.

"You have to get up there and stop him!"

"Stop who?"

"Your partner! Tom...Tam...uh.."

The Shadow cocked his head, a touch of wry amusement narrowing the corners of his eyes. "Termal? Why, what's wrong?"

"They've come back. The natives and their leader. He's going to attack them!"

"Great! We can get this over with."

"You don't understand." She clambered upright, one hand finding the familiar grip of her rod. "He can't see what I can. That warleader? He's got a Fragment alright. One Shadow doesn't stand a chance. We've gotta go."

"Too right we do, wouldn't want Termal to have all the..." Muted shouts drifted down from above. Percussive impacts on metal punctuated the outburst.

In a heartbeat, despite the weariness that she knew still clung to her, Heizl had fallen back within herself. Panic and guilt now tainted her own soul, but that didn't matter right now. Spiralling upwards, she watched the flickering change of soul as the Shadow made his move.

One native had gone down already, his light fading swiftly, while another recoiled, threads fading as agony overwhelmed them. Their rescued guilder broke and ran, a third Norjan giving chase, while Termal danced between the warleader and the remaining warrior.

Heizl had seen a few Shadows fight or train before, and could imagine the glint of knives and the spray of blood. She focused instead on the Fragment-bearer.

Shock and surprise rippled across his soul like blue tips of flame across a brazier. He retreated beneath Termal's assault, pain flaring bright several times as stabs and slashes connected. The Shadow gave him no time to react, filling every opening with cold steel. His attack intensified as the one native still with the warleader fell, Termal turning his whole attention to the task at hand.

After a dozen more swings, something in the Fragment-bearer snapped. As his inferno brightened, the Shadow's soul fell back as if thrown. It pulsed rhythmically. Pain filled the man.

Termal lasted perhaps a score of heartbeats beneath the fierce assault. Heizl didn't know if she should be relieved or not that she hadn't had to witness the mundane exchange between the two. She couldn't imagine that the Shadow had met a peaceful end.

As his soul flickered out, Heizl opened her eyes. Zecht stood in the doorway checking his weapons.

"Stop. It's too late." She sighed.

"Fuck. What happened?"

"Termal got the drop on him. I'm pretty sure he cut him up some. More than anyone but the champ managed on Elhin or Renyar, at least. After the last time, I'd've thought you'd be more careful."

Zecht ignored her. "How many are left?"

"Besides the warleader? Two, I think, but one's hurt. Pretty sure they got that guilder too. What was his name?"

"Who cares?" One by one, the Shadow loosened knives in their sheathes across his chest. "Come on then."

"What?"

"You said that Termal hurt our target and thinned out his guard."

"Yeah, and they killed him for it."

"They did, but if one skinny guy can manage that, imagine what the two of us can do." He flashed her a wicked grin.

"You don't get it." Crouching, she unwrapped another paper parcel. Mouth half-stuffed with what she hoped was dried meat, she continued. "That Fragment, you can't see it like how I can. It's like Renyar again."

"I can't see it, sure. We're not gonna get another chance like this though. He's hurt and away from his savages." He flicked her a smirk. "We'd get to go home again all that much sooner too."

Heizl stared at the Shadow. It *would* impress people if she returned successfully so soon. Her uncle, the Spire, the Court. A reputation for efficiency wouldn't hurt her ambitions. "Fine. How do we do this? I'm no battlemage."

"Yeah, you've made that obvious enough. Right, grab what essence or whatever you need." He waved a hand at their piled gear. "You said you can mess with people's heads, right? You get me an opening, keep him from thinkin' straight, and I'll do the rest."

She nodded once, and pushed past him in the doorway, stooping only to pick up another bundle of food. Tucking the paper packet under one arm, she waved her rod in front of her face, dispersing the tiny insects that buzzed around.

Heizl frowned as she realised that Zecht hadn't followed her out into the dark passageway. Turning, she opened her mouth to call to him before shutting it again. Things would go more smoothly if they stayed quiet. Just as she decided to walk back to find out what had delayed him, the flickering light of their single candle went out, plunging the corridor into blackness.

A hand fell onto her shoulder and she heard his whisper. "Take it easy, Fitz. Nice and slow now."

Heart pounding in her chest loud enough that she swore their target would hear, she crept up the cold, stone steps at Zecht's side. Dilute, grey light filtered down from above through the cracks in a wooden trapdoor. In the weary illumination, she could just about make out the man at her side.

Though she edged forwards as softly as she could, she still felt as clumsy as a drunk compared to the Shadow's silent movement. The smallest of their packs hung from one shoulder, and he cradled a small crossbow. Heizl had come to expect such weapons to resemble the heavy, assault models favoured by Sigren and much of the Imperial Guard. This looked delicate, almost fragile in comparison. Metal arms blued with some oil and stock brushed with soot and black sand, it blended into the darkness almost as well as its wielder.

At the hatch, Zecht stopped her with a tap on the arm before placing one hand on the trapdoor. At a glacial pace, he pushed it open and crept through, leading with his crossbow.

Heizl emerged after him a moment later, eyes squinting as they adjusted to the mid-morning light. Following the Shadow, they skulked into the cover of a broken wooden wall.

Since arriving the night before, she'd yet to come above ground. She'd yet to regret that choice. Cold fingers clawed at her through her clothes, and goosebumps rose on her skin. The whole world seemed made up of shades of dirty grey and dirtier brown. Her sorcerous scouting had given her an idea of what the place looked like, but had done little to prepare her for its harsh reality.

Every surface showed signs of fire. Blackened wood, drifts of ash, cracked glass, and warped metal. Outbuildings like the one that they'd hidden within resembled hollowed out husks, with scorched beams reaching skywards. An uneven line of shattered crates formed a crude barricade across the centre compound, while the outer palisade sported crooked gaps where axes had ripped it open.

Her gaze lingered for a moment on the heaps of corpses, burned almost beyond recognition. Stripped of anything useful – clothing, buckles, and straps – she'd no way of telling if she looked at dead guilders or natives. How the victors hadn't found the basement passages, she didn't know, but she probably had that oversight to thank for having made it this far.

"That must be him." Zecht whispered. "I thought he'd be bigger."

Heizl followed his subtle gesture. Half a dozen hunters, warriors, or whatever they were prowled the far side of the Outpost now. Fear and excitement seeping in, she hadn't cast her senses out since leaving the room they'd arrived at via the Nexus. If she had, she might've noticed the new band arriving. A few more wouldn't affect their ambush, she hoped. Most of them scoured the ruined compound, searching for any sign of more attackers. At least Termal had come from the far side, and none of them looked her way yet.

They wore a mismatched style of dress, of stitched hides bedecked with beads, bone, and feathers. All carried weapons, many of stone, wood, and antler, though bronze and steel glinted here and there. Such people made use of every part of their prey, be it a herd of animals or a group of encroaching merchants.

It took Heizl a moment to find their target. Like Zecht, she'd expected someone altogether more impressive. The warleader didn't loom over his followers, and those around him didn't shy away from a fearful presence. He didn't shout or berate them for letting an attacker through, but, even without her view of his soul, she couldn't miss him.

Painted with broad strokes of colour, he wore an incomplete set of dark, tarnished armour unlike anything the other Norjan's carried. It fitted the man poorly, covering half of his form with blackened iron. A handful of ornate studs and spikes protruded at his shoulders and elbows, the pale tails of animals hanging from them. Heavy gauntlets, engraved with triangular sigils and lined with fresh hides, covered his hands. Though the iron helmet upon his head, broad antlers tied to its crown, lacked any visor, she struggled to see his features. Fresh blood marked points at thigh and chest, and he walked with a barely perceptible limp.

Heizl eyed the spear in the native's grip. Though some oversized bone made up its curved head, the green sheen of its shaft revealed it to be of bronze or copper.

Not far from where he stood, Termal's corpse lay unmoving. Even against the dark leathers that the Shadow had worn, Heizl could make out the gaping wound near one shoulder. Blood, flesh, and bone glistened. Whatever had slain the Shadow, it had almost completely dismembered his arm.

Ducking back into cover, the mage glimpsed within herself. The spear shone as brightly as any soul. It had to be the Fragment that they sought.

"Right." Zecht whispered beside her. "You get them looking the other way, spread out as much as possible. I'll take down the big guy, and they'll probably scatter."

"Probably?" Heizl shook her head as she hissed back. "That doesn't matter. Are you sure a crossbow is going to do the job? You saw what Renyar did. That woman of his, Elhin, too for that matter."

"If not, I get the knives out. It's more fun that way, anyway."

"Even if he wasn't carrying a bit of Urathear, are knives really going to work against a spear? Or that armour?"

"Look, the longer we argue about this, the more likely we waste this chance." The Shadow didn't look at her as he spoke. "Get to it, Fitz. I'm gonna find a better angle."

Heizl scowled as he crept away. She had to hand it to the Shadow though, he knew how to move. Within barely a dozen paces she struggled to spot him herself, and she knew where he'd gone. Shaking her head, she turned towards her own task.

Threads reached out from the natives' souls like a blind man's hand groping through the darkness. Though several had grown bored with their task, complacently believing that the threat had passed with Termal's fatal failure, others sought vigilantly for other assailants. She worked on these first, gently nudging their attention to fine details that wouldn't matter. Even if she hadn't, Zecht probably would've gone unseen.

Two natives spoke as they searched. Though she hadn't the first idea of what the words meant, Heizl caught hints of boredom, impatience and frustration. It reminded her of the Imperial Guardsmen that she'd worked alongside over the years. Stoking such feelings didn't take long, leaving the natives irritable and distracted.

The warleader himself challenged her more. She'd already proved to herself that she could affect a Fragment-bearer. Her memory of Renyar inspecting her through the smoke and flames remained all too vivid.

Cold rage boiled within his soul where the spear's thread touched it. A thin veneer of calm wrapped around him, keeping it held within but liable to break at any moment. It reminded her of her uncle when he'd learned of one of her late nights outside the Spire. He'd had that same controlled anger while disciplining her. Where that had focused on a single misbehaving youth though, this felt aimed at the whole world, as if fate and the gods themselves had offended the man.

Catching a glimpse of Zecht's own threads swelling as the Shadow prepared to fire, Heizl pushed on. Jabbing and prodding at the warleader's mental poise, she drew his anger out. The emotion streamed through slender cracks, pouring a scowl over his face as he directed his warband.

Zecht's shot punched him in the small of the back, piercing through hides and flesh. Had the native's strange armour been complete, the steel bolt wouldn't have done much more than dent the stained metal. Instead, he let out a pained, bestial cry as he staggered away.

Through one blurred eye, Heizl watched the Shadow's attack. Lacking any true martial experience, she struggled to follow the exchange.

His crossbow left his hands, the stock bludgeoning one native. Zecht slipped past as blood blossomed from what had to be a broken nose. Somehow dodging the swing of an iron-headed axe, another hunter stumbled from his path with a knife protruding from his thigh. The fading light glinted from another flung blade an instant before catching a second native. Then, the Shadow faced the warleader.

She couldn't see how her partner planned on getting past a spear with nothing but his daggers. The difference in reach between the two weapons would be too much to overcome. If the crossbow bolt had done more, perhaps, or if Zecht had kept the element of surprise, but not like this. Most soldiers didn't choose to draw sidearms when facing a spearman.

Waving back the rest of his warband, the warleader engaged. Adjusting his grip upon his weapon, the spearhead probed out before him. The bone point, honed to a fine edge, danced up and down in a series of feints as the two men circled one another.

As Zecht lunged, intentionally overextending himself to get past the spear's weaving head, Heizl fell back within herself.

Relying on instinct, she twisted the native's threads even as the Shadow attacked. Beneath her spectral grip his rage snapped back and forth, a simple thing to manipulate. Focus blurred, the warleader's stab went wide, striking nothing but air. Zecht's own lunge skittered over hide-covered mail, ineffective.

The Shadow did all that he could to stay inside his foe's reach, grasping at limbs and face. His knife slammed in time and time again seeking unprotected flesh. For all his training, he struck iron plates with every attempt. With each stab, Zecht's cold control slipped further away. Visceral panic waxed to take its place.

Still gripping the warleader's threads, Heizl pulled this way and that. In ethereal fingers, his attention felt as heavy as a merchant wagon. Sweat prickling beneath her clothes and her insides clenching in on themselves, she kept going. The night Renyar had attacked she'd distracted two Fragment-bearers. She could handle a single native.

In spite of her efforts, she couldn't tell if she made a difference.

Gripping his spear with one hand, their opponent lashed out with the other. Black, iron gauntlet connected with Zecht's chest in an inexpert blow. The Shadow shifted at the moment of impact, rolling with the punch and redirecting the force of the blow as he stabbed upwards with one dagger.

At that ricocheting contact, the Shadow stumbled backwards as if struck a much more serious blow. Even over the distance and the jeering chants of the other Norjans, Heizl could imagine the crack of bone. Legs disappearing from under him, he rolled, coming up unsteadily. Drawing a replacement blade, Zecht shifted his stance and reversed his grip as he eyed the other man between strands of lank, blond hair.

The Fragment-bearer didn't let him recover, lunging after him again. Still gripping the man's threads, Heizl pulled just in time. Every muscle in her body strained with the effort as she attempted to shift his aim.

Zecht dodged aside at the last possible moment, ramming his blade ineffectually against the Norjan's strange armour. The knife snapped.

Even as he made contact, the warleader swung sideways. Both men grunted, one in shock, one in anger, as the bronze spear shaft struck Zecht's flank.

He crumpled around the blow, stumbling several steps as he collapsed. Burnt wreckage broke his fall. Splinters and shards burst outwards in all directions. A moment later, Zecht's gloved hand appeared as he struggled to stand.

Her own soul alight with fear, Heizl sank further within. The material world's hints of sound and colour faded as she relinquished her senses.

She sped past the warleader's inferno, coming to rest among his remaining followers. Their light marbled with pained emotions, never settling on one hue for long. Pride, fear, admiration, rage; every base human sensation flashed before her.

She ignored them, seeking something else. Digging deeper, she skirted past memories and impulses until she found what she sought. With immaterial hands, she grasped two native's roiling souls and pulled.

By the time she opened one eye again, the warleader stood over a prone Zecht. He said something then, but Heizl had no way of knowing what his words meant. Drawing back his strange spear, he made to stab downwards.

The javelin – a shaped length of local wood with a guilder's iron pocket knife bound fast to its end – staggered the armoured native as it struck the back of his helmet. His own strike launched splinters as it missed Zecht by a hair's breadth.

Stoking the envy and resentment of both Norjans further, Heizl broke from her hiding place. Another hunter cried out as he spotted her, but a sorcerous nudge turned him to face the sudden betrayal of his comrades.

As confused, hesitant fighting broke out – Heizl's charmed warriors launching themselves at the warleader – she reached the Shadow's side.

"Zecht!" she hissed, crouching alongside him. "We have to get out of here!"

"You don't have to tell me twice." The blond man took Heizl's hand and rose to his feet. A second later, he stumbled towards her, only keeping his balance with the mage's help. "I think... I think I hit my head."

"There's no time for that!" Heizl pulled one arm over her shoulders and reached around to hold his side. Only a few paces away, a couple of their foes attacked the warleader and one another, while others attempted to separate them. "I need you to guide me."

"Guide you? I can barely walk!"

She resisted the urge to dump the Shadow back to the ground. "I'll take the weight," Heizl murmured. "But I'll be concentrating on those behind us, not where we're going."

"Fine." Zecht glanced between the firelit remnants of the battle, a glazed look in his eyes. "Where do we go after?"

"Anywhere but here."

Blind to flickering flames and deaf to the Norjans' battle cries, Heizl set to work. Just as she had in her uncle's Throne Room, she danced around their thoughts, turning each questing eye aside. As she wove sorcerous webs, flies touched at her flesh and the chill wind picked up.

In her mind's blackness she had no way of telling how far they fled. By the time she risked opening one eye the sun's faint light painted the eastern horizon as the Outpost's rising flames marred the southwest.

Tooth and Nail – Chapter Ten

"Had one looked at the Imperial Second Army prior to the Civil War of 391 I.Y., few would find anything remarkable. Two and a half legions; four and a half thousand soldiers below Guard standards, but otherwise little different to its sister armies in other Provinces. The Fjujan rebellion proved a time of purification for the Second. A series of ambushes and defeats sorted wheat from chaff. Winters of holding mountain passes left their infantry as cold and hard as ice. Years of campaign forged them into something new, something stronger. It would be a veteran force that would serve to bring order to the region in the wake of the Empire's recent collapse."

Common Imperial History,
On the Imperial Guard,
Archimand Märchen (408 I.Y.)

27th day of Indern, 406th Imperial Year
17th Year of Emperor Rufenrich Konreig's Reign

Blue and gold rippled over grey, each surcoat a pale reflection of the approaching storm and the sunlit clouds above. The dry dust of the plains formed its breath, which, upon mingling with the inland sea's breeze, would rain down on the unfortunate souls below.

Blades the same colour as the impending storm waited impatiently within their scabbards. Chainmail rustled with the rise and fall of chests, while shields twitched as soldiers fought against the weight. Standards fluttered in the easterly wind, blue and yellow chevrons dancing above the companies of the Second Imperial Guard. Ranks stood shoulder-to-shoulder, while staggered lines of archers waited patiently behind them.

Their elements from the First – mixed infantry armed with axes, maces, and spears – held their right flank. They'd wait until the centre engaged, moving to counter or fallback as necessary.

A jagged, shallow ravine cut across the bare, undulating rock of Insel Drach to their left, anchoring that approach. Several squads of skirmishers roved the broken ground beyond it. They'd harry their opponents with crossbow fire given half the chance. Otherwise, they served to ward off any opportunistic archer that might attempt to strike with impunity.

The army's reserves – the Second's meagre cavalry and a hundred or so soldiers taken from the Crossing's garrison – formed a bristling wall of iron surrounding Thaun and his Royal Guard. He'd chosen a slight rise in the terrain, offering his officers and him a better vantage of whatever battle they now faced.

Advance units had seized the narrow, rocky passes that led to this field without opposition. Scouts had spotted bands of their unknown foe, but done little more than trade warning shots with one another. Those same scouts now manned their lines of retreat.

Thaun sighed, a long, drawn out exhalation of held breath, and hoped that his helmet hid his anxiety. Alongside him, upon her own horse, Lena cleared her throat.

"What's wrong?" she said.

He held back another sigh and surveyed his command. "Do you ever feel like you're meant to be somewhere else?"

"This is the place alright." The healer gestured, her movement smooth despite the weight of her armour. The wounds she'd taken during Renyar's attack had all but healed. "The Juncture site is somewhere beneath that outcrop. I can feel it from here. Like a ripple in a pool, bouncing from something sticking up from the water. Korten says that the old tunnels run under our feet even now."

"No, that's not..." Thaun shook his head, less to disagree and more to shake away the strange sensation running through him. "You know what? Forget about it."

Lena fell silent. After a moment, she spoke again. "It's a good formation. Sigren hasn't found anything to complain about."

Thaun's tongue grew thick. "Frida."

"What's that?"

"The Shadowmaster. She did a few lessons when Heizl and I were kids. I still preferred swords, but it was better than most classes. Brought in an old officer, did strategy with us for... we must have gone over it for at least a month. She made it hard to forget."

Thaun gazed out across the ranks of helmets and standards as soldiers awaited their orders. Beyond them, the jagged shapes of cut stone littered the ground. Someone had built here, once. He didn't know if those hands had been human or draconic. Either way, time and violence had broken them, leaving tumbled walls and masonry for the island's wiry undergrowth to claim.

That stonework hid the entrance to the Daericani ruins beneath, all the old reports agreed. He'd held back their outriders from investigating too close, and so had yet to locate the way in. Their scouts had all told him the same thing – their foe had fled that way, disappearing between the hollow shapes of long abandoned buildings.

"You don't have to give her all the credit, you know," said Lena.

"It's not that complicated. It's a bit like duelling, I think. You make a plan, you take your position, and you probe your opponent until you find an opening worth committing to." He thought for a moment. "Most people can only concentrate on one thing at a time. Sometimes you've got to present an opening yourself, getting them to commit, so that you can counter.

"This way," he continued, "We can respond instead of just reacting. If they dig in, we claim the entrances, lay siege. If they attack, we're in a formation the troops must've drilled a hundred times already. If we're outnumbered, they'll take long enough to assemble that we'll have plenty of time for a safe retreat."

"And what about positioning Korten where you did? Did she cover the tactical use of Highmages too?"

Beneath his helmet, hidden through its T-shaped slot, Thaun smiled. "I think she referred to them as Spire assets, but no." He glanced at her. "Just figured it made sense. If they're Thalans, then they'll have mages and he's our best answer to them. If they're not, well, Korten wanted a fight more than any of us. Only seems fair that he gets to make the first move."

"That's a lot of ifs."

"Heh." He kept his smile, though a sadness tainted it now. "I do a lot of overthinking when I can't sleep."

Lena laughed, catching Thaun off guard with the light, pleasant sound. "For all that you complain about it, you're actually pretty good at–"

Thaun held up a hand, cutting her off mid-sentence. "Sorry. Look, there's movement."

A ripple passed through the soldiers below as, one by one, they spotted the same disturbance. Messengers moved between officers, some already heading towards Thaun's command post. Sergeants barked at their squads, restoring order. Sheltz's Comet hung overhead, its hues so faint that Thaun wondered if he'd imagined it. Across the rocky, uneven field, figures appeared, scurrying out from the Daericani ruin beneath its rocky outcrop. First a dozen, then a score, until over a hundred stood opposite in a loose formation.

Without banners, Thaun didn't know their identity for sure. After Renyar's recent attack though, he had a pretty good guess. He couldn't be sure across the distance, but here and there he made out the same pale cloth over armour like he'd worn. Thala seemed a safe, if unwelcome, assumption.

Against the Imperials arrayed against them – fearsome, disciplined, and bearing fine steel – Thaun almost pitied them. Outnumbered by the Second alone, they had little hope of victory in a straight confrontation, and yet still they marched out.

They'd abandoned their only defensive position. It made no sense. Narrow tunnels would limit the advantage given by numbers if the Imperials forced the issue. Even besieged, holding that position would buy them time.

As messengers assembled, ready to pass along orders, Thaun waited. "I don't like this."

"The first time is always the hardest," Lena reassured. "You're doing fine."

"No, not that. I don't understand what they're..." He trailed off at more motion.

They shifted, men and women forming lines opposite the Imperial ranks. By their disciplined movement, no one obstructing another, these were more than just bandits. The line solidified, almost as long as the Imperial formation, but a fraction of its depth. A second later, gaps appeared.

Thaun sat in silence astride his horse, one hand out to forestall their messengers as he watched several figures walking out from between the warriors.

Across the distance, he could only make out so many details, with none hinting at the difference between those advancing now and the ranks that they'd left.

Down below, guardsmen cocked crossbows and raised bows, yet held their fire, the range still too great for anything short of a massed volley. The Second's own ranks shifted as Korten edged forwards beyond the shieldwall, accompanied by his Shadows. That simple action, the Highmage moving to respond without orders, told Thaun all he needed to know about their identity.

Lena's words only confirmed his suspicions. "They're mages. I can feel them from here." She paused for a second. "Permission to join Korten, Your Highness?"

Thaun barely even flinched at the formal tone in her voice. "You're a healer, Lena. What will you do if I say yes? You're not exactly a battlemage."

"I know more than just how to heal," she replied.

Nothing happened for several moments. Standards fluttered, men stamped feeling into their feet, and mages stood staring each other down. Thaun wondered what passed between them, what sorcerous battles they'd already fought in that unseen space between worlds. Motion pulled his thoughts back to reality.

A dozen paces out from the Second's shields, Korten took another step forward. His three Shadows stood behind him at a relatively safe distance. Across the field, Thaun couldn't make out the Highmage's actions, whether he spoke ancient words or wove arcane gestures, but a second later the ground before him began to smoke. Every eye fell upon the growing, billowing cloud. As the sparse vegetation burst into flame, the rocks glowed.

Insel Drach burned. Menar – god of dreams and fire – couldn't have wrought more destruction. The Highmage layered spell over spell and the dark stone grew slick as quenched iron. Flames burst outwards before dying, squeezed from the land itself. Dwarf lightning sparked across its surface. Rock melted into thick, luminous lava, and the air rippled as heat washed over the army's ranks.

Thalan mages answered. Beneath Thaun's mount's ironclad hooves, the ground trembled like a frightened child. He realised the source of the disturbance as several of the rocky field's boulders shuddered from their resting places. Smaller stones joined them as they rose in a tumultuous wall of moving debris. Dust drifted from their surfaces.

As the rising tide of banded stone hid the casters, it tumbled towards the Imperial lines. First at a crawl, before building speed until it matched any mundane landslide. Rocks fell the wrong way, as if the Architect himself had upturned the island.

Thaun couldn't take his eyes from the pure destructive force as it crossed the ground between the two armies. A voice within cried to draw his sword, or to dig in his heels and spur his horse to escape. The sickening weight in his gut stopped him from doing either.

The Second stood strong. Had one turned to flee, others might've followed, but none broke. It didn't matter what held them there – loyalty, training, or the opinions of their peers – they remained.

Stones hammered raised shields as if launched from a thousand slings. Some snuck through, breaking flesh and bone. The hands of comrades helped the wounded back, fresh bodies stepping into the gaps.

Korten bore the brunt of the impact. Flames rose as boulders struck his growing pool of molten rock. While some ground into the glowing surface, others skimmed and bounced for dozens of paces before losing speed. Stone cracked and smoke filled the air. As nearby soldiers flinched but didn't retreat from the sorcerous clash, their uniforms fluttered, passing a blue and yellow wave across the company.

Gouts of fire lashed out, intercepting stones in midair. Simple flame should've wrapped around the solid objects, providing little obstacle. Instead, these slammed against them like missiles, robbing the rock of momentum.

Dozens more rose from around Korten, the Highmage matching the opposing cadre blow for blow.

"Thaun," Lena's voice shook him from the mesmerising sight before them. "It's time. Orders?"

Nodding, he turned to her. "You're right. Go help Korten." Thaun swallowed, doing his best to ignore the smouldering terror he felt creeping into his belly. With a nod, she drove heels into her mount, and left.

He waved, and the messengers moved closer. "Those mages are concentrating on Korten and the Second. Have the First advance. Some pressure there might free up the centre."

The men saluted before sprinting away down the slight slope.

At the centre of a ring of Royal Guardsmen, Thaun suddenly felt very alone. He hated giving orders. The satisfaction of choosing correctly paled compared to the fear of getting them wrong. Without friends or family at his side, he now carried that burden alone.

He'd have rather given up. His officers had more experience than him. They'd make the right decisions. They'd know how to cope with that responsibility.

Pity he couldn't run. Even if his captains defeated this enemy without him, it would destroy what little faith they had in him. The troops would question his suitability, more so even than how much he doubted it himself.

Thaun clenched his eyes closed. Blood rushed between his ears. Pressure built.

Opening them again, he looked down on the battle developing below.

Ordered chaos swelled before him. Rocks cracked and flames roared at the centre. Their units from the First, in blue and white, marched, and soon steel and iron clashed. Soldiers screamed. Sergeants shouted. Swords rose. Bodies fell.

For their smaller numbers, the foe – almost certainly Thalan now – fought admirably. The occasional flash of green, grey, and red suggested lesser mages in their ranks. Discipline met destruction, and the right's advance slowed.

At some shift of the wind, smoke filled Thaun's mouth. His mind flashed back to his home, wreathed in flames and invaded by assassins.

Before he could shake those intrusive thoughts away, it grew worse. Mingling at the back of his throat, the sweet smells of cooking meat coated his insides. As Korten's inferno grew, Thaun's imagination painted disturbing images inside his mind.

He welcomed the distraction that came with a voice at his side. "Sir?"

Thaun looked down from his horse. An officer stood alongside him. He recognised the man from their briefing. "It's... colonel something, right? Colonel Harlech?"

"It's captain, sir," he cleared his throat, and patted down his uniform. Its colours had faded with use, and neat stitching showed old repairs in a dozen places. "Captain Halig."

"Ah, sorry."

"Easily forgiven, sir," said Halig. "Initial reports are coming in."

"Thanks. Let's get to it then."

A storm of information threatened to overwhelm Thaun then. Names and numbers blended into one another as he struggled to connect each report to the larger conflict. Here and there, officers arrived requesting instructions, which he gave as well as he could. The words felt clumsy in his mouth.

The reports formed a ghastly picture. Bowmen moved to arch their shots over the First, Korten's contribution hiding the centre in smoke and flame. Reserves reinforcing depleted companies. Wounded soldiers falling back through the passes to their rear, unable to fight further. Sections of ruins traded hands as cover was seized and lost.

Through it all, Thaun found his focus pulled to the meeting of magicks before the Second. The front lines had fallen back beyond the worst of the flames and stone. They stood as close as they dared, fearing the destruction unleashed before them, but ordered to support the Highmage nonetheless.

Fire, smoke, and dust rose into the air, obscuring half the battlefield. Stone cracked beneath the heat and drummed upon the earth. Bursts of flame, escaping the maelstrom roared. Korten was no more than a pale shape at its nearest edge. He'd heard stories of battles like this. Mages cancelling one another out, leaving it to the men and women of either side to decide on the victors.

"Voids take the Spire," Halig's muttering at his side caught Thaun off guard. The captain glanced at him sheepishly. "Sorry, sir."

"Easily forgiven, captain." He followed the officer's gaze. It was difficult not to look at that confluence of magicks. Thaun had only witnessed Korten's power once before, the night of Renyar's assault. The chaos of that evening hadn't allowed him to really appreciate the spectacle. If not for the dangers it posed, it might even be beautiful.

Now, Korten cut loose. Others had commented on his restraint within the Palace. Thaun believed them now. Less a man than an elemental force. Grasses burned. Metal glowed. Stone melted.

With some effort, Thaun turned away, taking in the continuing conflict upon the right flank. Archers had moved further forwards, finding their range against the indistinct shapes within the ruins' shadows. Though the centre had halted with mage against mage, this side at least seemed to be going well. He tried not to think about all the dead and dying that it had cost.

A hundred paces behind the loose lines of bowmen, two figures now stood, one in black and one in blue. As he watched, those two familiar shapes joined the fight. Across the distance, Thaun's imagination filled in the gaps that his eyes couldn't quite make out.

Lena placed one hand on Sigren, while holding her axe in the other. The Shadow aimed along his crossbow, unheard words passing between the two. He pointed almost skywards, far above the bead drawn by other men and women. Directed high and slightly off to one side, a passing observer might've thought that a bird or cloud had drawn his eye.

It took Thaun a moment to understand. The healer could do more than just mend flesh, as she'd protested. Magic was at play. He didn't know if she heightened Sigren's senses, propelled the quarrel over a great distance, or something else entirely.

From the command post, Thaun couldn't see the Shadow's individual shots. He trusted his friends though. More than he trusted himself. Their contribution would achieve more today than he would.

With the battle well underway, Thaun could feel his mind retreating even if he couldn't. Smoke obscured most of it, anyway. Complicated orders would do little now.

His gaze wandered, grazing over the centre, where squads of the Second had marched to join the brutal melee upon the right.

An ashen cloud shifted, and, for the first time since the battle had started, Thaun spied the fissure that protected their left flank. With the events unfolding on the far side of the field from it, he hadn't given it much thought.

Concentrating on anything other than Korten proved difficult. In the faint gust that heralded a coming storm, the smoke thinned. Through the dwindling, grey wisps, he spied their skirmishers.

Something tugged at him. He'd grown so used to one anxiety or another that it didn't register immediately. When every interaction or expectation prompted his stomach to turn, it could be difficult to listen to his gut.

"Um, col... captain?"

"Your Highness, sir?" Halig replied.

"How many men did we have holding that ravine?"

"A few squads, I think, sir. Would you like a message sent to them?"

"I don't know. A squad's got, what, a dozen men in it?"

"At full strength, yes. Not all of our units are at full complement."

Thaun stared through the swirling smoke, willing it to clear. A handful of indistinct shapes moved beyond the fissure.

"Then, captain, where are the rest of them?"

Halig turned, one hand raised to shade against Korten's blaze as he followed Thaun's gaze. "I'll have a runner dispatched. The Highmage's presence makes signalling difficult."

Insides twisting, Thaun said nothing. It felt wrong. More so than the unnatural clash of mages or the brutal violence inflicted by the Second. A sickening weight radiated through him as realisation descended upon him.

"Korten has to get back!" Thaun shouted and pointed. Those closest flinched away at the sudden outburst. Two messengers, little older than boys, broke into a run, not waiting to hear more. "Those aren't our men!"

Alarmed voices rose around him as officers and aides understood. Watching from atop his mount, Thaun barely noticed their controlled panic. Even if he'd had the clarity to make further commands, he didn't need to. Caught unawares on one side, his captains moved to respond.

Too late.

Dust rose before the handful of men on the left flank, rivalling the whirls of smoke drifting towards them. Untouched earth appeared a second later, bringing with it the weathered stones of Insel Drach. Ancient masonry and broken rock surged into a wave.

Whether he'd received the order or not, Korten answered. Flames shifted, and the ground erupted. Fire consumed the centre, incinerating those of the

Second that had remained close to the Highmage. Screams filtered through the inferno's roar.

Terror rippled across the Imperial Guard, discipline wavering beneath its onslaught.

"Orders, sir?" Halig asked from alongside him.

Lacking anything more coherent to say, Thaun swore.

"Sir, do we retreat?"

"Korten's holding," the words tumbled from his mouth. "If he can hold there a little longer, can we win the right flank?"

"It's risky, sir."

"If Thala wants this place so bad, they might not be willing to demolish it. We need to claim those ruins and–"

The roar of flames stopped. The grinding of stone ceased. Only the terrible sounds of close combat remained. Shouted orders faded to confused murmurs.

Smoke cleared with preternatural speed, drawn down into a single point. Korten appeared first, his pristine white clothes a stark contrast to the billowing darkness that he'd unleashed. Starting a few paces out from where he stood, the ground showed scars. A ring of uneven glass formed ripples on all sides. Gouges ran through the crystalline surface where opposing sorcery had reached close, their edges shattered.

As Thaun watched, even the distant sounds of men killing one another in the ruins faded. The ravine appeared next, along with the handful of Thalan mages that now held it. Here and there between the upturned earth, the blue and yellow uniforms of the Second's skirmishers appeared. Their killers stood as if in anticipation. Their ambush had lasted only a moment, but that had, apparently, been enough.

At the centre, the initial group of Thalan mages came into view as the smoke retreated. Thaun couldn't be certain, but he didn't think so many of them remained there now as had at first. Under calmer circumstances, he might've considered the pure destruction that Korten had let loose. Something else occupied his thoughts.

Like water draining through a crack, smoke collected around a single individual. They stepped forward, darkness gathering on one side. Halfway across the glassy surface before Korten, Thaun finally saw the distant figure more clearly.

Dark clothes. A shield on one hand. Blackness dripping like flames from the weapon in her other.

"Sound the retreat," Thaun said, his voice little more than a whisper.

"Sir?"

"You weren't there, at the Palace."

Halig's voice lowered. "Is that the one who attacked?"

"One of them. Elhin, I think." He turned to the other gathered officers and spoke louder. "Sound the retreat."

A chorus of affirmation rose as men and women leapt to his command. Thaun grimaced at that. It felt strange, being listened to so earnestly. He didn't deserve that sort of respect. What had he done to warrant such obedience?

"Sir?" Halig said, tone pitched low enough to not easily be overheard. "Can I speak plainly?"

"What is it?"

"We might be better pressing the attack. We might lose more troops withdrawing than if we stayed."

Thaun closed his eyes tight, face bunching up. How could people make such decisions? The weight of dozens, maybe hundreds of lives was too much to bear. "No, I'm sorry," he said eventually. "We're not ready for this fight. We need to get away, to regroup. If we stay here..." He shook his head.

"As you command, sir." Halig gave an uncertain salute, before gesturing down to where the black clad woman now stalked forwards. "I'm not sure the Highmage has heard the order though."

Thaun swore again.

Hands raised, white sleeves a distant shape, flame erupted before the Highmage. Even able to draw upon his full talent without fear of collateral damage, it wasn't enough. Incandescent pillars burst from the floor, but always a moment after Elhin had moved. Fiery bolts leapt the gap between them, forcing her away, but still she closed, and still the darkness in her hand grew.

"Captain," Thaun said, trying to hide the doubt that he felt. "See to the withdrawal. Have the surgeons move the wounded, and outriders secure our route west. Form up on the other side of the passes, and march doubletime. I want to be clear of this place."

"Sir? Are you certain?"

"Maybe." In his saddle, suddenly uncomfortable upon the soft leather, he looked down to where Korten fought Elhin. While he'd turned away, one of the Highmage's attendants had joined the fight. The explosion that destroyed the Shadow, black and grey, briefly eclipsed the fires that bloomed afresh.

Thaun wanted nothing more than to gallop down to the field himself, rallying troops, to rescue the Highmage. He'd heard it said that mages of Korten's talents were a rare thing, even in lands more magically inclined. The loss of such an individual would hurt the Empire more than that of any noble or royal. He doubted Thala would let them disengage cleanly. Someone had to cover the retreat.

Turning, he opened his mouth to speak. A weight settled upon his thoughts like a shovelful of damp earth. Halig had questioned him, but the feeling of someone else standing there settled upon him. No one stood with him to offer advice or comfort. No one placed a hand on his shoulder, or gave words of reassurance. For a second, that absence drowned out the noise of battle.

"You're right," Thaun said eventually. "Thanks. Send a word to whoever's in command of the cavalry. Cover the retreat, but don't commit to a full charge." As Halig signaled to their messengers, he thought. "I'll hold one of the passes with the Royal Guard. Find some intact squads and send them to the other. We'll withdraw when the cavalry gets free."

More salutes, flags, and horns. Soldiers responded, with men and women pulling back. In places, Thalan warriors pressed them, maintaining contact and reaping a bloody toll when guardsmen turned their backs to flee. Elsewhere, their enemies hesitated, wary of some trick or ambush. Scattered crossbowmen shot back towards the ruins, forcing the pursuing Thalan's into cover. Still people died, cut down as they disengaged. Dying because of Thaun's decision.

"I think, sir." Alongside him, Captain Halig's uncertain tone brought him round. "That your team's anticipated you." He pointed.

Thaun followed the gesture, squinting. Had the smoke not started clearing, he might've missed it. As it was, he spotted it a moment later.

The bulk of their cavalry still formed up, riders finding their positions and orders passing between the men. A handful of horsemen cut towards the centre though, where Korten's magic lashed out impotently towards Elhin. Figures rode double on two of the frontmost mounts. Spying a dark shape, their clothes not matching the uniforms around them, Thaun recognised them almost instantly.

Sigren and Lena had seen the same as he had, but had the freedom to do something about it themselves. He didn't know where they'd got the horses from, but, right now, Thaun didn't care.

They passed at a distance, not risking getting too close to either Elhin or her warriors. Bolts or javelins might have passed between them, but he couldn't see the exchange.

As the first soldiers streamed to either side of Thaun in semi-organised ranks, corralled by their squad leaders, he had to turn away. He'd have watched longer, hoping to glimpse some sign of Korten's rescue at the hands of his friends, but his own responsibilities loomed.

His Royal Guard fell in around him, and he wheeled his mount away from the battle. Though he'd never loved riding, Thaun appreciated the lessons that his uncle had forced upon him. At best, he'd describe himself as average, but breeding and training had left the beast beneath him more than able to make up for his own shortcomings.

Behind them, aides and lesser officers gathered up the last of the equipment that had made up their command post.

Forcing himself not to glance behind him, Thaun fixed his eyes on the rocky pass that they'd come through not long before. In a vain attempt to distract himself, he eyed the cracked stone where a path had formed from a weathered fissure. Starting so small, it led to the gouge upon the battlefield's left flank. Such a minute origin for something so grand. The clumsy poetry of that, in light of this defeat, chilled him.

He flinched at the sound of an explosion behind them. The discipline of those closest held, but many heads swivelled among the groups of injured limping before them. Thaun would've liked nothing more than to turn and see what had caused the noise. He gripped the reins tighter, and hoped no one saw the uncontrolled trembling that consumed his hands.

Reaching the pass, he seized the opportunity to look back the way they'd come. Past the retreating soldiers, he couldn't see the centre, where his friends attempted what he couldn't.

Royal Guardsmen, their blue surcoats untouched by the scorch marks and scars that so many others carried, formed lines on either side of the gap. Squads filed through between them, moving through the pass. He lost track of how many passed. Not as many as had come this way earlier.

Thaun tried not to think about it. He'd failed. His orders hadn't taken everything into account, despite a sleepless night. One bad decision after another, with others suffering for his shortcomings. His uncle should've seen that weakness, should've given the command to someone else.

The Second Army retreated. Thaun's numb senses only witnessed so much of it. Guardsmen limped away, uniforms bloodied and burnt. Notched weapons fell from hands as soldiers took the weight of their comrades. Those too hurt to march further pushed away from their friends, unwilling to slow down those that might yet survive.

Those images burning into his minds as surely as Korten's flames had marred the island itself, Thaun fought the urge to dismount. He could join the Royal Guard. Common wisdom told him that a few good swords could hold a narrow path like this. Their small group could stay here, and repay the sacrifice that so many had made.

Another part of his mind knew that such pointless heroics could only end in. Thalan mages had thrown the battlefield itself at them. Without Korten, they'd have lost this fight as soon as they'd started it.

Still, a final stand beckoned to him. Melodrama so often did. He didn't fear dying. As dark thoughts intruded, it seemed the easier option.

The Second's flow slowed. Those that could retreat had done so. Broken bodies and broken stone littered the battlefield. How many had died? How many now carried life-changing wounds?

Already they'd failed their Emperor's orders. The enemy held the only place of any importance on this island. An autocrat, with terrible magicks at his fingertips, would draw a broken elder god back into the world. At least those that suffered now might not have to for long.

The arrival of their cavalry helped draw Thaun from his self-destruction. Outriders and light cavalry reached them first, passing through to the far side to avoid clogging the rocky cleft.

Slower animals and riders came next. Some injured and limping, others carrying soldiers unable to walk.

Finally, a small rearguard. Heavy cavalry, with figures that he knew at their centre.

Sigren and Lena both rode behind other riders, bouncing uncomfortably without their own saddles. Though the Shadow sat awkwardly, twisted to look behind, his crossbow gripped tightly, the healer spotted Thaun as they passed. She whispered something to the woman at the reins, and they cut towards Thaun.

"What're you still doing here?" she asked.

"Where's Korten?" he replied, ignoring her question.

"We were too late. I don't know if he burnt himself out or..." The healer shook her head. She glanced down at something glistening in her hand, before gloved fingers clenched around it. Beneath her steel cap, a cut across her jaw slowly knit back together. "Nothing left to heal."

Thaun swallowed. "And Thala?"

"Gathering. They'll pursue if we stay here, I think."

"Hey!" said Sigren, finally moving up alongside them both and trembling with anger. The rider before him held the reins in one hand, their other arm hanging awkwardly with pain writ plain upon their face. "What're you doing? You shouldn't be here."

"We were just–"

"*Sir*," the Shadow spoke through his teeth as if hearing Thaun's own thoughts. "When mages are launching rocks at you, conventional wisdom doesn't apply. This chokepoint is a premade grave."

He was right, of course. Breath held, Thaun nodded. As much as his black thoughts demanded an end to all things, the men and women with him, those that had sworn an oath to his family, didn't deserve that. "You're right. Let's go."

Thaun didn't dare say anything else as they withdrew. Sigren rode at his side, fuming silently, while Lena and her rider zig-zagged through the column ahead. Surgeons would do what they could, but some wounds were beyond the help of bandages and mundane treatment. Though her part in the battle itself had come to an end, the healer's duties were far from over.

A moment later, they moved beyond the shadow cast by the pass' stone walls. Ahead, the Second formed up, ready to march. Half as many banners flew above them now, whether from the destruction of those companies or the loss of the banners themselves. Only a handful of guardsmen wore the blue and white of the First, and Thaun could see few who didn't carry wounds of one sort or another.

Guilt flooded him. His armour and uniform looked little different to when he'd put them on that morning. No blood, no soot, and no sacrifice.

In tight around him, the rearguard rejoined his battered army. Skirmisher squads, many now undermanned, formed ragged picket lines. More than a few guardsmen had collapsed to the floor, unable to stay upright despite their officers' commands. Cutters moved between them, doing what little they could.

Thaun couldn't look. Failure weighed upon him. He didn't much like himself at the best of times, but now a few hundred survivors would see him the same way. It was only right.

Guided by Sigren, the small squad of cavalry slowed at the command post. A flustered Halig stood at its centre with another man, giving and receiving reports to officers. Thaun couldn't see any of the other captains. He hoped they saw directly to their own companies, and hadn't met the fates of so many.

Murmurs rose around Thaun, and his beleaguered mind gradually caught up. He followed their gazes, and saw three banners propped up nearby. The Second's blue and yellow fluttered in the wind. Blackened on one side, the First's blue and white could still be made out clearly. The third took him a moment to recognise.

Red and blue, depicting a bird of prey in flight. It fluttered from a strange-looking polearm, half the height of the other two standards. A crest that he recognised.

As the man with Halig walked towards them, Thaun sagged, a fraction of the tension leaving him.

Pushing back long, dark hair, the other man smiled and adjusted his dark cloak, revealing the red and blue surcoat beneath. A crooked club rested in a holster at his right hip, while a sheathed blade hung at his left.

"Your Highness." Toland smirked as he bowed. Mint mingled with the faint scent of smoke. "I wasn't expecting to see you here, though it's truly a blessing." The young noble's blue eyes flicked to Sigren. "Would you kindly accept an escort from House Acquiel?"

Tooth and Nail – Chapter Eleven

"We do not worship; we fear."

Ulva, Norjan Shaman

27th day of Indern, 406th Imperial Year
17th Year of Emperor Rufenrich Konreig's Reign

One blistered foot after another, the lush, green landscape succumbed to grey. Rock and coarse plants extended as far as the eye could see, while a thin line of silver water glimmered beneath the morning sun.

Heizl trudged on, ever eastwards. At the start of their flight, she'd leant upon the Shadow at her side as she'd disrupted their pursuers' attempts. It hadn't taken long before she'd realised the flaws in such a plan. Carrying his own injuries, Zecht's condition had deteriorated with every step. A glazed look hung over the man's blue eyes. Whether shock or injury, he wasn't the same. Heizl could scarcely admit to feeling much better herself.

Now, her magicks all but spent and her stomach empty, Zecht's weight rested upon her instead.

Not for the first time that morning, she wished that Lena, or any other healer for that matter, limped along with her. For all the pleasure she took in being different to her sanguine colleagues, for all the joy she found in confounding her peers, she'd do almost anything for their more structured skills now. Surely there'd be a spell to heal, or to speed their journey along, or something. Seeing the lines binding people together compared poorly with the ability to cure injuries with a touch, even if spending the food in her stomach was preferable to burning the blood in her veins.

East, ever east. They'd find the sea that way, and, maybe, some kind of escape. She'd seen maps before they'd left Reiget City – had that truly happened only two days ago? Heizl grunted a laugh at the thought of her hopes and ambitions back then. It seemed far more probable that they'd simply die out here, by spear or exposure, far from salvation.

Still, she couldn't give up hope. On the coast, they might find a boat to limp south, or wave down a passing ship. A fleet operated in these waters out of Tarnac, and there were always merchants and the like besides. Even a Fjujan raider, or the mercenary Vigil, would be better than the alternative.

Free hand clenching her useless copper rod, Heizl drove it into the ground to help pull them up a slight rise. Overhead, gulls wheeled and cawed on the salt-laden air. The sea couldn't be much further. An age passed as she struggled up the dozen paces to the shallow slope's peak. Her training had done little to prepare her for this sort of environment.

Reaching the top, Heizl looked down at the rocky shore and halted.

In the earliest hours of morning, when the dawn light seemed more silver than gold, they'd passed an abandoned village. Plants had reclaimed the broken shapes of empty homes. Nothing valuable had remained within the ruined walls. At that point, Zecht had still seemed quite lucid, and they'd touched upon the idea of staying there, to use the site for shelter until the morning. The distant sounds of pursuit had killed that idea.

Now, rod-filled hand raised to shield her eyes from the low sun, Heizl looked down upon a similar sight. At first, she thought she stared at a second abandoned village – before the warleader had risen to power, the Guild must've forced more than a few of the native Norjan's from their homes – but gradually she realised life clung on.

Many of the squalid huts – sod-lined stone topped with stitched hides – stood empty. Their walls bore countless gaps where the village's few remaining occupants had salvaged materials to fix their own homes. Beyond the other buildings, a handful of small fishing boats lay above the shoreline. Squinting into the sun, Heizl could make out the moss growing upon their upturned hulls, revealing how long they'd rested undisturbed.

Coiled smoke twisted in the sea breeze from the chimney of one hut. Green eyes fixing upon it, she watched as its flap flicked back, and a man shuffled out clutching a wooden bucket. The native crossed between the shelters, and crouched down on the bank of a shallow stream that cut through the half-dead village. Lowering the container beneath the flow, he looked up, straight at Heizl, as he shielded his eyes.

Had she the strength remaining, Heizl would've dipped within to turn the stranger's attention away, or she would've fled back inland. She might have managed such a feat, but she doubted her ability to run afterwards, especially if she dragged Zecht with her. A sigh escaped her lips.

Leaning on her rod with one hand, she awkwardly raised the other, and waved.

She'd expected the old man to raise an alarm, or to flee inside. More of the native Norjans would've come out, and her ill-conceived mission would've come to an abrupt end on the bleak shores of the Tarnese Channel.

Instead, much to Heizl's surprise, the man struggled to his feet, and began picking his way through the rocky terrain towards her. She had plenty of time to consider this development as the elder hobbled across the gap between them. As she lowered the Shadow to the floor as gently as she could, Zecht didn't object.

By the time the native climbed the gentle slope to stop a short distance away, she smiled.

"Good morning," Heizl projected her voice over the wind.

Opposite her, the man paused, and cocked his head. Just as Heizl considered if they even shared a common language, the elder replied. Through a thick accent, he spoke words that the mage hadn't realised she wished to hear. "Water?" In both hands, he held out the bucket.

As she considered the smoothed wood and its lifegiving contents before her, Heizl felt the dryness of her mouth. Eyelids flickering as she attempted to see both mundane and magical at once, she passed over the Norjan's threads. A shiver of cold passed through her. Flies picked at her, scattering whenever she flinched. Past their creeping distraction, she saw more strands than she cared to count, many simply ending in midair. One though caught her attention. Broad and bright, it reached from the elder to her own tangled soul.

Trust.

Heizl didn't hesitate as she reached out and took the half-full bucket from the man. She nearly choked as she gulped down the cool liquid. At her feet, Zecht stirred in his dazed sleep. The Norjan stayed silent as she drank.

Lowering the crude vessel, Heizl wiped her mouth. "Thanks."

"You are most welcome," the savage, no, *native* replied in accented but near perfect Imperial.

The mage blinked several times as she took in this revelation. She'd expected broken sentences, if the man spoke a single word of Imperial. "You understand me?"

He nodded, a smile creasing his face with well-used lines. At that expression, Heizl realised that no elder stood before her. Weather-worn and hunched over, perhaps, but young eyes glistened. The native couldn't have been any older than Heizl's uncle. "Your Guild has visited these lands long enough. It is not so difficult to learn."

"I kinda thought you... you're not like the others I've met here."

"My brother no longer comes here," he shrugged, and began walking back down towards the cluster of huts. "Nor those that follow him."

"Wait, what? Your brother?"

"Come, I have food and drink. Guests are always welcome."

Heizl bowed and helped a Zecht to his feet. The Shadow grunted something that might've been gratitude, but said nothing. "Thanks, but I need to get home."

"Until then, I would be pleased to shelter you in mine."

"I appreciate it." Limping forward on her rod, Shadow resting his weight over her shoulders, she followed. "But my friend's hurt. We can't stay."

"I can offer healing."

She shook her head. "I don't even know your name."

"Okuaak."

"Heizl." She increased her pace. "Listen, Oku..Og..."

"Okuaak."

"Okuaak, listen, thanks for the offer, but—"

"But you have no other choice."

Heizl trudged down the slope in silence. She wished she could disagree. At least this would be an opportunity to rest. When had she last slept? Maybe a few hours after first walking into that damn trade post, but not much more than that. If she could get her strength back, then maybe a journey back to Imperial lands wouldn't be out of the question.

Okuaak stopped before the same hut that he'd left only moments before. As he held open the sealskin flap, Heizl squinted within. She could see little beyond the thick smoke that streamed out. Muted voices drifted to her over the sounds of the shore as other villagers awoke, muffled by the walls of their own homes.

She eyed the native. "And you're sure your brother won't come here?"

A flicker of sadness hung behind Okuaak's dark eyes, before he offered a wry smile. "Naqtuqa has not visited since his curse."

"The guy's cursed?"

"Come, there will be time for answers." He stepped within, the flap falling shut between them. "Now, your friend's needs must be seen to."

Heizl glanced down at the dazed Shadow leaning upon her. Zecht's face still held its pale colour, though she saw no fresh blood. Even she could see that his injuries went deeper than just the visible bruises and cuts. Swallowing, Heizl nodded, more to herself than anything, and stepped into the hut.

The smoke-laden air assaulted her senses as she entered. Eyes watering, wracking coughs escaped Heizl's chest. As her vision swam with each heady breath, Okuaak took Zecht's weight and guided the Shadow to a pile of furs.

"Fine." Heizl cleared her throat. "Can you help him?"

Their host didn't respond immediately, instead pouring water into a small cup to press against Zecht's lips. As she watched, Heizl considered her options. She liked the guy, but going home without any Shadows would mean she could tell her own tale. Colouring the mission to lessen her hues of failure might protect her ambitions further down the line. Heizl bit her cheek. Tempting as it might be, she knew she wouldn't leave a companion if she could help it.

"If you wish to be away from here, he is beyond the help of water and rest," said the native. "But I can bring those here who can heal him sooner."

"Are you talking about the warleader?"

In the dim light, a knowing smile tugged at Okuaak's lips. "Those I speak of are perhaps close to Naqtuqa, but they are not his."

Heizl threw up her hands. "I have literally no idea what you're talking about."

"Few beyond this land remember them. All places are home to the spirits, but your kind have long forgotten them."

"You're as bad as Hastigr…" the mage trailed off, aware that the native had paused. Okuaak's lips moved, but he stayed silent. "Uh, what are you doing?"

After a moment of silent whispers, he replied. "Bargaining. The land does not heal for nothing. Something must be given in return. I will find what is desired."

"Great," Heizl muttered, unsure what else to say. Fatigue wore her patience thin. Looking around, she gingerly lowered herself down onto another heap of furs and hides. "This is all happening a bit quickly for my liking, but if it works I'll take whatever help I can get."

"It has proved effective upon my other visitor."

"What other visitor?" A yawn punctuated her question.

"Such will wait." Okuaak turned. "You yourself are unwell. Exhausted in mind and body. Rest would serve you well; it is when the spirits do their best work."

Heizl pushed the heel of one hand into her eye, rubbing hard until colours blossomed. "I should stay on watch, in case those others come."

"I told you, they do not come here." He lowered his voice to little more than a whisper. "The spirits make Naqtuqa's curse unbearable."

"Good to know." Dragging her thoughts into line felt sluggish and slow. "Can your spirits help?"

"They yield to no man," said the shaman. "If they can help, they will demand something in return."

Heizl yawned again. "You're certain it's safe here?"

"They tell me that you already believe I can be trusted," said Okuaak. "The land is rarely so certain." He gestured to the crude bedding beneath Heizl. "Rest, they will see to your needs, while I see to the exchange of gifts."

The mage shrugged, and began to lie down. "Why are you doing this? If what you say is true, healing us will cost you."

"The spirits have whispered of those who will help free Naqtuqa from his curse," said the native.

"And I guess that's me...?" Heizl slurred, welcoming sleep rising around her.

No dream or nightmare disturbed her slumber, leaving her to the darkness. How long she slept, rolled in musty-smelling blankets, she didn't know. When she awoke, vision blurry in the hut's gloom, the fire's embers had died. Opposite her, Zecht still lay with eyes closed, his chest rising and falling. She saw no sign of the shaman.

Rolling onto her back, Heizl stared up at the smoke-blackened hide above her. Faint pinpricks of light broke through the coarse stitching overhead. For what must have been only a few hours of sleep, she felt more refreshed than she had since... when? Before the fire and chaos of Thaun's feast, at least.

She clawed, half-blind, out to one side until she found her rod, before clambering upright. Ducking slightly to avoid the roof's wooden supports, she glanced at Zecht's sleeping form before stepping outside.

Cold sea air sank claws into exposed skin, forcing her to pull her cloak tighter around her. The afternoon sun's grey light cast lengthening shadows out towards the shoreline. Somewhere nearby, over the swell of the surf, a child's distant laughter reached her. A couple of native women, old or weathered by a lifetime of exposure to the elements, wove nets near a low, crackling fire. Four mangy dogs ran back and forth, barking loudly at one another.

No one paid the stranger in their midst any attention. Heizl found no hint of the fear or disgust that she'd come to expect at home. For all the Court's claims of civility and culture, these villagers showed more humanity than any noble. That realisation should've relaxed her, but she only grew more wary.

Catching sight of Okuaak standing looking out to sea with another, taller native, the mage made for them. Her legs no longer ached so much beneath her as she walked. Short of Lena appearing overnight, she struggled to credit the improvement to the strange shaman. Heizl wondered if she should've paid more attention to Hastigr when he spoke about things other than her own scathe. Such talk seemed so irrelevant at the time, but she couldn't shake the feeling that he'd probably mentioned these so-called-spirits at some point.

Passing the women at their nets, Heizl glanced at the stranger standing with the shaman. She'd taken him as just another Norjan, but, as she closed the gap, details clawed at her that suggested otherwise. In spite of him wearing the same hides as Okuaak and the other villagers, he stood upright and straight, half a head taller than the native. Dark hair, a similar shade to the shaman, rustled in the sea breeze. Here and there, finer cloth hung out beyond the furred clothing he wore.

Heizl barely saw any of this, instead focusing on the sheathed sword at the stranger's hip. She'd seen weapons a thousand times, in the hands of the Royal Guard, or a Shadow, but this wasn't one of them. Broad and asymmetrical, in a black sheath bound in bronze, familiarity plucked at her.

Still a distance away, both men with their backs to her, recognition formed. Memories of smoke, fear, and sorcery.

Heizl's pace faltered before she pushed on. Neither man faced her as she reached out with her magic. The wind plucked at their strands. Both Okuaak and the other man spoke with one another, the bond between them ringing with colour as they talked. Other threads reached out in almost random directions, or back into themselves, but those didn't matter right now.

As she walked closer, Heizl stroked the chains between the two men. Had she tried the night before, still exhausted, she'd have failed. Even now, well-rested, it took more effort than she'd expected. By the time she stood close enough to physically touch them, the bond shone bright with raised interest though. Neither so much as glanced her way.

She'd had very little martial training, but wouldn't let that stop her. The man who'd crafted her useless focus for her all those years ago probably hadn't meant to create a weapon. On more than a few occasions over the years she'd considered getting rid of it. Most mages used such focuses to help channel the sanguine energies passing through them, to help reduce magic's unavoidable self-injury. Still, two and a half feet of metal had its uses.

As hard as she could, Heizl brought the rod down on the stranger's head. Blinded by arcane webs of light, she struck off centre, the swing bouncing down to strike into his shoulder. He staggered back, one hand clutching at the fresh wound as he reached for his sword with the other.

Heizl had limited experience of hitting another person, but a blow like that to the head should've done more than that, shouldn't it? Trembling, the mage drew back to swing again, only stopping as the shaman stepped between them, separating them.

"This man is dangerous!" Heizl cried, pushing against the outstretched hand.

"I have extended to him my hospitality, the same as I did to you!" the shaman hissed back.

"You don't understand! He attacked my home, my family! He's planning something here too!"

"You Imperials came here, exploited my people, and fought my brother. Your traders have plans for my home. All this, yet I did not turn you away."

She lowered the rod, but didn't put it down. Her heart pounded in her chest. Jaw bunching, she stared as the second foreigner straightened. Bronzed skin, straight teeth, grey eyes, and sleek, dark hair amounted to a handsome face, despite the blood. Heizl couldn't help but want to punch it.

With one hand resting on the blade at his hip and the other gently probing his head, Renyar glared at her. "I've killed men for less..." He narrowed his gaze. "I remember you. You helped the Crown Prince escape."

"And I remember you," Heizl snarled. "It's pretty hard to forget some insane, murderous, wannabe kidnapper!" She threw up her arms, and turned back to Okuaak, incredulous. "I can't believe you're helping him."

Arms still raised between them, the shaman glanced at Renyar before responding. "He came to me injured, just the same as you. I extended my protection to him, just as I did for you. You both came here for the same reason – my brother and his curse." He shook his head. "The only thing different between you is that the wounded man that you travelled with still lives." For the first time, Heizl's eyes tracked to the fresh pile of stones before the other two men. Other graves littered the hillside.

"Imperial," Renyar said, staring intently at Heizl. "Put down your weapon. Let us talk about this peacefully."

"This isn't a weapon," she spat back, a minor headache growing. "I'd have thought a murderer like you would recognise one."

"Put it down nonetheless," he commanded.

Heizl's hand, already trembling with rage, shook as she resisted the Thalan's words. After a moment, she flung her rod to the ground. "You're a real bastard, you know that, right?"

Renyar inclined his head, less than a nod, but said nothing.

Her different futures raced through Heizl's mind. Violence had almost worked. A hint of pride rose in her at having managed to strike him when the Royal Guard had failed. She doubted that she'd get lucky a second time, not with Okuaak now separating them. Successful flight seemed unlikely, even without her injured Shadow, now that Renyar knew of her presence.

Any plan she might have made screeched to a halt as the Thalan spoke. "You're a chained mage, yes?"

"What in the Voids are you talking about?"

"You are from your tower?"

"The Spire? Sure, I guess."

"Yet you access your kwen freely?" At the mage's indignant expression, Renyar continued. "Your magic is unimpeded?"

Heizl shook her head. She didn't know what she'd expected in meeting this threat to the Empire, but it wasn't this. "Even if I knew what that meant, why would I tell you?"

"Mine has been unreliable since coming here," he admitted, casting an appraising eye over the Imperial. "It's unlikely I'll be able to do much more than return home, when the time comes."

"Great, then leave."

"I can't, not yet." Renyar took a short step towards her, empty hands out to either side. "Your magic works?"

"Yours doesn't? I hear it happens to guys like you all the time..." Heizl shrugged, a dismissive sneer tugging at one corner of her mouth.

"Fascinating." He nodded several times to himself. "I knew that my magicks would be limited once here, but I never imagined it'd be this bad. Those that came with me couldn't conjure the simplest arcana."

"I guess I'm just lucky."

"I suspect there's more to it than that," he shrugged and turned away. "If not for the insistence of our most gracious host, I might compel you to tell me more."

"Try it." Heizl puffed out her chest and stuck out her jaw, willing Renyar not to test her in spite of her bravado.

They both turned towards the shaman as he spoke. "Guests." By the look on the Thalan's face, he'd dismissed Okuaak too. The native glanced between them, ensuring he had their attention. "I may be able to shine some light upon your weakness."

Still reigning in her disgust, Heizl stayed quiet.

"Please," Renyar replied. "Tell me."

"The spirits. The same ones that drove Naqtuqa and his curse from this place." He eyed Renyar. "The same that follow after your own curse too. They suppress such blood magicks throughout my homeland."

"That's really interesting, honestly, it is." Heizl half turned away, unwilling to take her eyes from Renyar. "But it doesn't really help me deal with sitting in the same village as someone trying to destroy the whole damn world."

"That's not my plan."

Heizl scoffed. "Well, not all of it then – you live here with the rest of us, after all."

"You speak bravely, if unwisely." Renyar's grey eyes narrowed. "What's your name, Imperial?"

For a second, Heizl considered a scathing retort, or literally spitting at the man. She sighed. There was little point in fighting something so minor, though she fought it anyway. And failed. "Heizl."

Without pausing, Renyar replied. "Heizl Fitzerin, Spire Third Class?"

"The very same. Got a file on me or something?"

"Something, yes." he smiled, though Heizl couldn't see any humour in the expression. "I hadn't realised that it was you who interrupted me at the Palace. It was suggested that you were unlikely to blindly follow your uncle's path. I must admit to some surprise to find you so far from home, carrying out his wishes."

"Why wouldn't I?" she scoffed. "He's trying to protect the Empire. Millions of lives depend on him."

"You truly believe he'll succeed in protecting anyone?"

"Oh, sinking to intimidation now?" Heizl gestured towards Okuaak. "So you stop me from hitting the guy, but threatening innocents is fine?"

"The spirits have little interest in your people, friend," the shaman replied, downcast. "Renyar's curse is another matter entirely."

"Do you have to keep it up with this 'curse' nonsense?" she growled. "He's carrying around a piece of some long-dead dragon. Who knows what else his pawns have got their hands on?"

At last, anger rising, some colour flashed in the Thalan's cheeks. "My hands are the least destructive option!"

"I'd figured you were a bit unstable." Heizl smirked at the heated reaction. "But that's quite an ego you've got there. I can see why Uncle thinks you're so dangerous."

"Only to a deluded man like him!"

"I've got to say, it's nice to know there's someone standing up to people like you."

"Urephor doesn't stand up to anyone," Renyar hissed. "If he comes back, he'll be destruction given form. Rufenrich will become Emperor of the ashes."

Heizl paused. "Wait, what?"

"If the dragon returns, he will bring only ruination. There's no one group remaining who could defeat him as Imes did so long ago, so he mustn't return. Ever."

"No, I get that." She shook her head. "What I don't understand is why you're suddenly being all theoretical in your doom-mongering. You're not summoning Urathear?"

Renyar reappraised her in return. "Only if no other options remain."

"Just what's that supposed to mean?"

"If his Heart is brought back into this world, I'm less likely to be outright corrupted by its influence than most."

"Then why bring it back in the first place?"

Renyar looked her up and down, as if for the first time. An unsettling smile spread across his face. "You don't realise what the Emperor plans."

Heizl held his gaze, a chill running through her bones that had nothing to do with the growing sea breeze. "If this is some kind of attempt to get me out of your way…"

"Heizl, if I wanted you out of the way, I'd tell you. It's better for us both if you understand the truth for yourself."

"And just what truth is that?" She held out both hands, mirroring Renyar's earlier gesture, as she stepped closer to better hear him over the sounds of breaking waves.

"Rufenrich will carry out a ritual to draw Urephor's Heart out from the darkness."

"Funny, he said the same thing about you."

"I imagine he would." The Thalan sighed, and looked away. "He means well, I'm sure, believing that it will give him the power necessary to maintain your family's grip upon your Empire."

"Let's say I believe you," said Heizl. "Ignoring the fact that he's no mage, just how do you know what he's thinking?"

"Why, he told me."

"I guess I should've seen that coming," she reflected back to a night with the Emperor's inner circle when she'd first learned all this.

"It's true. I sought out his help when I learned of Daericani-sympathisers within your Empire. For a while, we worked together to stop them, until he suggested another course of action." Renyar shrugged. "We parted ways after our disagreement."

"And so you tried to assassinate him in the middle of what could've turned into a decent party." Heizl couldn't help but smile a little. "Y'know, about all you managed to kill was the atmosphere."

"I have done regrettable things before, and am willing to do them again. My actions were unfortunate, but necessary "

"'course you'd say that."

"I say it because it's true."

"You know that no one thinks that they're the bad guy, right?" She almost laughed in disbelief. "Even if you're not lying through your perfect teeth, why shouldn't Uncle Rufenrich turn something dangerous to a good end? It's not like a sword cares who wields it. I'd rather it was in the hands of anyone but you."

"Friends." Okuaak lay soothing hands on their shoulders. Heizl fought the urge to flinch away. "The spirits dislike your tension. Such attention bodes poorly for us all. Please, grow still, let peace fill the silence. Your words will wait."

Renyar turned away from Heizl, facing the shaman fully. "As gratitude for your help, I yield to your wisdom."

The Norjan turned to regard her. "And you, Imperial?"

She considered storming away. She thought about arguing, like she had so many times with superiors or family back at home. Clenching both fists, Heizl looked past the native to Renyar. "Fine, I'll behave, but I have just one question first."

"What would you know?"

"Hey, Renyar?" she took a step towards him, the sea's roar filling her ears. "You said your magic isn't working here, right?"

The Thalan glanced at her before looking back out over the waves. "The arcanosphere is thin here, yes."

Heizl smiled. "Great."

Her fist connected with the side of Renyar's head bare inches from the dried bloodstain. The Spire had never seen any benefit in teaching its mages how to throw a punch or swing a sword, and Heizl couldn't say she disagreed with them. Her own strange style of magic had always proved effective enough. If he hadn't lay unconscious only a short distance away, Zecht might have pointed out the flaws in her technique.

Instead, the only thing she could think of was just how much her hand hurt.

Tooth and Nail – Chapter Twelve

> *"There are stories of men throwing in their lot with the Daericani since there have been tales of the dragons themselves. Indisputable histories tell of twisted sects, death cults, and opportunistic usurpers, both within and without the Empire. These pale in the light of the conflict that broke the Konreig Empire."*
>
> Cults of the Imperial Mainland,
> Archimand Märchen (409 I.Y.)

27th day of Indern, 406th Imperial Year
17th Year of Emperor Rufenrich Konreig's Reign

Rain hammered on the tent roof like falling spears, a constant susurration underlying all other sound. Out in the mud, demoralised soldiers fumbled with tents and shovels, preparing for their enemies' pursuit. Their surcoats held few hints of any previous colour, their uniforms growing as dark as the soot and ground that clung to them. The camp had shrunk since the morning before.

Events closer at hand occupied Thaun's attention more fully.

Sigren, hands firmly grasping Toland's shirtfront, slammed the other man into the tent pole. Years of drawing back bow strings had left him with more than enough strength to shake the noble like a dog with a toy. Canvas shivered above them. Dislodged raindrops ran down its sides. Mint's fresh aroma filled the air. "Say that again, Acquiel," the Shadow hissed. "I dare you!"

"I didn't mean any offence," he replied between grunting breaths. "I simply commented that it's days like these that it feels like the gods have left us."

"You want to see them sooner?" Sigren tightened his grip. "After today, what's one more?"

"Sigren!" Thaun stepped in, a hand on each man's shoulder. "Stop it!"

"With all due respect, sir, if this primary-coloured peacock had thought to tell us he was playing soldier here then we might not have lost all the lives that we did!"

"I'm..." Thaun swallowed, fighting back the first hint of tears. "I'm upset too. This isn't how things were meant to go, but taking it out on Toland isn't going to help matters. It's not his fault that we're in this mess."

Thaun left his last thought unspoken. It was his own fault. He'd done his best, and proven to everyone else what he'd always known – it wasn't enough. *He* wasn't enough. If he hadn't let Thala's appearance draw him in, then their scouts might've had the time to spot Toland's men. If he'd shown more caution and they'd arrived later, then the extra troops could've changed everything.

If anything, they should be glad for the unexpected reinforcements.

Sigren, and who knew how many more in the Second, had their own take on it.

"Besides," Lena broke the silence around a yawn. "I'm pretty sure that Shadows aren't employed to judge and sentence the noble class. Not in public, anyway."

None of the men spoke. A tense moment later, Sigren let go and stepped away.

Toland slumped down. "I suppose an apology is too much to ask for..." he muttered a little too loudly.

"I will punch you in the fucking neck." The Shadow's voice dripped with threat.

Thaun threw up his hands. "Sigren, stop, please! For all we know, Thala only didn't pursue because of Toland turning up. It must've surprised them as much as it did us. He quite possibly saved our lives today – the least we can do is hear him out."

"I don't know if you noticed," Sigren wheeled on him. "But you've lost half your troops and your only Highmage, all while Acquiel here gallivanted around with an unregistered private army mere miles away. For all we know he kicked the hornet's nest already, and that's why Thala reacted how they did."

"You're being irrational." Lena pushed herself more upright. "You didn't blame Vandel for not being there soon enough when Renyar attacked the Palace. We should be thankful Toland was here at all."

"Just what are you doing here, anyway?" The Shadow cast a venomous stare the noble's way. "Insel Drach isn't under Tarnese jurisdiction."

Toland shrugged. "Some accounting discrepancies shone a light on a merchant spending more than she could afford in Kreft. Father's been pulling on that loose end for a while, and we eventually found that some strangers had paid for transport with Thalan coin. After everything that happened in the Capital, we figured it was more than just coincidence, so I volunteered to come out here." His expression settled, hostility fading, as he turned to Thaun. "May I ask what brings the Crown Prince to a backwater like this?"

"We're..." Thaun hesitated. His head fuzzed with weariness. Had he ever had a day as bad as this one? Maybe once, and even then no one had died from it.

He liked Toland more than he did most nobles – his occasional irreverence reminded him of Heizl sometimes – but his uncle had spelled out the seriousness of the situation well enough. The more people that knew about the planar Rift, and all that it meant, the more likely things would spiral into disaster.

"After Renyar's attack, Uncle thought it best to hide me somewhere remote, until things calmed down." The half-truth clawed at his insides.

"And so you thought it best to attack known enemies? In an entrenched position?"

"I let Korten persuade me," Thaun mumbled.

"And see where his hubris led you?" Toland sighed. "As insufferable as he was, it'll be a long time before the Empire sees a battlemage of his calibre again."

Lena cleared her throat. "His contribution... I can't help but think that things might've gone even worse without him."

"Are you even listening to yourselves?" Sigren seethed. "If it wasn't for him, we wouldn't have marched without waiting to learn more. This is his fault."

"Was it the Highmage who cut down your men?" Toland raised his chin as he locked gazes with the Shadow. "Did Korten kill your friend? Blame should lie in one place, and one place only – Thala."

For a moment, Thaun thought Sigren might strike the noble. He wouldn't have had the strength to stop him if he had. Instead, the Shadow stormed from the tent, mumbling profanities under his breath. None of the others spoke, the sounds of the rain outside filling the space between them.

Toland's response drew his attention. Pushing back the red hem of his dark cloak, Thaun thought he'd draw the odd club at his hip. Instead, he held the cloth, preventing it from obstructing him as he plucked an untarnished silver decanter from a low table next to him. Letting his cloak fall free again, he took up a trio of cups in his other hand.

The sounds of tumbling brandy joined the sounds of the weather. Returning the vessel to its tray, Toland held out a cup.

Thaun shook his head. "I'm not in the mood for a drink."

"I thought we could raise a toast." He handed one to Lena, who took it with a wordless nod. "It seems the least we can do."

Thaun barely felt the cool metal as he accepted the drink. Opposite him, the healer grunted as she stood. None made eye contact.

Something coiled in Thaun's gut. He trembled almost imperceptibly. Heizl would've known what to say. Serious matters dogged him, often in the form of their uncle, but he'd avoided the worst of them. Talking about death, especially the death of so many, didn't sit well with him. He was glad when Toland drew some of the attention away from him.

"I didn't know those who sacrificed themselves today," the noble breathed in through his nose as sombre words formed. "I've known many loyal soldiers though, and I know what these men and women did at the end. They acted for the greater good. They protected those that they could. They played their part." He raised his cup. "Pragmatism, duty, and respect. All qualities that we can only hope to emulate. To their memory." He drank. Lena followed suit with a sip, and, a moment later, Thaun did the same.

As he lowered his glass, the tent flap ruffled. No one spoke as Sigren, significantly wetter than before, stepped back in. The Shadow took a mouthful from a tin flask that Thaun didn't recognise, hand trembling the whole time.

Their healer cleared her throat. She paused, and Thaun wondered if she might not say anything at all. Eventually, she spoke. "Thank you for doing your duty, and for paying its cost. It was an honour to march beside you. I swear to any god that'll listen – Judge, Witness, or Drowned – I'll help those comrades you left behind today." A tear welled in Lena's eye. "I hope that I can be as strong as you." An expression of distracted thoughtfulness passed over her features before fading again, like shattered ice rippling above a wave.

They all raised their drinks anew. As they lowered them once more, Sigren spoke, growled words breaking free.

"They didn't deserve to die like that." Head bowed forward to cast his eyes into shadow, he glared at Toland. "You and I are going to have a serious talk about all this sometime soon... but there's someone else who has to die first." He took a swig from the flask. "This isn't a toast, it's a promise. Even if Thala buries us all under a hundred boulders, *Elhin dies.* Understood?"

None of them felt the need to question him.

As Sigren sank down upon a stool, Thaun felt the other two glancing his way. None wished to push him forward, though he could sense their expectation pressing in on him nonetheless. He didn't know which was worse – the unspoken disappointment, or the all-too-brutal prompt.

Pulling the cool, damp air into his lungs, steeling himself, he forced it back out, attempting to send his emotions with it. It didn't work, but he spoke anyway.

"Thank you for..." His throat tightened, forcing him short. "Thank you. May your memories last as long as we do."

What else could he say? The others didn't expect truly to live through this, did they? It wasn't like words would make a difference anyway.

Thaun didn't make eye contact as he threw the glass back. A burning sensation struck the back of his throat, and he grew vaguely aware of the others following suit. Long after the brandy's warmth had faded, he kept the cup pressed hard against his lips, hiding his expression. It was safer that way.

He hid behind his empty cup for as long as he could. Glancing around, the other three looked into their drinks. In the lamplight, Thaun couldn't read their expressions.

As moments passed, and none of them spoke, Thaun felt the tension seeping back in. Lena's loud sigh cut through the quiet, the three men eyeing her as she dropped back down onto her stool. Toland lowered his cup and stood with his hands behind him, while Sigren crossed his arms over his chest, still gripping the flask.

Thaun couldn't help but eye the Shadow's clenched fist. Colour leached out by the cold rain, his grazed knuckles shone red. It was no stretch to imagine him punching the nearest solid object before skulking back in. The night's storm would hide the sounds of such an impact, but it did little to hide their grief.

It would've been easier to pretend not to notice. Guilt joined his grief at that thought. How dare he wallow in self-pity when so many others had legitimate pains? He'd at least had a choice in what orders to give. Every person beneath him had had no other option than to follow his commands.

Perspective didn't help. Thaun wanted to cry. That would only make it worse though. The others would react, coming to comfort him when others needed it more.

A few moments of awkward silence passed, broken only by the rain outside, and Lena cleared her throat. All three men turned to her.

"I think I should get back to the cutters," she said.

"With due respect." Toland glanced at Thaun before facing the healer. "Exhausting yourself now might do more harm than good. Rest could serve better in the long run."

Thaun swallowed. "How many injured are there?"

"Too many," replied the healer. "Even those who look unharmed carry inner wounds now. You don't have to see something for it to be real."

"You can't save them all," said Toland. Upon her stool, Lena slumped at the words. "Father always says that knowing who you can help is just as important as actually doing something for them."

Lena eyed Thaun. "What do you think?"

"I don't know. I don't have a better suggestion," he admitted. "I wish I did. You know your limits better than the rest of us. Maybe you should decide."

"Wise words," said Toland. "It takes a certain bravery to confess to such uncertainty. For what it's worth, I'll pray that the rest of us know the wisdom to do the most good for the most people."

"Give it a rest." Sigren rolled his eyes, his anger under better control this time.

Genuine humour seeped into the noble's smile, if only a little. "Rest is exactly what I just suggested." Sigren snorted a short, derisive laugh in reply.

The two said something else, but the words never reached Thaun's ears. Before he could sink into his own thoughts, Lena turned towards him and lowered her voice further. "Would talking about it help?"

He could only look away and mutter his response. "Later."

The healer nodded cryptically, and the conversation died.

Thaun leant back in his chair, its wood creaking beneath his weight. The tent's single crackling brazier did little to hold back the cold. Tired faces and weary glances held a suspicious vigil as distrust bound them.

Closing his eyes, not wanting to see those expressions, Thaun wondered at changing the subject. Trying a joke or an anecdote, so that none of them, himself included, would have to face the gloom head-on. Nothing came to mind. Heizl would've known what to say. When he'd struggled, she'd always had an answer.

Beyond the canvas walls that separated them from the rest of the island, the last glimmers of daylight fled the sky. Behind dark clouds, a glimmer of blue and green showed that even the Comet had grown distant. A handful of lanterns flickered to life as weary pickets stood at their posts. Darkness hung over much of the camp. Demoralised soldiers passed flasks between themselves, comforting one another the only way they had left.

Within the command tent, Lena broke their musing silence.

"If we're all now calm enough to discuss things professionally." The mage's face remained motionless. "We have work to do. Reports to write, messages to send, and questions to answer."

Thaun breathed out through his nose, any hint of rest going with it. "You're probably right. I just don't know where to start."

"I do." Sigren tapped his chin as he eyed Toland. "There have been rules about how many troops a noble can employ since the civil war. How doesn't the Forge know about the companies that are here with you now?"

Toland rubbed his face in some attempt to stall his own tiredness. "We've done all the required paperwork." He waved a dismissive hand. "It's a fraction of those that Strahl has hired of late. I can't stand the way he exploits selfish loopholes."

"I'm not going to hit you," Sigren said, sounding out each word as if instructing himself. "I am serious though. My briefing before we came here was thorough. I don't remember anything about a standing army this close to the Daer Sea. Especially not one provisioned like yours. That sort of thing stands out. It feels wrong."

"Sigren," the noble replied in an even tone. "I gave my statement to your organisation after the incident at the Royal Palace. I paid the fees and returned to Tarnac by the Nexus. There, I got sent here, to chase down stories of bribed ferrymen and merchants." He paused for a heartbeat, making sure his words had sunk in. "Our records aren't as substantial as yours, but I didn't go looking for details of troops movements, or Trade Guild contracts. No, with the few hours I had to prepare, I put my efforts into ensuring my men would have the supplies and intelligence that they'd need for the task at hand."

"What're you getting at, Acquiel?" growled the Shadow.

"Just that I had no reason to think I'd find the Crown Prince here, and so I don't know much about the army that you're here with. Why would you have looked closely at my family's regiment when you had so much else to learn before coming here?"

"I guess, it's just..."

"Strahl has thousands of men in his employ. Soldiers, scouts, spies – I imagine the Throne calls upon them themselves on occasion. My own informants suggest he's even tripled the number currently at his estate in the Capital. Does that feel wrong?"

"Don't turn my words against me," Sigren shook his head. "Gimme a break. What about these bribes? If they had Thalan connections, why risk coming here yourself? You should've passed it onto us. The Shadows, I mean."

Toland bowed his head, pinching the bridge of his nose tight before looking back up. Veiled frustration glittered in his pale blue eyes. "How long ago was that fateful night at the Palace? Three nights? Four? It feels like weeks. Even with my, ahem, funds, just how quickly do you think I can move around the Empire? I'm not a Highmage. Your Forge takes days to process a message, and that's ignoring the queue for the Nexus." He sighed, his shoulders rising and falling dramatically with it. "It could've been weeks before any Shadow even looked at the letter, and weeks more before they did anything with it. We saw something that needed doing, and so came here to do it."

The noble breathed, calming himself. "Despite all that, I'm glad to come across other Imperials, even if you're only here to lie low. When we first saw your banners, I'd assumed you were here to help us, not the other way around."

Thaun bit his tongue, just enough to remind himself not to say anything stupid. He couldn't see any way that Toland had ignored his silence during their exchange. Even the simplest minds would read something into the official explanation for their presence on Insel Drach.

Lena raised a hand while glancing between the three men. "I have a question, if you don't mind?" It took Thaun a moment to register she'd spoken. The healer's normal voice, balanced and calm, had changed. It was no longer just level. Now, he could only describe it as flat. Her efforts since the battle, stabilising the worst injured, had taken its toll.

"What is it?" said Thaun.

"Your men, Master Acquiel, are... strange. Why come here with just skirmishers? What did you hope to do without line infantry?"

"My Pinions?" Toland regarded Lena through narrowed eyes, raising his chin to look down on her. "They've proved themselves in the field, though perhaps not on this scale. I dare say they'd hold their own against the Royal Guard."

Across the tent, Sigren snorted in disbelief.

Toland sucked air in through his teeth. "My men may not have the storied history of the Royal Guard, but they're well trained, and uniquely armed. Warfare will change, and we hope to be at the forefront of it."

"*Uniquely armed*?" Sigren laughed harshly. "You can't just leave that hanging there. You're telling us you're carrying some secret weapon?"

"How you describe them is your decision." He shrugged, one hand patting the club at his hop as he spoke. "They're new. I don't really understand them myself. Father employed a team of specialists to develop them. An Imperial smith, a Daqini alchemist, a... Tszerrichan."

"You were going to say something else," Sigren growled.

"I believe both the magistrates and the church have something to say about self-incriminating statements," he sighed. "When all this is over, I will gladly submit them to the correct authorities for inspection. By then though, I suspect many people will be glad for Father's decision."

"Sigren," Thaun said softly. "It'll wait. Lena, you too." He rubbed his eyes. "Toland helped us. His troops' weapons don't matter right now."

"You're right," the healer admitted. "We shouldn't be distracted by that sort of logistics. What matters is if they can help us now." She turned to the noble. "Can they help with Elhin's mages?"

Thaun's ears fell deaf to Toland's answer. Melancholy beckoned. He'd held back the guilt of his failure, but cracks had formed in his weakening resolve. Mere talk – whether mourning, details, or tactics – could only distract him for so long.

Sigren argued with the noble again. Pushing his hands against his knees, Thaun stood. Silence blanketed his friends as they turned his way.

"Your Highness?" Toland made to stand, but stopped at Thaun's gesture to remain seated.

"It's okay." He rubbed his eyes. "I just want to get some air."

"Good idea." The noble rose anyway. "I'll come with you."

"No, I'd rather have some time to myself."

"Respectfully, Your Highness, but I don't think you should be alone right now."

"I'll be fine."

"Thala could return at any moment. We all saw what Renyar tried in Reiget City. They could have assassins in the camp even now. It's not *safe*."

Thaun hesitated. Not out of fear of unseen killers, but for those he'd leave behind. Toland, Sigren, or that officer in the Second would take charge. Any one of them would do a better job than he had so far.

Lena derailed his thoughts with a whisper. "If Elhin was to pursue, she would've by now. She's not likely to attack us until dawn."

"Still," Toland objected, "He shouldn't–"

"Knock it off," Sigren grunted a laugh. "We all process differently. Let him go and air how he feels. Hit something, scream, whatever." He leant back on the stool, balancing himself with his feet. "He'll be safe enough. He won't wander too far."

The noble's shoulders slumped, and he looked away. With a grateful nod to the Shadow, Thaun lifted the tent flap and stepped outside.

Rain twisted in the unseen breeze before sinking into his hair and clothes. The heat drained from his body, his skin growing cold, and so he walked.

Something told him that he should know the layout of the camp from some old lesson, but nothing came. Thaun didn't care.

He knew the self-destructive roads that his mind meandered down far better than the muddy paths between the tents. Indecision, doubt, guilt, Thaun lingered at each, and each took its toll in turn. Familiar feelings swirled chaotically through him, his throat swelling tight in answer.

Couldn't they *see*? Everyone said he'd be the next Emperor, something great, and that all this would be his. Didn't they understand how much of a mistake that'd be? If he couldn't even hold one little island, how could they expect him to look after an Empire? Having the Konreig name didn't make him worthy of all that it meant.

Huddled in twos and threes at their cookfires, soldiers mourned. A few raised fitful voices to the sky, singing dirges to one god or another as they sought salvation. Some drank until darkness overtook them, and yet others still roared into the night in a desperate challenge to the deadly promise that stood before them.

Some found comfort in the throwing of tiles and the reading of cards. The fashion for those decks had drifted down from the nobility it seemed. Printed and lacquered, bearing the coloured faces of gods and fates, they'd come with traders from lands far to the south. Children's games of skill and chance, grown men and women now credited events and experience on the way that they fell.

People would seek meaning in even the most disordered of things.

Passing braziers and fires, fitful beneath the wind and rain, Thaun reached the camp's perimeter. With the moon and Comet hidden behind clouds, visibility had shrunk to a dozen paces in most places. A few spots of light marked their pickets. The faint sound of metal on earth and stone hinted at troops digging in the darkness. He didn't know if they broke earth to excavate defences or to raise graves.

Standing there in the broken shelter of the camp's outermost ring of tents, Thaun felt more alone than the simple physical solitude dictated. Gusts plucked at the nearby canvas as much as it did his mood, pulling it this way and that.

He didn't know how to talk to them about it. Clumsy words couldn't compare to the thoughts weighing him down. At least here he knew that those closest to him – Toland, Sigren, Lena – would try to understand. Back home, every noble that crossed his path would pretend to listen, all in the hope of earning favour.

Someone should've stood there with him. He knew it deep within, but sensed nothing. A hole in his heart, a shape gentle yet strong, but with no reason for being there.

Muffled by the rain's murmur and drowned out by his own thoughts, Thaun didn't notice the guardsman step up alongside him until the man spoke.

"Y' thinkin' 'bout it too?" the soldier slurred.

"I'm sorry?" Thaun turned, wiping rain from his face, to look at the man. Taller than Thaun, he didn't wear any armour, leaving his blue and white uniform baggy beneath a dirty cloak. Older too, maybe as old as his uncle, with long, bushy eyebrows. Concealed by the waxed fabric, blood faded from red to brown as it dried. The waterskin in his hand dribbled with something dark.

"I se'n two go ou' there already," he continued, not looking directly at him. "They ain' comin' back."

Thaun considered this for a moment. He'd always wanted to talk to people without the pretence of his station, but now, in the face of it, he didn't know quite what to say. Opening and closing his mouth a few times, he tried anyway.

"Where've they gone?"

"They lef' their mail an' their kit," he eyed Thaun sidelong, his gaze glassy and unfocused. "They ain' taken shovels wit' 'em, so they ain' diggin' trenches." Silence, all but the weather, fell for a moment. "I'm thinkin' o' doin' th'same. Marchin' ou' there. Lettin' the storm, nigh', an' them bastard radicals fight over me."

"That's..." Years of training failed him. Courtly etiquette helped little when faced with circumstances like this. Thaun breathed in and out a few times, feeling his chest rise and fall, as he understood what the man next to him was considering. "It's not that bad. Maybe you should go back to your squad?"

The soldier laughed, a cruel sound railing against the dark. "Squad? Wha' squad? Thala cut 'em down. I made a bad d'cision, an' they paid. Hildrun wit' a spear through 'er gut, an' Gerwulf's 'ead caved in." His laugh faded to bitterness. "They didn't d'serve it. I shouldn'a been made sergean'. I din' even manage t' keep m'sword."

Unbidden, Thaun felt his lips press together, brows lowering, as emotions flooded his face. In the night, the other man likely didn't see. He didn't react, at least.

"I s'en a few go ou' there," the soldier repeated himself. "Joinin' 'em they lost." His words slowed, some inner conflict warring within him. "Thinkin' o' joinin' 'em too."

"I... I don't think you should do that."

"An' why not?"

"I don't know. It wouldn't help things, would it? I mean, we lost today, but that doesn't mean that we'll lose again next time." He steeled himself. "And even if we do, maybe it'll be a fight worth fighting anyway."

"If they're fightin', they'd be better off wit'out me."

"You don't know that. You obviously care. Maybe that's enough."

"Wha' good is a soldier wi'hout a sword?"

"Here." Thaun unbuckled his swordbelt, feeling his uniform's weight shift without it. He held it out, scabbard, blade, and all, towards the other man. "It's good steel, well-oiled and sharpened. Only a few small notches. Take it." As he spoke, regret flirted with an emotion he didn't often experience. Hope? Pride? Satisfaction? He wasn't quite certain.

"Y'sure?"

"No, but I think you should probably have it anyway." Thaun deflated, breaking eye contact while still holding it out. "I'll get another one." For a second, he thought that the guardsman wouldn't take the weapon. After what felt like a lifetime, he lifted its weight from Thaun's hand.

They stood next to one another for a few moments longer. The soldier fidgeted, looking at the weapon in his hand, to the man beside him, out to the dark, and back again. Any awkward silence faded beneath the whispering wind.

"Well, than's, I guess," he mumbled, eventually. "Squads'll prob'bly ge' reorganised tomorrow. Mayb' we'll end up in th' same one." He snorted, and it took Thaun a moment to realise that it was a laugh. "I'll try not t' ge' y'killed if so."

Thaun didn't reply. At that moment, indistinct memories of sermons came to him. His uncle had made him attend numerous church functions for as long as he could remember, for political reasons if nothing else. Still, even lacking any particular faith or belief, he couldn't deny the possibility that they'd preached some truth when it came to the meddling of gods.

The twists of fate that had led this grieving man here, now, was a hard thing to ignore. Its convenience and coincidence seemed so obvious. It felt easier, somehow, more clean cut, when facing someone else's problem. Knowing the right thing to do seemed so much simpler when the feelings involved tormented someone else.

"Than's again, trooper." Clapping one hand on Thaun's shoulder, the guardsman turned and stumbled back towards the camp, clutching his new sword.

Thaun turned, watching him walk away. Fitful fires, flickering beneath the storm, cast the soldier into silhouette, as a lone, dark figure walking towards light.

Other shapes stood in the darkness though, looking outwards. Stares rested upon Thaun, their weight growing as understanding dawned.

The soldier hadn't walked here completely alone. He might not have realised it either, but others had followed him. Several guardsmen and women guided him back to their tents, sharing low, comforting words.

More still watched Thaun. Nearest him, a woman – her head shaved bald – stood straighter, and tapped her fist to her chest in salute. One by one, others followed suit, and Thaun's eyes widened.

He'd seen the crisp salutes of commissioned officers many times before. Each time then, they'd held the motion until he'd returned it. It shared only a superficial resemblance to these gestures.

Used to the hardships of their duties on the frontlines, the infantry were sloppy and imprecise. Few held their stance, waiting for his recognition. Most, hands lowered again, offered a simple nod and returned to their squads. When Thaun saluted uncertainly, others stood firmer, shoulders back and their chests out.

To one side, three men stepped forward, saluting. It took him a moment to recognise them. Toland, smiling, with two of his men – Pinions, had he called them? – trailing behind.

"I only caught a little of that." His expression broadened into a grin. "But did you just give your sword away? In the middle of a warzone? To a drunken, suicidal infantryman?"

Thaun shrank. "Um, yeah, I guess I did." He closed his eyes, feeling tears threaten to well up past them to join the rain beyond.

"Respectfully, I don't know if I'd have done that." Toland whispered. "Are you alright?"

He looked away. "I wasn't hurt."

"Not in battle, no. But that's not quite what I meant, Your Highness."

Thaun replied with well-rehearsed speed. "I'll be fine."

"I understand, I think," he replied. "You don't want to lie to any of us, so you answer a different question. Most people probably don't even notice your deflection." He snorted a humourless laugh. "Or they're not stupid enough to point it out around the Crown Prince."

"I..." He started, feeling his throat tighten again. No more words came out.

"It's alright," Toland said in a gentle tone. "You don't have to talk, not if you don't want to. You might've done well tonight though. You should know that."

"What...What are you talking about?"

"That whole thing with the soldier just now."

"You just said–"

"That I wouldn't have done it? I wouldn't. But I'm not you. Some people might wonder if it meant you were giving up, surrendering your weapon like that. If we're lucky, this might be a better option than whatever I'd do though."

He coughed. "Just because something looks better..."

"It doesn't mean it is better? I know." Toland leant in close enough that not even his Pinions would hear them. "Look at them though. No, not so directly. Don't be obvious. Those soldiers from the Second who've taken him in. The way they're trying to find out what just happened. The way he clutches that sword."

"What're you getting at?"

"This is the way legends form, Thaun. A prince incognito with his people, sharing their pain, offering salvation. Look, even now, he realises who he spoke with."

"That's not what happened. I'm not trying to make some story. I was just trying to help someone."

"Tonight, you might've just saved that one stranger. Whether you meant to or not, you took that chance. The ends justify the means, after all." Toland reached out, clasping Thaun's shoulder. "Whatever you're telling yourself, that's what they see. You're better at this than you give yourself credit for."

"I don't know…"

"If you don't trust yourself, at least trust me." He squeezed. "You've made good choices with the information you had. Now we know more than we did, and we've survived to make the next decision. So, tell me, your most faithful servant, what do we do next?"

Thaun almost laughed. "You're crazy, and I should know."

"I'm serious. You might just be capable of great things, *commander*. Someday, if all this doesn't get turned into blasted wasteland, you'll sit upon your throne, and I'll govern Tarnon in your name." Through the waning gloom, the first light of dawn touching the horizon, Toland's blue eyes twinkled. "What would you have me do?"

Thaun drew cool, damp air into his lungs as he considered his response. He struggled not to reflect on their disastrous loss against Elhin, or how he now had one less ally than he'd had that morning. He forced aside his worries over Heizl, or the trouble she might be in. He tried to forget the things he'd felt under Renyar's influence back home, or the cavernous emptiness inside him.

His breath left his lungs in a single, long exhalation. "I just want to be left alone, but no one will let me." He locked gazes with Toland. "No, it's alright, it's not you. The Courts, Uncle, even Thala it seems. Whenever I try to get away, they come after me."

Grimacing, Thaun drew in breath between his teeth. He'd almost have preferred to face down Thala again if it meant he didn't have to do this. Voicing all this, admitting that a darkness clinged to him, scared him more than any fight.

It made no sense, but he'd grown used to that a long time ago. Everyone seemed to find it so easy, standing tall beneath the pressures placed upon them. The same burdens that they carried crushed him.

What did he fear would happen? Judgement and exploitation couldn't kill him. Still he shied away.

"No, I want you to help me do what I was sent here for. We'll protect those that are left here, we'll avenge those we've lost, and we'll face Elhin. We go back to those ruins, and we take them." He winced against the coiling fears within him. "At least, if we don't get ourselves killed first."

Tooth and Nail – Chapter Thirteen

"Beyond seven peaks and seven valleys, before scales and steel, there was a story. Giants ruled the nightlands, devouring flesh and soul. Fire birthed man and fire slayed beast, but before that occasion, there was a hero..."

Marsowy's Book of Children's Fables, Marsowy

27th day of Indern, 406th Imperial Year
17th Year of Emperor Rufenrich Konreig's Reign

Heizl threw up her hands. "I told you – I don't want to talk with Renyar."

Okuaak held up the hut's hide flap, the evening light behind him casting the shaman into shadow. "That's not why I ask you to follow. The things I need to show you will concern you both."

"Well *he* concerns me."

The shaman bowed his head. "Neither of you will come to harm while under my protection."

"Tell that to that snake's perfect face," Heizl smirked. She could still feel her bruised knuckles. Her cruel smile faltered. "Besides, I want to be here when Zecht wakes up."

"The spirits still watch over your friend," said Okuaak. "Neither your presence nor mine will speed his recovery. Come."

As her host walked away, letting the curtain fall back, Heizl sighed. She'd long thought of other mages, Hastigr not least among them, as some of the most insufferable people she knew. If all those who called Norjhost home could be this irritating, maybe the Trade Guild had the right idea civilising the place.

She shook the unfair thought away. At least no one had seen her anger flare across her face in the empty hut. The short nap she'd allowed herself had done little to improve her mood.

Heizl stood, and walked to the exit where she paused. She didn't look back at Zecht's still form – she'd spent long enough watching the Shadow's fitful sleep already. It'd be so much easier if their roles were reversed. Not that he'd have any idea on what to do, but a little blissful ignorance had a certain appeal right now. Well, she'd made worse choices in the past. Probably.

The sun sank toward the western horizon, its light painting the crest of every grey wave in gold. A dog, the same one as before perhaps, still barked beyond the other huts. Elders retreated inside from the first hints of night's chill. The village's few children had disappeared from sight. Ahead, at the settlement's edge, Okuaak picked his way between the abandoned shells of empty homes.

Stretching the tightness from her muscles, Heizl followed after him, doing her best to ignore the air's peculiar chill. The shaman followed a twisting path that hugged the shore long overgrown with disuse. Not once did he stop to check that the mage trailed behind him, nor did he slow down in the slightest.

By the time Okuaak halted upon a low rise overlooking the sea, the blue sky had faded to amber and grey. A single figure waited there already.

Renyar. A dangerous man bonded to a Fragment of Urathear. A foreigner who'd already attempted to murder and kidnap her family. A powerful mage seeking the same Fragment as she did. Heizl would have to deal with him, one way or another.

If she survived this whole mess, the Spire wouldn't be able to keep ignoring her. For years she'd dreamed of sitting on the Highmage's Council, to be recognised for her own merit. Now, an opportunity glimmered before her.

Both men watched her as she approached. She considered turning around and leaving there and then, but by the time she'd made up her mind, the moment had passed.

"Thank you for joining us." Okuaak smiled at her, well-worn lines forming around his eyes.

Heizl stamped her feet in an attempt to force some warmth into them. "I'm only here because I was getting bored waiting for Zecht to wake up."

"How's your friend?" asked Renyar, eyeing the Shaman.

"Why?" Heizl stuck out her chin. "Worried you might have to put him down before he comes round?"

"Guests, please," Okuaak groaned. "I grow weary of your strife."

"Then maybe you shouldn't keep dragging us together?" snapped Heizl.

Renyar glanced between them, "I can't help but agree. Time seems the best cure to her animosity."

Okuaak brought his hands together before him as he breathed deep. "Friends, I brought you here to tell you a tale."

Heizl arched an eyebrow. A handful of biting retorts sped through her mind, but she held her tongue. Of all the things she'd expected him to say, it wasn't that.

The Thalan did not stay silent. "Is this important?"

"I believe so," said Okuaak. "May I begin?"

Heizl rolled her eyes as Renyar replied, "Please."

"When Naqtuqa and I were children, travellers visited my village seeking out one of our elders," he began. "One of them, a hunter from the south, carried the curse that now afflicts my brother, and they sought her help in removing his affliction."

"You're saying an Imperial had the Fragment?" Heizl blurted out.

"Do you always interrupt people when they're speaking?" muttered Renyar.

She thought back to her uncle, and couldn't help but smile. It faded as the Thalan's accusations came to mind. "More often than you'd think. Go on, Oak."

The shaman inclined his head slightly. "He came from the Empire, but not all of his companions called it home. Another Imperial who worked metal. An edgewalker with the same skin as you," he gestured towards Renyar, "And a knight with ashen flesh. A cursed creature pursued them, and took the smith."

"Our elder offered the hunter freedom from his curse. Instead, with his remaining companions, he and my mentor went after the monster." The Norjan's eyes wandered. Following his gaze, Heizl paused at the sight of a low row of freshly piled rocks. "The knight died in the battle despite her ensorcelled armour, while the hunter held the monster at bay. Our elder called upon the spirits in a way that I could not hope to match, and they broke the monster.

"When the smith awoke, the edgewalker had left, now cursed himself. The two Imperials buried the knight." He waved towards the low cairn. "With nothing left to bargain with, the spirits were unwilling to heal the hunter, and so he did the only thing left to him. He walked into the sea, and let the waves claim him, rather than turn into that which they had fought. His friend mourned, before leaving with the knight's sword."

"That's all great," Heizl rolled her eyes. Despite her expression, she wondered what Hastigr would make of the shaman's story. "But, tired as I am, bedtime isn't for an hour or two, and I'm not in the mood for fairy tales."

"It's not a children's story," Renyar whispered.

"And just why do you think that?"

"The 'edgewalker?' He's one of my Melechs."

The shaman eyed Renyar. "Forgive me, Melech?"

"Elhin, Vinen, Ikkad, Razeen. My four lieutenants. They serve when I can't."

"You've got three more bitches like that one with the shield?" Heizl's mouth hung open.

Renyar smirked. "Elhin wouldn't react kindly to being described as such."

"So far, I've not seen her react kindly to anything."

"Regardless." He waved a gloved hand in dismissal. "I met Ikkad, oh, twenty years ago now. He had a different name back then. He'd returned to Thala with the Eye after a run in with an yrgol carrying several such Fragments."

"That's great, really, it is," said Heizl. "But I'm pretty sure most people have eyes."

"Not an eye, *the Eye*."

"Oh, I get it." Heizl arched an eyebrow again. "You're probably feeding me more lies right now, but just how many bloody chunks of dead dragon are floating around here?"

"I'm telling you all this so that you'll trust me, Heizl. Urephor fragmented into untold pieces. I carry the Tongue, Elhin a Fang, Vinen a Scale, and Ikkad the Eye. I believe that the warleader has a Claw, and a damaged one at that."

She didn't voice the collection of swear words she'd have liked to say at that moment. Four Fragments? Things had looked bad enough with just a couple of the Void-damned things in play. Instead, she injected as much confidence into her voice as possible. "What about your Razor guy?"

"Razeen doesn't need such Fragments. His power is purely his own."

"You are downright vexing, you know that, right?" Heizl pulled a face. "I could really see myself hating you even if you hadn't come close to killing my family."

"I could always compel you to like me."

"Friends," interrupted Okuaak. "I am not yet finished with my tale."

Heizl sighed. "Go on then."

"Thank you. The smith left, along with the knight's weapon, after his friend took his long walk into the sea, but things did not end there. Naqtuqa took to walking the shore, waiting for something. He never told me what it was. One day though, he returned home, cursed."

"Your brother found the Claw?" asked Heizl.

"Indeed. Though damaged, it changed him. Naqtuqa didn't recognise those he had grown with. He spoke of things that had never happened, and knew nothing of events that had." The shaman sighed. "As he grew stronger, he gained followers. When the traders encroached upon our lands, something snapped within him. With his chosen warriors he came here, to the ashen knight's grave." Okuaak gestured to the gathered stones. "Taking her ensorcelled armour, they attacked the Imperials at a gift-giving ceremony. Other tribes joined him after that day, with the promise that they would drive the interlopers from our home. Armed with the Claw, and protected by the knight's arcane iron, your Guild stood little hope."

"You keep talking about this knight's armour like it's important," said Heizl. "Ash-like skin – you mean a Tszerrichan, right? They don't like being described that way. Something to do with their religion, I think."

"That is correct. She had dedicated her life to hunting the monster, and had prepared her garb as such. A fortune spent upon it, a dozen mages pouring their blood and essence into each sigil. In defeating the monster, and in her death, she found peace from such a violent quest. The spirits did not take kindly to Naqtuqa disturbing her rest."

"Let me get this straight," Heizl tried to compose herself. "Some random hunter brought a Claw here, couldn't get rid of it, and so committed suicide. Your brother then found it, stole some enchanted goodies, and decided to wage war on the Trade Guild, which pissed off all your local ghosts or whatever. Does that sound about right?"

"You've quite the way with words," one corner of Renyar's mouth twisted upwards in what resembled a smile.

"Coming from you," the mage grunted a laugh. "I'll take that as a compliment." Remembering who she spoke to, Heizl felt her smile flicker and fade. Glancing at Renyar, she hesitated. Anything else she learnt now, the Thalan would know too. "But I guess I still don't understand why you brought us here to tell us all this."

"To help you see that it has all come before," said the shaman. "Two Imperials, a Thalan, and one of our people, all coming together to break a curse."

"I think you've missed the not-so-subtle animosity we've got going on. Besides, we've not got some magically-enhanced Tszerrichan with us to level things out." A distracted smile flickered over her lips. "Though it'd be nice to not be the only woman here. It might get a bit dull with just you boys trying hard to act mysterious."

"Her spirit will watch the breaking of a second curse with great interest."

"Do you have to keep talking like we're all on the same side? A week ago I thought my biggest worry was distracting my cousin from himself. A few nights ago, this snake tried to kill my uncle. Now? Now you're acting like the three of us are going to get all buddy-buddy in dealing with this Claw."

"Okuaak might have a point." Renyar shrugged. "His brother will probably try to kill him if he gets close. I can't defeat Naqtuqa with my magic as it is, and you've already shown that your own sorcery is only suitable for, ah, an indirect approach."

"Seriously? I thought I could at least count on you to try and cut me down."

"Come," said the shaman. "We should return to the village."

Heizl looked around them as twilight drained the world of colour. "I didn't take you for being afraid of the dark."

"It is said that the giants that once ruled this land still stalk the night." He shrugged. "But it is not that, your friend awakes."

Heizl didn't feel the urge to question Okuaak. If Zecht had recovered, she didn't really expect him to have any good ideas. It'd feel good to complain about circumstances though. And if he wasn't, well, at least it'd get her out of the cold.

Only the crashing sound of waves broke the silence as they returned to the village. Even Sheltz' Comet looked subdued, obscured behind clouds.

Each of them walked apart, Heizl only staying close to avoid getting lost on the way. She didn't believe the shaman's mention of giants, but most Norjans that she'd met so far had proved less hospitable than Okuaak.

Her thoughts meandered back towards their host's other words. Stories of monsters and heroes, with their swords and spears. The man spoke without the direct pragmatism that so many Imperials used, leaving Heizl unsure how to take him. She'd never paid much attention to the folktales back home, with their gods and dragons, but perhaps she should reconsider now she found herself part of one.

Okuaak's words rose in the wake of her thoughts. She hadn't expected to hear stories of curses and monsters while here. Frida's briefing hadn't mentioned anything like that. Did it change anything? Simply knowing the warleader's name did nothing to humanise him. Renyar on the other hand, now that was different.

The thought of competing with him in the hunt for the Claw didn't sit well. Even without his magic, the Thalan still had the Tongue. It was a miracle he hadn't compelled Heizl to leave, or something worse for that matter. If it came to a straight fight, the mage had no illusions as to how well it would end for her.

Maybe Okuaak's suggestion of working together wasn't as ridiculous as she'd first thought. It'd delay coming to blows with Renyar, possibly long enough for Heizl to get this Claw before him. With or without it, she might just get the chance to get the damn snake killed. There were more ways to see a man dead than in a direct confrontation, after all.

A meagre handful of lights glimmered in the twilight ahead of them. Smoke disappeared against the darkening sky. The lone dog no longer fought back the silence with its barks, leaving just the sea's dull susurration to accompany their return. The animal paused to sniff at her dirty boots. Bending, she scratched the mongrel behind the ears for a moment before it scampered away again.

Okuaak made straight for the hut in which Zecht lay. Heizl's own steps faltered as she saw Renyar pause. He turned towards her as the shaman disappeared inside.

"You want something?" She scowled, stopping just outside of the Thalan's reach.

Renyar shrugged. "I don't think my presence will help you in there."

"How considerate of you." She rolled her eyes and walked past. Okuaak had already disappeared within. Heizl didn't hesitate in following him.

Familiar, smokey air greeted her once more. A few short paces away, Zecht sat upright in the low bed of furs, head tilted back as he drank water from the cup clutched in his hands. After a moment, the Shadow threw it aside, retching violently.

"I would suggest slowing down, Imperial," the shaman whispered from his side.

"Shut up, savage," Zecht replied between wracking coughs. "Where in the Voids am I?"

"Hey, Okuaak?" Heizl didn't turn towards him. "Why don't you step outside? We need to catch up."

The shaman bowed his head. "The spirits' work here is done, for now." With just a single glance between the two Imperials, he left, the curtain fluttering in his wake.

"So..." Zecht looked around, his eyes bloodshot with smoke. "Last I remember, we were running from a bunch of filthy antler-heads, and then... What did I miss?"

Heizl dropped down on the other bed. "Pretty sure only Naqtuqa had antlers."

"I don't know who that is."

"Oh, right. I guess you've missed a few things." She leant back, lacing her fingers behind her head. "The big news is that Renyar's here in this village with us."

"He's what?" Zecht's coughing ceased as shock crossed his face.

"Yeah, I know, right?" Heizl yawned. "The local shaman or leader or whatever took me and him out to a grave where he told us a really interesting story..."

"Shit, he told you?" the Shadow's head drooped, his chin resting on his chest as he took a few deep breaths. "I thought he'd at least wait until after this whole Fragment mess was over with. I guess my sister doesn't matter to that guy as much as his own family does."

Heizl propped herself back up onto her elbows as she stared at the blond man. "What're you talking about?"

"I only did it because he helped me pass the tests." Zecht sipped what little water remained in the cup as he eyed the mage sidelong.

"No, I meant..." She shook her head, a pit forming in her stomach. "Go on."

"Well, I don't much like the fact she's been pegged as a mage." He shrugged. "Renyar paid my commission in return for dumping some stones where he asked. I wasn't really meant to get assigned to you," Zecht flashed her a dry smile. "But I guess it could've been worse."

Heizl ran her tongue over her teeth as she stood. "So you took Renyar's money, so that you could become a Shadow, in return for planting... These stones, did he talk about pairs, or beacons, or anything?"

"Oh, yeah, a beacon, like the Nexus."

"You know." The mage stood. "I'd got the idea that you weren't necessarily as good at your job as some of the other Shadows I've had, but I didn't really mind. It was nice having someone I could actually talk to, right?" She brushed her robe down for creases. Head bowed against the low ceiling, she took a few steps towards the still seated Zecht. "It's all starting to make sense now. What explanation is there for how else I end up with an incompetent, overconfident airhead other than him being a traitor!?" Heizl's knee connected with the blond man's jaw.

The Shadow half-turned with the impact. Credit to him, even still recovering from his injuries, his arms came up in a guard instantly. Left raised to protect his head from a follow-up attack, with his right he grabbed Heizl's leg and pulled. Flailing, a second later the mage lay sprawled on the floor. Another heartbeat, and Zecht had her twisted into a knot, pain lancing through Heizl's knee.

The hut's flap twitched open, two heads appearing in the doorway. For a second, Okuaak and Renyar simply looked down on them, before the shaman spoke. "I have little left with which to appease the land, but I will call upon a spirit of peace if I have to."

"No need," Heizl snapped, climbing to her feet as Zecht released her. She rubbed the back of her head the whole time. "I won't be talking with either of these bastards again. Find me a place to sleep and I'll leave in the morning. I'd rather take my chances out there with your brother's thugs than stay in the same place as either of these... these..."

"Bastards?" Renyar suggested, a cruel smile tugged at his lips.

"Shut up!"

"Fitz doesn't like that talk." Zecht smirked as Heizl stormed out, pushing past both men. She barely made it to the edge of the village when the Shadow caught her up, breathing heavily as he pulled his hood up against the cold. "Heizl, wait up!"

"Just what do you want?" snarled the mage.

"Look, I get this is all a lot to take in, but was hitting me in the face really needed?"

"Take in? You're working with the enemy! How did you expect me to respond?"

"Not like that, not after Renyar already told–"

"He didn't tell me, moron!"

"...Ah," Zecht clicked his tongue. "So what I said back there in the hut..?"

"Yup."

"What if I said–"

"Nope."

He didn't reply. A knife could cut the growing tension, a metaphor that left Heizl decidedly uncomfortable. The Shadow probably had a dozen such weapons hidden about his person.

Blood pounding in her ears, she unclenched her fists. As she spoke, she couldn't bear to look at Zecht. "You know that he's lying to you, right?"

"About helping me and my sister?"

"About what he's up to! That maniac is trying to resurrect a dragon that, last time it was around, went and ate half the damn world!"

The Shadow shrugged. "I'm a little hazy on the details. He mentioned some Imperials trying to bring a god back."

"Nobody thinks that they're the villain – of course he'll blame his schemes on someone else!" Heizl shook her head, strands of long hair shaking free. "You can't possibly believe him."

"Why not? He's already put his money where his mouth is."

"He's already *tried to kill both of us.*"

"What? When?"

"Seriously? At the Palace? After you apparently set up the beacon he needed so he could try and assassinate my uncle?"

"Oh, right. Well, him and Elhin wouldn't have killed me."

"You could've fooled me," Heizl growled.

A mirthless grin flickered over Zecht's face. "Pretty sure I did fool you, Fitz."

The mage fought the urge to hit him again. "Has he even shown you any evidence?"

"I didn't ask. So long as the money kept coming in, it didn't really matter."

"How very noble of you," she drawled.

"Come on, noble...ness doesn't come into it." Zecht threw up his hands. "You saw what he and Elhin did. No one should have that sort of power. Imagine what someone could do with the Heart."

"Exactly, he's already using the Tongue. Making people do things against their will, it's tantamount to rape. That's not even mentioning the Fragments his cronies apparently have. Do you really think it's a good idea to trust someone like him?"

"It's not like he's planning on keeping it."

"And what's that supposed to mean?"

"It means, Imperial," Okuaak said from a short distance away. Heizl hadn't noticed his approach. Nor the Thalan's, who stood just behind the shaman. "That removing the Tongue is a part of why Renyar has come here."

"If I didn't hate this whole mess before, I sure do now," Heizl growled. "I'm grateful for you taking me in, Okuaak. Really, I am, but could you not speak straight just once?"

"I felt that was quite clear, actually," said Renyar. "Accurate, too."

"And I'm supposed to believe you'd just get rid of the Tongue?"

"In return for an army, yes."

"Oh, so you're apparently worried about people having these Fragments, but you'll just give one away?"

"Better to corrupt an individual than to let the world burn. Besides, I have taken precautions."

"Sure you have," scoffed Heizl. "You realise that you don't make any sense, right? Why would you even tell me all this?"

The Thalan rubbed his temple, the bruise hidden by the dying light. "Because I'd rather not fight you, Heizl. Because if you truly understood what I'm trying to achieve, you might consider my offer."

"And just what offer is that?"

"Help me secure the Claw, stop your uncle's plan, and I will endeavour to give you whatever position you desire within your Empire."

For all Renyar's schemes and lies, Heizl hesitated. Ambitions, hopes, and dreams stormed through her mind, almost too fast to follow.

She'd been an outsider for almost as long as she could remember. The nobility had looked down on a child for no fault of her own. Her uncle had tried, but he hadn't known what to do with a bastard niece, not when he had a perfect nephew already.

No, that wasn't fair. Thaun had always treated her better than anyone.

But Rufenrich, as soon as Heizl's talent had manifested, he'd shipped her off to the Spire. He'd probably welcomed the opportunity to be rid of her, to be rid of his embarrassment.

The mages had treated her no better. Some had seen a royal thrust among them, yet another way to control their already limited freedoms. Others saw a rebellious child with little discernible talent. What good was seeing the connections no one else could, when they could burn people alive? Not until Hastigr had taken her under his wing had anything there improved, and even then they'd still stalled her advancement.

Always outside the circle, and now offered something as blatant as this. What position *did* she desire? There were so many. Every door shut to her now stood open... if she could trust Renyar.

Her thoughts returned to her cousin. Thaun had always treated her fairly. Even when others had avoided her for her magicks, or mocked her heritage, Heizl could count on him. The Throne was rightfully Thaun's – was she really considering claiming it? It wouldn't be right.

Beyond that man, whom she loved like a brother, only one other person had even come close to acting like she was worth something. The Court talked about them often enough, regularly in the same sentence as her cousin. It broke her heart to think that she could become Thaun's too.

Jilia.

Heizl shook her head. That wasn't something she wanted to think too deep on right now. Not with everything else happening.

She glanced at the men around her. An abandoned native, a traitorous Shadow, and an ambitious madman. Each seemed so sure of themselves. Heizl wished fervently that she did too. "There are going to be some ground rules."

Renyar smirked. "Go on."

"First up, I don't believe you guys. Well, maybe you, Okuaak, but I'm not convinced some fairy tale really affects the Empire that much. No offence."

The shaman bowed his head. "I am pleased that you are willing to listen."

"I don't seem to have much of a choice. It's not like I can finish this job by myself, but neither can any of you."

"Good to have you on board, Fitz." Zecht grinned.

Renyar's penetrating stare didn't shift from Heizl. "I'm glad of your change of heart, but you'll forgive me if I don't entirely trust it. I would hazard that, if we are victorious, you intend to seize the Claw for yourself."

"Well, yeah." She shrugged. "I'd be stupid not to. Think of this as a trade. Okuaak gets to see his brother's curse broken. You do the spirits a favour and get your Fragment removed so that you can get your army – which I still have questions about, by the way – and I get that spear."

Zecht narrowed his eyes. "And what do I get?"

"How about I don't execute you as a traitor?" said Heizl.

"Friends," said the Norjan, "If we're going to fight together, this bickering will get us nowhere."

"I don't know if you noticed, but we are fighting together. Seriously, so long as you get that this is temporary, I don't care one way or another who argues with who," the mage shrugged. Once more, she looked round at these unlikely allies. Shaman, Shadow, and... whatever Renyar was. "I've just one more question for all of you."

"What would you ask, Heizl?" said Renyar.

She arched an eyebrow, and couldn't help but smirk. "What's the plan?"

Tooth and Nail – Chapter Fourteen

"Before you are freed from here, to attend to your duties, you must understand your own talent. The teachings of others may give you answers, but your truth is an individual thing. You may share legacy, but your own unique experience will dictate the exploitation of your gift. Fail to build that relationship with your own being, and you will suffer for wasting that potential."

An introductory lecture to Spire apprentices, Highmage Nennein Ortharn (396 I.Y.)

28th day of Indern, 406th Imperial Year
17th Year of Emperor Rufenrich Konreig's Reign

More weapons than he could count surrounded Thaun. Swords in their scabbards, polearms in racks, and shields on hooks. For a small army far from home, he had to admit, his troops had come prepared.

"It's kind of you, thanks," said Thaun. "But the Second has more swords right now than it has men to hold them. I can get a new one from them."

"Your High... sorry." Toland brushed dirt from his shoulder. "Thaun, that's not why I brought you here. Well." He shrugged. "Not the only reason."

"My last sword was Guard-issue." He looked away. "I liked that sword."

"The sword will wait. Your morale problem won't."

"Morale problem?"

"You hadn't noticed?" The noble took a deep breath, as if preparing to speak to a child. "They're a long way from home, and yesterday almost one in three of them got crushed beneath the local terrain. Seeing their commander with a face longer than their supply train isn't doing them any good."

He looked away. "Oh... sorry."

"I don't want you to apologise, Thaun." Toland reached out and placed a reassuring hand on his shoulder. "No one blames you for feeling the way you do. You didn't ask to be in charge, and now you've got countless lives in your hands. You're responsible for them. Being responsible means doing the best that you can for the most people, even when that's hard. Even if people don't understand why you're doing it. Even if they hate you for it. Anyone would be low after all that you've been through, *but you can't let them see it.*"

"I..." He shrugged, and broke the other man's grip as he turned away. "I've never done this before."

"I can tell. So can they, but you've got to start somewhere, so let's begin by wiping that frown off your face."

"Korten died. So did a hundred others, because of me. You can't expect me to cheer up just because you tell me to."

"That's not what I'm suggesting. I'm just trying to help you see the effect you're having on those around you."

"You'd rather I pretend that everything's fine? That I don't feel like running off in the night with a sword in hand?"

"Well, you'd need a sword first."

At Toland's gentle laugh, Thaun felt his indignation wane.

"Seriously, everyone feels like that at times, and the men now more than ever. When with me, do what you need to do. Cry, sleep, whatever helps you get rid of those negative emotions, but in front of the men... They can't see you moping around. When they look at you, they need to see you confident and calm."

"I know, it's just–"

"Thaun, we don't have time for caveats and excuses. You need to look like you have command of the situation, whether or not you actually do. If you don't, any counterattack is only going to end with more death."

He took a deep breath, looked at Toland and then away again. "Is this what you pulled me in here for? To berate me?"

"Trust me, this isn't me berating you." The northerner smiled. "I'm just trying to help. God knows, you need it."

"Thanks for trying," Thaun mumbled as he turned away to scan the room.

"There were other things I wanted to talk about, while we have some privacy."

"Does it involve you pointing out my other flaws?"

"Only that you're bad at lying."

Despite the tension, Thaun could hear the reassuring smile in Toland's tone. He did his best not to react. "What're you talking about?"

"Why're you all here in the middle of nowhere? You're not telling me everything, are you?"

"I don't know what you mean." He took a moment to compose himself before continuing. "After Renyar attacked the Palace, Uncle sent me here to stay safe."

"You've got to stop it with your half-truths," Toland took the few steps to stand alongside him, both of them gazing unseeing at the steel-laden surface before them. "If that was the whole story you wouldn't have marched against Elhin. If they were pursuing you, even if you'd defeated them, their absence would've been noticed, and Renyar would just send more men. You'd have been better off avoiding direct confrontation."

Thaun pursed his lips. He trusted Toland. He'd known him long enough that he couldn't take even Sigren's concerns completely seriously. His uncle's briefing had left him nervous. The loyalty he felt to his friends didn't matter though. Anyone could fail, and say the wrong thing to the wrong person. Someone with even the least piece of Renyar's plan could try to copy it. An ambitious radical would only have to get lucky once to spell disaster. "...I can't tell you."

"I understand." The noble's voice dropped to a whisper. "It's related to Urathear, isn't it?"

Thaun's mouth crept open. "How did...?"

"I didn't. Just suspicions."

"Toland..." Thaun started, unsure what to say.

"There's more though, isn't there?" Toland continued, counting off on his fingers. "Daericani ruins, the Comet, Thala's appearance here, the incident at your feast, what Renyar and his lieutenant could do..." He laid a hand on Thaun's shoulder. "The Throne and Thala are warring over... something to do with dragons, aren't they?"

His mouth hung half-open. "How did you do that?"

"I wish I could say it was divine inspiration, but by paying the right people, mostly." Toland smiled, satisfied. "How close am I?"

"I shouldn't be talking about this with you," said Thaun. "Who else knows?"

"Just father, but if we worked it out, then others might. Do Lena and Sigren know?"

"Most of it. I wasn't at their briefings, but they can be trusted."

"I can't help but feel I'm still missing something."

Thaun swallowed. Would he get in trouble for this? He had no way to tell. "It's more than just Elhin's shield and Renyar's... whatever he has. They're Fragments of Urathear – the Daericani's dead god – and he's trying to summon its Heart."

A dozen distinct emotions flashed across Toland's face in half as many heartbeats. After a moment, he blew out a weary breath. "I know about Urathear. No wonder you look so depressed all the time."

Thaun couldn't help but snort a laugh. "It's pretty heavy stuff."

"You're not wrong." The noble shrugged. "Well, if the world's going to end, it'd be nice for some of us to survive, right? That'll be a lot easier with a better weapon." He gestured around.

"So you're giving me one of these..." Thaun waved a hand towards one of the strange armaments. "What are they called?"

"My Tszerrichan and Daqinese are both a little rusty, but my Pinions call them rifles, because of the way they go through their pouches to find their ammunition." He shrugged, but a hint of pride remained on his face. "They're as quick to learn as a crossbow, but with greater range and penetration, while weighing less. It's easier to beat someone over the head with one too."

Thaun drifted into thought as Toland continued. His swirling mind pushed aside descriptions of alloys and alchemy. He couldn't imagine his uncle would approve of him bringing the noble in on this. Hopefully he'd understand that that wasn't his intention. Renyar, Elhin, their ritual – all of it – they had to be stopped, and Thaun couldn't do it by himself.

As if the end of the world wasn't enough, Thaun hurt. He'd tried. He really had. Would others realise that? Or would they just see the end result. Hundreds dead after following his orders.

All those men and women had trusted him, and his mistakes had led to disaster. Even if they hadn't, their officers had. Soldiers knew the risks, but that didn't mean he could just throw their lives away.

On the table in front of him, Thaun's hands moved unbidden, the tactile movement of picking up and discarding weapons and parts soothing the conflict within. He'd fled from the authority thrust upon him for as long as he could remember, and it had crushed him as soon as he'd tried otherwise. Death, of both the many and the individual, cast a shadow over all of them now. Lena and Sigren likely weren't doing any better, but he didn't know how to help them. Calling out their behaviour – Lena's cold reticence and Sigren's barely suppressed rage – might only make them worse. He'd share their burdens if he could, but he already felt close to breaking under his own worries.

Maybe he should listen to Toland. Acting like he felt fine would give his friends, and by extension the rest of the men, one less thing to worry about. If it helped them to deal with this whole Thala problem, then he could grieve afterwards. Many deserved proper burials, after all. If they made it, he'd have to make sure they were buried under something other than ensorcelled stone.

Still running through his mind's well-worn tracks, Thaun recoiled as something sharp caught his meandering hands. Pulling back, distracted from introspection, he looked down as blood welled from a fingertip.

"Are you alright?" asked Toland.

"I'm fine." He sucked on the shallow cut. "Lena can fix it."

"You should be careful." The noble gestured around. "I hear some of these are pretty sharp."

"You're telling me." He didn't look up in response, eyes still on the weapon before them. One hand muffling his words, he picked up the offending steel and inspected the strange grey sword. A narrow tube ran the length of the short, single-edged blade "What's this? Another rifle?"

"That? I didn't even know it was here." Toland shrugged, and picked up one of the other firearms. "Here, these are much better."

He shifted his grip on the strange sword. "That doesn't really answer me."

"Our early prototypes were much more similar to the Tszerrichan example that we had. A sword with a secondary weapon, unwieldy things, the added weight making them impractical for anything more than intimidation. After a few attempts, we removed the blade completely, balancing it better for range."

"And that's what this is? A prototype?"

"I think so, though I couldn't say why it's here..."

Thaun lifted it by the curved handle, aiming its point away and looking down its length. Toland said nothing as he took a few practice swings. For all its added weight, it didn't feel much heavier than the weapons he'd trained with.

His original instructors had taught him the finer points of duelling, longswords, and other noble pursuits. They'd always described shorter blades dismissively, as butcher's tools and the arms of the common soldier. It had taken him years to persuade his uncle to let him loose with such weapons.

"Does it shoot?"

The noble sighed, but a faint smile remained. "I believe you trigger it by squeezing the bar running up the hilt. In later models we changed it to a small lever..." He trailed off at the faintly audible 'click' of Thaun doing as told. The two men made eye contact, a half-smile creeping onto both their faces. "We don't keep them loaded."

"Sorry."

"Stop apologising, it's fine." Toland gestured around. "You should try one of our newer rifles, they're much more practical."

Thaun didn't have a chance to answer. The tent flap opened as Lena stepped in. Colour had returned to her face, though a weary look remained in her eyes. Glancing between the two men, she managed a slow salute.

"Knock it off, Lena," said Thaun. "It's just us in here."

The healer slowly lowered her hand. "Sir... Thaun?"

The uncertain bravado left his voice. "What's wrong?"

"I didn't want to worry you, but..." Lena trailed off.

Thaun glanced at Toland, who gave him an encouraging nod. He turned back and tried to sound reassuring. "Go on."

"Sigren's acting strangely."

The noble raised a hand. "Is he threatening well-intentioned individuals? Because I'm pretty sure that's normal."

She didn't respond to the jibe, her face unmoving. "He's training."

"Toland's kind of right." Thaun narrowed his eyes. "That's not unusual."

The mage shrugged. "You'd best see for yourself."

They stepped out to find that the sun had shifted in the sky since first entering the small armoury. Thaun soon walked through their shrunken camp. When they passed the sixth tent, he realised he still held the strange, unsheathed blade in one hand. At Toland's suggestion, he wrapped the weapon in his cloak so as to not startle the troops.

A thin cloud of smoke hung overhead. Beyond the army's low hubbub, few other noises reached him. Where there should have been the cacophony of life, of sergeants shouting, and comrades laughing, silence reigned.

Thaun stared at the back of Lena's head as they walked. None of their small group were known as the most outgoing, but since their defeat he'd scarcely heard the healer say more than a sentence at a time. His attendant's new, cold nature weighed upon him. If not for the fact that most Imperials gave mages a wide berth he might have worried what effect Lena's downcast face would have on the men. The morale problem was bad enough, apparently, without their only surviving mage making it worse. Dealing with whatever issue Sigren had might help her, if they were lucky.

While neat rows of grey tents filled most of the camp, its centre consisted of an open space where soldiers could muster and train. A handful of guardsmen drilled, trading unenthusiastic blows, but few made use of the practice grounds.

Thaun stopped, and watched his men for a moment. Even from here he could read their low spirits. Toland's advice repeated in his head, childhood lessons on command echoing with them. He set his shoulders. Taking his responsibilities seriously had to start somewhere.

Right now though, he didn't have the strength to help a full army. His own grief still threatened to be too much all by itself. He might be able to do something about a single mournful Shadow, though.

"Thaun," Lena said, spotting his hesitation. "Sigren's this way."

Mud coated their boots by the time they stopped walking, halting at a coarse rope suspended between crooked posts. The scene before him reminded Thaun of the training grounds at the Palace, where he'd spent so long practising.

Beyond, several guardsmen shot at a line of crude archery butts downfield while two of Toland's Pinions looked on. After a moment of watching the guardsmen wind back their crossbows' strings, Thaun realised Sigren stood among them.

The Shadow blended in with those around him, a thin layer of dust coating his uniform. Sigren had yet to change from the previous day's battle. Lifting the weapon to his shoulder, he shot just as Lena cleared her throat. The furthest target, almost two hundred feet distant, shuddered as the bolt sank into the wood and leather.

"Dammit!" The word burst from Sigren's throat in a shout as he spun to face them. "What did you go and do that for?!"

The healer looked away, while Thaun raised an eyebrow. "You hit the target though, right?"

"Just hitting isn't good enough, *sir*." he half-turned and raised his voice to the assembled men. "Anything less than a killing shot means they're still alive, only angrier. Have any of you ever seen a pissed off radical mage? No? That's because people don't walk away from that sort of mistake!"

As the guardsmen muttered among themselves, Thaun took a second to inspect the chaotic scene before them. Quarrels protruded from the nearest butts, their fletching uniformly spread across each surface. Further targets stood almost bare. Colour flushed Sigren's face as he berated the downcast men, casting the dark bags beneath his eyes into sharp contrast. At his feet, the Shadow had trampled countless worn and stretched strings into the dirt.

He'd spent the whole night there. Standing beside Thaun, Lena leant in and whispered, "Talk to him." Then she turned away. Toland merely shrugged.

"Sigren?" Thaun spoke in a low voice, keeping his words from reaching the nearby soldiers. "What are you doing?"

"...so help me gods!" His shouts dwindled. "I don't want to see any of you stop until each of you have landed ten shots, got it?" He turned to Thaun without waiting for a response from the guardsmen. "What?"

Thaun took half a step away at the fierce tone. "I asked what you were doing?"

"Someone has to whip this lot into shape if you're going to lead us into another disaster tomorrow." Sigren turned his back to watch the men train. "They at least deserve a chance to take some bastards with them."

"Come on, Sigren, it's not that bad," he said, unsure who he was trying to convince.

"If they'd been up to scratch yesterday, then..." His shoulders sagged. "Then we wouldn't be in this mess."

Thaun sighed. "That's not what you were going to say, was it?"

"No, it wasn't." The Shadow glanced over one shoulder. "I was going to say that if they'd been better, then maybe we wouldn't have lost Korten. I didn't like him, but we'd be in a better spot if he was still here." He turned away again, and watched the men practice. "You could stand to have done your job better too."

"I'm trying, I really am. Toland's spoken to me, and—"

"Great, listen to someone else. I've only been trying to help you for... for as long as I've been stuck with you."

A false smile seeped onto Thaun's face. "I thought you were only here because of Lena?"

"Don't be so damn naive!" he hissed. Teeth and fists clenched, he faced the trio.

Thaun braced for the inevitable tirade, but it never came. Like the wind falling from sails, Sigren sagged. The fire in his gaze winked out.

Eyes downcast, he called wearily to the troops behind him. "Break. Fetch your bolts, see to your weapons, and be back here before the next bell." He didn't turn to see the weary guardsmen's relieved expressions as they followed orders. His chin gradually rose until he made eye contact again. Flames still smouldered behind his gaze, but something now held it in check. "Sir?"

The sudden change in his friend shook something within Thaun. "I... Lena was worried about you." He cleared his throat as he saw Sigren glance at the healer. "I mean, I heard you were overdoing it. When did you last sleep?"

"We don't have time for rest yet, sir." He gestured round to the camp. "Elhin's mages could turn up here any minute. There've already been skirmishes with their scouts, and we don't have a Highmage to sacrifice to them this time round."

"You're no good to us if you're dead on your feet though."

"It won't matter if we're standing or lying down if Thala follows us here." The Shadow eyed Toland. "With or without your buddy's fancy Pinions."

"He's trying to help us."

"*I'm* trying to help. You think I want to spend my last hours shouting at a bunch of uniforms who couldn't stop a force a quarter of their size? Toland here is just trying to curry royal favour in case we somehow make it out of this mess alive."

"Sigren." Thaun did his best to harden his voice. "We're all going to get through this, but not by arguing. You're pushing the men too hard, you're scaring them."

"They should be scared. You know as well as I do what we're up against."

"I do." He sighed. "And we'll stand a better chance if both of us stop distracting the men."

"That might be the first sensible thing that you've said since we left home." Despite his words, his tone didn't change.

"Sorry, what?"

"Owning up and taking charge is a good first step." The Shadow crossed his arms over his chest. He spoke more precisely and stood straighter now. "What's next?"

"I..." Thaun stammered. "I don't know. Go back there and do our job, I guess." His grip on the wrapped sword tightened. "If we're lucky, we'll avenge Korten too."

"Now that." Sigren grinned, revealing a few too many teeth. "That is something I can get behind."

"I've been thinking about that," said Lena. "If we go back the same as before, the outcome's certain."

"Even as hopeless as they are now–" the Shadow gazed off towards the nearby cluster of guardsmen, "–your rank and file are capable enough to deal with any mundane warriors Thala might throw at us. They've the steel, training, and numbers. It's just a matter of convincing them to stand and fight."

Toland grunted a laugh. "Do you have a better plan than shouting at them?"

"I thought maybe seeing a mouthy noble get his teeth kicked in might raise some spirits."

"I don't know about that. Proving a Shadow isn't invincible won't do their morale much good." He flicked a strand of dark hair from his blue eyes as he thrust his jaw out.

"Not in front of the men," interjected Thaun. "You can threaten each other once we've worked out what we're going to do about Elhin and her mages."

Before either of them could respond, Lena raised a hand and cleared her throat. "I went through Korten's effects. I think I have a plan for her."

"What are you going to do?" Sigren smirked. "Heal her to death?"

The mage shrugged, but said nothing. A pregnant pause grew between them, broken only by the sounds of camp on all sides.

Thaun swallowed. "In all seriousness, are you sure? She basically ignored Korten back home, and he's... he was a battlemage."

Lena bowed her head. "I can do more than just heal. I'm fairly sure that I'm the only one left here who can do something about her. I should play my part."

"There's got to be a better way." He placed a hand on the healer's shoulder. "I don't want to lose another friend on this island."

The Shadow grunted a disbelieving laugh. "You do realise, even if we do come up with a way to neutralise that bitch, that we won't all walk away tomorrow?"

"I know, but shouldn't we try to not get everyone killed?"

Toland flashed a wicked smile. "What we should be doing is trying to leave each and every Thalan interloper dead."

Thaun didn't share his friend's cruel mirth. "That's not so easily done with their mages throwing boulders at us."

"My Pinions can deal with them," said the noble.

"Those contraptions of theirs aren't going to make a difference against a wall of rock." Sigren shook his head.

Toland rolled his eyes. "The distance your men say they started casting at is well within rifle range."

"Sure, they can fire that far." The Shadow glanced down at his crossbow. "But can they do it accurately?"

"Throw enough slugs downfield and it doesn't matter how accurate they are."

Thaun found himself stepping between them again. "Sigren, why don't you try one for yourself?" He held out the wrapped sword.

The Shadow seemed to consider for a moment, before gently putting his own weapon down and taking the bundle from him. Passing its wrapping to

Lena, he held the prototype in both hands. "This isn't like the others. What is it?"

At Thaun's insistent gesture, Toland sighed. "It's an early model, made obsolete by our current rifles," he said with a dry smile. "His Highness seems to have taken a liking to it."

Sigren didn't respond immediately, shifting his grip several times before looking down its length. "Well, he likes useless things." The Shadow smirked at Toland before returning his attention to the weapon. "You can't aim this thing worth a damn," he muttered. "And the weight of the blade pulls it down. You're not going to hit anything much beyond arm's length." He looked at the noble. "It's decent steel, but I wouldn't count on this levelling the field with any mage."

"Like I said, it's an old model. My men's current equipment is significantly more suited to such a task."

He handed it back to Thaun. "I'll stick with mine, thanks."

"I gather it served you well in your last battle," Toland drawled.

Sigren clenched his jaw. "Shadows aren't meant for a straight fight."

"Protect your mage, guard against radicals, or something, yes?" said the noble. "Perhaps that prototype isn't the only thing made obsolete by firearms."

Thaun shook his head. "Stop it, both of you. We're all on the same side here, so could you act like it, please?"

"His Lordship might have made a point," the Shadow shrugged. "Maybe I should let his Pinions take point tomorrow, but there's something they can't do."

Toland frowned. "And what's that?"

"Go out there tonight and thin their numbers."

Thaun blinked rapidly. "You're kidding, right?" No one spoke. Somewhere in the distance, a soldier began a mournful song. A few voices joined her. "Lena, talk some sense into him!"

The healer turned to leave. "I should go and get ready."

"Toland? Help me out here."

The noble paused as if considering his words. "We're all here for the same reason. Doing the best we can for the most that we can." He glanced sidelong at Sigren. "For all our disagreements, I must admit that there are few things as pure as doing one's duty."

Thaun looked between his three friends, mouth hanging half-open. "I can't believe you're all so eager to go and die out there. A lot of people gave their lives so we could get away and come up with a better plan. What would they think?"

Toland laid a hand on his shoulder. "They were doing their duty, and so are the rest of us. Whether you like it or not, this *is* our better plan."

He sagged, and watched the healer as she walked away. Did he imagine seeing Lena's shoulders slump? As long as he'd known her, people had commented on the woman's flat voice and reserved nature, but this all seemed different somehow.

Thaun looked to Sigren as the Shadow returned to the archery butts. He couldn't help but notice the uncharacteristic tremble in the northerner's aim. When night fell, he'd go to face the mages alone – his anger wouldn't help him there.

Finally, he turned to Toland, who met his gaze. Without the noble, they might not be standing here now. Faint guilt rose in his stomach. Though friends, the Court had often painted them both as rivals, and perhaps Thaun had let that taint his view of the man. In spite of all that, he was still here, helping him. When all this was behind them, he'd have to make amends.

Thaun nodded. "I guess we've all got our duties."

Tooth and Nail – Chapter Fifteen

"It's not as simple as drawing a sword. The art lies in drawing the sword that complements its wielder."

Dallan Gildur, former Imperial Champion (387 I.Y.)

28th day of Indern, 406th Imperial Year
17th Year of Emperor Rufenrich Konreig's Reign

Tawny flames twisted over crumbling wood. Deeper within the fire, branches crackled as men fed the blaze. Dark broth bubbled in hammered copper pots, while amber juices dribbled down scarred chins. Golden light poured over those closest, revealing the countless tribespeople gathered close.

Norjan men and women spun and danced between cooking fires, a fleeting reflection of the stars peering between clouds high above. Dressed in sealskin, clad in leathers, or adorned with shells, the natives mingled. Their old rivalries smouldered low, held at bay by one man.

At the largest fire, surrounded by chiefs and elders, the warleader preened. His promises of wealth and glory had drawn these tribes together. Plundered crates bearing the Trade Guild's spoked-wheel crest lay scattered, their contents given freely to those most loyal to his zealous vision.

A superficial return to old ways, Okuaak had said, of showing power and securing alliance. Agreements and betrothals would be made tonight that'd shape the peninsula for years to come.

"This place stinks," Zecht muttered as they walked between the celebrating tribesmen.

Eyes half-closed as she turned the natives' attention from them, Heizl ignored the Shadow. He'd done nothing but complain since they'd got here. In borrowed clothes, the three of them would only pass as locals for so long, even with her efforts. Only the Thalan's coarse mantle hung outside their hooded garb. It hardly seemed necessary between her own weaving sorcery and Renyar's compelling voice, but Okuaak had insisted on the disguise.

Renyar seemed more than happy to respond to the Shadow. "Quiet, you'll draw attention."

"I thought you could just tell these savages to avoid us?"

The Thalan turned towards the Shadow, mouth opening to say something before closing it again. Rolling his eyes towards Heizl, he shook his head and looked away. She couldn't deny it – with everything they'd planned, she was glad that her temporary ally had chosen not to compel Zecht. Though an inarguable advantage for their attack, she still didn't like the idea of anyone bending to another's will so completely.

Heizl considered asking her companions what they could see; her own mundane senses rarely caught everything when she probed the weave of souls surrounding her. The mage got a few syllables out when she noticed both men gazing towards the camp's centre.

Sat among Trade Guild crates, surrounded by his most-trusted warriors, Naqtuqa watched over the ceremony. He looked much the same as during Heizl's singular, violent encounter with him. His salvaged armour still bore its original dark tarnish, but someone had replaced the fetishes and painted colours upon it. Blackened iron hid the man's scalp and hands, and the bronze Fragment lay across his knees. Among fur-skinned hunters and hide-clad fishermen, he would've looked out of place in such mail if not for the satisfied smile that he shared with so many of his followers.

Heizl narrowed her eyes upon his spear. How many had died because of it already? To a mundane eye, it looked little different to the scores of other hand-crafted weapons on show here. Its cracked, ivory head almost identical to the trophies so many carried, its bronze shaft so similar to the cold-hammered copper that adorned throats and hair. A month ago she wouldn't have thought a physical manifestation of an elder god existed, let alone threaten all that she knew.

She thought about saying something. A warning, perhaps, that Naqtuqa had recovered from his injuries. Or maybe some encouragement at what they hoped to achieve. Heizl closed her mouth, teeth tapping together. Was it truly such a loss if either man didn't last the night?

"'ware," Renyar whispered, flicking his chin towards one side of the warleader's bonfire. She followed his gesture, though saw nothing of interest. As she turned back towards him, a chill wind caressed her senses, and Okuaak appeared from among his people.

Hastigr's training, away from the sanguine majority of the Spire, had often felt similar. Even the Highmage could only push her threads away for so long. Those times when she'd found his soul, the source of his meddling, his reappearance had looked much like this. The same wavering focus, the same delayed reactions of those surrounding him. In her chest, each breath even felt cold in the same way, though she'd never noticed that from her own sorceries.

The shaman halted several paces from his brother. Firelight revealed a figure unlike the weathered native Heizl had met just a few days before. No longer did he huddle beneath old, salt-stained hides. His hair and the clothes now glittered with uncountable beads, bones, and baubles. Lit by the crackling, amber flames, he looked as impressive as any jewellery-bedecked nobleman.

He held in one hand a wooden rod, even shorter than Heizl's focus. With its age-smoothed carvings and dangling strips of fur, she hoped it'd prove more effective than the copper that she gripped.

As Okuaak spoke, his brother's hunters rose, but Naqtuqa himself remained seated. Unseen or ignored, Heizl's green eyes narrowed on a woman beside their warleader. Where most shook weapons at the shaman, she carried nothing in her hands. Though pale in comparison, something in her attire echoed Okuaak's.

"Zecht," she whispered.

"Aye," the Shadow replied. "That's my cue. See you on the other side, Fitz." With a nod to Renyar, the blond man pulled his hood tighter around his head, and disappeared into the milling crowd.

The Thalan didn't take his eyes from Okuaak, who still spoke in his own tongue to his cursed brother. "What did you see?"

"Oh, just a mage." Heizl shook her head as she turned back to the warleader's fire. "Or shaman, or whatever."

"I understand your Shadows are trained to deal with such threats."

"A knife in the back'll do that to you," she drawled. As Naqtuqa finally rose, responding to his brother in a deep, carrying voice, Heizl cocked her head. "I thought Okuaak said the spirits had rejected him or something?"

"In any family, some choose a different path," Renyar whispered as he watched the pair speak. "Every god, king, and mortal has their own path. These spirits are much the same."

Heizl shook her head. "If I wanted a lecture, I'd have stayed home. Does it actually matter?"

Still turned away, she caught the hint of humour in his voice. "Perhaps not."

A few dozen paces away, shaman and warleader continued speaking. In between Heizl and the two brothers, hide-hooded heads shifted uneasily, blocking her vision. An itch here, a distraction there, and hunters parted, letting her see.

Throatal words drifted to Heizl's ears above the growing silence, though she didn't understand a single syllable. "I wonder what they're saying. Should we move?"

"Not yet. Okuaak deserves this chance."

"The chance for what? To piss away any advantage?"

"To reason with his brother. Even Naqtuqa might be worthy of such an opportunity. He could be a valuable ally."

"You would think that," said Heizl. "How do we know that barbarian isn't swaying our new friend back to his side?"

"Their reunion follows a different path," replied Renyar. "The *warleader* is confused, slow to recognise family. Okuaak is appealing to him to scatter the tribes, and to end his campaign of vengeance."

"How can you be so sure?" Heizl spoke in a low voice. She had no reason to risk drawing attention to them, even with magicks and disguise to help them blend in. "I've barely picked up a dozen words of their language since getting here."

The Thalan paused before replying, one hand brushing dirt from his mantle. "Urephor's Fragments bring with them many changes. Gifts and curses, strength and weakness, clarity and madness."

"Riiight. You're saying that some insane dragon has spent the time learning to speak Norjan, or whatever they call it."

"Must you be so sceptical? You've witnessed more magicks than most, and this is what confounds you? Now's not the time to be contrary."

Heizl suppressed a smirk. Part of her had hoped for a bigger reaction.

Cocking her head, the mage returned her attention to the man that they'd come to murder. She didn't much like the thought of taking another's life, but her other options seemed to be fewer every time she counted them.

"What're they saying now?" Heizl asked, as much to distract herself as from any real interest. She doubted mere words would change tonight's outcome.

Renyar eyed her sidelong for a second. "Naqtuqa's mind has cleared, and he recognises his brother now. He seemed pleased... until asked to discard the Claw. His words reveal confusion and anger now. I believe that the warleader expected Okuaak to join him."

She gestured off to one side. "I guess that was that outburst just now? And why those warriors are moving to surround Oak?"

"Exactly. Okuaak is grieved. He came with us willing to do what was necessary... but I think he still believed that his brother could be saved."

"I thought you said that he could change too?"

"No, I merely said that Naqtuqa deserved such an opportunity."

"There's no need to split hairs." Heizl rolled her eyes and nudged aside the hunters blocking her view once more. "Come on, we should–"

Half-sunk within her web of binding threads, Heizl felt the spirits rise a moment before she saw them. Had the strands surrounding them hung in the material world, they might've shivered beneath cold winds or sagged with ice forming upon them. She struggled to describe what she saw.

Those closest to Okuaak succumbed first. The light of each soul dimmed and wavered as lethargy descended upon each. An external force – no, *scores* of external forces – descended, sapping vitality from flesh. Warriors staggered, covering their faces and struggling to stand.

The shaman's magic washed outwards like a wave, passing over Heizl within a handful of slowing heartbeats. A deep chill sank into her muscles as a weight settled upon her soul. Next to her, even Renyar shook as he resisted the effects.

Trembling, Heizl dropped deep within. Faint threads, cold and hungry, reached towards her from all sides, clawing at something intangible. With a sorcerous sweep, she cut the net that the spirits had cast, feeling warmth trickle back through her body.

"Snap out of it," she hissed, elbowing the Thalan in the ribs. Fine chainmail flexed beneath the sharp blow. At the quiet groan, Heizl repeated the arcane motion, releasing Renyar from the hungry land spirits. As he straightened, she wondered if she might come to regret freeing him, but regrets would wait.

"It's time," said the Thalan. One hand on his silvered scabbard, his blade leapt free in the other. Stabbing it skywards, sorcerous, green lights danced along its steel.

Had Heizl not seen his intricate preparations through the night, she might've dismissed the gesture. He'd never used quite the same words twice, but his message remained clear. *"When emerald light shines, yield to self-interest."*

As ghastly green shadows fell outwards from those closest, Heizl felt her web shiver. For a few heartbeats, each strand grew tighter still.

Opening her eyes, chaos greeted her. The first few shouts rose from those furthest from Okuaak's spirits. Old rivalries burst into new life from those that Renyar had enthralled. What started as raised voices and shoves soon turned to screams and violence.

Heizl spun a slow circle, taking in the expanding brawl. Whereas the closely-packed natives had blocked her view before, many now fell to their hands and knees beneath the shaman's sudden summoning. Completing her turn, she faced the warleader's fire, where he now leant heavily upon his spear, weathering the assault.

At Naqtuqa's side, his own shaman stepped forward. None there saw the spiritual exchange, though few would miss its effects. Only those most distant wouldn't feel the temperature plummet.

As if struck, Okuaak staggered backwards, barely remaining upright. In that same moment, something metallic arced through the air.

More arrows followed in rapid succession as Zecht revealed himself. The warleader's shaman dropped to the ground moaning, fletching protruding from her belly, as another projectile ricocheted from Naqtuqa's arcane armour.

"Heizl, concentrate." At her side, Renyar's voice shook her from her swelling panic. Latching onto that solid presence, not caring for its eldritch source, she watched as, blade in hand, he stepped forwards. "It's time."

Sweat marring her grip upon the copper rod, she watched as the Thalan stalked forwards. Before him, Naqtuqa struggled to stand beneath the torrent of unseen, gluttonous spirits. Had she thought this through? Perhaps allying with someone who'd already tried to kill her family hadn't been her best move. In the handful of heartbeats that she considered sabotaging Renyar, he reached Naqtuqa. Perfect poise and martial prowess promised the warleader a swift death.

The Norjan had other ideas. One hand clutching his head, he swung the Fragment in his other with wild, half-blind fury.

Lit in the swaying flames of the nearby bonfire, Renyar flowed like water as he struck the reeling Naqtuqa. His curved blade, its steel an extension of the Thalan's arm, hammered time and again against the warleader's guard as he sought openings. Even protected by layers of sigil-marked, ensorcelled armour, the native reeled beneath each expert blow.

Renyar's sword caught Naqtuqa's visorless helmet a glancing blow, opening a shallow cut across the bridge of the Norjan's nose. Graceful as a dancer, a metallic shriek filled the air as his backswing skittered down the spear's bronze shaft a second later. Beneath razor's edge and lean strength, the old gauntlet failed. Iron rent, leather parted, and flesh tore as the sword slashed into the warleader's hand. Cold despite the cookfires, the night air chilled further as the spirits swarmed close, feeding upon spilled blood.

With a pained, bestial snarl and a single word in a language that Heizl didn't understand, Naqtuqa lashed out. All attempts at defence abandoned, he swung the bronze spear in a wide arc, blood streaming from the stump of a missing finger.

Despite parrying, Renyar still staggered beneath the blow. More fierce swings followed, forcing the Thalan swordsman back as he defended himself. Heizl scarcely followed the exchange as steel whipped out ineffectively between each strike.

Only at the sight of a swirling green half-dome coalescing into existence did she realise the danger Naqtuqa still posed. Angled to redirect the warleader's overhead swing, Renyar's arcane shell still shattered at the impact. Green shards span out in all directions like molten glass before fading into nothingness.

Preoccupied with strumming her web, Heizl didn't notice Zecht's arrows cease. Even subsumed by her sorcery, she would've struggled to miss the Shadow's timely arrival. Zecht's knives, Imperial steel at its finest, struggled against the old Tszerrichan armour. Still, his presence bought Renyar valuable time, even if it proved ultimately useless.

Stab and slash. Parry and block. Spear and sorcery. Perhaps a soldier or Shadow could describe the three-way duel as steel, iron, and bronze pirouetted around one another in violent exchange. Heizl, though, saw just their emotions. Zecht's growing panic. Renyar's fierce focus. Naqtuqa's wild outrage. Heartbeat by heartbeat, the anguished faces of conflict flashed through her mind's eye one after another.

"Our friends fare poorly," Okuaak spoke, appearing alongside her. "I fear that the land will comprehend soon, and demand more for its assistance."

"Firstly," Heizl said as she drew upon another native's deep seated hatred of another, "They're not my friends. Second, what do a bunch of hills care? No, don't answer, I don't care either."

"Naqtuqa has grown stronger than I dared imagine," the shaman continued as if she hadn't spoken. "The spirits sap his cursed strength, but the spear sustains him."

Heizl grabbed him by the arm. "Then let's leave the murderers to their fates and get out of here!" she hissed.

Okuaak shook his head, the beads in his headdress ringing with the movement. "Without our assistance Renyar will fall, and your companion shortly after. Takuq has revealed it to me. My brother's curse will grow as he adopts the Tongue. He will become a threat not just to my people but to yours too." He turned towards Heizl. Glittering eyes, nestled among weathered wrinkles, locked with hers. "They might still prevail if I remain, but, should you stay, the spirits remember a victory yet to be realised."

"Look, I've got no intention of dying in some godless backwater. I'm not done living!"

"The spirits agree, and so do I." Okuaak gave a wry smile before turning back towards the melee. "And that is why you must stay."

Heizl followed his gaze in time to see Zecht fall backwards as if struck by a charging buck. Naqtuqa, moving as if ignorant of the dozen wounds he'd already suffered, turned in time to block another of Renyar's swings. To the mage's untrained eye, she would've sworn it looked more like an attack in its own right rather than any form of block or parry.

Looking back and forth between Okuaak and their failed attempt upon the warleader, Heizl stamped her foot. "Dammit!"

Turning back towards Naqtuqa, her rod trembled as her sweat-slick grip tightened. One uncertain step at a time, she started towards the melee.

In the shadow of half-lidded eyes, Heizl's imagination moved quicker than her feet. Choices flashed before her mind's eye in rapid succession, each worse than the last. Attempting to enter the vicious three-way melee would end in disaster. Twisting Naqtuqa's perceptions and senses would only buy time. The mage lived, second after second, a dozen versions of herself that manipulated threads one way or another. Regardless of which man's attention she grasped and which way she pulled them, it'd all end in disaster.

She wished Okuaak's spirits could be wrong, and, in hindsight, she'd hate it when Hastigr was right.

One unsteady foot after another, Heizl urged herself forwards. Picturing all the ways things could go wrong wouldn't get her anywhere. If she hesitated then her fear might catch up with her. She spared the twisting strands at her fingertips only the barest attention.

Eyes fully open now, drinking in the light of a dozen cookfires, she searched as she sidestepped around the edge of the fight.

Dew hung from coarse, trampled grasses. Blood stained the ground. Smoke and mist mingled in the air. None registered to her for more than a single panicked heartbeat.

Skirting the fight, she brought her hands up in time to catch Zecht by the shoulders as he dodged beyond the warleader's reach. The Shadow grunted the faintest of acknowledgements as she struggled to keep upright.

Stumbling beneath his weight, Heizl reached out to steady them both against the cool earth. Knuckles sinking into the dirt, she didn't release the grip upon her focus' cold metal surface. Teeth grinding together, she pushed with her other hand, propelling Zecht back into the fray.

Even that effort sapped something innate from her. Whether from weaving through the souls of a hundred Norjan warriors, her recent lack of rest, or from the pressure of Okuaak's summoned spirits, she didn't have a whole lot left.

Had she not felt so empty, she might've had a fraction of a chance of getting out of Naqtuqa's path. Spinning the spear into a two handed stance, he lunged for the Shadow, missing Zecht by a knife's edge. Snarling, the warleader reversed direction, and slammed the spear's tarnished, bronze butt into her chest.

Her feet left the ground and air escaped her lungs. Every bone in her body shook as she struck dirt.

Coughing and groaning, Heizl rolled onto her front. Had she a clear enough head, an open enough mind, or enough breath to speak, she might've voiced a grateful prayer to any god that would listen. The warleader didn't follow her further, engaged once more by Renyar. In spite of the trickle of blood matting his hair, the Thalan fought on.

Something pressed against Heizl's knuckles. Harder than the copper focus, and colder than the earth beneath her, it dug into her fingers. When she'd leant upon the ground to prop up Zecht, she would've sworn she'd only touched soil. No reasonable thought could explain an object's presence now. Sapped by the night, her senses played tricks on her. No other explanation sufficed.

Pushing herself upright, she scooped it up with her free hand. She might've wondered at that choice, if not for the sharp pain shooting through her chest. Teeth and fingers clenched, she barely felt the cold, bloody object in her grip.

Still holding her focus, she wrapped an arm around herself and squinted at what she held. Past the struggling shapes of enchanted natives, the amber glow of firelight wreathed a crooked oblong. Indistinct in the violent night, she focused on a dismembered, iron-wrapped finger.

She sank back onto her haunches, head spinning, and glanced to where Renyar backpedalled. Even his masterful swordplay struggled to fend off Naqtuqa's onslaught. Zecht lay nearby, struggling to rise while clutching his shoulder.

Clenched fist trembling, Heizl's gaze flicked to her copper rod. She'd carried it for so long. Why? Other Spire mages used similar objects to channel their magicks safely. It gained her nothing. Sure, she could hit a guy with it, but under the current circumstances that'd be almost useless. She only kept it because they expected her to. Most Imperials already kept their distance from mages – why give them one more reason by standing out?

The thought passed in an instant. Her hand gripping tighter still around the bloodied finger, a growl rose in Heizl's throat. Muscles tensing, she flung the rod to the ground. Digging into damp earth, her focus bounced once before rolling to a stop.

Heizl clapped both hands together just as Naqtuqa backhanded Renyar. Blackened iron met the Thalan's angular cheekbone, sending him sprawling.

She saw none of it. Armoured finger pressing against both palms, she reached out. Faint threads reached from its cooling flesh to the warleader as he glanced towards her and Okuaak.

Heart pounding in her ears, and neck itching as if swarmed by insects, Heizl's memories turned towards a balcony a thousand leagues away. A motheaten old man locking every muscle with just a single strand of hair. If Hastigr could paralyse her every muscle in such a way, then she could do the same to some dirty Norjan in stolen armour.

She grasped the threads, feeling them as surely as she did the finger in her hands. Heizl didn't twist, pull, or push this time. Instead, she just held. More and more, she leant into that grip, channelling every ounce of strength into that singular bond.

Drifting back to her mundane sight, she watched as Naqtuqa, midswing towards a downed Renyar, froze.

Iron pressed into her palms. Even backed by her sorcery, she felt the warleader's strength push against hers. One by one, she relinquished her grip on the other natives, trusting to human nature to maintain momentum. The most strong-willed of individuals hadn't resisted her like this. Blood dripped as her flesh wrestled with corroded metal, and her soul struggled against Naqtuqa's.

Poorly-lit and half-turned away, still she saw the warleader's face twist into a bestial scowl. Spear inches from the back of Renyar's neck, the Norjan pushed against her sorcery. Though he remained motionless, Heizl felt his strength against hers. As if pulled by a team of labourers, her feet slipped through damp grass and mud.

Redoubling her efforts, the gap between them shrank. Half a pace from her, Zecht looked up at her, wincing in pain and clutching his shoulder.

"Hey, Fitz." The Shadow's mouth twisted up at one corner in what might've been a smile. "Here." Shifting his weight, he held a dagger up towards her, hilt first. "Prolly easier to put y'self out of y'misery."

If not for her inexorable slide towards Naqtuqa – his physical might overpowering her magicks – Heizl might've hesitated. Only a moment before, she'd considered sabotaging both Zecht and Renyar. Now, it looked like all of them, Okuaak included, wouldn't last the night.

For a second, still grasping the bloodied finger, Heizl's grimace matched Naqtuqa's. Muscles trembling, she snatched the weapon from the Shadow's outstretched hand. Its well-worn hilt almost slipped through her grip.

As surely as if she bodily wrestled with him, Heizl lurched forwards and let go of his bloodied finger with one hand. She all but fell towards him, as if the iron-wrapped flesh was still attached to the raging native before her.

Fear took her, eyes widening at the warleader's growing shape. She raised both hands to protect herself.

Her sorcerous grip upon Naqtuqa failed. Renyar forgotten, the warleader spun towards her, spearhead glowing in the firelight.

Heizl slammed into him. He barely moved. A bolt of sharp pain lanced through her chest. Her vision blurred.

Zecht's blade pierced the warleader's right eye. The ancient helmet, visor missing for gods-knew-how-long, did nothing to protect him. Flesh tore beneath sharp, notched steel. The thin layer of bone at the back of the socket resisted for the briefest instant. Heizl might've struggled to break it with just her own strength. Propelled by Naqtuqa's own resistance against her sorcery though…

Even as the Norjan died, Heizl bounced from him. The mage struck the cold, muddy ground a split second after the corpse did. For a moment, she blacked out at the pain, a rib cracking. When the darkness rose from her vision, Naqtuqa's unmoving, destroyed visage greeted her.

She only saw one thing though. Beyond his motionless shape, Renyar climbed to his feet, sword in hand. His cold, grey eyes flicked between her and Naqtuqa's corpse. No, not Naqtuqa. The Claw.

Heizl had seen the murderous look upon his face before. In the Great Hall. When she'd blindsided him near some dead Tszerrichan's grave. Neither time had he looked quite like this. In all her years, twisting minds and souls, she'd not seen anything so intent. Death loomed.

That same deadly grace lunged towards her now.

She glanced at the spear. It didn't look like a dead dragon's claw. Sure, its ivory head could've come from something living, but still. Eh. What did it matter?

Without hesitating, she rolled, only regretting the pain of bruised bones for a second, and rose into a clumsy crouch. As Renyar closed, Heizl flashed the Thalan a sardonic smile.

Her hand, so used to the presence of her copper focus, wrapped around the Claw's shaft.

Renyar, foe, ally, whatever, connected with her as soft skin touched cold bronze. Darkness descended.

Heizl had succumbed to hallucinations and visions more than once. As the subject of other mages practising their spells. In the depths of Hastigr's Nexus. In certain bars and venues within Reiget City. Few of them compared to what she saw now.

How long she stayed in that realm, Heizl didn't know. Her vision returned though as she skidded backwards across the mud. The spear trembled in her hand where she'd blindly blocked Renyar's slash. In her chest, the sharp stab of battered bone seemed distant somehow.

As the Thalan paused, harsh necessity glowing silver in his eyes, the mage straightened. They locked gazes.

"You lack the substance to master that Fragment," Renyar growled.

Heizl shrugged. "Tell me something new."

"I'll kill you if necessary."

"I just killed a guy myself." She shuffled her feet, bringing the spear around between them. "I'd rather not do it again, but I will if I have to."

From where he remained propped up on the ground a short distance away, Zecht drawled, "Eh, it gets easier."

Heizl opened her mouth to snap back. Her gaze tracked past Renyar to a multitude of dark shapes half-lit by flickering cookfires. Bruised and bloodied faces turned towards them, eyes glittering with uncertainty as natives faced them. She didn't know if she preferred their fearful expressions or the looks of hatred, fear, and envy that so often had come with the Imperial Court.

The Thalan followed her gaze. As he saw the hunters and warriors arrayed against them, he shifted back into a ready stance. His sinuous movements didn't betray the multitude of injuries he'd suffered.

Considering the beating he'd taken in fighting Naqtuqa without his magic, Heizl had to give him credit. Maybe all deluded megalomaniacs had the same unwillingness to die. She risked a glance down at the bronze spear now in her grip. Somehow, the might of a dozen tribes against her, she'd won. The power of an elder god in her hands. Maybe she should test Renyar's mortality.

A few paces away, Okuaak helped Zecht to his feet. The air didn't seethe with cold hunger anymore. Shouldn't the spirits beswarming her? Just one more group shunning her. No, more likely the shaman's deal had come to an end. Understanding the man's strange magicks might help, but other details drew her attention.

"Our feud'll wait," Renyar spoke over one shoulder. "Hold my left, and resist the Claw's influence. Its violence has tempted greater men than you."

"Says the man brandishing a sword." With some effort she lowered the spear, and stepped past Renyar, standing between him and the gathering Norjans. "Hey, Okuaak? You wanna translate? Unless this stick is likely to let me talk like the snake here?"

"What are you doing, Heizl?" the Thalan hissed in an impatient, almost singsong tone.

"You're the one who was willing to give the armoured maniac a chance." She cleared her throat. "Sorry, Oak, no offence."

"Pay it no mind." The shaman shuffled up alongside her. "What would you tell them?"

"That we're done here. Spent. None of us have got a whole lot left, and we just want to leave." She eyed a native warrior marginally closer to them than the others. "Between the lot of 'em, they'll probably cut us to pieces. One of them has to get to us first though. Probably a second and a third too. For them? It doesn't end well." Heizl risked a glance at Okuaak. "Unless they walk away."

"And if they don't?" asked the shaman.

Heizl bared her teeth, gripping the spear more tightly as she leant her weight upon it. "If they don't, then we find out what happens to the first of them."

She thought Okuaak might stay silent. After a moment though, raising his voice, he turned to his kin. She didn't understand a single throaty word that he said. Eventually, after longer than she'd expected, he stopped speaking.

None of the other Norjans reacted straightaway. Several spoke in low voices, fears whispering among the gathered tribes. Weapons, many still dripping with the blood of rivals, trembled in calloused hands.

"Snake, looks like they're not going for it," Heizl mumbled back over one shoulder. "Get the big guy on the right, put him down dramatically, and I'll–"

She trailed off as she saw a single shape in the crowd step back. A moment later, another Norjan followed suit. One by one, the tribespeople edged away. Murmurs still flowed among them as incomprehensible as the land's spirits that had retreated only moments earlier. An occasional shout or jeer rose from them, and Heizl couldn't help but feel that her words hadn't fully convinced them all.

"Snake, make sure that traitor of yours limps out of here with us." She considered for a moment. "Or don't. Probably easier if we leave him. Come on, before our new friends change their minds."

Renyar chuckled as he stepped alongside her, Zecht's arm draped across his shoulders. "I'm impressed. Gods have chosen saints with less cunning."

"Ugh, don't say that. Getting a compliment from you is like... like... ah, forget it. Let's just get out of here."

He at least gave her the courtesy of not replying, even if she did have a burning urge to cut his answering smile clean off his face.

The injured Shadow's weight still leaning against him, Renyar led them from the gathered tribes. Even after she turned her back on them, Heizl felt a hundred native eyes track them beyond the campfires' light. Even with the sun's cold light licking the eastern horizon, and a mile or more separating them, still that watchful presence carried with it the promise of violence should they return. If not for the familiar weariness filtering through her bones, then she might've faced the way they'd come just to challenge them.

"...Fitz?" Zecht's voice, as tired as she felt, sifted through the fog that had descended upon her thoughts. "You alright? I know he's kinda dull, but Oak asked you something."

"Huh?"

Still supporting the Imperial, the shaman let a soft, reassuring smile seep into his features. "Friend, you dropped this."

Heizl's gaze sank to the dirty object in Okuaak's hand. Sore eyes settled onto her focus' familiar shape. Its copper no longer shone, instead scuffed and stained with dirt. Several strands of coarse grass hung from one end. Had he carried it this whole way? It looked so similar to the wooden totem that he'd held before.

She glanced at the spear. The Claw. Dirty, scratched bronze, so alike the rod that she'd carried for so long. The same, but different. She could feel it.

"...Keep it."

"Come," Renyar interjected, stepping closer, sword in hand. "We're not finished."

"I'm happy to finish anything." She shook the spear in his general direction.

"You misunderstand. You showed restraint." Renyar shrugged. "We might've slain those who stood against us. Instead, you showed reason. Let me show reason in return. I'm a man of my word, Heizl. Should you trust me, I will endeavour to secure you whatever you wish for... after the Comet has passed."

"Yeah? And if I don't?"

"Then we'll have a different conversation somewhere that I'm... not so limited."

She eyed him, lips pressed together. Despite his perfect posture, he looked weary. Bags under grey eyes, skin sallow, she might not get this chance again.

Heizl shook the idea away. Even with a Fragment herself now, she probably looked no better.

"I was always told not to take rides with strange men," she said. "Especially when they're suggesting travelling directly into the Nexus. You know the place, right? The sensitive little room at the Empire's beating heart?"

"I'm not going with you. Even if your Spire would permit me to use one of their beacons, my business here remains."

"Your..? Oh," she glanced at the shaman who stayed quiet. "I still don't believe that you're getting rid of that Tongue of yours, y'know. Anyway, the Nexus needs a beacon at each end to work, and I don't see one here."

"Huh?" said the Shadow, somehow managing to look even more damaged than the rest of them. "Oh, that?" Zecht reached into a pocket. "Just one more broken bone, right?" He opened his hand to reveal a bleached fingerbone.

"Fine. So we've one of Hastigr's beacons. If you're not gonna send me, then I sure as Void don't know how to use it."

"I gather that your scathe is quite advanced. You should be able to sense the bond between this beacon and its pair."

Heizl's nose whistled with the force of her frustrated indrawn breath. Just another arrogant bastard trying to show off all they knew. She'd practised plenty dealing with that.

A sickeningly sweet smile spreading onto her face, she cocked her head as she spoke. "I know the theory, thanks. I just can't sense it. It's too small."

"Until now, you've crawled blind." He gestured to the bronze spear. "Look again, this time by the fire you now hold."

Teeth grinding, Heizl bit back a sharp reply. Forcing herself calm, she let her eyelids half-close, and looked within.

She didn't know a stream of colourful enough curses for how she felt. Renyar was right, about this at least. Before, when Hastigr had shown her an inanimate object in the reflected light of mortal souls, she'd barely seen it. Now, illuminated by the broken piece of an elder god in her hand, it seemed so obvious.

If the average people all around her were blind to the bonds between souls, then she'd been blind to the depth that they went. She could barely look at the Claw, so close now. Sickly light burst out through jagged rents in its cracked shell, like flames, undulating and all too organic.

If not for the distant, blue-green orb, she'd have struggled to liken it to the paths out of the Nexus. Heizl lacked the words. Threads, strands, chains, webs, none of them matched the thing's solid feeling. As broad as any city road before her, she couldn't shake the sensation of movement beneath it. Like ice upon water, she knew that she could move upon it, somehow, but that destruction lay mere breaths away.

"I see it," she spoke, eyes still closed. "What if this goes wrong?"

"Then one more piece of Urephor returns to the Voids," said Renyar, voice deadpan and distant.

Heizl grimaced, and nodded once. Time to go home.

Tooth and Nail – Chapter Sixteen

"Ladies and gentlemen, I will not bore you with folktales and religion, nor theories and technicalities. No, I shall teach you how to recognise the most common paths of sanguine magicks. Learn, and you might just avoid being burned alive by an angry radical."

An address to officers of the Imperial Guard's First and Third Armies, Highmage Aidan Orecalin (404 I.Y.)

29th day of Indern, 406th Imperial Year
17th Year of Emperor Rufenrich Konreig's Reign

"You must realise that this isn't what I meant," said Toland, arms crossed over his breastplate. "Lena, tell him."

The healer didn't so much as glance up from where she tightened the straps on Thaun's armour. "It's logical enough, nor's the risk much higher than if he was anywhere else."

"That's not what you were meant to say," said the noble. "If Sigren was here, he'd talk sense."

Lena continued speaking in a monotonous voice, checking buckles and straps again and again. "Sigren's mission is important. Even if he only gets one of their mages, his absence could be a worthwhile trade. It might clear his head too."

"I much preferred it when you weren't talking," Toland muttered.

"Hey." Thaun looked up, catching the noble's eye. "Don't take it out on Lena."

"Well, apparently berating you doesn't help."

"This solves it all." Thaun raised his hands, gesturing around their command tent at nothing in particular. At his side, the healer paused, waiting for him to stop moving before continuing to adjust his armour. "My stepping up to lead, the morale problem, everything."

"Maybe, but there's a reason that only stupid or desperate generals lead from the frontlines. This is borderline suicide."

He flinched at the word. "How far do you think the men's spirits are going to fall if they see me hiding behind them on a horse again?"

"That's where you're supposed to be!"

"Last time I did that–" Thaun stepped away from Lena, open palms raised towards her. "–it didn't go so well. If we do the same thing again, how can we expect it to end any differently?"

Toland looked around the command tent in search of support. None appeared. Placing his gloved hands together in front of him, he eyed Thaun. "A lot's changed since then. We know what we're up against, we've got a plan, and you've got my Pinions. You don't need to do this."

Thaun sighed, before whispering, "I'm honestly getting fed up with other people telling me what I need."

"I know you are, I know," said Toland. "I can't speak for everyone else, but I'd rather not see people die unnecessarily. That includes you."

"Thanks," Thaun murmured, glancing over his armour himself. The plates and chainmail hid the worst of his nerves. "I've already compromised with you. I won't be in the frontline itself."

"If Thala spots you within the ranks, they'll come for you. Every stone and sword, aimed at your royal throat."

"Then we'll wear the same colours as the rest of the Second." He watched as Toland crossed his arms over his breastplate again. "Don't look at me like that. I thought you'd be pleased I was taking responsibility."

"'Pleased' is hardly how I'd describe it. Responsibility is about more than just looking like you're in charge. Lena, is there nothing you can…" The noble trailed off as he looked to the healer. A moment later Thaun followed his gaze to see the mage peering out the tent's canvas flap. "What is it?"

Lena didn't look at either of them as she replied in a flat, dry voice. "It's time."

As he grew aware of the growing noises outside, Thaun felt the distinct sensation of the pit of his stomach *not* dropping out from under him. Instead, stony resolve filled his veins. At his sides, leather creaked, almost inaudibly, as he clenched both fists. Checking the unfamiliar sword sheathed at his hip, he followed Lena out.

His Royal Guard waited in an attentive line outside. Upon seeing him, they saluted with fists to chests, waiting for him to return the gesture, before falling in on all sides. As they walked, the soldiers kept hands on swords, their boots striking the hard ground in unison.

Passing by the ordered rings of tents with Lena and Toland in tow, Thaun soon looked out over the assembled ranks of his army. His escort parted, and a gentle but firm hand propelled him forward to face the ranks.

Many uniforms bore bloodstains and the damage from their last battle. Notched blades, torn mail, and dented steel. The men beneath undoubtedly carried their own scars, both inside and out. Their company standard hung limp in the still air, its blue edges frayed and tattered. Off to one side, Toland's Pinions stood in a smaller group, their rifles resting upon their shoulders.

Thaun half-turned his head towards the noble. "Should I... say something?" he asked quietly.

"Did you have something in mind?"

"I don't know." He did his best not to show his uncertainty. "Aren't leaders meant to say a rousing speech or something before a battle?"

"Baby steps, Thaun." Faint humour, twisted with exasperation, echoed in Toland's whispered voice. "Call for your officers, and give them your orders. Your men down there? They'll see you taking command. That's enough for now."

"Now you're going easy on me?"

Behind him, Toland's armour rustled in what Thaun could only assume was a shrug. "I'm just doing whatever helps the most people."

"Thanks for the support." Thaun raised a hand, gesturing a messenger over. He raised his voice. "Have Colonel Harlech distribute the order to march."

The aide looked uncertain. "Do you mean Captain Halig, sir?"

"Just tell him," said Thaun, heat rising in his cheeks, though his helmet hid the worst of the colour. Forcing himself past his embarrassment, he turned to Toland. "Where do I stand?"

His friend paused before replying. "Right this way, Your Highness."

Within a bell, he marched shoulder-to-shoulder with two members of the Royal Guard. Dressed now in spare, almost clean uniforms of blue and gold, three more formed a line before him with another directly behind. Beyond them rose the sound of the Second, a martial cacophony of boots on shallow earth. The faint beat of a drum broke over them, and Thaun found his own pace falling in time with the army's steady pulse. Dirt rose with each step, coating the inside of his throat. Raising his hand to cover his mouth, his mind, for an instant, travelled to their rearguard – they'd breathe in ten times as much dust in the back than here near the front.

Thaun had spoken to his escort on occasion, but hardly knew one from the next. Now he walked among them, ready to draw steel and face their enemy. Was this what it meant to be a soldier? A duty to guard the person at your side? A readiness to march into the unknown? The thought humbled him. More of the nobility should experience this.

Glancing about, he sought distraction. His friends had left him. Though Thaun knew that they didn't mean to abandon him, it couldn't help but hurt. Sigren among the enemy, attempting to thin their mages before battle joined. Toland ranging out before them, or to the flanks, with his Pinions. Even Lena had disappeared along with what little essence Korten hadn't burned up, unwilling to share her plan for dealing with Elhin. Each had good reason to be elsewhere, but he'd have felt better with one of them at his side.

Somewhere off to his left, a horn sounded and the march stopped. Unprepared for the signal, Thaun bumped into the armoured back of the guardsman in front of him. He bit back an apology. The soldier barely moved with the impact.

He'd barely noticed their army moving through the pass, and now they stood upon an all too familiar expanse. Glassy stone, impact craters, and upturned earth told the story of what had happened here last time.

On all sides, men and women adjusted shield straps or loosened swords in scabbards. Separated from him by several thin lines of men, Thaun watched runners jog past their front ranks of infantry, helping them find their formations. Dust, disturbed by their march, drifted to the ground. Anxious sweat filled the air.

Past the helmeted heads before him, he made out Toland's Pinions, forming a skirmisher line before the main force. Red cloaks fluttered in their wake, so dark they might as well be black. For a second, he imagined a murder of bloodied ravens. Thaun shook the thought from his mind, dismissing the omen.

He didn't risk turning around to face his officers overlooking the battlefield. If the men saw any uncertainty in him, it could be disastrous. Besides, he already knew that the company's banner would stand above them, or that messengers would run to and fro. The Imperial Guard would run just fine without some meddling royal.

A low murmur grew among the Second in spite of the shouts and scowls of their sergeants. Thaun didn't notice it until they fell quiet, caught up as he was in his own thoughts. Even his bodyguards turned slightly, stares parallel to the rest of their small army. Following their gazes, he watched as, as if from nowhere, a line of men climbed from unseen cracks in the rocky ground.

Beneath swathes of pale cloth, bronze scales glinted in the late afternoon sun. Iron flickered in each warrior's hands. They didn't need any colours for every Imperial there to recognise them. Few members of the legion could claim not to have lost a friend the last time they had clashed with these Thalans and their mages.

The men across from them spread out, forming a shallow line. Thaun felt a bead of sweat trickle down beneath his armour. The warriors opposite them had had only so much to do with their recent defeat, but still he felt his nerves rising. His self-absorbed anxieties flickered away as Thalan mages appeared along with the others.

As events fell into motion before him, for the briefest of moments Thaun wished he'd stayed with the other officers.

The mages, perhaps emboldened by Korten's defeat, spread out quickly to leave a dozen paces between each of them. Though hard to tell over the distance, more of them had come to face the Imperials than the last time. Whatever their motive, none now hid among the shadowed tunnels below.

A violent shiver ran through Thaun, followed by another. At the third quake, he realised that it wasn't his body that trembled. He glanced down. The ground rumbled, and he braced himself. A nearby soldier stumbled, but his squadmates steadied him.

As dirt and rock erupted to the surface, despair rose with them. Curses, laments, and prayers rose from the men all around him. Their training held though – none broke or fled.

Breaking free of its earthen grip, the first jagged boulder burst into the light. With dust drifting from its cracked skin, it began its slow advance. The front row of guardsmen raised their shields, for all the good it'd do them, and Thaun followed suit.

More stones appeared before them, forming a more intimidating army than any of flesh and bone. Like the rising tide, they tumbled and shuddered towards the Imperial ranks.

A sharp bark broke over the low rumble of stone-on-stone. Thaun flinched as cracking noises filled the air. The last time he'd heard anything similar, the keening retort of fireworks, the Royal Palace had exploded. A visceral shudder ran through him at the memory.

Still uncertain, but too scared to risk looking around for the source of the noise, he gripped his shield more tightly. A second verse of detonations sang out over the company.

At the third volley, feeling the ground's rumbles subside, Thaun understood what he heard. He craned his head to see past the guardsman directly before him. The nearest of Toland's Pinions lowered the rifle from his shoulder.

As rocks skidded to a halt, and the dark-cloaked skirmishers reloaded their weapons, a confused murmur passed over the ranks. With the dust settling, similar uncertainty rippled over the distant Thalan lines. If any mages remained, they hid now among the bodies. Pinions retreated to the sides, out of the Second's path as they began the slow process of reloading their rifles.

In spite of the battle going to plan so far, Thaun had little idea what to do next. As nearby sergeants barked commands, he stumbled into step with the guardsmen around him. He knew that the different battalions and companies communicated with runners and flags, but he'd spotted neither.

As he marched, shifting his grip on his shield, he drew his sword in imitation of the man beside him. Through the jostling gaps before him he could make out the Thalan line. Though a handful ran forward to help their fallen mages, the others closed ranks. Outnumbered and without magical support, they began a slow, measured retreat. None fled. They remained shoulder to shoulder with their comrades. It seemed the Empire didn't hold a monopoly on discipline.

A few Pinions fired again, but the Thalan formation held. Men fell and blood blossomed. As their shrinking ranks fell back, a single figure remained behind.

No Imperial step faltered. The gap closed. More shots harried the retreating Thalans. Rock-dust and shouts of pain filled the air in equal measure, but not as many as Thaun would've expected.

He watched a handful of skirmishers join the Pinions, crossbow and rifle alike levelled at the Thalans from the flanks. Following their aim, he eyed the single warrior covering the enemy retreat. Black clothes, and wielding sword and shield, familiarity dawned on him. Something dark flickered in their distant hand.

"Wait, no!" The words escaped his lips before he knew it. Outright terror thrust aside any worries of how the troops around him might react to his outburst.

Separated from the Second by empty dirt and stone, the black-clad Thalan stepped forward.

Rifleshots cracked the air, twisting smoke rising from them. A handful of crossbows joined them, quarrels springing free to chase the retreating men.

Thaun didn't truly see the arc of each shot, but his imagination filled in the gap. One after the next, projectiles curved unnaturally towards the warrior in black.

Elhin paused in her inexorable advance as the volley flowed into her raised shield. Onyx fire burst along the length of her sword, and she broke into a sprint. As fast as a collapsing sand dune, she charged the Imperial ranks. Skirmishers and Pinions scattered from her path. A handful of shots flew wide as she crossed the ever-shortening distance. Back in the palace, Korten's smallest flames had given her enough force to break solid stone. Now, empowered by Toland's men, only flesh and steel stood to resist her.

Too late, Thaun opened his mouth to shout another warning. She struck their front rank like the Void given physical form. He felt more than heard the blast. Sable flames pulsed outwards, vapourising the unfortunate soldier at the centre of her charge.

Uniforms turned to ash. Red and gold sparks flew from flash-melted steel. Flesh crackled and blackened beneath the sorcerous explosion. Bodies – bloodied, broken, and dismembered – tumbled through the air to slam into former comrades, knocking them from their feet. A shockwave of smoke-tainted air washed over those that stayed standing.

Thaun staggered sideways, the world growing mute as the stench of burning flesh filled his nostrils. Blinking away the tears blurring his vision, he felt a single Royal Guardsman catching and steadying him as the rest of their squad collapsed. Flailing in the soldier's arms, Thaun grabbed a handful of scorched surcoat before trying to push him away. The veteran simply held on more tightly.

"We have to retreat!" Thaun shouted, but he heard only silence.

The soldier opposite him – dirt smeared over his face and blood dribbling down from a cut above his ear – said something. His lips moved, but no sound came out. Past the man's shoulders, several survivors fled while a single guardsman stumbled through the haze as if lost.

The low hum that had settled over the battlefield gave way to a deeper drone. Gradually, it yielded to a sound like rain as pieces of broken rock fell back to ground. Shards shattered into splinters upon impact. As the air cleared, a single figure loomed at the centre of the newly-formed crater. Elhin wiped sweat and dirt from her face, rolled her shoulders, and stalked after the regrouping Imperials. Whereas before she'd flowed like water in her movements, a hesitancy clung to her now. The way she favoured one leg, and held her blade in an only almost perfect stance hinted at the injuries she'd sustained through their recent clashes. Beyond her, drifting ash concealed the Thalan retreat.

Smoke filled Thaun's lungs. Helplessness threatened to overwhelm him. He hadn't felt such terror and confusion since Renyar's attack upon his home.

The rain-like pattering of debris faded as the world's breath returned, all at once flooding Thaun with sounds. Words grew clear over the chaotic sounds of retreat. "Sir!" The Royal Guardsman gripped him tighter. "We have to leave."

He didn't look at his bodyguard, instead watching the rest of his dwindling escort picking their way towards Elhin. Her clothes smoked, with patches of skin revealing angry, lustrous burns beneath. Korten was gone, but his flames weren't so easily forgotten.

The formidable woman paused in her stride, turning to face them. Edging closer to her, the three Royal Guardsmen – all that remained standing after the blast – separated in an attempt to limit the damage another explosion might cause. Thaun stared as the Imperials halted, heads flicking towards movement at the army's flanks. After a moment, Elhin risked turning to follow their gaze.

Smoke swirled as it settled, limping shapes casting long shadows through the grey. Lena emerged at a sprint, silver-inlaid axe in one hand and a shield in the other. In the eight years Thaun had known the mage, he'd never seen her move like this. Training together had revealed her as a reliable attacker, a poor match to Sigren's fury, but skilled in her own way. Few members of the Spire chose true weapons for their foci, preferring rings, wands, and staves, but the healer had proven to be a competent, if unimaginative, fighter.

Now she moved like a woman possessed. Fast as an avalanche, her entire body glistened as she crossed the gap. The last time Thaun had seen someone move like that had been, well, Elhin herself only moments ago. Lena had mentioned a few times that she knew more than just how to heal, in spite of where her strengths lay. Seeing her now, Thaun could believe it.

The axe, a swirl of silver and steel, forced Elhin back one shocked step after another. Each time she raised her shield, the mage pulled back, expertly avoiding the Fragment's bronze surface. Her own small buckler, bearing the Imperial crest, bashed aside Elhin's blade, though the healer found few openings.

Settling into her opponent's rhythm, the Thalan recovered. Despite her injuries, she danced and whirled before her, dodging powerful blows and peppering the healer with shallow cuts. Lena didn't slow as red trickled into her uniform. Almost too brief to be sure, Thaun could've sworn he saw, through the growing slashes in the hardened leather armour, flesh knitting back together.

As hands dragged him back, Thaun resisted. He couldn't tear his gaze from the martial display.

A handful of cloaked men jogged past, abandoning the relative safety of the Second as soldiers regrouped. Toland appeared alongside Thaun a moment later.

"At ease there, soldier." He held his own rifle in both hands, eyes fixed on the duel. The young noble glanced at Thaun. "You should get out of here. We'll support your mage."

"I can't leave her." Thaun stooped, picking up his new sword with a stony expression upon his face. Reverberating horns sounded on either side as their flanking units advanced. At the edge of the smoking crater, he couldn't tell if they'd crossed swords with the Thalans or not, but he didn't really care. They marched to fill their duty. Thaun didn't face Toland as he spoke. "Help me, or get out of my way."

His heart hammered for a second as he saw Toland hesitate before replying.

"With me, Your Highness." Turning, he shouted, "Pinions, encirclement but hold fire. The rest of you, just what're you waiting for?!" And with that, he nodded towards the fight, before pushing through the dwindling ranks of retreating Imperials.

As Thaun watched, Lena threw several rapid swings down upon the Thalan, one stroke smoothly arcing into the next. Elhin's own blade spun as she deflected and dodged each blow, before slamming her shield into the healer, staggering her back. She stepped forwards, not giving the mage time to recover. The slender sword whipped back and forth, and blood spouted between the gaps in Lena's armour.

Catching a slash on her axe's haft, both combatants froze for the briefest of seconds, matching strength against strength as bloody slashes knitted shut. Jabbing a toecap into her opponent's shin, Lena broke free. Elhin stumbled, her blade slipping from the lock as the two separated.

As pale-clad warriors stepped through the dust, the Royal Guardsmen leaped forward to meet them. Several of the Second, less injured or more stubborn than their comrades, joined and soon a desperate melee grew beyond the duel.

Over the sounds of battle, Thaun couldn't make out the words that passed between the two women then. As Elhin spat to one side, the healer rolled her shoulders and set her feet, wounds closing as she prepared to meet her charge.

Lena reluctantly gave ground. Unwilling to risk a swing that might land upon Elhin's draconian shield, she fought defensively. Her wooden, blue shield bore an expanding hatch-mark pattern, while tatters of leather armour sloughed from her. Fresh blood clung to smooth, pink flesh. For just a moment, the unstoppable Thalan force met an immovable Imperial object.

As Thaun pushed apart the nearest two soldiers to rush to the healer's aid, his fear took form.

Lena's axe, metal scarred and pitted, connected a glancing blow to Elhin's shoulder. The Thalan shuddered under the force of the swing even as she stepped into the opening that the healer had left. Her bronze shield pushing her aside, she lunged. Her curved sword dropped from her hand, a steel-pointed dagger appearing in her grip as Elhin drove through the mage's damaged armour. The short crossguard slammed against Lena's gut. Its tip pushed through the other side, barely slowing as it broke through the second layer of hardened leather.

Thaun opened his mouth wide and shouted, "No!" The word did nothing to stop Lena's own cry of pain.

The healer said something then, but through the pounding in his ears, Thaun heard nothing. Stepping forward unsteadily, as if pushing through tar, he watched the healer slump forwards, buckler tumbling from her grip. Though she made no attempt to attack, she held her axe tight. The mage's failing body leaning against the other woman, Elhin didn't move beneath the weight. Lena struggled lightly, taking hold of her foe's arms to keep herself upright. Elhin stood firm, her only acknowledgement a wrenching twist of her blade.

She half-turned to stare at Thaun, who still held his sword. He saw no anger nor hatred in her brown eyes, only cold resolve. Her expression slowly curled into confusion, and she risked a glance down at the dying Imperial.

In the blink of an eye, shock gripped the Thalan's features. She took a step backwards, as if retreating, though Lena stayed with her, steel blade locked within her flesh. Thaun watched in growing horror as the healer's body continued knitting back together. Skin bubbled and muscles swelled around the wound until tumourous meat engulfed the weapon's hilt. And Elhin's hand along with it.

The Thalan flexed and struggled, but the mage's face set as she gripped tighter. A second later and her gloves burst, her hands expanding in swollen growth. Lena screamed as her flesh melded with her opponent's. Whether at the sight of the mage's uncontrolled magic, or out of fear of the woman's black fire, the soldiery held back, unwilling to close.

To her credit, Elhin didn't cry out as she fought to break free of Lena's death grip. A knee rose into the healer's groin, a headbutt bloodied her nose, but the Thalan couldn't break free of the mage's writhing flesh.

Toland brushed past him, rifle levelled as he sought a clean shot. Though their foe seemed trapped, she proved far from helpless. The two pivoted around one another like entwined lovers, the romance long gone, neither saying a word as they locked murderous gazes.

As if determined to do something despite the consequences, Toland fired. Thaun flinched at the firearm's bark. The metal slug moved too fast to see, but the results were clear enough.

Elhin's shield rang, and her dagger – still buried within Lena''s flank – flickered like the sunlight through a raised hand. Black flames writhed over Lena's side, disappearing beneath crackling, growing flesh. The Imperial hissed through clenched teeth, but held on.

Seeing Toland falling back to reload, Thaun stepped up close, sword arm raised. Different techniques flashed through his mind too brief to truly grasp. Lunge, slash, or shoot, he hesitated on each. Fortunately, Sigren made up his mind for him.

A heavy quarrel appeared in Elhin's back with a sickening sound, its leather fins poking out over one shoulder. The Shadow stepped through the settling dust, his black uniform stained grey, reloading as he walked. He didn't take his eyes from her as he slowly closed the gap.

Though Elhin didn't look towards Sigren, she spun. A kick broke Lena's balance, and she moved the healer between her and this new threat. She raised her shieldarm as much as she could, blocking the aimed rifles of Toland and his Pinions.

Thaun saw his opening then. As he lashed out he saw the Thalan woman flinch as if trying to bring her own blade in to block the slash. The sword cut across her chest, dark cloth slicing apart to reveal the fine, scorched chainmail beneath. If not for her armour he would've separated her arm clean from her shoulder. He drew back to strike again, but, her weight on Lena, Elhin's boot came up to strike the inside of his wrist. Bones jarring from the force of the blow, the blackened sword fell from his hand.

Stepping out of reach again, Thaun hesitated. Her toe dipped under his fallen blade and flicked it away.

No one there would learn what she would've done next. A second crossbow bolt slammed into the side of her hooded head, from much shorter range this time. The light left Elhin's eyes as the steel point drove through flesh and bone. Fire and panic rose in Thaun's gut like caustic lightning as blood sprayed over him.

The Thalan went limp, collapsing onto Lena. Still melded together, the pair staggered and fell towards Thaun. Throwing his shield to the floor, he stepped in to catch his friend. Their combined weight proved too much for him, and he tumbled to the floor in a pile of dying, writhing flesh.

On striking the ground, the air fled from his lungs. He wrapped bloodstained fingers around the rim of Elhin's shield, and pushed. Still winded, he managed to move the pair a few inches, but not nearly enough to free himself.

In another life, Elhin might've made history. Perhaps in Thala the people knew and feared her. They might someday raise statues in her memory, this loyal servant and protector. Such noteworthy individuals deserved a better death. Instead, her lifeless form pressed down upon him, unmoving.

Through thick leather, the shield's metal rim, as keen as any blade, sliced into Thaun's palm. He recoiled, but he found his hand stuck to the surface by more than just dried blood. The pain, like lightning in his veins, ran up his arm.

Thunder resounded in his head, and Thaun blacked out to dream of fire and darkness.

Tooth and Nail – Chapter Seventeen

> *"Firesand slew many sons of Velast upon the back of Birka's Serpent. His iron crescent shed their mead upon heroes' soil. His flint mind cut short their skein.*
> *But Firesand could not stand against Fjarl's Champion."*
>
> Verses of Steinar, Steinar, self-proclaimed Champion of Fjarl, regarding the Snake of Birka (388 I.Y.)

29th day of Indern, 406th Imperial Year
17th Year of Emperor Rufenrich Konreig's Reign

Heizl had never tasted anything quite like it. Well, she had, really. Most marketplaces sold pears at this time of year. Still, after what felt like weeks out in the Norjan wilderness, the novelty of eating something other than trail rations wasn't lost on her.

She took another bite. Sweet, watery juice ran down her chin to soak into her dark collar. Under other circumstances, such a stain would've irritated her until she could change. Things were different now though. She cast an admiring eye over the bronze spear lying across her knees.

Its damage – cracks, scuffs, and dents – mattered little to her, for she saw within. Fire burned in her mind's eye, fierce enough that she almost looked away. Souls might shed their own light, but this? It *blazed*.

Heizl shook her head. She found it hard to concentrate with such power in her hands. The weapon whispered to her, though in words she couldn't quite hear. If only she could push past all the distractions, surely she'd understand it then.

The polite clearing of a throat made her look up. This was one distraction she could live with. On the other side of the low table of drinks and refreshments, Jilia Strahl eyed her with genuine concern. Petite yet womanly, with gently curling hair, and wearing a dress the colour of a summer sunset, Heizl shook her head at the thought of having turned away from the governor's daughter for even a second.

Heizl took a deep breath. "Sorry, did you say something?"

Jilia painted a wan smile upon her lips. "I asked you how you're feeling."

"Never better."

"Are you sure?" The young noble's eyes narrowed, though she held her smile. "Not only did you waltz past our house guards, openly armed, in the middle of the day, but you've eaten..." She gestured towards the bare plates and empty bowls. "Well, everything."

"Come on, I've always had an appetite." She grinned at her.

"For a lot of things, or so I hear, but this... Something's changed."

"Jilia." Her grin broadened. "You've no idea."

Leaning her elbows on the table, Jilia leant closer. Heizl couldn't help but mirror her, unable to break eye contact as she spoke. "So tell me."

The mage surprised even herself with her willingness to talk. Starting with when she'd last seen the noble at the feast, she spared no detail. She did however modify a few to reflect better upon herself.

Her own intervention against Renyar during the attack had let the Imperial Champion, Vandal, chase the Thalans off. Rufenrich's explanation of elder gods, extraplanar realms, and dragons had little to do with Thaun's absence. The initial clash with the warleader? If not for Zecht, and having to save the Shadow's life, she might've emerged victorious there and then.

As her story came to Okuaak's shelter and his mastery of strange spirits, she slowed, drawing out each syllable. Soon, she'd have to make a decision. How would Jilia react to Heizl's meeting with Renyar? With Zecht's betrayal? With the treason that she now considered?

Jilia would understand. She had to. That level of trust, that symmetry of thinking, why else had she come to speak with her? Heizl had missed the woman sitting with her in the small garden, of course, but it was more than that.

Some in the Courts had underestimated Jilia before. Even the Trade Guild's dealings with her remained cautious. Many nobles planned a page ahead, but Jilia had outlined the later chapters of her plans. It was sometimes said that she ran more of Kragiv-Stal than the Governor himself. That it was her designs that had brought their family so close to the Emperor once more, after her disastrous betrothal with Thaun. If Jlia couldn't give Heizl sound advice, then few could.

The Claw writhed beneath her hand. And if Jilia didn't understand? Well, with Governor Strahl at the Imperial Palace, discussing who knew what with the Emperor, Heizl could simply deal with things here. One way or another.

At a lull in the details, Jilia opened her mouth to speak, but Heizl plunged onwards. Renyar, and his stories, lies, and promises. Okuaak's tale of foreign travellers a generation before. Their ambush and battle with Naqtuqa. One by one, it all spilled from her mouth. A warm feeling rose within as she saw Jilia's eyes twinkling in response to her words.

By the time she spoke of using the Nexus herself – surely an influential noble would recognise what power that implied – Jilia had gained a thoughtful, faraway look. Heizl let the garden fall quiet. Insects droned, birds sang, and the sounds of the city drifted over the estate's wall.

Jilia's eyes gradually focused as she turned back to Heizl. "Is Renyar here? In Reiget City?"

She nodded. "Zecht's with him."

"And they know you're talking to people about all this?"

At the implication, Heizl felt sweat mar her grip on the spear. "They'd be sorry if they tried anything," she growled.

"I..." The noble's gaze flicked to the Claw, and she swallowed before changing the subject. "Have you spoken to anyone else? Like your uncle?"

Heizl nodded slowly. She winced as her head throbbed. Too much sweet food, most likely. "I saw him almost as soon as I got back."

"And you told him all this?"

"Not all of it, no." She rubbed her forehead. It didn't help; her thoughts remained thick and sluggish. "I considered it, but I figured it wasn't exactly something I could take back. The Emperor doesn't know I met Renyar."

"But you told him about...?" She struggled to keep her eyes from Heizl's spear.

"I did." She followed her gaze. "I even suggested we destroy it."

"Is that even possible? You said it's a dragon's claw."

"They weren't immortal. They'd still be around if they were. Anyway, it's damaged already though, look." She ran a finger over the jagged crack in its head. Jilia leant closer. Heizl's heart beat a little faster.

"I see, it's like it's missing a piece."

"Right? But he all but ignored me." The spear rolled in her grip, like muscles shivering beneath skin. "What if he's plotting to collect all these Fragments? That's what Renyar said."

The noblewoman leant back. Placing her hands in her lap, Jilia breathed deeply as she composed herself. Heizl considered speaking – to tell her more of her concerns, or how she truly felt – but a thoughtful look in the noblewoman's eyes made the mage pause.

Frustration blemished her soft, serene features. "Heizl, why're you telling me all this? What do you think I can do?"

"Jilia... Honestly, I don't know what to do, or who to believe..." She swallowed. "What do you think I should do?"

Jilia smiled sympathetically and, just for a moment, Heizl felt like it would all work out. "It sounds like you don't know who to trust."

"Exactly! Both uncle and Renyar say the other is trying to summon Urathear. Can more than one person be planning the same? It's not like any of this is common knowledge."

"Heizl." Amusement tugged at the corners of her mouth. "I wasn't finished."

"Oh. Sorry."

Dismissing the apology with a wave, Jilia continued. "There's someone you're forgetting."

She arched an eyebrow. "I'll always trust you."

Jilia sighed but kept her wry smile. "I'm talking about trusting yourself, Heizl." She raised a hand, and a maid appeared to refill her cup. The girl frowned at the mage but moved to pour anyway. Heizl could well understand the servant's confusion – few commonfolk understood magic, let alone Heizl's own scathed flavour of it.

The mage smiled as Jilia continued. "You've made it this far by yourself, and I'm not talking about your journey to Norjhost. You never knew your father, your mother disappeared, and we both know how most people feel about the Spire."

"You don't have to remind me," Heizl muttered distractedly, though her mind wandered to her parents. For a second, she considered telling Jilia about a meeting just a couple of short years ago. In the end, she decided against it. There'd be time after all this.

"But look at yourself, you got through all that. Through your choices, you're respected at the Spire. People know who you are."

"I guess…"

"Heizl, I'm trying to tell you to make a decision and stick with it. That's part of what responsibility is. Making the best choice for those that you care for. It's what you've done this far. It's all any of us can do. You'll either be right, or you'll be wrong. You won't know until afterwards, so trust yourself to make a good decision. No one's going to make it for you."

"Well, I know that…"

"Then why're you asking me?"

Heizl sighed and looked away. Jilia was right of course. What *did* she want to do? Whatever she chose, history would remember.

Steeling herself, she came to a decision. Heizl stood. "I need to go."

"I'll need a coat." Jilia got to her feet.

"Sorry, what do you mean?"

"I'm coming with you."

"But you don't know where I'm going, or what I'll do."

Jilia shrugged, and Heizl couldn't help but notice the delightful way in which her chest bobbed up and down. "Then I suppose I trust you too."

Heizl swelled and her throat tightened at those words. They said little as servants appeared with Jilia's travelling cloak. The maids, after a sorcerous nudge, promptly forgot that the two women still stood there. Heizl still encouraged her to stay quiet as they left, though less for the sake of stealth and more to better hear the Claw's alluring whispers.

Shifting the gaze of two souls felt a little easier than it had in the past. Heizl still felt the same sapping as energy left her body to fuel the sorcery. With it came something else though, a warmth, a hint of the Fragment's power just beyond her reach.

Unseen by most, the pair crossed Reiget City. It took them twice as long as it should've to travel through the capital. In more peaceful times, Heizl would've followed the Old Imperial Way eastwards, but, even with her magic, it'd draw too much attention. Instead, they did their best to skulk down side streets, alleys, and narrow roads.

Warehouses of wood, stone, and brick loomed over them as they walked. The capital's industrial sector couldn't compare to that of other cities. Decisions were the only thing created in Reiget City. Trade and wealth passed through, and ended there in tax and revenue; it didn't start there. Thin wisps of smoke rose skywards before bending and streaming north as they caught the faster winds higher up. As steady as a temple's bell, the sounds of smiths beating on iron rang out over the warehouses and workshops. Stone-on-stone sounded as mills worked, laying a low susurration below the clamour of labouring tradespeople.

Heizl hadn't visited Renyar's safehouse before, but Zecht had described its location to her at length. As it transpired, she'd no need for any directions. Her sense of the Thalan, now that she'd grown familiar with him, shone almost like one of Hastigr's beacons.

She didn't knock or call out, instead pushing the old wooden door open with one hand. Something within resisted for a second. Heizl barely noticed her own grip tighten on the ancient spear as a tremble passed through her. With a cracking noise, the door jerked open beneath her strength. The mage paused mid-step and glanced at the splintered beam that now lay at her feet.

Emotions as varied as the gods themselves greeted her, along with almost as many weapons. Shock, fear, outrage, and a host of others. Though she only understood a handful of them, muted shouts of alarm rose on all sides in myriad different languages.

Jilia placed a hand on Heizl's arm, and the mage looked down at where she'd raised the spear towards one of the nearest figures. She didn't remember reacting, but the Claw stood ready.

The noble gave a reassuring squeeze, and a blanket smothered the flames of anger kindling to life in Heizl's veins.

"Heizl?" Jilia whispered aside to her, though loud enough for the motley collection of rebels and outlaws to hear. "Aren't you going to… introduce me to your friends?"

Before the mage could respond, a new voice spoke from behind the militia's spear wall. "Heizl? What took you so Void-damned long?"

She suppressed a sigh. "Zecht, is that you? Want to call your dogs off?" As she spoke, Heizl edged sideways to stand between the noble and the nearest men.

"No need to act tough, Fitz," the Shadow chuckled as he pushed through the line of men and women. "Though I guess I understand the urge to impress your girl there. Hey, I'm Zecht."

"I am not *her's*," muttered Jilia.

Heizl waved a free hand. "Not now." She ignored the icy look Jilia shot her. "Where's Renyar?"

"Someone shut the door," drawled Zecht. "And find a new bar or something." On either side, weapons slid back into sheathes and pockets, though more than one hand stayed close enough for a quick draw. "Come on, he's in the back. He wasn't expecting you to bring a guest though."

"Yeah, well, I wasn't expecting you to betray me, but here we are."

"Fitz, you realise you're here to join us, right?"

"Dunno about that." Heizl glanced down at the Claw. "You saw what the warleader managed against a bunch of ill-prepared militia." A few of those closest to her edged away.

Zecht grinned. "Maybe you didn't notice, but these aren't a bunch of backwater savages. Raiders, revolutionaries, anarchists – they all know how to swing steel better than those barbarians did."

"If you're finished." Jilia stepped forward. "We came to see Renyar."

The Shadow's grin only widened. "I like her." He pointed a thumb over his shoulder. "Come on."

Heizl glanced at Jilia, though she couldn't read the expression upon the noblewoman's perfect features. She smiled anyway, as much to reassure herself as to encourage her friend. As Zecht turned his back to walk towards an old foreman's office, they followed. Passing rows of cheap wooden bunks, the mage took in the warehouse interior old – shelves and boxes pushed to one side – and dismissed it just as quickly.

The blond man didn't knock on the worn door that he came to, shoving it open with one hand instead. Clean, green light – flowing, not flickering – shone out past the wooden frame. As they stepped in, Renyar didn't look up from the paper-strewn desk between them. His sword, black and silver scabbard and all, lay upon the table's surface a few inches from his hand, weighing down several stacks of notes. A dozen tiny, glowing orbs in characteristic green orbited his head, illuminating the curling script upon each sheet with a steady, even light.

Beside her in the doorway, Heizl heard Jilia's sharp intake of breath. She considered saying something to her, before shaking her head and stepping into the room.

Heizl started to speak, but Renyar beat her to it. "You're late." The Thalan glanced up, grey eyes flicking between the trio of Imperials before returning to his papers. "Why aren't you alone?"

For the second time in as many moments, the mage began to answer. This time however, it was Jilia who interrupted her. "It wasn't Heizl's decision." She eyed her sidelong in defiance. "I wanted to meet you."

"A pleasure, Lady Strahl," he replied distractedly, without looking back up. "Though you understand that I can't let you leave here now. Our strategy relies on secrecy."

Unbidden, Heizl felt her grip on the Claw tighten and she found herself edging forwards. Jilia's hand on her arm, not for the first time, stopped her.

"I haven't come here to undermine you, Patriarch. I'd like to talk."

Renyar slowly looked up. His gaze fixed on Jilia and, to her credit, she returned the hard stare. A wry smile flickered to life upon his lips. "You may've heard that talking is a talent of mine."

"There are... rumours." A hint of uncertainty crept into the noble's tone.

"Tell me–" He stopped mid-command as the Claw's bone-tip pressed against his shoulder. His gaze shifted sideways. "I'm sorry, Heizl, did you have something to add?"

Her hand trembled, the point wavering where it rested against Renyar, dragging at the fine fabric of his shirt. The Thalan didn't seem to notice. "You're not giving any commands today, snake."

"I'm not so callous as to discuss anything unnecessary with the young lady. That'd be irresponsible." He stood, chair sliding backwards and a hand coming up to grip the bronze haft. "However, please don't think you could stop me if you turned against me."

Heizl's jaw bunched as she struggled not to thrust the Claw straight through the man. Beside the pair, Zecht's hands dropped to his sheathed knives as he glanced between them. Sweat beaded on the Shadow's forehead, though he didn't move.

"You couldn't handle some fur-skinned savage with this thing, so what makes you think things would end well against me?" Heizl said through clenched teeth.

Renyar smiled and, ever so gently, drew his free hand through the air. Arcs of pearlescent green formed on all sides of the spear, holding it in place as he took a half-step away. "There are no spirits here to hinder me." He gestured past Heizl to where men filled the doorway. "Besides, I'm not alone."

"You don't have enough," Jilia spoke in a quiet, thoughtful voice.

"More than enough to deal with young Heizl here," Renyar replied.

"Perhaps. I don't know as much as I'd like about magic, or dragons, or anything," she mused. "You'd probably lose a lot of them though, and might get hurt yourself, which I don't think would help, Patriarch. That's not what I mean though."

For the first time that Heizl could remember, Renyar's face twisted in confusion. Jilia continued. "You've maybe a hundred men in here, and you can't have more than a dozen of these safehouses anywhere else, or someone would have noticed."

The Thalan slowly turned to face her directly as she spoke, and Heizl couldn't help but do the same. She knew that Dasimir had trained Jilia to someday succeed him, but still.

"Even with however many Seorsans are in their embassy – assuming their actions are related to you somehow – the garrisons will outnumber you at least... three-to-one? You've not got enough men to take the city."

Zecht snorted a disbelieving laugh, but no one else spoke. After a moment, Renyar shook his head. "I see that I'm not the only one with a silver tongue, my lady."

Jilia blushed and turned to pull a seat over. She sat, adjusting her skirts, and looked between the two Fragment-bearers. She gestured, and Renyar sat down opposite, eyes narrowed but a faint smile twisting one corner of his lips.

Heizl had all but forgotten the green shells holding the spear until she tried to sit down herself. For a second it refused to budge, like a boot stuck in thick mud. With conscious effort, she yanked it free, Renyar's spell shattering.

Flashing a proud grin, Heizl sat too. The Thalan rolled his eyes at her feat, though his own smile faded at the sight of his magic so easily defeated.

"I assume you have other assets, Patriarch? Those willing to make sacrifices for your cause?" said Jilia. "If you're here personally, you must feel confident that you're ready to stage... what, an intervention?"

"I trust, my lady, that your questions are benevolent in nature? Your paramour's attitude led me to believe that there was a confrontational element to your visit."

"Heizl and I are friends," she said, though the mage saw a glint of something in her expression. Mischief, caution, or regret, she couldn't be sure. "The Empire's on the verge of collapse. I hoped that you might provide a better alternative."

Renyar leant back. "I have no intention of taking Rufenrich's crown, merely in..." His gaze strayed to Heizl, and then to the Claw. "...Reducing collateral damage."

"May I ask who'd lead after?" said Jilia.

"I've already spoken of this with Heizl."

"Patriarch," Jilia smiled, a coy tone coming to her voice. "Respectfully, I'd like to hear it from you."

"Whether he abdicates or is removed in a different way, an appropriate regent would be required, my lady, until I have the opportunity to assess the Crown Prince. Someone with ties to both the Konreig family and one of the Empire's most renowned institutions." His eyes shifted to Heizl before returning to the noblewoman. "Or a skilled administrator who understands the Court's wiles."

"Good." She nodded thoughtfully. "You still haven't answered my question though."

"I've provided you assurances, Miss Strahl."

"No, I mean about your other assets. Individuals? Mages? People like him?" She pointed towards Zecht, who flinched back at the attention.

Renyar took a calming breath as he leant forward onto his elbows, steepling slender fingers. "I admit to desiring some reassurance myself. What's to prevent you two upstanding citizens from delivering such answers into the hands of the Emperor and his Shadows?"

"The Empire's in shambles." Jilia mimicked his movement until their faces lay less than a foot from one another. Seeing the proximity, Heizl's hands balled into fists and heat rose in her cheeks. "Fjujhost is in open rebellion. Rumour has it that Seorsa has broken both the Third Fleet and the Fifth Army. The Vigil beg for support against the Stricken. If something doesn't change, there won't be an Empire for much longer. You might just be better than the alternative. Besides–" A cold smile spread across her face. "–I thought you weren't foolish enough to let us walk out of here unescorted."

"Good enough," said Renyar. "Anything to add, Heizl?"

Heizl blinked several times. She'd always prided herself on her cunning and charm, but, for the first time in a long while, she felt almost out of her depth. Crossing her arms over her chest, she raised her chin. "Jilia's said everything worth saying. You gonna answer her now?"

Renyar wasted no more time. He slid several sheets of paper across the table separating them. "We've resources. Both Spire and radical mages, a few Shadows, and a number of troops. I believe it's enough to disrupt an organised response long enough to remove the Emperor as a threat."

Jilia passed a finger down the first sheet, glancing over a list of names and numbers before pushing it aside. "How many more men do you need?"

"What're you implying?"

She smiled. "My father has signed contracts with several mercenary companies since your appearance at the Palace. Including our existing house men-at-arms, there are probably almost a thousand men in the city dressed in Strahl colours."

"Lord Strahl is also among the Throne's most ardent supporters," Renyar replied.

"Yeah, Dasimir's an utter killjoy," drawled Heizl without thinking. "There's no way in the Void that he'll throw his lot in with you. Jilia, I know you two are family, but sometimes I don't get how you two are related."

"Love *can* make people do strange things..." Jilia nodded in thought.

"Wait, can we go back a step?" Heizl raised a hand as her conscious mind caught up with her glib tongue. "You're going to just *remove* the garrison? That's over two thousand men. You can't possibly command all of them." Her gaze fell to the spear and a whisper escaped her lips. "...Though I bet with that Tongue of yours I might manage it."

The Thalan ignored the implication. "I just need to order a number of officers. Enough to make them suggestible when a series of forged orders arrive on their desks."

"Okay, fine." Clenching her eyes shut, she shook the violent urge away. "That might work, but what about Vandel? Word on the street is that last time you tangled with the Champ you didn't come off so well."

Renyar cleared his throat. "I was not aware of your Imperial Champion's identity during my last visit. The two of us have... history."

"Yeah, about that. You've the Tongue, and all that magic of yours besides – just how did an old man with a sword chase you off before?"

"I'm curious about that too..." said Jilia distractedly, head tilted back to study the low ceiling.

He leant back in his seat. "We can discuss my relationship to 'Vandel' another time. Know simply that I'll lure him away, and thus leave the Emperor open to more direct assault."

"And just who do you think's gonna do that? As if I need to ask." Heizl shook her head.

"I'd hoped that Elhin would return from her own task in time to lead the assault, but contact with that particular lieutenant has been... sporadic. We must do the most good that we can with the choices before us."

"I wouldn't mind knowing a little more about her myself." Heizl mused. At the shocked but amused expression on Jilia's face – eyebrows high and a faint smile on one side of her mouth – a brief flash of embarrassed panic shot through the mage. "No, I meant that–"

Renyar saved her from herself with his interruption. "Even with your Claw, a direct attack would not be guaranteed."

"That's just one reason why you haven't sold me on this insane plan."

"And the others?"

"Oh, I don't know. Selling my country out? Betraying my family? Still not buying your whole story? Pick one!"

"Your Empire, Heizl, is divided, with the wealthy prepared to clash over their claims to power. It might last a generation without intervention, but I doubt it will stand any longer than that. Your family? The Emperor ushers destruction and dominion into the world, while his heir is untested and consumed by his own inadequacy. I offer you a chance to set right what others have done wrong. I offer you a chance to build a better world, where people are recognised for who they are, not for their heritage and the opportunities that they seize along the way."

"I think he's right," Jilia said in a low, measured voice before she had a chance to respond. "Even if your uncle isn't about to do something dangerous, you know how things are. There's so much judgement in the Court, and the people in the streets aren't any better. The Empire hasn't always been united – it's only a matter of time before someone breaks it further. If we're involved, we can at least steer it towards the best outcome."

Heizl grimaced. It wasn't that she didn't believe the things being said. For as long as she could remember, she'd had thoughts that ran in much the same direction. Her issue was more with admitting them. If it was true – every imperfection in every system that surrounded her – and she only decided to do something about it now that someone offered her an incentive, what did that say about her? Was she truly the sort of person who stood by until they could gain from it themselves? Did it even matter?

"Please, Heizl?" said Jilia, eyes wide. "If we've got the chance to do some good, isn't it down to people like us to try to improve things? At least think about it? For me?"

"Dammit! Fine." Heizl stamped her foot. "It's got to be done, I get it. It doesn't mean I have to like it though. Neither does it alter the fact that it's not going to work in the first place!"

The noblewoman looked up, a sly light in her eyes. "You're right, we need more men."

"Jilia." Heizl reached out and placed a hand upon her knee, feeling her own conflict subside. "We know. It's not like either of us can wave a hand and magic up an army."

She brushed her hand away. "We just need to persuade my father to join us."

Heizl arched an eyebrow. "We've already discussed that, haven't we? I don't see how–"

"I'm not finished, Heizl. Maybe persuade isn't the right word. Coerce." Jilia winced slightly. "He'd do anything for me." Across the desk, Renyar leant upon the surface again, but didn't speak as he waited for her to continue. "It's simple, really. I don't go back home. If you can forge orders that will move an army, your people can manage a ransom note, I'm sure. I'll want to see it before it gets sent – no one knows a father like his little girl."

"Void take me," Zecht muttered. "Lady, that's pretty dark."

She shrugged. "Father is blinded by his ambition. That, and his relationship with the Emperor. Too many of his decisions have been shortsighted and impulsive. Someone has to do something, for the good of both Kragiv-Stal and the Empire."

"I'm not sure I'd describe our choices here today quite like that–" Renyar cocked his head as he regarded her. "–but I'm glad you have joined me so wholeheartedly."

"Yeah, yeah, keep it in your breeches." Heizl waved her free hand. "We've probably found you an army, and my Claw gives you the muscle to spearhead all this. Now what?"

"Now?" Renyar smiled. "Now it's time for you to commit treason."

Tooth and Nail – Chapter Eighteen

> *"There were almost as many reasons for the war as there were men fighting it. Lord Kuhlner claimed he would put power into the hands of a parliament, enforcing checks upon the Throne, and restoring political power to the Church. Across the divide, the Royal Family maintained that dire times rose upon the horizon, and that only the clear vision and single purpose of the Crown could protect the Empire and its peoples. Regardless, upon the death of the Royal heir, Myron Konreig, any calming influence between the two factions was lost."*
>
> Common Imperial History,
> The Second Imperial Civil War,
> Archimand Märchen (408 I.Y.)

2nd day of Ehnaln, 406th Imperial Year
17th Year of Emperor Rufenrich Konreig's Reign

"Y'know, I can't help but feel like we shouldn't be here," Heizl whispered from the corner of her mouth.

"Having second thoughts, Fitz?" Zecht replied, a little louder.

"Keep your voice down," she hissed as they stepped beneath the open gates to the Imperial Palace. Guards in blue uniforms eyed them warily. "The only thing I'm reconsidering is whether you're actually going to be of any help."

"Ah, lay off." The Shadow punched her in the arm. "You wouldn't have made it this far without me."

Heizl sighed, and brushed down her finely tailored grey shirt. "Do you think Renyar'd silence you again if I asked him nicely?"

She dismissed Zecht's reply with a wave. The Claw had grown quiet as if in anticipation. Heizl didn't even feel the need to nudge aside the attention of those around them. With the familiar surroundings and the veiled looks of servants, it felt like coming home.

They passed the Great Hall, where labourers carried out the finishing touches on its repairs. Only a handful of nights had passed since Renyar's surprise attack, but already the signs of chaos and destruction had almost disappeared. Imperial taxes hard at work. Elsewhere, messengers carried word from one wing of the palace to the other. It wouldn't be long before they spread news of Heizl's assault. One problem at a time though.

Febrile with rising fear, the air in her mouth grew as thick as morning fog and clung to her throat. A street crier had announced an advancing Seorsan army to the general public just that morning. By the time the pair had reached the Palace, few talked about anything else. The whispers of the noble courts had finally reached the commonfolk. Perhaps it'd helped to persuade much of Reiget City's garrison to leave the capital on training exercises. The Nexus would be filled with mages and their Shadows at the news, helping Hastigr send men and orders across the Empire. Heizl couldn't have planned it much better herself.

A blue-clad guardsman pushed open a door and waved them through without saluting. Neither of them reacted. Flickering flames replaced the light of day as they walked down the stone steps within.

It didn't feel like she'd stumbled this way little more than a week ago reeking of sweat and smoke. In spite of the things she'd suffered, Heizl felt significantly better than when she'd last walked to the Emperor's private office. It was probably for the best too, with what they hoped to accomplish.

Down the short passageway, and the pair stopped at another door. Two more Royal Guardsmen stood to either side of its reinforced wooden panels.

Heizl paused before them both. "The Emperor's expecting us." The soldiers looked from mage to Shadow doubtfully. Their meeting was today, right? Rolling her eyes, she gestured to the closed door. "You might get in trouble if you keep me waiting." That was true, at least, if a little misleading.

In her hand, the Claw stirred. Heizl gripped tighter, willing the guards not to notice. They were probably close enough now for them to just kick the door in and seize the Emperor. She'd seen the destruction it had wrought in the hands of the Norjan warleader. The idea held a certain visceral appeal, but the slightest mistake could spell failure. Gently moving her hand down the shaft, Heizl readied herself to lunge.

One guard raised a fist and rapped upon the door. As she recognised the tired voice that emerged a moment later, Heizl relaxed.

"What?" called Rufenrich.

The soldier didn't take his gaze from Heizl as he answered. "Your Majesty, your niece is here to see you."

"What? Now?!"

A flurry of movement drowned out anything else he might've said, and the door flew open. The Royal Guardsman stepped aside as the most powerful man in the Empire barged past to wrap arms around the mage. Heizl flinched at the contact, and didn't immediately return the embrace. Before she'd the chance to even decide whether or not to return the hug, Rufenrich stepped back to look her up and down. "Come on, join us. We've a lot to talk about."

Heizl shrugged, freeing her shoulders from the Emperor's grip. She glanced at the strange knife at his belt, with its discoloured metal, but nodded anyway. It'd take more than a dagger to stop her plans coming to fruition. "That's... I'd like that." She forced a smile and allowed herself to be ushered into Rufenrich's study. "Zecht should come too."

The Emperor slowly nodded. "You're right. A second, firsthand, point-of-view might be helpful. Frida's here – he can report directly."

Renyar had said that the Shadowmaster would be at the Forge, outside the city. Would her presence change things? Too late to change her mind now.

Within, the room had changed little since Heizl's last time there. The same scattering of souvenirs and belongings lay upon the desk, the same books sat unread on their shelves, and a mostly untouched tray of refreshments rested upon a low table. Only the chairs and their occupants differed. Four of the six plush, cushioned seats rested in corners or against the walls. The remaining two faced one another near the office's centre.

A mage and a Shadow, neither of which Heizl recognised, stood against the far wall. Her gaze lingered on the two unfamiliar women. With the Spire spread thin by news of Seorsan aggression, it seemed that a Highmage couldn't be spared, not even for the Throne's safety.

A week ago she'd have flashed a smile or found the time to share a word with one of the other women. Now though, Heizl's mind instead kindled upon thoughts of Jilia. She never would've imagined that the noblewoman might've even hinted at sharing her feelings. Distractions like that right now though could get them all killed.

For a second, Heizl felt like she'd stepped back in time, so similar to stepping into this room with her cousin. Just a week ago it had all seemed so much simpler.

"There aren't enough seats," Zecht mumbled, uncertain.

Frida stood from her own chair, brushing down her dark uniform. Heizl took a short step back, shaking her head. She hadn't spotted the Shadowmaster there, she'd sat so still. "Shadow, I trust that you recognise the honour His Majesty shows in inviting you here. You may stand until called upon."

The blond man had the sense not to aggravate the Shadowmaster further by replying. With a quick salute, he moved to stand beside the reinforced door.

Rufenrich ignored their exchange and pulled up another chair to join them. Turning, a concerned smile upon his lips, he gestured towards his own seat, and sat upon the one he'd dragged over.

As Heizl edged towards the chair, she thought she caught Rufenrich glance towards the Claw. She squeezed a little tighter as she sat. She wouldn't let him, or anyone else, take it from her. Not now, not ever. With them both seated, Frida joined them, staring intently at the young mage. Still standing by the door, Zecht shuffled his feet.

After a moment, Rufenrich broke the waxing silence. "New dress, Heizl?"

She glanced down at the clean, grey fabric. "After living in the same clothes the whole time I was travelling, I thought I'd try something fresher."

"Well, I can empathise with that, though I preferred your old clothes," he said. "I'd have preferred it if you'd come straight here after getting back though. What happened?"

Heizl hesitated. "How... I told you all about it already."

All faces – royal, Shadows, and mage – turned towards her. Rufenrich opened his mouth a few times, the words slow in coming. "Heizl... I don't understand?"

"I..." She glanced past Frida. Zecht stared back at her with the same confused expression as the rest of them. "We discussed this already, after I got back."

Rufenrich composed himself, holding his hands in his lap. "This is the first time I've seen you since you left." He glanced at the Shadowmaster before looking back. Across the room, the Spire mage and her Shadow straightened. "Where've you been?"

Heizl ignored the question. Against the palm of her hand, the Claw's bronze shaft felt warm to the touch. "You saw me just a few days ago."

"No." Rufenrich leant closer. "I didn't." He held up a hand to forestall a response. "You reached the Nexus a few nights ago, but disappeared between there and the Palace. We've had people out looking for you. I was worried."

The Fragment's warmth grew, its heat becoming almost unbearable. Heizl's scalp prickled with sweat, and her head throbbed. With her free hand, she reached up and pinched the bridge of her nose. It didn't make sense. "I came and spoke with you," she whispered.

"Frida," Rufenrich said softly. "Contact Highmage Ortharn. I think we're in need of a healer."

"She's currently stationed in western Tarnon." The Shadowmaster's eyes narrowed. "I'll have a message sent after our meeting."

The Emperor nodded. "Heizl, it's clear you've experienced a lot. I can't begin to imagine what you must have gone through in Norjhost to get back so quickly with..." His gaze drifted to the Claw and back, and Heizl felt something instinctive sweep through her. "If I'd known it would have this effect on you, I'd have sent someone else... But we haven't got long. Seorsa continues to march through our territory. The Comet'll be at its peak in a few days. We all need to be at our best. Why don't you go rest?"

Her vision blurred, her skin crawled, and her head spun. Rufenrich was lying to her, but she didn't know why. It wasn't like he had to keep up appearances for anyone here. There was more going on than she knew, that much was obvious. She'd have to be careful. "Are you sure? I remember talking to you." Behind Frida, Zecht frowned in confusion; it wasn't much different to his usual expression.

"It's alright, you're probably just tired from your ordeal. Why don't you tell me all about it... again."

This wasn't how it was meant to go. How could he just lie like that, and pretend to still care? Had her family always been this way? The rest of the Imperial Court were a bunch of backstabbing, brown-nosing deceivers, but she'd never thought that of Thaun or Rufenrich. How wrong she'd been.

"Why are you doing this?" Heizl whispered, eyes not rising from her spear. "I wanted to be wrong, but I guess lying to your niece isn't such a big deal when you're betraying the whole damn Empire."

"Betrayal?" He replied. "I'm not–"

"Don't bother!" Heizl surged to her feet, looking down on the Emperor. Across from them, Frida rose more gracefully, muscles tensed as if preparing to pounce. "I know what you're doing! However you justify it, summoning Urathear is damn stupid!" She kept talking, growing in volume as she spoke over the Emperor's reply. The Claw shivered in her grip. "Haven't you thought about anyone else? How your pursuit of power will endanger thousands? How making me question myself might hurt me? I thought you were better than that. You don't deserve to lead."

"You're not well, Heizl." Rufenrich stood too. "I don't know what happened in Norjhost, but something's wrong with you. Is it the Fragment?" He gestured towards the spear.

"I'm better than I've been in a long time," she growled. "Frankly, I'm pissed off with people thinking there's something wrong with me. Just because I'm a mage, just because mum's gone, everyone treats me like I'm less than them. Well, they can't do it now."

"I've never treated you differently," said Rufenrich, hurt creeping into his voice. "Just put the spear down and we can talk about all this."

"Never treated...?" She barked a laugh. "Thaun was always your favourite. Admit it, I've always been an afterthought to you." The Emperor took a short step back as if struck. "You only sent me off to find this cursed thing to get me out of the way. You probably thought I'd fail, never coming back to embarrass you." The caustic lightning in her veins smouldered, and one corner of Heizl's mouth twisted up in a sneer. "Well, here I am."

"None of that's true." Rufenrich steadied himself. "This isn't you, Heizl. That spear, I never should've sent you to find it. It's done something to you."

"It's done more for me since I got it than you've done for me my entire life!"

Heizl never discovered what response he might've given. The door flew open and a Royal Guardsman rushed in. Zecht jumped away from the soldier's path, while Frida half-turned to face the disturbance. She didn't leave Rufenrich's side, unwilling to abandon him to Heizl's growing revelations. In the room's corner, the Spire mage and her Shadow nodded to one another before edging apart.

"Your Majesty!" the soldier panted. Heizl hid a smile. It was about time.

"How expedient," said the Shadowmaster, eyeing Heizl. "Captain, call for the guard."

"Impossible, ma'am." He shook his head. "They're engaged already."

"What?" Her composed expression slipped. Tearing her gaze from Heizl, she looked at the guardsman. "Where? And with who?"

"Everywhere, sir. There's chaos in the streets. The City Watch are fighting fires and riots. The Spire's under attack by Thalans, and men in Strahl colours have assaulted the gates."

"Dasimir? Really? Acquiel maybe, but... That can't be right," said Rufenrich, his attention slipping from Heizl. "What about the garrison?"

"They're out of the city–"

"What?!" All of them?"

The guard had the decency to look abashed. "Most of them, Your Majesty. The officer corps received your orders to carry out training and manoeuvres outside the city in preparation for a Seorsan offensive."

Rufenrich spoke a crude word that Heizl had never heard him use before. She blushed as the Emperor composed himself. "Captain, take a squad and relay my orders. Recall the garrison from their exercises. Get someone through the lines to the Nexus – we need the First back." He hesitated, and glanced at Frida. "Have the Champion attend me."

"Your Majesty..." The officer winced. "Sir Vandel left the Palace an hour ago. He said that someone had seen Renyar down in the city. You didn't know?"

Frida pointed out the doorway behind the soldier. "The other orders. Go. Now."

Heizl fell within herself at the Shadowmaster's words, and so missed Frida's flinch. Her own thread to the soldier was a weak, nascent thing, but it'd be enough. With her grip tight upon the warm surface of the Claw, she barely noticed the trickle of power fueling her sorcery. Travelling the short distance along the strand, she wove confusion and doubt into the man's bond to the Shadowmaster. She couldn't afford any orders getting out. A united resistance would end their plans all too swiftly.

Mundane vision returning to her eyes, Heizl smiled as she saw the soldier standing numbly, rubbing at his head. Her expression faded as cold steel stroked her throat.

A punching dagger's short blade protruded from between the knuckles of the Shadowmaster's clenched fist. Its point grazed Heizl's skin, and a thin trickle of blood ran down her neck and its growing scathe.

"No magic, Miss Fitzerin," she whispered. "Drop your weapon, and sit down with your hands where I can see them and your eyes open." Frida turned her head a fraction of an inch towards the officer. "Follow your–"

A grunt interrupted Frida's commands as Zecht threw a knife. Its blade cut across her ribs, slicing cloth and drawing blood, before skidding away to disappear into a dark corner.

The blond man followed a split second later, wielding a pair of daggers. His first slash caught Frida's shirt front, drawing blood as she dodged away. The pair, both dressed in black and with blades in hand, joined in a twisting, violent dance.

Heizl shrugged nonchalantly despite how close to failure that they'd come. With the Claw's power at her fingertips, the thought of failure scarcely crossed her mind. She would've liked to talk a little more, and maybe even to enjoy some of the refreshments before them, but that would wait for now.

She levelled the spear towards the Emperor. The time for sharp remarks and final pleas had passed. Rufenrich seemed to understand this just as well as she did. He pulled free a familiar, ancient-looking dagger. The man – did she even know him? – shifted into a defensive stance, holding the blade as if it were much larger.

In a heartbeat she found the fledgling threads joining the Claw and her Emperor. A fledgling, hollow light flickered in his blade. Darkness descended, dimming her vision, but not as much as it had once. She could almost see the room's other occupants.

A thousand times before, she'd read people's emotions to better predict them. A hundred times before she'd manipulated such bonds to her own ends. A dozen times before she'd toyed with minds and emotions to satisfy her own needs. None of those approaches would work here.

The spear's raging core glimmered through its cracked shell. Its light cast more threads into silhouette, linking the Claw to every soul in the room.

As naturally as stroking an ego, Heizl drew power out of the Fragment and sent it running the length of the thread that reached towards Rufenrich. She'd only ever felt a trickle of the Claw's power before, hinting at some deep well of destructive strength. Now, it emerged as if she'd opened a floodgate.

Through half-lidded eyes, she watched as a bolt of grey energy wreathed in purple lightning leapt from the weapon's ivory head towards the Emperor. Heizl wondered, just for a moment, if the warleader – or anyone else for that matter – could've done the same.

Her wonder faded as it curved unnaturally towards the pale dagger in Rufenrich's hand. Not the gentle arc that Korten's flames had towards Elhin's shield, but a distracted redirection as if spotting an old friend. For a second, a dark chain formed between spear and blade. Heizl blinked, checking that she still looked out through mortal eyes. Her attack winked out, and the Emperor stepped back, weapon held before him. It glowed for a moment, as if fresh from the forge, before fading to a dull ivory.

"This isn't you, Heizl." Rufenrich kept his eyes on her as if an antique dagger hadn't just saved his life. "It's not too late. Put that thing down and we can talk it all through. We can get you help."

Anger welling back up within her, Heizl pointed at Rufenrich once more.

The Spire mage interrupted. With one hand holding open a small book, she stretched her other out towards Heizl, a fine chain dangling from her wrist. Faint mauve light rippled in her palm, and her shirt whispered in an unseen wind. That glow, violet-tinted and nebulous, turned to something solid that leapt from her hand. The air cracking, three more of the darts followed in rapid succession.

Moving from the missiles' path, Heizl didn't dodge quickly enough. Sorcery sliced through her new, grey clothes and impacted her flesh like needles.

Letting out a bestial roar, Heizl pivoted and aimed at the Spire mage instead. Grey and purple filled the gap between them.

The loyal mage threw up her hands. Her focus, that slender chain of silver, glinted between graceful fingers. Palms out, the destructive force struck her swiftly-raised wards. Sickly, green light flashed for an instant before disappearing within the dark cloud. Here and there, like cheap glass through fog, her protective magicks flickered within Heizl's attack. Beneath the assault, the Spire Mage's partial-dome was driven back, its jagged, emerald edges slicing into the leather and parchment of so many books. Her Shadow wisely dove away from the sorcerous clash.

Another growl escaped Heizl's curled lips as she called upon more of the Claw's power. The other mage screamed. Golden sparks spiralled out as her green shield, riven with cracks, swirled with blue. At her feet, carpet and floor disintegrated, and sweat poured from her paling skin.

With a final cry, the mage's magic gave out. She could hold off the Claw's inexorable assault no more. Heizl's blast struck raised hands first, blistering and cracking flesh. The loyal woman's arms disappeared into the rolling wave of grey and purple even as she recoiled. Her shriek ceased as the sorcery enveloped her, and her desiccated corpse struck the wall behind her.

Heizl looked down at the Fragment in her hand. She'd never seen or felt anything like it. Even Korten, the Spire's most promising battlemage in a generation, would've struggled to do anything so impressive.

The loyal Shadow gave Heizl no more time to appreciate the power that she held. Spire mage dead, the woman lashed out in vengeful desperation. A slender sword, fine Imperial steel, swept towards Heizl. Retreating, her chair skidding away as her legs struck it, she raised the spear to block more quickly than she knew how. The bronze rang at the impact, and the weapon jerked in her hand like a dog pulling at its leash.

The spearhead lunged towards Heizl's foe, twisting around a parry to slice into her forearm. As if struck by a mighty blow, the Shadow staggered back. Pain and anger tainting her features, the other woman dodged a sweep of the weapon and stepped in to strike. The spear's butt flew up, dragging Heizl's grip with it, and struck the Shadow in the chin. As she recoiled, Heizl stabbed again, and felt the sharp point penetrate the woman's chest. The Shadow collapsed to the floor, tumbling from the ancient ivory.

Breath heavy in her lungs, Heizl leant on the spear. Sweat marred her grip, but it kept her upright. She hadn't realised how tired she'd become.

Turning, she caught the end of Frida and Zecht's duel.

In spite of her injuries and his ambush, the Shadowmaster had proved her suitability in leading the Empire's secret police. Administration and age had done little to dull her edges. Her empty hands struck out, turning aside the younger fighter's slashes and cuts as they circled one another. Blood continued to pour from her wounds, but damp patches now marred his clothes as well. She'd reduced Zecht to a single knife, the floor around them littered with several more blades where she'd disarmed him.

After an ill-timed lunge, the Shadowmaster struck. One arm wrapping under and around his arm, Frida slid in and twisted, launching her rebellious subordinate over one hip. The Shadow slammed into the table. Refreshments scattered as glass broke.

Heizl watched as Frida half-crouched over Zecht, still holding his arm. She pulled it back, her knee pressed against his elbow, and began pushing it towards an unnatural angle.

As Heizl drew once more on the Claw, the Shadowmaster looked up. Her knees bent to jump away from the attack, but she stumbled as Zecht's hand latched around her ankle.

The cloud of purple lightning consumed Frida in her entirety.

Ignoring Zecht's attempts to struggle to his feet or the corpses around them, Heizl turned to where Rufenrich had stood. Nothing but empty space greeted her.

"Where is he?!" she demanded. The room lay in chaos, the only movement that of Zecht struggling to rise. She saw no sign of the Emperor.

The Shadow shrugged before wincing in pain at the movement. "He must have scarpered," he said.

"I can see that!" snapped Heizl, before lowering her voice. "He was actually here, wasn't he?"

"Something wrong with you, Fitz? 'Course he was here."

The mage slumped down into Rufenrich's chair, exhausted. "It should've worked."

"It prolly would've if he hadn't blocked that purple thing of yours." Zecht leant heavily upon the back of Frida's empty chair opposite. "Damn impressive what y'did there. How'd he stop it? Is he a mage or something?"

"I'd have known before now if he was." She reached down and picked up a broken piece of biscuit before shoving it into her mouth. "No, that dagger..." Heizl blinked several times, another headache growing behind her eyes. "I... What was I...?"

She didn't hear the Shadow's immediate answer, for darkness overtook her. Swirling violet patterns flooded her vision. Shattered shapes and broken lines in a dozen shades she couldn't describe made up that brief world. A moment later and they faded, replaced by a flickering flame of the same colour upon an endless, grey background. For a while, an eerie silence accompanied the fire, but, after what seemed an eternity, a whistling, wind-like noise grew.

Heizl nearly stabbed Zecht when he shook her awake. Still, the Shadow guided the spearhead away from him with the back of one hand. "Fitz? You alright?"

She rubbed at her eyes. "I'm fine. Come on, we should look for Rufenrich."

"No point." Zecht shrugged, and for the first time Heizl saw the fresh cuts over his black uniform. A guardsman's sword hung from his hand. "He'll be long gone by now."

"Don't be stupid." She struggled to rise, before slumping back into the cushioned chair. "He can't have got far."

"He left here like an hour ago. You were out cold the whole time."

She'd only blacked out for a moment, hadn't she? Her gaze sank to the Claw and its many dents and cracks. Even discounting the Emperor's lies, she'd begun to realise that her memory couldn't entirely be relied upon.

She narrowed her eyes. "What did I miss?"

"Just me heroically fending off half the Royal Guard while you caught up on your beauty sleep."

"Shade..." Heizl hissed a warning.

"Fine." He let the sword drop from his hand and slumped into the late Shadowmaster's chair. "The city's ours, pretty much. The gates, Spire, and Palace, anywhere worth having. Renyar's not shown up yet, but his boys are clearing out the corners and looking for your uncle. He can't have got far."

"What about Jilia? Is she okay?"

"She's our hostage, right Fitz? Why would we bring her out in the middle of all this?"

"Zecht..." her tone became a growl.

"Yeesh." The Shadow rolled his eyes. "She's probably fine. Can't you relax just a little? We've won. No way he'll summon that demon now."

She fought the urge to blast her companion through the nearest wall. "It's a dragon, idiot. While the Emperor is still out there, that ritual can still happen. This isn't over."

"And here I was hoping we could put our feet up for a bit." Zecht did exactly that, balancing his boots over the edge of the upturned table and closing his eyes. "Dunno if you noticed, but it's been a rough week."

Grey and purple lanced out towards the nearest bookshelf, passing the Shadow by mere inches. As the outburst subsided, paper drifted to the floor. "I said that this isn't over. Now get out there and *find him*!"

Tooth and Nail – Chapter Nineteen

"Who can say what observer first wrote of Sheltz's Comet? Certainly there are ancient records from the time of the Urlanst Empire that describe an ominous star amongst the Void. Scholars the world over prescribed meaning to such sights, be they Oesel, Thalan, or Daqini. It was Sheltz though who first postulated that each celestial event was but the return of the same portent."

Astrology and the Uloric Church,
Father Goland of Tarnac (370 I.Y.)

3rd day of Ehnaln, 406th Imperial Year
17th Year of Emperor Rufenrich Konreig's Reign

Thaun jerked awake, one hand shooting out to seek reassurance. His fingers touched only air. Someone should've sat with him. That absence lingered for a moment before he remembered where he'd fallen asleep.

Lena lay upon a low bed at the tent's centre, the sheets soaked through with old blood and fresh sweat. Even with so few living left to use it, they'd run out of clean bedding the day before. The mage lay in the same position as she had when they'd dragged her away from their hard-won victory over Elhin. Beneath the covers, her flesh twitched and writhed.

They'd cut away the remnants of her bloodied armour, and heaped it in one corner. Her silvered axe leant against the wrecked cloth. Both Thaun and Sigren had added almost all of their own equipment to the pile. Only the strange shield that they'd taken from the Thalans remained with Thaun, resting upon his thighs. He didn't feel ready to discard it.

The Shadow himself perched at Lena's feet. Since the healer's injury, Sigren had yet to leave her side. A few half-eaten meals littered the floor.

Victory held a bitter taste.

Thaun stood, scratching at his patchy stubble while pinning the bronze shield beneath one arm. "Any news?"

Sigren shook his head without looking up. "A cutter came and forced some honey and water down her throat. Some willow bark for the pain too. She hasn't woken though."

"What about her... swelling?"

The Shadow grunted a harsh laugh. "Seriously?" He cast him a narrow glare. "Lena healed herself so much that her own flesh grew beyond its limits. 'Swelling' doesn't cut it."

"I know." Thaun sighed. "If she was awake she'd probably tell me the right word."

"Yeah, well she's not awake. I could give you a few choice words if it'd make you shut up."

He flinched back. "Sigren, I'm sorry. If I'd known what she'd planned, I never would've let her go through with it."

The Shadow responded in little more than a whisper. "Repeating yourself for the hundredth time doesn't make it any better." His voice softened, though only by a fraction, as he gestured towards the bronze shield in Thaun's arms. "Toland wanted to take that thing off you while you slept. Dunno why you don't just put it with the rest of your junk."

He tightened his grip on the Fragment just a little. "You saw what this thing can do. I can't just leave it lying around." With a deep breath, he loosened the embrace. "Did Toland say anything else?"

"His Lordship produced a little more essence. Dunno where he got it from, but I don't really care right now. Lena's already drained it anyway. You'd think, with all Toland's riches and secrets, he'd have some more stashed away somewhere. He's probably just holding out on us."

"He wouldn't do that."

"And I wouldn't withhold it from you, if I did." The rustle of the tent's canvas flap accompanied Toland's voice. "I know how much Lena means to you both."

The Shadow slowly rose from where he sat, facing the noble. Thaun stepped between them, one arm still clutching the shield as he raised the other to prevent the Shadow from moving closer. His hand met Sigren's chest and he stopped short.

Toland didn't respond to the Shadow's aggressive posturing, instead nodding towards Lena. "Has there been any change?"

"I don't think so." Thaun glanced to where the healer lay unconscious and barely breathing. "She must be trying to heal herself. She can't have much strength left."

"Her tenacity does her credit." Toland followed Thaun's gaze to the mage. "I wouldn't believe it if I hadn't seen it myself, even if she is a Spire legacy. She's exhausted all of Korten's essence, as well as what we salvaged from the Thalan mages. God willing, our messengers will return from the Crossing and its beacon soon – perhaps they'll have found some more."

Thaun nodded slowly. He didn't believe his friend's words for a moment. Few mages on active duty had the chance to store up much essence personally. Most came from apprentices within the Spire, or those with less practical skills. Even with her position, Lena had been no exception. If not for Korten's cache, her healing would've given up days ago. Still, he appreciated Toland's attempts to reassure him.

"Did you want something?" Thaun asked.

The noble turned back to him. "I was hoping to persuade you to come with me for a walk."

"I... I can't leave. I want to be here when Lena wakes up." He wanted to say so much more. How he didn't know how to respond to Sigren's own grief. How he didn't know how to live up to his family's expectations. How he didn't know how to keep going with everything he felt.

"With all due respect–" Toland's eyes flickered to the healer's still form. "– you being here won't help her recover any more quickly. The men's spirits will improve at seeing you."

"They don't need me. I led them into this mess. More of them would still be alive if I hadn't." Thaun turned away.

"I'd suggest that they'd disagree with that opinion." Toland gave a bolstering smile. "They saw you on the frontline with them, willing to face Elhin even after... I think I was wrong about your choice to march with them. Come on, you should see for yourself." Mischief glimmered in his eyes. "Besides, the weather will change soon. There's more shelter in the ruins, and some of your men are refusing to leave here without you. Lena will be more comfortable there too."

Thaun rubbed at his face one-handed. They couldn't blame him that some stubborn soldiers didn't want to go inside before the weather worsened. Still, Lena couldn't make that sort of choice herself, not like this. He blew out a frustrated breath. "Fine. Sigren, will you make sure Lena's moved safely?"

The Shadow grunted something wordless in reply.

Toland shook his head, whether at Sigren's impertinence or Thaun's own reluctance, Thaun didn't know. "Thank you. We'll have the men sheltered by nightfall." He gestured to the tent's entrance. "Shall we?"

Thaun nodded reluctantly, and moved to follow.

"Hey." Sigren's voice made him pause. "At least take that stupid sword of yours. We don't know who else is still out there."

Thaun gave another nod, but said nothing as he buckled on his sword belt. Pulling on a raincloak, he followed Toland from the cramped tent.

Their camp, even smaller now, rested upon the hard, torn-up ground not far from where they'd first faced Elhin's forces. Disturbed boulders still loomed up here and there, tents pitched on their lee-sides. Soldiers in blue and yellow patrolled in reduced numbers around the perimeter, while others huddled close to fires. Tattered standards and company colours fluttered in the breeze like revenants.

Guilt welled up inside Thaun as he realised how the camp had clustered close to Lena's tent. Against normal procedure, the men and women of the Second had formed a protective ring around where he and his retinue had rested. His decisions had led to the deaths of hundreds of them – he didn't deserve such loyalty.

Thaun's only surviving Royal Guardsman and two of Toland's Pinions fell in behind them as the noble guided him towards the camp's perimeter. More of his escort had survived the battle, but without a competent healer their wounds had proved too much. No one spoke as they walked, but he soon noticed how each campfire grew quiet as they neared, weary eyes tracking their movement.

At one such ring of light a sergeant struggled to his feet. The man evidently hadn't washed, shaved, or changed since the battle, and the smell of strong liquor filled the air around him. Toland stepped before Thaun, blocking the man's path, one hand falling to his slung rifle. For just a second, Thaun wondered if his friend had exaggerated about the soldiers' opinion of him, and he found himself reaching for his own sword. Then, the sergeant saluted.

It was a sloppy gesture. The man couldn't stand straight, all of his weight upon one leg. Bandages wrapped his hand as it touched his chest, while an open clay bottle hung from the other. Still, little more than a faint glimmer in the dawn light, earnest sincerity shone in the veteran's eyes.

Toland visibly relaxed and stepped aside. Others turned towards them, and Thaun felt the collective weight of a dozen soldiers' attention upon him. As a second man stood, the royal threw a hasty salute of his own, followed a moment later by the rest of the squad.

He held their regard for what felt like an eternity, but was probably no more than a few heartbeats. They were wrong to show him such respect, but the only thing worse would be to point that out to them. He wouldn't place that burden on anyone else.

Finally lowering his hand, the soldiers followed suit one by one.

Half-turning away to better hide his words, Thaun whispered to his friend. "Can we go?"

He could hear the proud smirk in Toland's reply. "As you wish."

"Shut up," he growled, before spinning and marching away. Somewhere behind him, murmurs erupted among the guardsmen, though he couldn't make out the words. A second later they were drowned out by the sounds of Toland and their escort. His friend did him the kindness of not commenting further.

The Royal Guardsman led them onwards, their path winding through disorganised tents towards one of the few remaining outcrops of cut stone. Most of the others had crumbled in the wake of the Thalan sorcery. The broken blocks now stood testament to that as cairns and headstones for their many losses.

Where two walls of tumbling cyclopean blocks met, half a statue stood. Time and the elements had won out against grainy stone. What had once likely been a draconic figure standing in a heroic pose would be difficult to distinguish from a man now, its details so weathered down. Somehow though, it had still sustained less collateral damage than most of the ancient site.

An almost intact squad of soldiers stood watch in the meagre shelter that it provided. As Thaun, Toland, and their guard approached, each of them rose to stand at attention. After a moment they saluted, and Toland returned the gesture.

With a tug, the guardsmen pulled back a large piece of loose canvas to reveal the jagged hole underneath. Damp stone steps led down into the earth, their edges rounded by centuries of exposure. Perhaps some kind of door had protected the opening once, but they saw no sign of it now. Thin topsoil clung to its edge.

Thaun gratefully accepted a lit lantern from one of the troops and followed Toland through the trapdoor. Dirt brushed his shoulders, though he kept his attention upon the uneven footing and the encroaching gloom. The guards above waited a dozen heartbeats after the last of the nobles' escort descended through the opening before returning the canvas cover. If not for their lantern's weak flames, the darkness would've been absolute.

The tunnel twisted as they walked in silence. Beneath their feet, the steps improved, their stone surfaces escaping the worst of the elements. The walls changed as well, raw rock giving ground to crafted blocks and masonry. If Thaun had dared relinquish his light, he could've touched both damp sides with outstretched hands, while the ceiling loomed out of reach. Had they walked through an ornate, brightly-lit tunnel of the same size he wouldn't have spared it a second thought. Surrounded by darkness though, Thaun couldn't imagine anything but hulking, inhuman shapes covered in scales. Everyone had heard the stories, but, until recent events, he'd doubted that the Daericani ever really existed.

It took him a moment to realise that fire shone somewhere ahead, his night vision burned away by his lantern's light. In front of him, Toland didn't slow as he stepped past the ancient, long-destroyed door fittings, and out of the tunnel's confines.

They stood upon a platform, separated from a steep drop by a low stone wall. Far below, Toland's surviving Pinions fed a raging bonfire at the chamber's centre. Others disappeared in and out of various tunnels leading off from the single, huge room like the spokes of a wheel. Tremors and fallen masonry had blocked many, though it seemed the domed room had survived more or less unscathed. With the distance, Thaun struggled to find a sense of scale, but the openings appeared at least twice the height of any man. High above, a single beam of dying natural light shone down through a newly formed crack. It petered out long before reaching the ground.

"Impressive, isn't it?" Toland murmured. "This central chamber alone is as big as Ulora's Cathedral in Tarnac, and built without any supporting pillars. A single unsupported dome beyond anything our architects have accomplished."

"That's... great," Thaun mumbled. He had no real understanding of construction, but even he could appreciate the room's truly massive scale.

"Come on, there's more to see down below." His friend gestured to one side where more stairs continued down. The crumbled remains of a wall ran to their side, and might have once separated them from the chamber entirely. "This way."

Thaun followed. His tired gaze scanned the floor as they descended further. Piles of rocks lay in heaps where the roof had collapsed inwards. Chunks of ancient stonework blocked several of the broad passageways, with soldiers working to clear them under the direction of sappers. Elhin's mages had damaged more than just the Imperial Second.

The bonfire's flickering lights caught the edges of shapes on the surrounding walls. At first, Thaun thought the recent quakes had revealed fresh patches of raw stone. As they walked though, starting down the curving stairs and then across the open, mostly flat floor, he understood. Forgotten, clawed hands had worked the carved blocks, creating sweeping murals that ran the entirety of the room. Fresh cracks ran through some from the recent conflict, but did little to hide its ancient artistry.

From where he stood, he could make out the jagged grooves in the stone. The sharp edges between each gouge had broken in places, blurring the once clear lines. Still though, pictures formed, like faces and images coalescing from clouds. Ancient pigment, discoloured and flaking, hinted at empty vistas on which floated jagged mountains bound by chains. Smaller shapes, details lost to the ages, floated around each one.

Figures, humanoid but inhuman, dominated each scene that had survived the ravages of time. Here and there, wings and snouts made it clear what these people were. Others lacked such distinct markings, but stood too small of stature to be mistaken for men or women as Thaun knew them.

Distorted by quiet weathering, everything focused upon the centre. Silhouettes pointed, while chains and storms radiated like a sunburst. Whatever had lay there though was nothing more than rubble at the wall's base.

"I hear they're as old as the Empire itself." Awe tinged Toland's voice. "Scholars and adventurers have visited here over the years, hoping to find some new answer to their dreams of riches and renown. Not all of them have come back again, but some still risk it."

Thaun didn't reply as Toland guided him into a broad circular path.

"There's another ruin near Tarnac with some of the same styles; my father took me there once when I was young. I always thought it fascinating, seeing another perspective on a different culture's history."

"I thought that the Daericani came here to wage war centuries ago, or something." Thaun glanced down at the shield cradled in his arms. "Does what they thought at the time matter right now?"

Toland shrugged. "A historian would answer that question better than I can. It's still interesting though. Think of it like hearing a new story when all you've heard before are the same old sermons."

"You're really into this stuff, huh?" For the first time in days, a smile tugged at his lips.

Toland offered a sheepish grin. "Everyone enjoys a good story, Your Highness."

"I guess..." Thaun waved one hand towards the nearest stone image. "Go on then, what does it say?"

"I hope you understand that I'm doing this to try and distract you. It's for your own good, really." He threw him a sidelong glance through dark strands of hair. "But thanks. Not everyone indulges me." He slowed, stepping closer to the nearest section of surviving carving. "You know that Urathear sleeps below the world of men, ready to awaken in fire and judgement?"

"Sure. I've been preached at."

"Well, the Daericani that made this place, that entered the Empire from the Voids beyond, they remembered when he flew above the clouds. The world back then was a different place. False gods warred among themselves, breaking nations and scattering peoples. One family of abominations were worse than the rest though, shaping the land itself in their efforts to expand, enslave, and to escape. Had they succeeded, the stars themselves would've been theirs.

"When he arrived, all those years ago, Urathear found himself at odds with that twisted family. A few Daericani tales speak of a great battle between the great dragon and the abominations that shook mountains and broke nations." Toland's lips crooked into a wry smile, and he ran a finger over the ancient mural. "I always thought that bit odd."

"Hmm?"

"The timing. The Daericani arrived here a few centuries ago, when their distant home was closest. They say that Urathear was broken well before that arrival."

"I guess. Does it matter?"

"Perhaps not." He shrugged. "Anyway. Those abominations, they warred with sorcery and steel and against fang and flame. In the wake of their battle, Urathear lay broken, but in turn his foes were defeated and scattered." The noble pulled a sceptical face. "In a twisted way, the dragon fell so that the enslaved could be free of those tyrants.

"Eventually, Urathear's people came looking for him. Across the world, the Daericani crossed the expanse between the stars and in places like this they hid, for a time." Toland gestured to the chamber, his sardonic smile lingering. "They grew strong, swelling their numbers, here in the depths. Heroes don't often hide in darkness, but still there are those like Renyar who'd attempt to make use of them for their own, impure ends." He shook his head. "One day they broke the surface though, and left. The Daericani slew all who stood in their way, believing that, when he returned, he'd separate those he favoured from those still tainted by the abominations' bloodline. Maybe they thought that places like here would protect them? Their crusade to revive their lost god led directly to the alliance that birthed our Empire."

"Crazy stuff, huh?" said Thaun, still gazing at the carved images before them. "That last bit's familiar, at least. Must've heard it in a lecture or sermon or something. I didn't know all of the rest though."

"I'm not surprised." Toland eyed him sidelong, an amused smile returning to his face. "I hear you never paid much attention during your lessons."

Thaun smirked. "That was Heizl's fault."

"I can believe it." The noble slowed and gestured around them at the massive chamber. "You hear rumours occasionally that some Daericani survive in isolated spots. Mountains, swamps, that sort of thing. Apparently they built this place to, when the stars are right, try to bring Urathear back." He lowered his voice. "And now Renyar wants to do the same. He probably thinks that he's doing the right thing. Villains seldom think otherwise. Do you think he's found whatever it was that the Daericani lacked? Some key or ritual to open up the path back to that Void?"

Thaun didn't know what to say, and so he stayed silent. The whole thing had felt beyond him even before they'd started discussing the philosophies of perspective and motive. As their circular wandering came back to the bottom of the steps where they'd started, the first soldiers of the Second filed into the chamber.

A few unladen squads entered first, moving to cover and reinforce the Pinion-held tunnel mouths. Their injured followed, some under their own power, others leaning on comrades, and yet more carried on stretchers. Thaun paled as he watched them limp in, all thoughts of dragons forgotten.

He'd spent almost all of his time since the battle at Lena's side, and so had yet to truly appreciate the Second's losses. When they'd first landed on Insel Drach, the battalion had numbered over five hundred strong, not counting their support units. There couldn't have been a third of that before them now, and most of those bore wounds.

Uncle Rufenrich should never have given him command. With an actual officer at their head, rather than an inexperienced royal, they might have avoided half their losses.

In spite of that grievous mistake, soldiers still glanced his way, whispering like school children as they passed.

"Maybe someday," Toland mused, "Two friends will discuss the things you'll do. Hard decisions, terrible sacrifice, brave advances. They're certainly already talking about you."

Thaun shook his head. "Not this again. Don't they get it?"

"Perhaps they don't want to. Ignorance soothes the masses, after all."

"That's not fair," objected Thaun.

"Sorry." Toland pursed his lips. "You're right. They've earned our respect. A lot of their losses came after the battle itself, down here. Thala retreated and tried to collapse the ceiling. Your men stopped them. Even half-dead after facing Elhin, they marched in here. Rifles aren't nearly so effective at room-to-room fighting, so your Second took the brunt of it."

"Why are you telling me this?"

"The troops knew what they were here for, and so they did as expected of them." He gestured around again, his dark red cloak falling from his arms like wings. "What are you here for, Thaun? What are you going to do?"

He didn't respond, still watching the guardsmen. They'd left only a few on the surface to guard the entrance, bringing the rest of them inside. The huge chamber could have fitted them in ten times over.

Several cutters and bonesetters worked among the injured, doing their best to comfort them and ease their pain. Until then, Thaun had almost forgotten about Lena. He saw no sight of either the healer or Sigren. He could picture the Shadow's outbursts, refusing to let anyone else move the mage.

Many of those trained at the Spire reflected the more pragmatic aspects of Imperial life. Most tried to learn how to mend a flesh wound or to set a broken bone. Something as simple as a grazed knuckle could distract a mage from their careful calculations – it only made sense to limit that risk. Few among them showed the talent necessary for more advanced restoration. The rupturing of organs required a different order of skill.

Losing Lena would be bad enough, but the healer's death would lead to the losses of dozens more.

"Your Highness?" said Toland, a formal tone creeping back into his voice. Thaun turned towards the noble, before following his gaze. A young woman whom he didn't recognise, dressed in a creased, muddy Second Army uniform, approached. "After the battle, I took the liberty of despatching your scouts back to the Crossing as messengers."

Thaun straightened as the soldier approached. He felt something distant, almost like amusement, as he returned the young woman's salute, both of them as fatigued as the other. "Yes?" he managed.

She broke eye contact. "Uh, Your Highness, sir, we've news."

After an uncertain silence, Toland answered on his behalf. "Well? Spit it out, soldier."

The messenger nodded, well-used to the voice of command. "Word from the capital, sir."

"Good." The noble nodded, and glanced towards Thaun. "When can we expect reinforcements?"

"Sir." She swallowed down her nerves, "I doubt they're coming."

"Don't stop on our behalf," said Toland as she trailed off. "Finish your report, please."

"Sorry. We sent a message through to the Spire, updating the Throne on our status, and waited until we got a reply. The response came from a Shadow stationed at the Nexus." She hesitated, swallowing again. "Reiget City is besieged."

"What?!" Thaun exclaimed. The bottom of his stomach had dropped as if he stood at the edge of an abyss. "Who is it? Renyar? Seorsa? Who?"

"It's not Thala, Your Highness. Not just them, anyway..."

"We didn't say 'stop.'" Toland waved to continue.

"Sorry, sir." She inclined her head. "Thalans, Seorsans, Fjujans, some old Kuhlner loyalists... and several mercenary companies flying Strahl colours."

"How did–" started the noble.

"Is my uncle alright?" Thaun interrupted, holding up a hand to forestall his friend.

"No word from the Palace. Sorry, sir."

"Toland." Thaun turned from the scout, eyes wide. "What're we going to do?"

Before he could answer, the soldier cleared her throat. "Excuse me, sirs? There's something else." She glanced between the two men. "It's about your cousin."

Tooth and Nail – Chapter Twenty

"Whatever nation you look to, history repeats itself. Seorsan children inherit their parents' privilege. Tszerrichan Lairz will fall from favour only for the pious and promising to be appointed to their lands. And Imperials, when they run out of horizons to invade, will wage war upon themselves."

Of the Lands Beyond the
Rampart,
Yu Zhi, Daqini Imperial
Calligrapher
(391 I.Y.)

4th day of Ehnaln, 406th Imperial Year
17th Year of Emperor Rufenrich Konreig's Reign

Sliding a little on the old jetty, Thaun trod upon damp wood slick with algae. His last surviving Royal Guardsman held out a steadying hand, but he pushed it away. Their journey back across the Daer Sea had proved less comfortable than their original trip. His worries about the friends that he'd left behind and the family he travelled towards hadn't made it any easier.

Half a dozen soldiers of the Second clambered out of the small boat behind him, before jogging towards the Crossing's fortified structure. They'd asked for volunteers to accompany him, with Lena unable to move and Sigren unwilling to leave her side. The resulting list had proved too long to be practical. In the end, they'd selected several of the least injured guardsmen to join him. Toland had practically had to restrain one particularly injured corporal.

Dark clouds filled the sky from one horizon to the other, but the rain had yet to fall. By the time he left the Crossing, the impending storm still wouldn't have reached them. Winds however plucked at the waves upon the inland sea, cresting them in white and rocking the Trade Guild ship upon which they'd sailed.

A few soldiers ranging out both before and behind, Thaun marched towards the Crossing with his new escort. Though his footing shifted beneath him in the well worn, muddy path a few times, they made good time.

Fewer sounds arose from the small fort than the last time he'd visited. He guiltily thought back to Korten intimidating the garrison commander into giving up half of his troops for their mission. Both the Highmage and most of those soldiers had died since. Still, merchants and travellers continued their business under the watchful eyes of inspectors and tax collectors.

It didn't take long to reach the Crossing's beacon. An almost orderly queue of couriers and messengers greeted them, but, as soon as the officer organising them saw Thaun, he rushed them to the front. The man could've taken ten times as long to let them into the locked underground room, and it wouldn't have made much difference. Without their own Spire mage to manipulate their link to the Nexus, the garrison relied upon regularly scheduled collections and deliveries. The men guarding the beacon reported that these had continued even since receiving news of the trouble in the capital. Mind racing, Thaun waited, perching upon his pack for their allotted time.

Without any of his usual companions to confide in, Thaun couldn't help but worry about those he'd left behind.

Lena had still lived when he'd departed, but, if he was honest with himself, he'd already started to mourn the healer's loss. It was a miracle that the mage had lasted as long as she had. Either her wounds or the rampant growth of tumours should've killed her outright. Winning out against both was unthinkable. The part which hurt him the most was that his friend couldn't reply – whether she slept to rest or she'd fallen into some meditative trance, Thaun's words fell upon deaf ears. Leaving now was easier than waiting for her to awaken. He wondered if that made him selfish.

He'd argued with Sigren before leaving. A voice inside him said that they'd be the last things he shared with the Shadow, but he pushed that feeling down. His friend's habitual contrary attitude hadn't stopped them from growing close. They'd argued this time over how foolish it was for him to return home. A part of him agreed, but admitting that wasn't so easy. Thaun didn't want to leave things as they were between them, but he couldn't just sit on an island and ignore all that he'd learned.

Toland at least had shown him some support. The noble had spoken at length about the strategic issues that he might encounter, about the risk his return might pose to the Empire itself, but he'd never made Thaun doubt his decision. He'd volunteered to join Thaun's remaining captains in securing the Rift, not that any of them had seen any sign of its opening. He'd even suggested that there might be a few Pinions at his family's own estate in the Capital, and the advantage their presence might provide.

Thaun was no less worried about those he hurried towards now.

The talk of Heizl's involvement made him more uncomfortable than anything he'd experienced since that fateful night at the Palace. Anyone who knew his cousin would label her as ambitious and maybe even a little resentful. The rumours of her joining forces with Thala was all but unthinkable though. Renyar had made a good go at killing them, and had hurt countless others.

No, something had to be wrong. Enough of the nobility looked down on Heizl that someone would benefit from slandering her. Besides, she'd still be hunting for another Fragment beyond the frontier, wouldn't she? Thaun couldn't see another option other than going home to find out what had really happened. A question dogged him though. If he truly thought Heizl had nothing to do with this, would he really be going back now?

He'd question anyone who told him that his cousin would do something like this. Renyar on the other hand... The Thalan Patriarch had already shown a willingness to cut straight to the root of a problem. Fear bubbled within Thaun. Not for the first time, that root was his uncle.

Rufenrich surrounded himself with some of the most skilled people the Empire could offer. Most days, Thaun would rather bet on Frida, Hastigr, or Vandel than against them, but–

"Your Highness? It's almost time." The Royal Guardsman snapped a crisp salute before pointing towards the final grains of sand in the nearby hourglass.

When the last of it tumbled into the bottom chamber, Hastigr would activate this strand of his Nexus.

Thaun stood, as did his volunteer escort. In a perfect world, two of the Second would go through before him and the Royal Guardsman to secure their destination, but this backwater outpost would only have a single contact each day. Once home, he might end up alone. What he wouldn't do to have Sigren, Toland, or Lena with him now.

He breathed in deep. "I'm ready."

His bodyguard nodded, and the pair stepped into the ring denoting the Nexus' reach. Before it, a short plinth rose from the ground with a polished pebble placed upon it. Half the Empire away, an almost identical stone lay a short distance from Highmage Hastigr.

As darkness rose up to envelope them, Thaun felt glad that his anxiety had stopped him from eating much that day.

The solid ground disappeared beneath his feet. A few stomach churning moments of blackness and brimstone later, Thaun stood in Reiget City once more. He blinked several times as his eyes adjusted to the torchlit gloom of the Nexus, wracking coughs escaping his chest.

Much as he had before, Hastigr knelt in a trance a short distance away at the centre of the engraved map like some sleeping god. The others sharing the room with them differed from what he remembered from his last visit though.

The ring of troops closing around them no longer wore the blue of the Royal Guard or the black of Imperial Shadows. Each wore a different uniform, with some not showing any colours at all. As he turned to take them all in, hand falling to the hilt of his sword, Thaun saw a few he suspected were Thalan or Seorsan among the mismatched squads. They numbered more now even than when the royal family had all stood within.

Boxes, bags, and scroll cases lay in disorganised heaps against the room's walls. In a few places, someone had moved some of the crates into rough lines, creating cover from both the centre of the Nexus and its single entrance alike.

Beside him, he heard his Royal Guardsman pull free his own blade.

"Put it away," Thaun whispered, before facing the nearest of the approaching rebels and filling his words with every ounce of command that he could. "I'm here to see my cousin. Take me to the Palace."

To his ears, the order sounded laughably weak, but the man – a Seorsan in well-cared for leathers – paused. The others followed suit, and the ring around them shrunk no further.

"Of course," he spoke in accented Imperial. "If you'd kindly relinquish your sword, we will provide you with an appropriate escort."

Thaun fought the urge to draw the blade at his hip and to fall into a duelling stance. Though he'd rarely had the chance to use it, he'd always found the weight of a scabbard reassuring, and didn't like the idea of surrendering it.

"I assure you," the rebel continued with a polite tone. "You'll not need it here. We'll look after you."

Forcing open a fist he'd instinctively clenched tight, Thaun nodded. In a reverse grip, he inched the sword free of its sheath with his left hand. He hesitated, running his eyes down its dark edge. So far, the blade had done him little good. It wasn't like his previous weapon had served him any better though. Hopefully its new owner would have more luck with it.

Pommel first, he handed it to the lead rebel. The Seorsan accepted it with a grateful nod. After a moment, the Royal Guardsman likewise gave up his sword, though more reluctantly than his charge.

The Seorsan smiled. "Thank you. Right this way."

The last time he'd walked through the Spire's bowels it had buzzed with mages walking between projects and classes, and Shadows watching over them. Now, armed men and women stood in every doorway, guarding entrances and checking their weapons.

Mercenaries and warriors eyed Thaun as he passed. From the quick glances that he managed, he couldn't tell if they looked curious, afraid, or triumphant. Perhaps it was all three.

Stepping outside, the light struck him first. He'd left the Crossing less than half an hour before and the sun had still shone high overhead. Here in Reiget City though, dusk approached and the first few stars twinkled in the sky. He could just about make out the sign of the Wanderer, hanging half-hidden above the western horizon. Upon the Spire's outer curtain wall, more men – mostly mercenaries wearing Strahl brown and yellow – patrolled. He didn't see a single Shadow.

Moving through a small postern gate, Thaun stepped back into his city. Smoke rose against the red sky in more places than he could count. The violent sounds of fighting and riots drifted upon the autumnal evening breeze. He could see that this rebellion was far from over.

Looking down the short, winding path to the bank of the River Reigan, he saw a small patrol boat awaiting them. Ushered across the wharf's slick stones and up a gangplank, he soon stood among even more men in mismatched uniforms. He recognised the armour of Imperial guardsmen, even if they no longer wore the First Army's blue and green surcoats. Others he didn't know, but the sight of House Strahl's brown and gold sent a shiver down his spine at all it implied. The armed men and women kept their hands on their weapons, their attention focused as much on outside threats as upon the two men that they escorted.

Thaun had never spent as much time beyond the Palace's walls as he would've liked, but still he'd never seen Reiget City like this. Its people, *his people*, should be full of life, sharing their homes with one another. They shouldn't be cowering in fear or smashing shop fronts.

That injustice, at normal people suffering due to those fortunate enough to be born near power, stayed with him as they crossed the river, just one more passenger on their small vessel.

Moving against the river's current, debris bumped against the boat's prow. Above the banks, scorch marked brickwork and wooden buildings lay in ruins. A single watchtower loomed above one of the city's stone bridges. Men moved upon its ramparts, though it now stood stripped of its loyalist Imperial colours.

As the crew guided them against a wooden jetty, Thaun looked up at the Imperial Palace. Above the stone tunnel before them, fissures marred its once fine flagstones. Sentries lit torches upon the walls as they continued their vigil.

He let the men with him guide him through the bowels of his home. Doors opened at his approach, and the Seorsan waved him inside. Thaun could have shown the rebel the way to the Throne Room better himself, but allowed himself to be ushered through the Palace's various passageways instead.

Its corridors bustled with activity. Armed revolutionaries moved from barracks to walls and back again as patrols ended. He soon lost track of the different factions that crossed his path. Seorsans, fair-haired Fjujans, renegade Imperial guardsmen, even a couple of Shadows still in their dark uniforms.

At the sight of a trio of bronze-skinned Thalans, he tightened his grip upon his shield. If they recognised it on his arm, none of them spoke. It might've been nice to acknowledge that stroke of luck, that only their weapons had been confiscated, but Thaun struggled to appreciate much of anything in the shadow of his growing fear.

The Great Hall's double doors stood shut before him. None of the Seorsan insurgents knocked, instead pushing open one side. With a loud creak, the wooden barrier swung open.

The room beyond shared little with Thaun's memory of it. A single table remained within, the others from the feast removed, probably for more barricades and firewood. Most of its seats stood empty. Guards lined the walls, the tapestries and banners now likewise missing. His uncle's throne sat empty upon its raised dais. A score of faces turned towards him as he stood in the doorway, but Thaun focused on just one thing.

Heizl sat in the centre chair in clothes so dark a grey that they might as well have been black. She held Thaun's gaze as she chewed on a mouthful. Recognition dawned in his cousin's eyes more slowly than he would've liked, and she stood, leaning slightly upon an archaic spear. She rounded the table as their guards stepped away, and looked Thaun up and down.

With a smile, the mage crossed the gap between them in just a few strides. Thaun flinched as Heizl spread her hands, spear still held in one, and wrapped her arms around him. After the shortest of moments, he let himself fall into the woman's embrace.

Everything felt right. The familiar smells of home. The welcoming warmth of family. The loving support of a lifelong companion.

Almost everything at least. Still attached to his left arm, the shield seemed to twitch and pull him forwards, a frenetic energy running through his veins.

"You're home," whispered Heizl before breaking the hug, free hand still on Thaun's shoulder. "Are you okay? Are you hurt?"

"I'm fine." In spite of everything that he'd heard about events in the capital, and for everything he'd experienced, Thaun couldn't help but smile. "What about you? Why aren't you in Norjhost?"

"Come on." The mage turned and waved towards the food-laden table. "We've a lot to discuss, and it'll be more comfortable to sit while doing it. We can eat, too."

Thaun looked over those already seated.

His cousin's Shadow – hadn't she left with two? – sat with his feet up and fingers linked behind his head as he leant back. An empty plate rested upon his stomach, rising and falling gently with each relaxed breath. Though Thaun noticed the stark contrast the young man's pale hair struck against his dirty, dark uniform, he paid more attention to the collection of knives and blades at the Shadow's belt.

He passed over several more faces that he didn't know. An auburn-haired Seorsan in a fine suit, a red-bearded Fjujan dressed in oft-repaired armour, an elderly Imperial noblewoman whom he vaguely recognised, and a man who had to be Thalan from his clothing's cut. Each in turn returned a cautious nod as he walked towards the last empty seat.

He made it halfway there before one of Heizl's guests blocked his path.

"Your Highness!" Dasimir Strahl's customary booming voice stopped him short.

Thaun flinched back at the sudden noise, looking the Governor up and down. The past week hadn't treated the nobleman kindly. By the grime around his cuffs, he'd worn the same clothes for several days, and sweat coated his face. Fresh wrinkles and folds had formed around his mouth and eyes, as if something that had sustained him now dwindled.

"With you back, we can–"

A hint of menace undercut Heizl's tone as she spoke over Dasimir. "Strahl, sit down. I don't want to remind you again."

The Governor trembled at her words, hands bunching into fists. Resisting for just a moment, he did as told, and returned to his seat next to the Thalan.

Thaun didn't speak as he continued towards the table's single empty seat. He shook aside the sensation that someone else should have accompanied him. With an awkward motion, he slung his shield onto his back and sat down opposite Heizl. His empty scabbard knocked against one leg of the bench. An aide swiftly appeared, filling his cup before shuffling away again. Such people cared little for who ruled them.

No, that was unfair of him. Of course people cared. In their place though, how would he have felt? Helpless, frustrated, and spiteful. What could they hope to change by themselves when an unfair twist of fate had refused to bless them with power or opportunity?

Thaun smiled at the servant in what he hoped was a reassuring way.

His cousin leant towards him, a relieved smile upon her face. "I'm so glad you're back. We can finally sort this whole mess out now. Where're Lena and the others?"

"They..." Thaun swallowed down his grief. "Lena's hurt. We fought Elhin, and she got wounded. I... I don't know if she's going to make it."

The mage's smile flickered in shock at the news. "Elhin was a canny bitch. I guess that explains why you're carrying around her shield though." Her green eyes tracked to where it rose over one of Thaun's shoulders, lingering there for a second before returning. "It's another Fragment, I hear. How does it feel?"

"A lot of others got hurt too," he continued in a whisper. "If her wounds are too much, a lot more are going to die. They might die even if she lives."

His cousin paused, a pained look crossing her face as she glanced again at the shield. She sighed as she turned away. "I'm sorry. I always liked her. It sounds like you went through a lot. No wonder you came home."

"I came back because of you," Thaun murmured, unable to hold eye contact with anyone. Gaze to the floor, he didn't see Heizl's flash of anger. "What happened?"

"Norjhost was good for me," she mumbled, picking up a piece of bread from her plate. "The people I met there helped me gain some perspective. If it wasn't for them, I wouldn't have got this."

Thaun's eyes tracked upwards at the sound of her moving. She smiled down at the spear as she raised it into view.

"Uh... huh." He didn't know what else to say. "Is that what Uncle sent you to find?"

"It is." She grinned more broadly than before. "You've not come back empty-handed yourself."

"Oh, yeah, that..." Thaun rolled his shoulders, feeling the shield brush against his back. "I've not put it down since we fought Elhin."

"Sounds about right," she spoke around another mouthful. "Mine's much the same. These things are harder to get rid of than the pox."

"Have you tried?"

"Give up this power? Not likely." A sly look rose in Heizl's expression. "Can I try it?"

"What?" Thaun edged away. "Uh, no, I don't think so."

"Figured." The mage cocked her head before returning to her food. "I wouldn't let someone try my Claw out either."

"Your Claw?"

"Yeah, that's what this beauty is." She shook the spear slightly where it now leant against her shoulder. The others on either side shrank back. "A Claw of Urathear. There's something very cathartic about doing good with a piece of destruction incarnate. I'm told that you've got yourself a Fang there, by the way."

Thaun didn't know how to reply. He knew so little about the thing he carried, and now his cousin had answers. Right now though, he had more important questions.

He pushed his plate away. "Heizl, where's Uncle?"

"I wish I knew! All this would be a lot cleaner if things had worked out as planned."

"...As planned?"

"Why, to protect everyone." Heizl straightened in her seat. "Wasn't that what we both set out for? Void knows I didn't visit some primitive wilderness for the culture and cuisine. Rufenrich was right that someone is out to summon the rest of these Fragments. He just blurred the truth a bit on who it actually is. Renyar's not so bad."

"As in the Renyar who attacked a party, killed a dozen guests, and twisted the minds of everyone else? The guy who had us all acting like puppets? Me included?"

"We're not the only ones toting around Fragments, you know. He's got the Tongue, at the moment at least. That's how he did it."

"You're missing the point, Heizl."

"The point, Thaun, is that the Emperor can't be trusted."

"The Emperor. Our uncle. The same uncle who raised us both, after my dad..." Thaun took a deep breath, something hot welling up inside his chest. "After he died, and your mum left?"

"Unless we've another uncle I don't know about." Heizl's eyes glittered at some private joke.

"The one who had sweets smuggled into the Spire for you? Who paid to keep trouble from catching up with you? Who got you the best tables in the best restaurants when you were entertai–"

Heizl's fist struck the table, and the entire surface shuddered. Her other guests fell silent, none of them quite willing to look directly at her. Even Thaun closed his mouth. After a moment, as the mage's willpower overcame her anger, her fingers uncurled.

"What's wrong with you?" Thaun asked in a low voice. "Why are you doing this?"

"I've only done what was necessary," Heizl whispered, rubbing her brow. "If I hadn't, everything'd be so much worse. Rufenrich would've ruined everything by now if I hadn't stepped in."

"Don't you remember?" Thaun rose slowly, pressing both hands against the tabletop. The gaze of every guard in the room tracked to him. Several laid hands on weapons. "Renyar's the one who's going to summon Urathear. We have to stop him."

"I'm trying to stop Urathear. I hoped that you'd help me." Heizl turned slightly in her seat. She gestured towards the empty throne perched above them on the dais. "I even saved you a seat."

"I've never wanted that." At his words, Thaun saw his cousin's features flash with anger once more. "No, I mean I'm not interested in the Throne. You've always known that–"

"Now who's missing the point? I just offered you a chance to do some lasting good in this world, and you ignored it."

"It's not too late. We can end all this. Turn things around on Renyar, and break whatever spell he has over you." He took his turn to gesture around at the Hall. "You saw what he did right here. He'll have said something to you, some command, and you're just confused."

"I'm getting pretty pissed off with people telling me that I'm confused," Heizl hissed, rising in turn. "Renyar's got nothing to do with my choices. He's getting rid of the Tongue." She waved offhand at the Seorsan ambassador. "It's the whole reason they're helping us. Without it, he won't control anyone, least of all me." She threw up her hands, and began pacing. "The Tongue doesn't even work on me now I have this..." She lowered her voice as she lingered on the Claw before continuing in a whisper. "It probably won't work on you now either."

He sighed. "Who are you trying to persuade?"

Any recognisable sense of familiarity left the mage's voice. "I don't have to persuade anyone of anything anymore."

"Heizl..." Thaun wrung his hands out in front of him. "I'm worried about you."

"I don't *need* anyone to worry about me either," she hissed in reply.

"But... we're family. Isn't that what we're supposed to do?"

He watched as Heizl hunched in on herself, arms hanging limp at her sides. "Always so worried about what you're supposed to do, aren't you? Well right now you're supposed to be helping me! Oh, sure, you stress that you're not going to reach everyone's expectations, but you still care. Then you get upset because you don't live up to your own unreasonable standards." Heizl's voice, already a dry whisper, sank lower and sharper. "And then you try to make yourself feel better by looking down on me."

Tears welled in Thaun's eyes, and his throat tightened. "Heizl, that's not true."

"You won't even listen to the truth."

"You're just confused! Listen, we can–"

"I'm disappointed in you." The quiet words, appearing from her wrath as suddenly as calm after a storm, hit him like a physical blow. "I thought you were better than all the others." She snorted a sharp breath from her nose. "Zecht? Find my cousin somewhere safe to stay until I can talk some sense into him."

Stretching, the Shadow placed his plate upon the table, and rose. "I told you it'd come to this. We all told you. You could've saved a lot of time by just locking him up in the first place, Fitz."

"Just get on with it."

"Ugh, fine," the Shadow muttered.

Opposite him, the bench creaked and cutlery shook as Dasimir Strahl likewise stood. "Miss Fitzerin," he said in a stately voice. "May I kindly remind you that I help you willingly. Please do not make me reconsider our agreement by making such a rash decision." Along each wall, the handful of guards and mercenaries in the Governor's colours tensed further, eyeing the other rebel soldiers.

"You help me because you're willing to be an ambitious jackass!" Heizl shouted, a cruel smirk coming to her face. "That, and because you have no idea where I've hidden Jilia."

"I tell you, girl." The noble pushed his broad chest out as he stared at the mage. "One day you'll get your comeuppance, and I'm going to be standing over you when it happens."

"Your Lordship," her smirk widened. "I highly doubt it. Until then though, you and your men will do exactly as they're told. Sit. Down."

For a second, Thaun thought that he might raise his voice again. After a moment though, Dasimir sat, hands trembling. The other guests backed away slightly, as if worried they might suffer merely from sitting too close.

Distracted by the Governor's outburst, Thaun hadn't realised Zecht stood at his elbow until a strong grip latched onto his arm. "Come on, Your Highness, let's—"

Before he knew it, Thaun had spun, flailing his outstretched arm to backhand the Shadow back a step. The blond man looked shocked at the response, pulling free a slender dagger mid-movement as if from nowhere.

Zecht lashed out, steel flashing in his hand. Thaun recognised the instinct. A knee-jerk reaction to discourage a foe from following too closely.

It didn't land. Faces winced at the subdued screech as the blade ran over his shield. He hadn't even noticed himself pulling it free.

Shifting back, empty hand behind him for balance, Thaun raised his shieldarm again in time to deflect any follow-up attack.

"Zecht!" Heizl snapped.

"I know, I know," the Shadow drawled, not lowering his blade. "But he hit me first."

"No, not that." The mage rolled her eyes. "Look at his damn hand."

Thaun risked his own glance down at his right glove, at where the others stared. Across from him, Zecht hesitated. Only at a second look did he comprehend. All too familiar black flames glimmered along his gauntlet. Fire dripped like ink to the tiled floor below where it winked out after finding nothing to consume.

Thaun shook his hand as if to flick away water, but nothing happened. He suppressed the panicked reflex to grab at his other hand. Flexing his fingers, he returned his attention to the Shadow opposite him.

"Want to put that thing out, Your Highness?" drawled Zecht, reversing his grip on the dagger and pulling free a second blade. "We wouldn't want anyone to get hurt."

"I, uh, don't know how to," he admitted.

"Fine, have it your way."

Before he knew it, steel flashed towards Thaun's head again. Faster than he knew how, he raised the shield into its path. As the knife fell motionless to his feet, Zecht arrived, dagger twisting past his guard to skitter across his chainmail. A fist struck upwards, catching him in the jaw, and Thaun staggered back, arms swinging.

As his stance crumbled, his flaming fist clipped the Shadow's shoulder.

Zecht flew sideways as if dropped from the Void. He almost managed a roll as he struck the hard floor, taking at least some of the impact from his fall. He rose unsteadily, hands out for balance, before dropping back onto the flagstones. Dazed and rubbing one hand at his face, he didn't immediately stand back up again.

Thaun ignored Heizl's Shadow, still struggling not to overreact to what had just happened to his hand. He'd seen Elhin do similar a few times, but he hadn't foreseen it doing anything while unarmed. This Fragment, the Fang, was just full of surprises.

Across the table, his cousin didn't focus on Zecht either. "Well, I don't know what I expected." She waved her empty hand. "Men, please find His Highness somewhere to rest. He's had a long trip."

At first, the various rebels hesitated, having just seen one of their number defeated in a single blow. As Heizl tapped the butt of the Claw on the floor the first man stepped forward, pulling free a sword. Cowed by his example, others soon followed and a ring, bristling with steel, formed around Thaun.

Between the shoulders of two mismatched rebels, Thaun eyed his cousin. "So what? Are you going to kill me now?"

Heizl laughed. "No! Don't be stupid. I'm hoping they won't even hurt you – with Lena gone we're pretty limited when it comes to decent healers." She tapped the spear against the floor again. "What about you? We've both seen that Fang in action. You could probably kill every single person in this room."

Thaun swallowed, his hand still clenched in a fist. His gaze danced to Zecht, who lay nursing his head. He glanced at the rebels surrounding him, and the uncertain looks upon their fearful faces. As he turned back towards his cousin, his stomach tightened.

"I don't want to hurt anyone." Thaun closed his eyes. "I'll come quietly."

Tooth and Nail – Chapter Twenty-One

"The disastrous uprising that led to the Incident reminded the commonfolk of their own power. In its wake, many took up arms, fighting for their own freedoms. The quenching of such revolutionary fires by the new Imperial powers was swift and brutal."

> Memoirs of Kaimund Tembrane,
> First Citizen of the Kuhlner
> Republic
> (445 I.Y.)

4th day of Ehnaln, 406th Imperial Year
17th Year of Emperor Rufenrich Konreig's Reign

Heizl bowed her head, eyes closed. It wasn't meant to have gone like this.

The Great Hall's unyielding stone floor sapped the warmth from her flesh, even through her trousers, but she barely noticed. Her neck itched, but she kept both hands in her lap where one gripped the Claw, and the other held the strange sword taken from Thaun. Sweat stuck clothes to skin, but a small voice at the back of her mind insisted that no one would notice through the dark fabric.

None of that mattered right now though. She'd felt so excited when she'd learned of Thaun's arrival in the city. It had almost made the costs of occupying the Spire worthwhile by itself. If her cousin had just listened to her instead of being so damn stubborn then none of this would've happened. She could've put Thaun on the throne and pulled in enough support to not worry about any retribution from Imperial loyalists. Instead, the Void-damned fool had forced her hand, and now he was locked in a tower like some fairy-tale princess.

It wasn't like Heizl wanted to put him there, but what other choice did she have? Thaun would stop being so stupid sooner or later, but she could hardly have him wandering around the city. People would question her authority if they saw the Crown Prince free, and she couldn't have that.

But what if Thaun didn't understand? Renyar might have magic in his words, but the Emperor could be persuasive too. The promise of wealth, power, and respect could twist even the strongest will, and her cousin stood to gain a lot after the Comet passed. Heizl would just have to keep him safe until then.

And then there was the sword. The Fang she could understand. Even if Thaun had turned up wearing Thalan armour she could've explained it. But this? A single-edged blade of dark steel with some mechanism attached to one side of it? She didn't know where to begin, and their interrogation of his Royal Guardsman had given them little of use.

Heizl would have respected the soldier's loyalty and reluctance to tell them anything helpful if it hadn't angered her so much. The idea of torture turned her stomach, but she'd no way of telling when Renyar would return. If the bodyguard knew something valuable, could she really afford to wait for the Thalan and his Tongue? Besides, if the man could give her answers, even costly ones, then it'd spare her having to order the same treatment of Thaun. She was protecting him, really.

She stood. She didn't like making choices like these, but such was the burden of leadership.

"I hear my father nearly ruined things again," said Jilia from a short distance away. Heizl hadn't even noticed her entering. Only a handful of their insurgents stood around the room, not a single one wearing Strahl colours. "What exactly did he do this time?"

Heizl's worries sloughed from her mind. "Oh, he was just about to try and incite Thaun to attack me. Nothing out of the ordinary."

"Hmm. Well." She perched on the edge of the long bench. "I'm glad he failed. I don't think injuring the Crown Prince would endear us to many right now."

Heizl dismissed the thought with a wave. "He'd have been fine. He's gone and bonded with Elhin's Fang. You know, that shield?"

"I don't, but I heard a little about it," the noble mused. "You're certain?"

"Absolutely. I can see these things, remember?" Heizl grinned. "I still don't know how he managed to get hold of it. I guess Elhin's in a shallow grave now. Honestly, I'm more concerned about the Emperor's dagger."

"Maybe Renyar will know more about it," she spoke in a slow, measured tone. "Have we heard from him yet?"

"Not since he left to draw Vandel out," said Heizl.

"Maybe that's for the best. If he's around too much, people might think all this is an attack by a foreign power. At least this way everyone knows Imperials are in charge."

"They'd have a nasty shock if they tried anything."

"I'm sure." With a wave of her hand, Jilia dismissed the thought. If she saw the brief flash of anger upon Heizl's face, she didn't react. "Are guards in place? I don't think risking Thaun getting out will help matters."

Heizl shrugged before replying. "He's disarmed and locked in his room, and the guards with him are reliable. Some of them were stationed here in the Palace before. I'm hoping he'll hesitate before trying anything foolish if he recognises them."

"What about the Fang?"

"Locked away safely. He didn't take too kindly to us taking it from him, but he saw sense. Eventually."

"That's wonderful news! Who'll you give it to? Or will you keep it yourself?"

"My training didn't really involve weapons."

"You seem to be doing fine with a spear."

"Heh, honestly, I've tried the Fang already. It didn't seem to do anything for me. Or when any of the troops tried for that matter either."

"So it only works for Thaun?"

"Seems that way."

Jilia paused for a moment, her eyes shining as she thought. "Have you tried getting someone else to use the Claw?" Something must have crossed Heizl's face then, as she flinched back before composing herself. "Renyar must've had the Tongue for a while. Maybe he can tell us more about how they work."

"Stop dismissing me!" Heizl snapped. Even as the instinctive words leapt unbidden from her lips, she regretted them. At the shocked expression upon the noble's face, the mage took an involuntary step back, and lowered the Claw. She could think of few things she wanted less than to hurt this woman. "I'm sorry if I scared you, I didn't mean to shout." A sharp ache rose behind her eyes though she resisted the urge to rub at her face. "It's just all this was possible because of me. I should be in charge, not Renyar."

Jilia took a moment to centre herself, though her gaze lingered on the spear for a few heartbeats. Along both walls, their guards straightened as they eased off from drawing their weapons. "It's fine. Everyone respects you. No one thinks that this is just because of Renyar. We should discuss the layouts of…"

Heizl heard little of what Jilia said next. Something about troop movements, defensive positions, and appealing to potential allies. It took all her restraint to merely look like she paid attention, nodding at the right moments and making reassuring noises.

The pain in her head grew. Where her skin touched the Claw, lightning raced. It hadn't hurt much less when Thaun had insulted her. The spear had struggled against her then, to strike down the threat that her cousin posed, urging her to take the Fang for herself. Maybe it would've pained her less just to give in rather than resisting. At least that way, with two Fragments, there'd be no question of who was in charge between her and Renyar.

"…the Church too, if we approach them the right way. They lack the manpower of the others, but they hold a lot of sway over the lower classes. It could help recruitment. What do you think?"

"Do whatever you think's necessary," Heizl said without hesitating. "We'll deal with any who come."

"Honestly, I'm not sure we will." Jilia stood and began pacing, her expensive dress flowing around her legs. For just a moment, at the sight, Heizl forgot about her headache. "There are still groups loyal to your uncle throughout the city, and it won't be long until the garrison retakes the walls. After that we'll only have a few pockets of resistance. We should consider consolidating our hold on the Spire – it's just as defensible as here, but the Nexus gives us a way out if things don't work out."

Heizl couldn't help but glance at the empty Throne. "We're not abandoning here. Not after everything we did to win it."

"Heizl, I know how much this all means to you, but we should consider what to do if the Emperor's forces take the Palace back. We should repeat what we did with my father. If Rufenrich believes that Thaun is in danger, it'll at least stall the garrison's assault."

"I doubt it." She rubbed at her brow with the back of her hand, the Claw weaving through the air around her as if of its own volition. "The Emperor's only interested in summoning Urathear. If anyone stands in his way, even Thaun, he won't hesitate." Her headache intensified, pulsing behind one eye worse than the other. "You're right though, we should make plans for this place to fall. I even have an idea."

Jilia's wry smile narrowed her eyes. "I'm glad to hear it."

"I'll need a scribe, and a merchant not affiliated with the Trade Guild. We'll send a letter to Baron–"

The door slammed open, wood resounding against stone as Renyar flung them wide. He strode in, halting at the centre of the room, still breathing heavily. Sweat marred his brow, and dried blood caked one sleeve. His sword hung notched from his hand.

"You know." Heizl bowed her head, pinching the bridge of her nose as pain flashed behind her eyes again, "I think I'm beginning to understand why Rufenrich always got so annoyed at being interrupted."

"Where is he?" the Thalan demanded.

"My cousin? Probably pacing back and forth, trying to come up with a way to sneak out."

"Your Crown Prince will wait. Where's your uncle?" As he growled, he enunciated each word.

"Mind how you're speaking, friend." Heizl cocked an eyebrow. "You might still have that Tongue, for now, but don't forget who took this place. Without me seizing the Spire, Rufenrich would've gone through the Nexus already all while you ran around the city playing tag."

Renyar drew a breath, and his face softened. "I'm proud of your achievements so far, Heizl." Across from him, she flinched back. Too few people had said anything like that to her before. She didn't know quite how to react. "I've sang your praises to our allies, but let me remind you that we're not in Norjhost anymore. My magic works perfectly well here. Well enough to take that spear from you if necessary." Heizl's frustration flared back to life.

"We don't have time for this," Jilia growled in a manner unladylike enough to make the pair turn. "We hold the Throne and the Spire. That's it. There's a whole Empire out there who haven't taken kindly to our coup. If we waste our time on threatening one another then we waste our opportunity. We'll be remembered as traitors and rebels, rather than as patriots."

"That doesn't matter!" snapped Renyar, all prior semblance of civility fading. "Fragments of divine destruction fall into the hands of men. Hunger grows in the darkness. Scions of broken gods walk among us." His volume grew as he continued. "Families break apart over the future! A flaming portent hangs over us all!!" The Thalan's voice dropped to a whisper as he clenched his fists tight. "All that, and you worry about politics and mortal legacy."

Jilia stood, tilting her chin upward in defiance. "That may be. Every word you've said might be the truth. Or maybe you've lied to us this whole time. None of *that* matters if we don't start communicating with one another."

For a moment, no one spoke. Chainmail and cloth rustled as the guards along either wall shuffled their feet, uncertain of where their loyalties lay.

Renyar slammed his sword back into its scabbard without cleaning it. "Understand that we're only having this conversation because I still need your connections."

"I understand," Jilia replied, her voice lilting strangely for a moment as his magicked words washed over her. She wiped her brow before inspecting the Thalan's injuries. Heizl leant back against the stone steps. "Where's Vandel?"

"I'd have thought he'd have charged in here by now." Renyar rolled his bloodied shoulder, his armour giving off a muffled clinking. "He must be somewhere in the city. His pursuit lasted longer than I'd anticipated, and he proved more dangerous than I care to admit."

"I don't get why you're so freaked out by the guy." Heizl smirked. "He's just one man with a sword."

"Everytime you open your mouth, you further prove your own ignorance." Drawled Renyar. "My... His presence is at the centre of all this."

"Yeah, well, everytime that you open your mouth–"

"Heizl..." Jilia spoke in a gentle but firm tone. "Renyar, I appreciate that by withholding information you maintain a degree of control over us, but it'd be in everyone's interests to be honest with one another."

Renyar bowed his head the barest fraction of an inch. "My lady, I trust that you know how grateful I am for your presence here. If only all Imperials shared your wisdom." He took a deep breath before looking up. "Send your guards away."

"Really?" Heizl sneered. "You've threatened me at least once since you busted in here. Just why should I do a single thing that you tell me?"

"This again?" the Thalan Patriarch rolled his eyes. "I'm showing you a courtesy in allowing you to send them away. Refuse, and I'll command them to vacate this room myself." A cruel smile flickered across his face. "Better yet, I'm sure they'd help me relieve you of the Claw if I simply asked them politely. There are other candidates that would prove worthy of it."

A low growl escaped Heizl's throat, but Jilia stayed her with a raised hand. "We've nothing to fear from an ally. Men, leave us." After a moment's hesitation, the soldiers – former guardsmen and foreign insurgents alike – filed out. As the last man left the Throne Room, the noble turned back towards Renyar. "You were about to say something?"

"I was." He nodded once before glancing between the two Imperials. "I was considering telling you about my grandfather."

"While we're at it, I could tell you all about my grandma. Now there was a lady who knew how to get people to do as she said." Heizl grinned.

"Understanding the scope of our situation may well cause you to better appreciate the circumstances." Renyar looked down his nose at Heizl as he started pacing. "It was my grandfather who banished Urephor into the darkness between worlds in the first place."

"See? He's not taking any of this seriously." Heizl waved a hand.

Jilia cleared her throat. "We're already dealing with pieces of dragon. Maybe it's not so ridiculous."

When Renyar smiled at Jilia, Heizl felt a heat rise in her chest. She had to restrain the urge to lash out at him.

"My thanks," the Thalan continued. "My grandfather couldn't face the full power of Urephor. Even with kin and country at his back, victory was not guaranteed. So he chose to avoid direct confrontation. Instead, at another's suggestion, he came upon the dragon while it slept, and created an opening into the Void outside our realm. Holding its Heart, with it he stepped beyond, and so saved the world."

"That's just great," said Heizl, pulling a face. "What story are you going to tell us next?"

"What she means," Jilia said quickly, "Is that we'd like you to explain why this is relevant."

"I remember my paternal grandfather as an ambitious, complicated individual. He was no self-sacrificing hero, and had no intention to abandon all that he'd built here. His pupils were left with the means to reopen the path that he'd taken, to allow him to return. It is that path that lies at the centre of Rufenrich's ritual and his ambitions."

"You're telling me," Heizl dragged out each word, "That Rufenrich is going to use your secret family recipe to cook up a fresh batch of dragon?"

"Not in so many words," replied Renyar.

"Void take you, snake, I didn't realise you had it in you," Heizl laughed. "You nearly had me for a moment there." Still on the bench, Jilia didn't seem to find the story of monsters and men quite so amusing.

"We're past the time for jokes, Heizl."

"Not that I trust a word you say, but just how do you suggest the Emperor got hold of this ritual? I can't imagine that sort of thing is just left lying around."

Renyar shook his head. "I can't answer that question. Rufenrich has held together an Empire that's intent on breaking itself apart, and has discovered long-forgotten secrets. It is not beyond imagination for him to have found that as well."

"Tell me about it – you should've seen how quickly he found out I'd snuck someone into my room at the Spire." Heizl thought for a moment, and glanced at Jilia. "I mean–" She never knew she could be so glad as the instant when Renayr interrupted her.

"This is hardly the time for such levity." Renyar scowled. "Now, in the interest of sharing, where's the Fang? I'd honestly expected you to have attempted to seize it by now, what with your corruption."

As the noble replied, heat rose within Heizl, her skin prickling. "...What corruption?" She glanced at Jilia before turning back towards Renyar.

"When the Claw was in Thalan hands I recall it in significantly better condition. Fragments take a strain upon their bearers even when pristine. Traditionally, my Melechs have trained for months, if not years, before bonding to theirs. Carrying one with such damage could have unforeseen consequences upon an unprepared mind."

"So you're saying that the spear might hinder Heizl's judgement?" Jilia asked, holding her gaze steady upon Renyar.

The Thalan cocked his head and regarded Heizl. "I'm saying that her mind might already be broken. Maybe I should take her with me to Norjhost, and give Seorsa her Fragment rather than mine."

"You have to realise I'm standing right here." Heizl growled, tucking the shaft of the Claw under one arm, its cracked head scraping the floor.

"Renyar, I have a question," said Jilia.

As the Thalan shifted his grey eyes back to the noble, Heizl felt her grip loosen. She hadn't realised how tightly she grasped the ancient weapon. The logical part of her mind knew that how hard she held it didn't change how she drew upon its power. It made her feel better though.

"We took Thaun's shield away from him, and it doesn't seem to do anything now. Is it broken too?"

"It's bonded with him." Renyar replied with a wave of his hand. "It requires death in one of its many forms to break such a link. Until then, only the Crown Prince can use it fully."

"So there's no benefit to him—"

"I've got a question." Announced Heizl, interrupting and drawing frowns from both Renyar and Jilia. "Don't get me wrong, I've only got to play with this thing for a few days now." She shook the spear. "But I've worked out how to hit things with it pretty good, watch." Levelling it at one end of the long bench, she let loose a tight blast. The varnished wood disappeared into the cloud of grey and purple. As her magic dissipated, it revealed charred splinters and ash. "At the risk of you making a performance jibe, it didn't work against the Emperor. What went wrong?"

"Do you Imperials always talk so much?" Renyar waved his hand through the air impatiently. At his disregard, Heizl fought the urge to repeat her demonstration with a living target. "A divinitesimal's intricacies and mechanics are tiring to discuss."

"A what?"

"Such will wait until another time. I must leave for my meeting with Seorsa soon, but I intend to speak with the Crown Prince before I depart."

"What do you need to talk to Thaun for?" asked Heizl.

"He arrived here carrying Elhin's Fragment," growled the Thalan. "I intend to learn more of my lieutenant's failure."

"That might not be the best idea." Though her headache had returned, Heizl spoke in a steady tone. "We can get any answers that you need from the guardsman that arrived with him. There's no need to get unpleasant with someone who might be a useful ally."

Renyar didn't reply straight away, but Jilia continued on Heizl's behalf. "I agree. Thaun's presence is a good thing even if we can't talk him round. So long as we hold him it forestalls any strike by the Emperor's men."

The Thalan worked his jaw with one hand. "I do all of this for our long-term benefit, but don't let that overshadow the importance of short-term gain. Having the Fang back in our hands is just as valuable as your cousin's influence. Kingdoms have fought and fallen over the rumour of such Fragments." He half-turned away, as if to start for the door. "Your Shadow friend has proved himself both loyal and effective. Perhaps he would benefit from such a gift."

"Who? Zecht?" Heizl almost laughed. "He's out cold again. The guy doesn't know how to pick his fights."

"Then I'll find someone more suitable."

"Come on." She smiled disarmingly, and almost didn't notice her headache receding. "I can bring Thaun over to our side, promise. We get the best of both worlds that way. Someone competent with another Fragment, and enough political pull here that things won't fall apart in the long run."

"Just like you promised me that you could seize your uncle?"

"That was different," said Heizl, still smiling. "He had some knife or something that we didn't know about. You know, I'm pretty sure that's something to do with why the Claw didn't work properly."

"Heizl," Renyar spoke with barely concealed impatience. "I'm fully aware that you're dragging out this discussion because you know I have time sensitive obligations towards Seorsa. If I don't leave soon, our entire bargain may well fall through, and then our long-term strategy will fail."

"You say that you know what I was doing." Her smile turned to a smirk. "But you still fell for it. You've got to be running late by now, right?"

The Thalan turned away fully, but didn't move towards the door. He glanced over one shoulder. "Seorsa is my priority right now. You have one chance to do as you say. Don't disappoint me."

Before Heizl could craft a retort or Jilia could attempt to diffuse the situation, a twisting black orb formed around Renyar. Just like in the Nexus, a sulphurous stench filled the air. A moment later, it burst apart under its own energies, revealing nothing but empty space and a hint of brimstone.

"Considering he almost literally has a silver tongue." Heizl turned to the noble, still perched with folded skirts upon the bench several feet from the smoking wreckage of one end. "That guy's a bit of a jerk. Do you think all Thalan's are that annoying?"

Jilia smiled and shook her head. "You almost sounded like your old self just then."

Heizl couldn't help but smile back, despite the strange comment. "Why wouldn't I?" Things were going to be alright.

Tooth and Nail – Chapter Twenty-Two

*"By love or fear imprisoned,
Make one, prepare another,
For guidance you should listen;
Chain yourself, chain your brother."*

Verse to Inheritance,
Guiare the Filidh (214 I.Y.)

5th day of Ehnaln, 406th Imperial Year
17th Year of Emperor Rufenrich Konreig's Reign

Through bleary eyes, Thaun awoke to a ceiling of pale stone. The morning sun filtered through wispy curtains to break across his face, highlighting the dust drifting in the air. He held up an arm, casting his view back into shadow, and blinked several times as he adjusted to the light.

Sinking back into the soft pillow, Thaun closed his eyes. Despite everything that had happened, he'd dragged a few hours of sleep out of the night just past. He didn't feel any better for it. Letting his arm drape back across his face, he plunged into amber-hued darkness once more.

Oblivious slumber soon reclaimed him. When he opened his eyes again, the sunlight seemed little different. He couldn't have slept for long. Too many nights had felt like that of late. Maybe not just of late – sleep rarely came easily, even on his better days.

He ached. More than that, he *hurt*. His head pulsed with pain. Tightness gripped his jaw. Tension strobed along one cheekbone. It felt like someone had punched him in the face. Or what he imagined that'd feel like, anyway.

Thaun stared at the ceiling, hand breaking the beam of light cast across him. He'd recognised the familiar stone of the Imperial Palace in an instant, but he didn't know this place. His own suite had a roof of dark wood, separating his bedroom from a rarely used office on the floor above. For whatever reason, his cousin had moved him somewhere else.

Unwilling or unable to succumb to sleep, he propped himself up onto his elbows to take in his surroundings.

At the sudden movement, his head spun. Eyes clenched shut and chin tight to his bare chest, Thaun waited for it to pass. It took a moment longer than he might've expected, but the feeling faded and he risked looking around again.

An empty fireplace filled half of one wall, while a dressing table and a single bookshelf lined another. Other than a pair of doors and the window, the room held little else.

Memories gradually filtered in as he took in the sight. He hadn't come here much before, but a child's trauma rose in his mind. Crawling into a father-figure's bed, crying for lost family. Servants trying to coerce him away from an uncle dealing with his own grief. A civil war brewing so unlike Heizl's rebellion. A child confused by the flight from their home under cover of night.

These were the Emperor's quarters.

Thaun sat up a little straighter. It felt strange to be here, for more than one reason. Deep down, he knew that someday he'd inherit this room, along with everything associated with it. The Throne, a crown, and a thousand other responsibilities. He'd pictured that day in a dozen different ways, but none of them looked like this. Dead gods, missing and traitorous family, and the city up in arms. None of this was meant to be this way.

What little of his training he'd actually paid attention to had little to say on such matters. At the very least he'd always assumed he'd have Heizl with him to help.

He couldn't believe it. His cousin had always been ambitious, and more than a little ruthless when it came to her own desires, but she'd never do something like all this. Not without someone forcing her to, anyway.

Thaun shuddered at the memory of Renyar's attack upon the Palace, and the way that he'd commanded and enthralled those around him. It couldn't be a coincidence, not with the Thalan's plans and Sheltz's Comet so near. The idea of someone manipulating Heizl made so much more sense than her doing this by herself.

And here Thaun lay, in a gilt cage while the world burned all around him. Normally he would've expected melancholy to wash over him under such circumstances. Instead, anger smouldered in the pit of his stomach.

He rose, tossed the blankets aside, pulled on some clothes, and started pacing. Soft carpets of blue and green parted around his bare feet. With each step, the fibres pressed down a little more, and sprang back a little less. Lost in his thoughts, Thaun didn't notice the way that the blues soon carried the scars of his passage, while the twisted strands of green bounced upwards behind him.

His path carried him around the room, from window to each door in turn. Beyond a gratefully received change of well-tailored clothes and a jug of cool water, nothing else caught his interest. Heizl's men had taken everything that he'd brought with him. His armour, new sword, and the Fang not least among them. He hadn't felt this naked or useless even when facing Renyar through the flames.

Thaun sighed. More than just those belongings were missing. It looked like he might've lost his relationship with his cousin, too. He would've found it a little easier if he didn't have other burdens to consider.

He'd left behind one set of responsibilities for another. Rufenrich, wherever he'd gone, had tasked Thaun to hold Insel Drach, and he'd abandoned it to run home. He'd tried to show initiative, and instead he'd rushed into danger. He'd fled from failure, yet it had followed him. It was meant to have been the safe option, and still he'd failed.

He'd left his friends behind to face the consequences of his actions. Lena lay dead or dying. Countless loyal guardsmen had given their lives. He'd cast them all aside. What he wouldn't do to have one of them here with him. Any of them would do a better job at... at whatever this was than he had so far.

For all their years together, he'd never seen Lena fight the way she had against Elhin. Magic had lent her unnatural strength and speed. Like every mage, or so Thaun was told, the healer walked the balance of trading blood for power with every spell and incantation. She'd strayed too far though, and spent more than she could afford. Corruption had repaid her for her attempts to halt their foe. Had the healer come here to find out what had happened instead, no number of rebels could've caught her.

Toland would have talked Heizl down, Thaun was sure. This whole time, the noble had known the right things to say. Whether that was in quiet answer to Thaun's own issues and insecurities, or a stern command to their soldiers, his words made a difference. At the very least the northerner would've found a way to cast some doubt into the turncoats that had rebelled – maybe that would've been enough to stop this madness.

And Sigren? He probably wouldn't have been caught in the first place. The Shadow had spent almost as much time in the Spire and the Forge as he had in the Palace with the rest of them. He'd paid much more attention to the things around him than Thaun ever had. That said, Heizl's death by crossbow bolt wasn't really the resolution Thaun had had in mind when he left Insel Drach.

Then there was... who, exactly? Someone he didn't know. Someone that should be there with him. A barely remembered face that he couldn't put a name to. A figure no one else thought existed.

Thaun sagged and his pacing ceased. Even if Heizl had left his weapons he probably still would've felt disarmed. It was hard to admit how much he relied on those around him, and how much faith he had in them. If he got out, he vowed he'd tell them just that.

That meant escaping, and self-reflection and sulking wasn't likely to help.

He pushed open a door to another of the Emperor's rooms and began exploring further.

A plate of meats, cheeses, and soft bread sat upon the private dining table, along with several bottles of wine. Tearing free one end of a loaf and stuffing it into his mouth, Thaun continued past without another glance. As much as drunken oblivion tempted him, now wasn't the time.

He vaguely remembered a couple of old swords hanging on walls from his youth, but saw no sign of them now. No hidden weapons or secret doors revealed themselves either. His uncle had trained as a Shadow once, before having the Throne thrust upon him. Rufenrich knew the value of an unexpected blade. If one lay in the small suite though, Thaun didn't find it. He even checked various books for hollowed out compartments with no luck. The rebels had had the sense to go through this place before locking him up. They'd left him with a fortune of art, books, and gold-threaded clothes, but nothing he could use to free himself.

Bars blocked each window – he could remember them being installed throughout the Palace after a particularly bad episode of his in his youth – but he found no locks on any door. The wood still bore the marks of where someone had removed the latches. Each of the side rooms stood empty.

Thaun paused at the heavy door that led from the suite. After disarming him, a dozen guards had escorted him here. Still, he didn't see many other options at this point. With a shrug, he took hold of the handle and pulled.

The subtle creak of its hinges accompanied the raising of four crossbows. Light glinted off steel bolts as half of the rebels standing outside levelled their weapons at him. Thaun hesitated. When faced with such a threat, it seemed the safest option.

The man furthest from him cleared his throat. Too old to be a green recruit, he wore his Imperial steel and faded black and red surcoat – the Kuhlner family's old colours – like a second skin. More than just idealistic rebels and foreign agents had joined Heizl's rebellion. For the first time, Thaun took his uncle's words of instability through their Empire at face value. "Your Highness? Did you need something?"

Thaun let his mouth hang open slightly. Did he know this man? There was something familiar about him at least. He could probably say the same about a hundred souls within the Palace though, joining the staff for the predictable pay rather than any sense of patriotism. "I... uh..." The weapons he'd expected, but the unlocked door and the almost-polite response came as something of a surprise. His eyes flicked across their faces, taking in the mixed expressions of respect, fear, and even a little hatred.

"Sir?" the former-guardsman repeated.

For a moment Thaun considered trying to shove past them. Though he'd tried hard not to take it for granted, soldiers and servants had always got out of his way before. With a little confidence, maybe they'd do the same now. After another glance at the weapons that each of them carried – swords, axes, and even an archaic-looking hammer – he reconsidered. It had been years since he'd once tried to take his own life, and today didn't seem like the time to have another go. "I was just going to see my cousin."

The veteran's hand fell to the head of the axe hanging at his hip. "Not an option I'm afraid." A touch of malice crept into his voice. "Your Highness, do you require an escort back to your quarters?"

Thaun didn't respond as he inched the door shut and backed into his uncle's suite. As the latch clicked, he leant against the wall and sank down to the carpeted floor.

Something febrile built within him. Static ran up his arms as his fingers tingled, and his scalp prickled with anxious sweat. His stomach convulsed as if acid boiled in its depths. A deep self-loathing came with each sensation. At his sides, his hands crept into fists.

Anyone else would be a cell right now. Many probably were already, or had lost their lives during the uprising. Heizl's uprising. That was the only reason they'd locked him away in here. His talent meant nothing to them, just his name. A thing he'd never earned for himself.

Reflection dogged him, as it so often had.

Heizl had succumbed to some madness; by the Claw, by Renyar's words, or by something else, it didn't matter. Their uncle had fled, disappeared into who-knew-where. Reiget City, largest city in the entire Konreig Empire, rioted while engulfed in flames. None of this should've happened, and he couldn't help but feel it was all his fault.

It'd be so easy to sink further, to bow his head and to accept the fate that fast approached. Thaun couldn't deny the temptation to give up. No one would blame him, but then, they never had. Friends and family, those closest to him, had always supported him. Faces flashed through his mind in lightning quick succession. Rufenrich, Heizl, Toland, Lena, Sigren, Jilia, Korten.

In spite of his every failure, they'd shown faith in him.

Thaun tilted his head back and opened his hands. The tendons in his arms ached. Scratches marred his palms where nails had cut them. His throat tightened and tears welled in his eyes, but none tracked down his cheeks. Maybe it was about time he began trusting in their opinion of him.

He wished he'd come to that decision sooner.

Wiping his face with one hand, he pushed himself upright with the other. Closing his eyes, he drew in a deep breath. The quiet and the darkness calmed the turmoil within him. Not by much, but by enough.

When Thaun looked around his prison a second time, it was with a fresh perspective. The fine craftsmanship of the furniture no longer spoke to him of dead ends and poor choices, but with promise and potential. He'd find a way out. Failing that, he'd make enough ruckus to get Heizl to come see him. Maybe it wasn't too late to talk her out of things.

His uncle had never meant to sit on the Throne; that responsibility had always fallen to Thaun's father, Myron's. As a second son, Rufenrich had shared in much of his elder brother's education. However, while the Court had groomed the heir to rule, they'd sent Rufenrich to join the Shadows at their Forge, with a view to one day leading the organisation in their family's name. After Myron's death, and the disastrous civil war that had followed, the man that had ascended to the throne knew more of blades and secrets than he did administration. The new Emperor had made many changes in his attempts to hold their fractious Empire together.

Not least among those had been the Palace's redesign. Every Imperial Shadow knew the value of a concealed way in and out of, well, anywhere. He couldn't imagine Rufenrich's private quarters to be an exception. He hadn't found one yet, but that didn't mean there wasn't one. Thaun just needed to search harder.

He checked the window first. Even if inch-thick iron bars hadn't dug a handspan into the stonework on either side, it seemed like exiting that way would be a bad idea. He suspected that ropes made of bedsheets wouldn't work so well in real life, even if he knew how to tie knots. If nothing else, he didn't want to start making a habit of leaping from windows. Rumours had got around after he tried the first time, all those years ago, and he couldn't imagine what people would say if he did it again.

He moved on. Old paintings hid only plain walls, and no secret doors swung open as he tilted every book and sconce.

Running out of inconspicuous hiding places, he turned his attention towards less convenient objects. Thaun felt his fresh resolve wavering. Deep down, he knew that failure could spell disaster. Not just for everything going on with Renyar's ritual. He'd felt before the mounting of minor obstacles and the way they could build. Too many, and even the smallest thing could trigger another unpleasant episode. Self-loathing and despair hung close enough to touch.

With one shoulder braced against the stone wall, he dug his fingers in behind a heavy-looking bookshelf and heaved. For a moment hope flared within him at the ease with which he moved the tall piece of furniture. Someone must have made it that light for a reason. Anything could be behind it. Weapons, a safe room, a passageway, his mind raced. Its dark wood creaked as it tipped to its balance point. For a precarious moment it stood there, before, with what felt like the smallest of nudges, it crashed to the floor, scattering its contents across the carpet. The soft fabric barely muffled the noise at all.

Within a matter of seconds, the heavy front door flew open and a familiar set of rebel guards rushed in. The first pair held their shields raised, shoulder-to-shoulder, while those behind them aimed their loaded crossbows out between them. More rebels crowded the corridor outside.

Thaun froze, one hand still reaching towards the collapsed bookshelf, the other braced against the wall. He returned the soldiers' stares, unsure of quite what to say. After a moment the older soldier who had spoken before risked looking at the scattered furniture beyond.

"Having trouble, Your Highness?"

"I, uh, couldn't reach the book I wanted." Even Thaun couldn't imagine someone believing his lie.

"...Right. Maybe you should pick something within your reach next time. It'd be a shame if a noise surprised one of the men while they held a weapon."

"Umm, sorry," he replied distractedly, looking down at the wreckage at his feet.

"That's alright, Your Highness." Impatience painted the veteran's voice in a slick tone. "We'll have someone up later to deal with you... and this mess."

Thaun kept his gaze downwards as his captors backed out of the room. Rebels muttered unpleasant things to one another. Only as the door nestled into its frame did he dare to look up.

Thoughts trickling down like sand in an hourglass, he sat down at the suite's broad table and slowly poured a small cup of wine. He didn't drink it, instead swirling the red around the crystal. His eyes glazed over, blind to the way that the viscous alcohol clung to the vessel's sides, as he thought. Familiar paths beckoned him forwards, those same self-destructive tracks he'd spent so much time upon, but he hesitated at muffled sounds.

For a second, he thought the noise came from outside, down in the city below. After everything that had happened recently, riots or skirmishes didn't seem too far-fetched. It took him a moment to cast that image from his mind.

Voices and noises still came from the other side of the door, but the tone had changed. His jailers had fallen into arguing with one another after leaving him. Their dispute had faded now. In its place came sounds of confusion, followed swiftly by shock and outrage. The metallic screech of violence joined them a second later, and Thaun's uncertainty twisted into pain and fear.

He froze. There was no way to tell who fought outside. The last week had exposed him to sounds more violent than he could've imagined before. He'd witnessed a distant battle while on his tour of their Empire, but miles of Kragiv-Stal's mountains had muted the clash of soldiers. Listening now, the rapid rhythm of sword blows punctuating cries of pain, it sounded like the rebels fared poorly. Even with the element of surprise, any less than a full squad would've struggled to achieve such an advantage so quickly.

Thaun willed himself to stand, placing the glass down just as the sounds of fighting stopped. Sweat prickled under his clothes, but he didn't move. He hadn't found any new source of bravery or strength, so much as being just so tired of all of it. It was easier to stand his ground.

The last moans of pain from outside ceased. A shiver ran down Thaun's spine as the door opened to reveal the devastated waiting room beyond.

Thaun's gaze fell across one corpse after another. Dropped weapons, broken armour, and even a few dismembered body parts littered the floor. Bile rose in his throat and the colour left his face. Images of the Second's disastrous battle against Elhin rose in his mind despite his efforts to push them back down. He'd hoped to never see such carnage again.

"Your Highness." The man standing at the centre of the bloodshed wiped his notched and bent longsword clean. Blood soaked into the front of his blue uniform and dripped from the huge pommel that protruded past one broad shoulder.

"I..." Thaun swallowed as recognition dawned. "Vandel? What are you doing here?"

The Champion's grey eyes scanned over those at his feet, checking for any signs of life. None of the unfortunate rebels so much as twitched. "Give me the Fang."

"What?" His mind couldn't keep up with events. He almost asked how the veteran knew about the Fragment, but reconsidered. The Champion, covered in blood and sweat, didn't look in the mood to be questioned. "It's not here. They took it from me."

"You're no good to me then." He didn't look at Thaun as he turned to leave.

"Where's my uncle?" he blurted out, his feet propelling him into Vandel's wake. He held his breath as he passed the motionless corpses, letting it out again as he entered the corridors that made up the veins of the Palace.

"He avoids confrontation."

"Where is he?"

"Less talking, more walking."

Another voice joined them. "Leave him be, old boy."

Thaun started as he turned to find an elderly, dark-skinned man walking at his side with the help of a cane. A foul, sulphurous smell filled his nostrils, and the breath in his lungs chilled. Despite the jangling charm bracelet, Thaun hadn't noticed him join them. Though he vaguely recognised him too, he couldn't quite place the man.

"Leave him be?" Vandel scoffed. "If he'd been strong enough to keep that Void-damned Fragment we'd be having a very different conversation right now." The Champion lengthened his stride, disappearing around another corner.

Though he didn't appear much healthier than some of the broken bodies they'd passed, the old man kept pace with Thaun. Despite his age, his voice came through deep and sonorous, though pitched low enough to avoid being heard. "You'll have to forgive Vandel. He's always had a one track mind. Never appreciated all the nuance of circumstance. If he knew everything going on, I suspect he'd be even worse. The stories I could tell you…"

"I know you, don't I?" asked Thaun, his mind thick and his headache returning.

"Highmage Hastigr, Your Highness. At your service, I believe." He smiled warmly. Beneath the collar of his dusty robe, several sharp lines of a tattoo poked out. "Now, if you'd please, we've been asked to retrieve you. A boat awaits us." The mage gestured forwards. "We should continue."

"No, wait," Thaun said, halting. "I'm not going anywhere until I get some answers!" Hastigr walked a few more paces before looking back. "Just what's going on? Is my uncle safe? Where's Heizl? Where are we going?"

"Your Highness." The Highmage offered a not-quite smile, "I was unfortunate enough to meet a traveller once. A regrettable encounter for all involved, I assure you. I learned something important from their tempestuous, misguided mind though."

"Unless it's an answer to one of–"

"There are occasions," Hastigr continued, ignoring his protests, "When it is in your best interest to wait for a satisfactory answer. I assure you that all will be answered in time. Now." He gestured again. "We should continue, and I fear that the rebel might not take kindly to our plot."

Tooth and Nail – Chapter Twenty-Three

"All magic is blood, but not all blood is magic."

Kraze the Scathed (386 I.Y.)

5th day of Ehnaln, 406th Imperial Year
17th Year of Emperor Rufenrich Konreig's Reign

Heizl kicked out at a broken piece of masonry the size of her fist. She barely felt the contact as it disappeared down the dim corridor and bounced out of sight. Their seizing of the Palace had probably bashed the rock loose – she'd have to see that her servants cleaned up properly.

One weary foot after another, Heizl stalked the bowels of her ancestral home. Her scathe itched, her palms sweated, and her shoulders ached. She ran a finger under the leather strap that held her cousin's shield, the Fang, against her back. How did Thaun put up with this sort of thing all the time? Heizl herself had carried a satchel that weighed twice as much for their trek across Norjhost and it hadn't felt this bad.

That had been... when, exactly? She wiped her free hand over her face. Her memory had proven to be less than reliable of late.

"So, where are we goin'?" asked Zecht.

She glanced at the Shadow limping along beside her. A mismatched squad of their revolutionaries followed behind at a short distance. "I've already told you twice. I'm not just gonna say it again."

"Yeah, I know, but I like asking you lots of times to see you get all pissed off." He glanced sidelong back at her. "Did you know you've got a vein in your–"

"Knock it off and hurry up." Heizl lengthened her stride.

"Eh, what's the rush?"

"I understand why Thaun punched you now." She paused for a second. "Wait, he didn't hit you in the leg. Why are you limping?"

"Yeah, I tripped up the stairs this morning." He shrugged.

"You've got to be the worst Shadow, you know that, right?"

He grinned, and hurried up just a little. "I get by."

Heizl shook her head and resisted the urge to blast a Zecht-shaped hole through the nearest wall. The Palace staff already had enough to clean up after their coup without adding to it with more debris. Besides, as unlikely as it seemed, he might still be helpful.

The soldiers escorting them drowned out the silence with the noise of armour rubbing against armour. Sounds of life drifted down through the ceiling. The Palace buzzed with uneasy activity. Rufenrich's loyalists massed at the Shadow's Forge, beyond the city walls. It had cost Heizl's revolutionaries enough to take the city even with the element of surprise. Holding it against a numerically superior force wouldn't end well. For those without a Fragment, at least.

That was before planning how they'd protect the Spire as well. It shouldn't have surprised her that their latest reports said that Hastigr had somehow disappeared from the Nexus itself. They were fortunate he'd kept it running from his trance as long as he had. If it wasn't for Thaun himself breaking free, Heizl would probably be searching for her old mentor instead. She wasn't sure which would be worse.

It wasn't meant to go like this. At least Renyar had already left for Seorsa. Dealing with traitorous, ritual-obsessed Imperials was one thing, but Heizl didn't know if she could put up with the Thalan's complaining much longer. When the snake came back, he wouldn't have the Tongue anymore – another exchange with him wouldn't end the same again.

As they neared the Emperor's suite of rooms, the itch at the back of Heizl's neck grew maddening. She'd noticed it doing that more and more lately. She'd heard a few of their men whispering about how she scratched at it all the time. They spoke of insanity, inhuman outsiders, and treason. If she caught anyone spreading rumours, she'd put a stop to it in a way people wouldn't ignore.

As calmly as she could, Heizl unslung Thaun's shield from her shoulder. She felt no more ready to deal with the situation this way, but at least she had her hands full – resisting the urge to scratch seemed easier like this. It wouldn't stop them from talking behind her back, but she preferred it to the alternative.

Heizl rounded a corner and the visceral sight before her scoured all vengeful thoughts from her mind. She hadn't given much thought to what this place might look like. Her cousin's escape had occupied her fully.

The corridor to her right opened out onto the waiting room outside the Emperor's own quarters. She paled as she counted eight corpses lying among the furniture. Beyond the blood, she didn't know what she looked at. Lena might've learned more – did a wound like that count as clean or messy? How recently had they met their fate? She'd miss the healer.

Two of her insurgents, both loaned Seorsan troops, guarded the bodies. If Heizl herself felt shocked at the scene before them, this pair looked positively broken.

She could feel the weight of her escort's expectations on her back. This wouldn't stand.

"Damn." At her side, Zecht let out a low, impressed whistle. "All close-up work, and only ours downed. No signs of magic, and it don't look like they had to drag any wounded or anything away... I'd say at least a dozen guys."

Heizl stared at him, mouth agape.

He shrugged. "What? I told you I get by."

Shield hanging from her arm, Heizl rubbed at her face. "Just... I... Which way do you think they went?"

"Well, yeah, sure." The Shadow gestured back the way they came. "There's another corpse over there, and where there's one..." He shrugged again, and limped away in the direction he'd pointed. "What? Aren't you coming? I thought you dragged me down here to deal with your cousin's mess?"

"Shush." Spear butt tapping the floor, she began after him. "Just show me which way they went. We need to find Thaun."

"You know I was I gonna follow them anyway, right? What did you think, that I was doing this for my health?" Zecht snorted a laugh. "Void, you really are–" The Shadow flinched as an exploding patch of wall showered him in masonry dust.

Stride faltering, Heizl opened her eyes and lowered the Claw. "I might not be able to control you like Renyar would, but I can still make you regret ignoring me," she seethed as she caught up. "I told you to shut up."

"Fine, shutting up." He threw up one hand as he leant against the wall with the other. For a moment, Heizl thought he was going to say something else, but nothing came.

They walked. For how long, she couldn't be certain, but it felt like Heizl only had time to blink before the Shadow stopped her again. Behind her, their escort halted with the clattering of armour and fastenings. They wisely stayed quiet.

Heizl stomped her foot. "Why've you stopped? Have you found him?"

Before her, blocking her view further up the corridor, Zecht cocked his head as he looked down. "Found something."

"Get out the way," she replied, pulling her companion back and stepping past. A week ago the horrific sight that greeted her might have turned her stomach. Her experiences in Norjhost had tempered something inside of her.

The stone wall on one side of the passage had cracked around several points, the centre of each spot now dark and glassy. Pieces of chipped tile and stone lay upon the floor from where something had struck the ceiling. A powdery, soot-like substance coated the surface for several feet in both directions. Opposite the scarred masonry lay a single corpse bearing two wounds – a jagged cut to the chest and a gruesome impact across the face. Between their dead feet lay a bent, scorched length of steel that might've once been a sword.

Heizl tapped the Claw against the flagstone as she pieced together the scene before her. She found it hard to concentrate, the Fang's unfamiliar weight pulling at her arm. After what felt like an age, she half-turned her head towards Zecht. "I recognise her..."

"D'you associate with corpses often? I heard a few rumours about your preferences, but–"

"She was Spire, I think," Heizl continued, ignoring the Shadow. "I don't remember her from any lessons or anything, but she was one of the first to join us after everything happened. Ciarra or something? Remember? She fried her Shadow when he refused to see sense?" Witnessing that had sent a sweet chill up Heizl's spine.

"Don't remind me." The blond man shuddered. "I closed my eyes and I'm still pretty sure I saw her lightning."

"Did we find her another Shadow from ours?"

"Nah, not enough to go round. Some Shades linked up with the First, so are probably out with their camp at the Forge. After we dealt with Frida, most of the rest are lying low, waiting for the dust to settle."

"Your loyalty is an inspiration to us all." She rolled her eyes and looked back to the corpse at her feet. "She didn't go down without a fight... so whoever broke Thaun out must be carrying their dead with them. That'll slow them down..."

"So what?" he replied.

"So we use that, idiot. Didn't they teach you anything when you signed up?"

Zecht grinned. "They taught me how to stick radical mages real good."

"I know that sounded like a question, but I didn't really expect an answer. Look around. They're not making towards the gate, and we've not found any hidden passages or anything down this way. Thaun's gotta be heading for the dock."

"Makes sense, I guess."

"Stop guessing." Heizl spun on him, shooting him a hard glare. "Take two men, and go that way. There's a service corridor that heads down to the river. Find it, use it, try and cut them off."

"You're the boss, Fitz." Zecht threw a mock salute, and limped away. Two rebels – a tall, bearded man with a woodsman's axe, and a lean woman with slicked back hair – peeled off to follow him.

Heizl let them get a dozen paces away before calling after him. "Shade, be careful."

The Shadow slowed slightly, but didn't turn around. He simply waved one hand in the air before disappearing around a corner and out of sight.

Breathing deeply, Heizl set off again, stepping over Ciarra's corpse. She could hear the remaining members of her escort falling into step behind her. They knew their place at least.

She didn't regret sending Zecht away. Whoever had stolen Thaun from them, they'd slain a battlemage. The Empire still had three more Highmages; any of them might've managed such a feat. In a straight fight, no dagger could hope to make a difference against such a foe. The Claw on the other hand... She'd probably just saved the Shadow's life.

They passed several more corpses as they walked, but she didn't recognise any of their unmoving faces. The passageway sloped downwards, passing torn paintings and smashed windows. She noticed a few more weapons damaged beyond what she'd have expected, but didn't slow to investigate them. Other thoughts clouded Heizl's mind, distracting her from the carnage and her guards' whispered murmurs.

It was the Wanderer's own luck that Renyar had already departed for Seorsa. The Thalan wouldn't be happy with any of this. He'd view Thaun's escape as another failure on Heizl's behalf. He already blamed her for losing the Emperor. Maybe Rufenrich's treasonous loyalists wouldn't have made a move if the snake and his Fragment hadn't left the Palace.

Still, she could turn this to her advantage. Thaun would meet with Rufenrich. This trail would lead them straight to the Emperor, and then all this would be over. With a little luck, that'd solve a lot of her problems. With the two royals removed, and Renyar trading the Tongue to Seorsa, there'd be nothing to stop her from taking the Throne.

Heizl's foot caught an uneven flagstone, but she stopped herself from tripping. Still gripping the Claw, she rubbed at her temple and shook her head. She didn't want the Throne, not really. She'd just lock them both away until after the Comet had passed. Those entitled boys in the Imperial Court could deal with everything else after. That was the right way to solve it all. Jilia would be more impressed with that... right?

She looked down at the shield strapped to her arm. They'd seen it in action, both in her cousin's hands and Elhin's, not that it seemed to have done either of them much good. Heizl had wondered if it might react to the spear in some way – both came from Urathear, after all – but she'd had no luck getting it to do anything.

In spite of all that, holding it made her feel a little better, a little clearer-headed. If she'd had to explain the sensation, she might've claimed that without it Thaun was less of a threat. In all honesty, she didn't know if she believed that herself. With her cousin's disappearance, she had other priorities.

At a rippling sound echoing up the corridor, she looked up. She'd walked halfway across the Palace without paying attention to her surroundings. Glancing down, a fresh corpse, mangled beyond all recognition, lay at her feet.

At least she'd managed to keep following the trail of blood – Zecht wouldn't have let her live it down if she'd lost her way.

From behind her, the sounds of her escort drawing weapons was like a lens pulled before her thoughts, focusing them onto a single point.

The Royal Docks awaited them, with a handful of boats moored against its jetties. Beyond, the Reigan River flowed from right to left, another trio of small craft paddling in different directions. Upstream, downstream, the far bank – it didn't make a difference, she'd caught them now.

A single figure stood upon the damp stone. Heizl spared him a dismissive glance. Blood covered their arms up to the elbows, while red speckled the rest of their blue uniform like stars in the night sky. Resting in its scabbard still, he carried a large sword on his back. On one arm hung the shattered remains of a guardsman's shield – little more than a leather strap – while his other hand held a damaged axe.

Heizl ignored the single surviving soldier. She'd bigger things to worry about than some suicidal old veteran playing rearguard.

The three fleeing boats looked no different to those still docked. A single sail, a couple of oars, and a crew of just half a dozen or so. The sides came up high enough that Thaun could've hidden in any of them. Glancing from one vessel to the next, Heizl shrugged. It took more than some painted wood to fool her.

She began falling within herself, drawing upon her sorcery with eyes half-closed to see the chains binding all things together. Streams of light hung in the air, linking soul to soul and plank to plank. In her hands, the Claw raged and the Fang smouldered.

Faint threads, barely visible in the light of the twin suns at her side, stretched out from her chest to each boat. Men plied the waters, but she lacked the relationships with them to form strong bonds. She pushed and twisted, seeking one that she might recognise, but they recoiled from her touch.

Eyes half-closed, Heizl had only the barest awareness of her escort moving past her, or the old soldier stepping into their path. She ignored them all, mind racing as her arcane eye wandered.

Rufenrich's traitors couldn't have penetrated their defences with naked steel alone. The Empire had few enough mages, let alone ones capable of entering her Palace unseen. It all made sense, the defeated mage, the trail of carnage with no enemy losses, there being no trace of her cousin after following him all this way. Only one mage could hide things from her like this. Hastigr had to be here, Heizl was sure of it.

She stumbled back as something heavy struck her. The lines of light faded from Heizl's vision as she opened her eyes. One of her escorts, a man in Strahl colours, had fallen against her with a gaping wound where his face should've been.

Heizl shoved the fresh corpse away, straightened her shirt, and looked up as the last of her insurrectionists collapsed to the wet floor. Heizl arched an eyebrow at the old-timer still standing upon the quayside. None of her rebels moved, their bodies scattered in a semi-circle around the loyalist soldier. A single body floated face down in the river's shallows.

The soldier spat to one side and opened his mouth to speak. Heizl didn't give him the chance. Her revolution had given her plenty of opportunities to practice with the Claw. Once or twice she'd even used it as an actual spear, rather than the power source she'd come to view it as.

Grey and purple filled the space between them, raw power tearing apart the nearest corpses. Uniforms turned to ash, and flesh followed. Stone flaked as if having lived an age beneath desert winds, and wood shrank back. Even the river's flow twisted away as if blown upon by a mighty wind, fresh currents rising upon its surface.

Heizl opened her eyes as the blast faded. It seemed almost a pity to destroy such an expert soldier in such a brutal fashion, like defacing a masterpiece, but she didn't have time for hesitation.

She walked forward, blinking through the falling dust as she struggled to make out the boats that she'd seen before. Even if she couldn't sense Thaun on any of them through Hastigr's interference, the Claw would make short work of the fleeing vessels. They could fish her cousin out of the water after.

Tugging on a random thread, Heizl bound it to the Claw's blazing centre, and watched as destructive power flowed along it.

It never reached the river craft.

Something struck her in the chest hard enough to launch her back several paces. Her head rang as she bounced from a wall. Heizl didn't get the time to appreciate how little the blow hurt. Strong hands grasped her shirt and threw her sideways to skid and roll across stone and wood.

Blood dribbled from a split lip as she pushed herself upright. Her vision swam for just a moment, before focusing on the figure standing a short distance away. Smoke rose from the scorched flesh of the old soldier that had faced down her escort.

"A Fang," the man said in a familiar voice. "A Claw." He stooped and picked up a long object trailing tattered straps. "Two Scales." Something gouged at the inside of Heizl's stomach as half-buried memories rushed back to her. "A Wing..." The soldier drew the two-handed scimitar from its damaged sheath. "...Bone, and Hea–"

Heizl's next blast slammed into the raised blade, enveloping the Imperial Champion in an instant. The loyalists she'd encountered during their coup had died in heartbeats. The mage that had bought Rufenrich time to escape hadn't survived more than a moment.

Hairs standing on end, scathed neck itching, and mouth dry, Heizl didn't relent until a section of roof fell in above where Vandel had stood. Both Renyar and Elhin had fled when confronted by the veteran soldier. Even with the Claw's untold power at her command, she'd no interest in taking any chances.

A cloying smell, not unlike ash-laden smoke, filled her lungs. Stonework cracked and shifted as the Palace's weight settled. Dust drifted down like snow, and the mage let out a cough. Everything hurt, but she pushed aside the aches, stings, and maddening itches. The Fang hung from her arm as a heavy, useless weight.

Heizl hesitated for a moment longer before turning back to the shrinking shapes of the three boats. Motion in the dust rewarded her caution.

She lacked the words to describe Vandel's charge from the shifting ash and dust. A galloping horseman didn't carry the same promise of death. Bears lumbered towards wounded prey with less mercy. An avalanche might be more easily pushed aside.

Heizl failed to find a suitable analogy before Vandel was upon her. His oversized curved blade danced in big sweeping arcs, razor-sharp edge swinging towards her. The Claw leapt to meet it, writhing in her grip as if in an attempt to destroy the slashes themselves. Between attacks her mind flashed back to Norjhost and the way Naqtuqa had fought. Did she look like the warleader had, lashing out at whoever came near, face and mind wrapped in rage?

She didn't believe it. The Norjan had held off three men, even while his brother's bargains with the spirits kept him dazed. Heizl struggled to survive beneath the martial attentions of a single soldier. She fought with a skill and strength that wasn't her own, yet Vandel forced her further back along the wooden dock.

More by luck than by any sort of intent, a couple of blows landed upon the bronze shield strapped to her left arm. Much like the unyielding blocks she'd made with the spear, the Fang absorbed the strikes with only the slightest damage upon its old surface, but no black fires grew in response. Whatever magic fuelled the Fragment, she couldn't make it function. It ignored her just like everyone else always had.

Growling, Heizl retreated another step beneath the onslaught. Water seeped through her shoes and sweat soaked into her dark shirt. She squeezed the spear's leather-wrapped grip a little harder.

The Champion stepped in past a wild stab, each of his swings leading into the next like a dance, his every movement poised, perfect, and conserving unnecessary effort. His blade ran along Heizl's side before whipping upwards, slicing through cloth with the ease of a tool honed to the finest edge. Heizl threw herself backwards, and felt a burning brand slide through the flesh of her left arm. Blood ran between her fingers. If she hadn't abandoned her own lunge, she probably would've lost the entire hand.

Leather straps cut, her cousin's shield swung wildly from her one-handed grip on its handle. Face contorting into a snarl, Heizl threw it at her opponent's head, missing by several inches as Vandel dodged deftly aside. The Fang bounced from a wall before sliding across the slick stone and out of sight.

Rage burning hot in her veins, she launched herself after the shield. Vandel rewarded her by stepping into the lunge, the Claw's amber head breaking the few remaining chain links across his side to score a wound along one rib. In return, the Champion reached out and slammed the crossguard of his sword into the side of Heizl's head.

At such a blow, anyone else, even Renyar, would've fallen. Her vision swam as she fell backwards, barely keeping upright on the smooth planks, flailing blindly in an attempt to prevent a follow-up attack. She needn't have bothered. Vandel stood where she'd left him, scimitar resting in a one-handed grip upon his shoulder. The old veteran ran a gauntlet along his side, fresh blood coming away at the touch.

Penetrating, grey eyes flicked up to Heizl, an unreadable depth behind them. Head clearing, she flashed a smile back, a look that had infuriated family, friends, and rivals alike for years. This man, this soldier without equal, could be hurt. Sure, he'd survived beneath the Claw's destructive onslaught where stone and magic had given way, but Heizl could put that down to Hastigr's interference. Vandel bled like any other.

That flickering hope winked out as the Champion returned her smile, one corner of his mouth twisting up in a cruel scowl. Heizl swallowed. She understood. This whole fight, Vandel had toyed with her. The Champion could've ended it at any time.

"A Fang," the veteran began again in his gravelly voice. "A Claw, two Scales, a Wing, Bone and Heart." He glanced over her shoulder towards where Thaun's shield had disappeared into the shadows. "Yield–"

As he turned back to face Heizl, grey and purple erupted from the Claw. A smell like stale smoke filled her nostrils once more. She didn't really expect it to do much good, but she did it anyway. Through the dark cloud, she made out Vandel's indistinct shape. The Champion stood his ground, sword raised before him.

"Sorry." She shrugged, feeling her sweat-soaked clothes peel away from her with the movement. "I've always been told that I interrupt people too much. Were you saying something?" She let the blast fade and watched Vandel straighten. What little armour that had survived before had disappeared almost entirely, revealing blackened, soot-stained flesh. Blood no longer trickled from the wound in his side. In his hands, the huge, curved blade gleamed faintly, looking no less the worse for wear.

His newfound, muscular nakedness didn't seem to bother him in the slightest. He shifted back into a stance, blade held out before him in steady hands. "Yield the Claw."

"It seems like you keep claiming to already have one." Heizl leant upon the spear, feeling the planks creak slightly beneath her. "Don't you think it's greedy asking for more?" Vandel took a step towards her. "Woah! Wait up! We both know I can't beat you in a straight fight, and you refuse to die against this thing. You've got me, I'm dead, I get it." She sighed. "Can't we just talk for a minute?"

"You sound like my brother," the Champion growled. He didn't lower his stance, but neither did he move towards her. Heizl took a couple of steps back anyway, unwilling to get too close.

"Family, right?" Heizl tried a disarming smile, anything to keep her alive for a few moments longer. She edged back a little further, and the veteran followed, always just beyond reach. "Look at mine – they're trying to summon a god to help destroy the world, or something."

Vandel's eyes narrowed. "You're wrong. Things aren't so simple as dragons and destruction."

"Yeah? Why don't you tell me about it? You're going to kill me anyway it seems, so what's the harm?"

"That's not how this works." The tip of his sword wove a figure eight as the Champion drove her further back along the jetty.

"You can't blame a girl for trying," Heizl drawled, her weariness catching up with her. Sliding one foot backwards, she almost slipped as she reached the end of the dock. Another pier ran parallel to this one a few paces to her right, but, even if Vandel would let her, she wasn't sure she still had the strength to jump between them.

For a second she considered throwing herself into the rushing current beneath, the waters further out deep enough to accept larger boats and barges. Heizl shook her head – she'd never been a strong swimmer. Better to end this. "Want to get this over with?"

"No more words?" Vandel looked almost shocked, and then shrugged. "I'm not cruel. Accepting your end will be much easier for both of us."

"Oh, that's not what I meant." Heizl let out another blast, ash coating the inside of her throat. Above the sound, she heard the Champion's dry, amused laughter. She couldn't help but join him with a satisfied chortle as energy crossed the distance between the two of them. Grey and purple struck, but not into her indomitable foe.

The wet stone and planks beneath the veteran's feet disappeared in a heartbeat. Vandel plunged into the water, his laugh twisting into a shocked yell. Heizl didn't stop, destroying the nearest supports and beams to prevent any chance of the formidable warrior climbing back up, before turning her attention to her target himself. The blast itself did little to hurt the Champion, but anything to disrupt his attempts at swimming would buy her time.

After a moment, sweat pouring down her brow and into her eyes, Heizl let the attack fade. She blinked several times as she stared at the spot where Vandel had stood. None of their fight should've been as difficult as it was, but she could work that out later. She'd come down to the docks for... something.

Slowly, she looked around. A small boat pulled up onto the opposite bank of the river, men rushing to disembark. It came to her then. Thaun. Heizl had followed him, and couldn't afford to let him get away.

Vision blurring from sweat and fatigue, she levelled the Claw at the distant shapes. She fought to focus, the world spinning still from the blow to her head.

She hesitated, something drawing her attention further upstream. It didn't feel right, but something in her gut called her to look aside, to search for something hidden. The sensation was familiar somehow.

Understanding came too late. For much of her Spire career she'd manipulated men and women's thoughts and emotions, growing accustomed to her scathe being unique. It wasn't often that she'd been on the receiving end of such an arcane bond.

Eyes growing wide, she turned to look back, searching, along the destroyed jetty.

Hastigr stood at the far end, almost in the shadow of the Palace's tunnels, staring back at her. Despite everything that had happened in the last few moments, she swore she could smell mothballs.

Heizl opened her mouth to speak, Claw coming round to aim at the old mage. She never got to find out for herself what she'd have said to her mentor at that moment. It probably wouldn't have mattered anyway.

The sword, a well-used piece of Imperial steel dropped by one of Heizl's own escort, slid along her side, just beneath her ribs. Fire erupted as flesh and cloth parted around the honed edge.

She spun, balance giving way as hot blood left her body, taking her strength with it, just as the follow-up attack connected.

Both hands upon the hilt, Thaun's thrust pushed the blade's point through her gut. Legs already weak and growing cold beneath her, she fell backwards as the tip burst out of her back and the crossguard slammed into her stomach.

As Heizl struck the water, she looked up in shock and pain at the man that she loved like a brother. The river rose to consume her, but through it she saw tears streaming from her cousin's face. A few moments earlier she'd almost come to accept her own death at Vandel's hands, but this hadn't once crossed her corrupted mind.

She fought to say something, anything, but nothing came. Instincts kicking in, she struggled to tie bonds from one piece of shredded flesh to another. Every thread unravelled at her touch.

Blood, dirty water, and ash filled her mouth. Fluid fought with smoke in her nostrils as cold crept into her arms and legs.

Closing her eyes, the darkness claimed her entirely.

Tooth and Nail – Chapter Twenty-Four

"There is not a healer in all Seorsa who could mend the harm I have caused. The pains of knowledge plague me night and day. I understand now the inner workings of those with silver in their eyes, and that which they made me do. First among sinners, I do not deserve the quiet mercy I now bring upon myself."

The High Inquisitor's Diary,
Final entry, Daen (386 I.Y.)

6th day of Ehnaln, 406th Imperial Year
17th Year of Emperor Rufenrich Konreig's Reign

Smoke rose in a dozen places over Reiget City. The plumes rivalled the Spire's looming spectre, dark forms rising to block out the blue sky. Its northern gates lay in ruins with scorch marks scarring roads and walls alike where the Imperial Guard had re-entered the city. Forgotten corpses still lay in dark corners, though press-ganged clean-up crews had removed most. They'd killed or captured all but a handful of the rebels, the remaining few going into hiding.

High above, a dark cloud drifted, and the sun's gaze broke through to illuminate the Palace. Thaun's eyelids fluttered open as soft light touched upon him. Wrapping one arm over his face, he willed sleep to claim him again, but no release came. He pressed a little harder until faint stars bloomed across his vision.

That brief moment of pain, like a weight pushing his eyes into his skull, seemed the most real thing in the world. It didn't last long enough. A deeper agony, crushing and all-consuming, pressed in on all sides.

Heizl. His cousin wasn't just gone. No, he'd killed her himself. Thrust and slash, just as he'd practised. Cold water, hot blood, and hotter tempers. He could count the number of times he'd drawn a blade in anger on one hand, but he'd never killed anyone, not even when fighting Thala. Not until now.

Thaun wished he'd never picked up a sword in the first place. How different would all this have turned out if he'd shown an interest in his lessons, rather than wasting time in a duelling ring? Had he shown the slightest competency elsewhere, how much better might things be now?

He scratched at his face, eyes still clenched shut. His fingers found coarse, patchy stubble. How long had he gone without shaving? Or washing properly? Sleeping through much of the day and crying for most of the rest hardly encouraged good timekeeping.

Thaun cracked one eye open, letting it adjust to the light before opening the other and taking in his surroundings. The same room that he'd fallen asleep in. The same bed, furniture, and decorations. The same barred window. The same books and old mementoes resting upon dusty shelves. His own room.

Some member of the Palace staff had cleared away his heaped clothes from… had that only been the night before? It was hard to tell. Thirst and grief had scoured his throat raw.

He rolled over and sank into the soft mattress. One eye pressed into the too-warm pillow, his other focused upon the Fang where it lay upon a chair. When servants had removed his dirty and damaged clothing, they'd tried to take it with them too. His brief outburst had put a stop to that, and they'd fled the room. The resulting fear in their eyes was just one more in a long line of regrets.

With great effort, Thaun swung his legs off the bed. He didn't stand straight away, sitting instead with head bowed.

Heizl was gone. Stabbed, cut open, and knocked into the Reigan River's murky flow. Even knowing what his cousin had done – to the Empire, to the city, to their family – none of that excused Thaun's own actions. He should've found another way. They couldn't ignore Renyar's influence, but Thaun couldn't find it in himself to put aside his own guilt.

There must've been something else he could've done. Maybe if he'd returned home sooner, said the right thing, or done something differently, then he could have prevented it all. Then they could've locked Heizl in a cell or beneath the Spire, and she wouldn't be dead and gone.

Those same thoughts had echoed through his mind since he'd... he struggled to even think the word. Since he'd killed her.

Thaun forced his ever-tightening fists open. Surging upright, he took two quick steps and seized the Fang in both hands. Clutching it to his chest, he sighed. Its metal surface felt lukewarm through the coarse shift that he wore. Almost instantly, he felt a little better. The pain still pulsed within him, but now as if at a greater distance. If the shield could seemingly handle any attack thrown at it, somehow Thaun could find a way to persevere a little longer.

He held it tight, like a child's toy. Looking down, he was surprised at the fondness and calm that burgeoned within him at such a reunion. Thaun hadn't realised how empty he'd felt without it.

Straightening his arms, he held the Fang at arm's length to admire it. The battered bronze surface caught a hint of his reflection, twisting his features into something barely recognisable. A bitter voice in the back of his mind told him he wouldn't much prefer what he'd see in an actual mirror.

Breathing heavily, hands trembling ever so slightly, Thaun placed the shield back down on the chair. Simply seeing the Fragment gave him a faint sense of relief, but the way it made him feel left a bitter taste in his mouth. As if he didn't have enough to worry about.

Still, for just a moment he could forget at least some of his pains.

Thaun turned his back on the shield and wandered towards the window. It hadn't opened in years, but standing there, dull light streaming through the glass, represented something final for him. Jumping had always been a stupid plan – he wasn't even sure it would've been a big enough drop to... He probably shouldn't be thinking about it. Such thoughts only ever seemed to spiral, getting worse before they got better. *If* they got better.

His gaze, not really focusing as he scanned across Reiget City, settled on the Comet's blue-green shape. It had grown brighter since he'd last seen it, appearing clearly even by daylight. Even in this difficult time, most Imperials would go about their business. Only a few would glance up at the once-in-a-generation sight. If only they knew what it represented, what its arrival meant, then they might worry as much as he did.

All this death already, and they'd yet to win anything resembling a clear victory over Renyar. It was like the Thalan Patriarch knew their every step, as if someone had told him how all things might turn out. If they couldn't find him, could they hope to defeat him? The window – broken glass, bent bars, and a long drop – seemed almost preferable to finding out how this would end.

He didn't know if he was grateful or not for the hesitant knock at the door that distracted him from his thoughts.

An unfamiliar, muffled voice came from the other side. "Your Highness? His Majesty has requested your presence for a private audience." Thaun kept his mouth shut, and his shoulders sagged. Any hope that whoever it was might leave if he stayed quiet quickly left him as they spoke again. "Your Highness?"

"Go away," he said in a low voice.

"I'm sorry, sir, but we were given specific instructions to ensure your presence." They at least had the decency to sound appropriately apologetic as they raised the latch. "The Emperor was very insistent."

"I said to leave me alone!" Thaun snapped over one shoulder, still standing at the window.

Two figures stood clustered in the doorway, a man and a woman. For a second, his heart raised into his throat at the almost familiar silhouettes. The sensation passed just as quickly.

"Sir." The woman stepped forward and saluted despite wearing no armour. The young mage, barely out of adolescence, wore expensive but functional clothes with her hair tied back into tight braids. A cudgel-like rod hung from a ring on her belt, its wooden surface engraved with curling patterns. "We're ready when you are."

He sighed and turned away again. "And if I'm not ready today?"

"We're sorry, Your Highness. We were told that if you refused then we were to escort you regardless."

Thaun couldn't help but laugh at that, even if it didn't last more than a breath. "It's fine," he mumbled. He had a lot of practice at doing what others wanted him to, even if he'd managed to forget that while away from the Courts. "Can I get dressed first?"

"Of course." Her shoulders relaxed in relief. "We'll be outside. Please don't tarry, sir." She closed the door, the latch clicking shut, and Thaun briefly wished that he'd remembered to draw the bolt across. Next time.

The clothes he pulled from the cupboard felt as heavy as his armour. He didn't bother to try and brush the creases from their blue linen and stumbled towards the door. Halfway there, he paused to collect the Fang. For a second he considered the sword that Toland had given him where it hung from a chair back. Insel Drach seemed so long ago. So much had happened.

In the hallway beyond, his two new escorts waited along with a full squad of Imperial Guard. He barely registered their blue and green uniforms, cheaper and simpler than the Royal Guard's brighter hues. Heizl's coup had cut the best out of many of their Empire's most recognisable branches.

Heizl...

Thaun shook his head and kept walking. He could think of only one place where his uncle would hold a 'private audience' with him, and so he did his best to maintain an even pace as they made their way there. Most of the infantry squad followed in his wake, though periodically two or three of them would jog ahead to post guards at corners, doors, and branching passageways.

The pair, that he soon had labelled as a Spire mage and her Shadow, kept closer to him than he would've liked. He could almost smell the tension that radiated from them, though he tried to ignore it.

After several more twists and turns, walking along corridors and through the Palace's countless halls and galleries, Thaun paused at the top of a short flight of stone stairs. His escort hadn't tried to stop him once on his way here. This had to be the place.

"Everythin' alright, sir?" The Shadow assigned to him, a lean, middle-aged man with a scraggly beard and a mismatched pair of short axes through his belt, stepped a touch closer still.

"I'm fine," he replied a little too quickly, and made his way down. Soldiers lined both walls of the short corridor, a sharp contrast to the Royal Guardsmen that had stood there last time he'd visited. As much as he wanted to, Thaun didn't hesitate as he reached the door. He could almost hear Toland's voice in his ear. Words of reassurance and advice, of how looking like he was in charge was as important as actually being in charge. He wished he could disagree.

He didn't wait for a response to his single knock, and entered. His uncle's office bore little resemblance to how it had appeared last time he'd come here, but the Emperor didn't give him a chance to take in its details. Rufenrich wrapped his arms around his nephew in a tight embrace, one hand coming up to hold the back of his head.

Thaun went still, every muscle seizing at the contact. The Fang hung heavy across his shoulder. Deep in his gut, a slow urge to push his uncle away grew. A moment later and the feeling passed. Breathing out at least some of his tension, he sank into the hug.

Rufenrich's clothes smelled of sweat and smoke. As Thaun pulled his uncle further into the embrace, neither man spoke. He lost track of how long they stood there like that, but he relished the relief that seeped into him at the contact.

The Emperor didn't break his grip to speak, his voice coming out weary and thick. "I'm sorry I didn't come to see you. Hastigr told me what happened."

Thaun's throat tightened until words could barely escape. "It's alright..."

"You shouldn't have had to go through all that. I thought I had it all in hand," he spoke quickly. "Insel Drach was meant to be safe. I didn't know Thala had already reached there, and–"

"Uncle..." Tired as he was, Thaun found stone seeping into his voice. A crumbling, weathered pebble, but stone nonetheless. "It's fine. You couldn't know everything that's happened." He struggled for more to say, but the words failed him. "It's fine."

"I won't lie to you." Rufenrich finally broke their embrace, revealing tears welling in his eyes. "It's not all fine. We're in trouble, Thaun."

His throat seemed to finish closing up all the way, and so he made a show of looking around the room. For the first time he registered that his uncle wore a dusty but functional black uniform, so similar to what Sigren tended to wear. A single knife, hardly long enough to be a dagger, rode his hip.

The room behind him lay in chaos. A bookshelf lay upon the stained rug, books scattered everywhere, to reveal a hidden, closed door. Patches of wall, once covered by paintings, maps, and more shelves, had turned to powder, while an upturned table and chairs rested where they'd fallen. Thaun didn't know what had happened here, but his uncle's office looked to have seen as much violence as the rest of the Palace during the rebellion.

Behind Thaun, the door remained open. His temporary escorts waited outside with a clear line of sight within. Other guards – soldiers and Shadows both – stood within the small chamber. Following Heizl's betrayal, it seemed that the Emperor was unwilling to take any chances, even with his heir. Few of them looked directly at him, but only a couple didn't appear tense enough to draw their weapons.

"Thaun?" said Rufenrich, tone tainted by worry. "You had a sort of distant look on your face for a moment just then. Are you alright?"

"I'm fine," he choked.

"We're in trouble... but we can take care of this." He lowered his voice. "Renyar, Seorsa, Urathear, all of it." The Emperor began pacing around the room. "More's on the horizon too, but..." He trailed off as their guards shifted to face the doorway in answer to a series of shuffling noises and mumbled apologies. Thaun followed their gazes and, for a second, wondered if it had been a mistake to leave behind Toland's gift. Rufenrich didn't move.

Hastigr stopped in the doorway, leaning on a cane as he looked around. The Highmage had never looked young to Thaun, but years seemed to have fallen upon him, highlighting every wrinkle and bowing his back with their weight. "My apologies for my tardiness," he said in a low, tired voice. With short steps, feet scuffing the ash-laden carpet, he passed the two royals and sank into one of the surviving seats with a sigh. "I've been preoccupied."

"The Nexus is important." Rufenrich nodded, and gestured for Thaun to sit before moving to his own seat. "But we can run messages the old-fashioned way for a while. Thank you for joining us."

"The Nexus, yes." The old mage nodded but didn't make eye contact. "Its reach was less vast when the Comet last hung in the sky. I hadn't anticipated the changes it would bring to the arcanosphere. Can we make this quick?"

The Emperor leant forwards, his head resting in one hand. "Yes, sorry, I'll try. It's hard to think about such practical matters with..."

Thaun couldn't remember ever having seen his uncle this way. He'd always seemed so in control, like everything went according to some unspoken plan. Seeing him this way, unbalanced and distracted, left him feeling uneasy himself. It would be so easy to sink down into a chair, to shed tears until Renyar spelled out their doom. Only an hour ago, with just his own grief to bear, he probably would've done just that. Now though, seeing his last remaining family member so close to collapse, a glimpse of something came to him.

Perspective. Every time he'd lost the words, every time he'd felt like crying, someone had stood alongside him. Each of his friends had done their best to distract or comfort him in their own way. None of them had ever truly managed, but they'd always tried anyway.

Tensing his shoulders, Thaun blew out a forceful breath, and moved to sit at his uncle's side. He reached out a hand, and grasped Rufenrich's.

"Heizl wasn't your fault." He didn't know what went through the Emperor's head, but a flash of something like recognition came to Rufenrich's eyes at those words. "You couldn't have known what leaving here would do, or that Renyar would get to her." Thaun sighed, the corners of his mouth tightening. "I should've talked her out of it. At the least I shouldn't have killed her. There must've been a way to, I don't know, subdue her or something."

"If you think mere words could've helped push past the corruption that she experienced," Hastigr said slowly. "Then you are sorely mistaken. Such resistance must come from within. My mentorship could have prepared her for such a challenge, but I shirked my duty to her. I've lost apprentices before, but few with such promise."

"Don't be stupid," said Rufenrich, a hint of anger creeping into his voice. "If I hadn't sent her to Norjhost none of this would've happened. If she hadn't gone, she'd still live, and she wouldn't have..." he trailed off again, eyes holding on a bloodstained patch of carpet not far away. He shook his head, and when he continued he sounded more like himself. "Arguing over who's the most to blame for what she did isn't going to get us anywhere. As hard as it might be, we should look to the future. We can mourn afterwards. We'll have a small funeral. Something quiet and private. Maybe we can downplay her role in the rebellion."

"I agree," said the Highmage, straightening in his seat. "No loss, no matter how personal, is enough of an excuse for us to give up. Renyar can't be allowed to do as he wishes. It'd spell the end of our legacies. The stakes are greater than that."

Rufenrich nodded. "You're right. We only have so many pieces left on the board. We've just one Highmage available." He ticked a list off on his fingers, glancing at Hastigr as he did so. "One's dead while three more are too distant to recall, we've lost contact with Tarnac, Frida is dead..." For a moment, Thaun thought his uncle might choke up and grow mute, but, after clearing his throat, he continued. "And we've not yet recovered the Claw from the river."

"It can't all be that bad," said Thaun, though he wasn't sure if he was trying to persuade his uncle or himself. "Toland and Sigren are holding Insel Drach, we've taken back the city, and we beat Elhin." Neither of the other men looked convinced. "And what about Vandel? Somehow he lasted against... when he fought Heizl."

"He can't be here right now," said Rufenrich. "But you're right, he'll be a valuable asset before all this is over."

"How did he do it?" Thaun glanced between the other two men. "If that spear was another Fragment like my shield, or whatever Renyar has, it should've... I dunno, but he lasted longer against Heizl than he should have."

The Highmage cleared his throat to speak, but the Emperor beat him to the answer. "You remember how long Korten held Renyar off for? Hastigr was close enough to intervene against Heizl. He's only one man though, and with the Nexus, and everything else..." He glanced at the mage, though the old man turned away from them both. "We should be wary of playing all our cards before the final hand."

Thaun raised an eyebrow before forcing a passive expression onto his face. Concern crossed through the front of his mind, but his uncle continued before he could voice any of his questions. "Now, there's a lot still going on. I know how difficult you find this sort of serious business, but we need you."

"You need me?"

"You should know by now. All this is going to be yours someday, maybe even sometime soon. If you don't help me fight for it now, you won't be able to fight for it later. Besides." He smiled, though fatigue filled his eyes. "With that Fragment of yours, you're one of only a few who can face Renyar."

"You want me to... Uncle, this is all too much. Send the Imperial Guard and let Toland deal with Insel Drach. We should stay here until Heizl's found."

"Until..." Rufenrich rubbed at his face. "Heizl's gone, but Renyar's not. We can deal with mourning, the funeral, and what's left of their rebels when we get back."

"When we get back? We can't go anywhere, not now, not before we find her."

"It's good to hear you speak with such passion, I just wish I could agree." His uncle leant across and placed a hand on Thaun's arm. "The Comet reaches its peak tomorrow. Renyar only has a few days left. All we have to do is stop him from reaching Insel Drach."

"Isn't that what the Imperial Guard's for?"

"And it's our job to lead them. He's marching towards Insel now at the head of a Seorsan army. The Fifth Army moved to intercept, but were forced to retreat. We think Renyar assassinated their command structure while his Seorsans made an assault under cover of darkness."

"I can't believe I'm saying this, but couldn't I stay here? The city must need leadership too, and I can help look for Heizl's body."

"You'd rather lead people, and stay near the ruins of the Imperial Court, than go and fight someone? What's wrong?"

"I don't know." Thaun turned away. "Toland said some things, everything's changed." He shook his head to himself. "No, it's all the same. It all still hurts, and confuses me, and I feel overwhelmed... But you can't expect things to get better if you're not willing to change yourself."

Hastigr leant in a little closer, studying him through narrowed eyes. "You have the most interesting relationships with people, Your Highness." The Highmage hesitated. When he continued, Thaun couldn't help but feel that he'd intended to say something else. "Which of them helped you come to this realisation?"

He blinked a few times. "All of them. But Lena was willing to go through horrible things, and Toland listened to me. Even Sigren kept me in line when I only thought about myself." Thaun laughed at himself, no hint of humour in the sound. "Maybe I just needed to open up."

"Thaun..." For the second time since arriving, Rufenrich looked like he could weep. "You sound like your father. I'm so proud to hear that you're finally starting to take all this seriously, and I'm happy that you're talking about how you feel." The Emperor stood and began pacing the chaotic room. "You can't stay here though. With the Fang, you represent a unique tactical advantage now. We need you, or Renyar will roll right over us."

"Then I'll give it to someone else." His stomach twisted with acid at the mere idea, but pushed on. "Vandel, or a Royal Guardsman, or someone."

"You haven't tried passing it on, have you, Your Highness?" said Hastigr. "Few can bear such a Fragment without developing a certain obsession. Fewer still are able to give one up without outside assistance."

Painful memories rose of Heizl's rebels tearing it from him. He wouldn't wish that feeling of loss upon his worst enemy. The confusion, the hunger, and the sickness that came with its absence rose again in fuzzy recollection. "No, I guess I haven't." He glanced at Rufenrich. "Do I have another choice?"

"I wish I could give you one." One corner of his mouth rose in an attempt at a comforting smile. "I need you to come with me. It'll all be worthwhile in the end."

"Fine." Thaun let out a sigh. "What about here though? We can't just leave Reiget City like this."

The Emperor shrugged. "It'll still be here when we get back. The garrison is recruiting to make up for our losses, the Spire's recalled every mage we can, and there are only a couple of rebel cells still holding out. With Heizl's passing, Renyar's absence, and Dasimir's house arrest, there's no one left to stir up too much trouble."

"I forgot about Strahl," said Thaun. "What happened to Jilia? Is she okay?"

"She's fine." The Emperor waved distractedly. "The Uloric Cathedral has taken her in. You can go see her when you get back, if you want, but I didn't think..?"

"No," he snapped the reply. "It's nothing like that. I just thought... Nevermind."

As both Konreig men fell quiet for a moment, Hastigr cleared his throat to speak. "Highmage Aurus will be the first of our Council to return from his duties. He's been left with instructions to investigate the disappearance of the treasury and the Spire's essence stockpile both."

Rufenrich continued for him. "And Governor Tresig is travelling here from Schieliche to oversee the rest. The Capital will survive without us for a while." He eyed his nephew meaningfully. "The rest of the Empire might not, not if we don't stop Renyar."

Again Thaun felt like the Emperor left something unsaid, though he couldn't place what. "Fine. What do we do now then?"

"Oh, I know exactly what we're going to do." An uncharacteristically bitter smile awoke upon Rufenrich's lips. "We get to Insel Drach, we dig in, and we let Renyar grind himself into dust against us."

Thaun arched an eyebrow. "But don't we just need to hold him off until after the Comet passes?"

"If stopping his ritual is all we're trying to do." Something hard fluttered in his eye before he turned away. "It's his fault that we lost Heizl and Frida, and it's his fault that everything has spiralled beyond control. I don't know about you, but I want justice. Failing that, vengeance will do."

"I guess... I just wish this was all over."

"Me too, Thaun. Me too." Rufenrich stood and held out a hand. "Every choice I've made so far in this has been for you. Let's do this last step as a family."

Thaun paused. For all his talk of wanting to change things, of saying what others wanted to hear, he could think of nothing he'd like to do more than curl up and let the world roll over him. Something told him that, if his overbearing but well-meaning uncle had anything to say about it, he wouldn't get much of a say in the matter. He took the other man's hand. "Fine. Together."

Tooth and Nail – Chapter Twenty-Five

"Pride and grief, bittersweet, mingle within one cup,
Sour water flows hence, twisted hist'ry supped.
Nescient eyes blinded, legions paw these shallows,
Sharp few heed our fell song, for the deeps are gallows.

Attend these heroes' tales, revel in majesty,
Harken to their troubles, destined for tragedy.
Men as dread as shadows, from marbled voids they spring,
Fated for sacrifice, against absent god-kings."

The Urlungenlied,
Act One, Extract

7th day of Ehnaln, 406th Imperial Year
17th Year of Emperor Rufenrich Konreig's Reign

Thaun stumbled, dropping to one knee as he succumbed to wracking coughs. Faint streamers of smoke rose from his shoulders, and tears trickled through closed lids. As he fought back the urge to vomit, he clenched his fists hard enough that pain pulsed through him. Somewhere in the darkness he could hear his uncle reacting no more elegantly.

Hastigr's Nexus offered the Empire the chance to match their more magically-inclined neighbours, with their dreamscapes, portals, and windwalks. Thaun still would've much rather found passage by ship or saddle.

By the light of lamps and candles, figures rushed to assist both royals. Thaun batted aside the first few supportive hands before relenting. Men more used to inspecting farmers' wagons than nobles' clothes pulled his smoking cloak free and presented him with another. In that moment, Thaun didn't have the heart to say anything – the old replacement, some veteran's worn rain cloak, felt more comforting than any fur-lined garment he owned.

"Come on," wheezed Rufenrich. "Hastigr will come through soon. We should get clear."

Thaun nodded and allowed them to guide him from the enchanted beacon at the dusty room's centre. He'd heard a few rumours of those unfortunate enough to stand too close to an active Nexus beacon, and had no desire to witness such horror firsthand.

They followed a sergeant through passageways lined with old wooden doors and out into the rain. Grey drops fell like clouds' tears over the outdated checkpoint. Puddles rippled beneath the downpour as men and women ran from shelter to shelter. A handful of Royal Guardsmen oversaw the Outpost's undermanned garrison, driving them towards efficiency in their Emperor's presence. Above the wooden peaks of the fort's two towers, the Konreig crest hung limp, wet, and uninspired.

Their guide hunched down beneath his helmet in an attempt to shelter from the weather. He crossed the yard, leading them towards a squat building opposite the small keep. Thaun mimicked the movement, though water still ran over his loaned cloak and down his neck. The rain and the noise alike faded as they stepped back into shelter.

Someone had done their best to turn the storeroom within into... something else. Thaun couldn't help but question its suitability as a war room. A set of large planks – possibly the bed of a wagon – rested upon a pair of boxes at the slightest angle, while old chairs and stools ringed the makeshift table. Though one of the garrison had shown the floor a broom, clumps of straw still hung around in corners, and the dull light outside struggled to break through dusty windows.

Hastigr had only sent a small contingent ahead of them, two at a time, but one of their staff had laid out several local maps upon the impromptu table. Pewter mugs held down their curling corners. Thaun only glanced at the papers as he came in and shed his borrowed raincloak, though he recognised Insel Drach's jagged coastline from his last visit.

A single Royal Guardsmen stood sentry just within the door, matching his less-fortunate colleague outside in the rain, while a pair of aides laid out papers and poured drinks. The Outpost's commander, an impatient man that Thaun couldn't quite remember the name of, loomed with two of his officers over the makeshift table. None of the garrison looked at all prepared for another royal visit. The room held only one other man, leaning against the back wall with arms crossed over his dusty uniform. Through the dust-strained light, Thaun made eye contact, and a relieved smile crept across his face.

In a few quick strides, almost without thinking, he'd crossed the room and wrapped his arms around the other man. Beneath the dark cloth, he felt ropey muscles tense at the contact before relaxing. A moment later, his friend patted him on the back, a reluctant response to the gesture.

"Sigren, what're you doing here?" said Thaun, breaking the embrace to inspect his friend. Dark lines hung under the other man's eyes, and a fresh set of straight, shallow scars criss-crossed the back of his bare arm. "I thought you were staying with Lena? Is she here?"

The Shadow didn't reply as he looked away. Behind Thaun, Rufenrich spoke with the commander, his voice strained but controlled as he gave out orders and asked questions. Thaun paid his uncle no attention.

"...She..." Sigren's voice cracked as he spoke. "She didn't make it."

Sickness pulsed through Thaun. "I..."

"You weren't there." His friend still didn't look at him. "She gave everything she had to stop Elhin, everything, and you picked up that damned shield and left."

"Sigren, I'm sorry." Thaun didn't know what hurt more – the news of Lena's death, or the raw edge in the Shadow's voice. "If I'd known–"

"You'd have done the exact same thing." Sigren gave him the briefest of glances. "We had things under control, and you had an Empire to look out for. One dying mage who couldn't even heal herself had to come second. It was smart."

"But I should've stayed, I could have..." He shook his head, unable to find the right words.

"You could've done what? You're no healer. You didn't have some hidden supply of essence to keep her going." Sigren's voice gradually rose in volume. Around the room faces turned towards them, but even Rufenrich didn't say anything in the face of the Shadow's anguish. "What you did have was some magic shield, and a problem that you could fix. You did the right thing!" He sagged and turned away, revealing Lena's silver-inlaid axe hanging from his belt. "You did the right thing... and I wish that you hadn't."

Thaun raised a hand to clasp his friend's shoulder but paused before making contact and lowered it again. Words failed him, though apparently the same couldn't be said for his uncle.

"Shadow," said the Emperor. "We're stretched thin here, and you've lost your mage." Sigren bridled but said nothing. "You'll join Highmage Hastigr's staff until further notice. Understood?"

The Shadow blew out a short, sharp sigh laden with anger. "...Yes, sir."

"Good. You can wait outside until we're done."

"I'd rather stay for the briefing, sir." He made eye contact with his ruler for the first time.

Rufenrich frowned and stared back at Sigren. When he finally spoke, his voice came out as little more than a whisper. "Frida would've cut you down in three words, and then probably beaten you down by hand for good measure. Don't go thinking that the Empire owes you anything just because you've lost someone. We've all lost someone."

Sigren flinched as if struck. A moment later, fire burning in his eyes, he brought his fist to chest in salute. When the Emperor returned the gesture just as sharply, the Shadow marched from the room.

Thaun watched his friend leave. It felt like he had fewer and fewer people in his life that he could describe that way. He still didn't know what to say.

"Are you alright, Thaun?" murmured Rufenrich. "I wish we had the time to worry about everyone's feelings, but our legacy depends on more than a single Shadow."

"I guess." He turned away, still watching the door that his friend had left by. He opened his mouth to comment on the two men's similarities. The desire to look out for people, the willingness to do whatever was necessary, even the recent loss of companions. Thinking better of it, Thaun closed his mouth again.

"Take a seat. We'll reach Insel Drach tomorrow, just as soon as a Trade Guild ship big enough for the crossing arrives." The Emperor walked around the makeshift table, and glanced at the other men sharing the impromptu war room with them. "The rest of you can leave. Not you, Commander. I imagine we'll have your troops run messages before all this is all over, too."

The officer, a middle-aged man with a bristling moustache, halted halfway to the door and gave a clumsy bow. He moved to stand near the table and glanced at Rufenrich before making an exaggerated show of inspecting the curling maps.

Thaun sat heavily, and eyed the commander. In the brief time he'd met him, both now and before, the officer had struck him as fairly typical of his breed. Commission paid for by family or a patron, resenting the fact that he'd ended up at some backwater rather than one of the fronts, and ready to preen before the powerful. In one shape or another, he'd seen his type enough times before.

"I dare say Hastigr knows all this already, so we'll start without him," said Rufenrich after a moment. "With everything that's happened, I don't know how much has sunk in. You'll have to forgive me if I repeat myself.

"Renyar's marches at the head of a Seorsan army that's defeated the Fifth Army in the field twice already. Our latest intelligence suggests the bulk of that force is marching this way, presumably for the ships and facilities needed to mount a large-scale crossing. A smaller – but still considerable – group approaches the shore further west, where we believe they've secured alternative means to reach Insel Drach."

The commander cleared his throat. "Your Majesty? May I suggest that all available ships sail to prevent the invaders from seizing them?"

"It's already done, Commander." The Emperor didn't look up. "When we sail in the morning, every other vessel will leave here too. Once we disembark, all available patrol vessels will attempt an intercept course for the smaller, western group. Even if Renyar reaches Insel Drach alone it could spell disaster."

"A sound strategy, Your Majesty," said the officer.

Rufenrich waved the compliment away. "In addition, we'll put this place to the torch as we depart."

"What?!" The commander spectacularly failed to hide his surprise.

"This Outpost hasn't got a chance of holding out against Renyar short of Ulora herself thumbing the scales. Even if we hold them off on Insel Drach, we can't afford to leave a foreign power a secure foothold within Imperial borders."

"Uncle? There are more than just soldiers here," said Thaun, looking up from his less-than comfortable seat. "I saw them when I visited before. Merchants, sailors... normal people. We'll be destroying their home."

The Emperor sighed and smiled weakly. "You're right. You've got good instincts, Thaun, even if you don't put them to use often enough. Commander? Offer the chance to volunteer on the ships. Anyone who chooses can join in intercepting Renyar's advance force at a guardsman's wage. You'll escort any who won't fit on board overland to Poludaer Keep. Even with civilians, it shouldn't take you more than a couple of weeks."

"Sir." The Commander regained something resembling composure. "Respectfully, with the weather coming in, and on such short notice, people will die whether we confront Seorsa or not. Maybe if we had some time to prepare, but—"

"This is greater than a few hundred civilians and a dozen soldiers, Commander." His voice held none of the patience that it had when he spoke to his nephew. "Please don't confuse my desire to protect my Empire with an inability to make necessary sacrifices. We'll save all that we can from what's coming, but some might not make it."

"Sir, I'm so—"

"We haven't got time for apologies." He waved a gloved hand. As if the gesture held its own sort of magic, the door swung open.

Hastigr shuffled in, the growing wind outside picking at the hem of his robe and blowing the smell of mothballs into the room with him. "The sun must be close to setting," he mumbled. "I gather that my Shadow has grown." The old man dusted a few raindrops from his collar. "Am I late? It feels like I'm late."

"I'm glad you could join us," said the Emperor. "The Nexus?"

"It won't operate effectively without me." Hastigr shrugged, looked around, and found himself a seat. "I suspect that my presence here is more important than accommodating travel arrangements."

Though Rufenrich kept his head down, facing the maps upon the table, his eyes tracked up to shoot the mage a sharp look. "I hope that our present circumstances won't last so long that we have to make that choice."

Hastigr mumbled something then, but Thaun didn't catch it, just his uncle's reaction. He'd seen the frustrated expression a few times, but rarely aimed his own way before. Heizl had earned it with her questionable antics on more than one occasion. That thought of her caught him unawares, and he pushed the conversation to one side. He hadn't thought about his cousin since arriving.

So far, he hadn't found an option less painful than ignoring it. Denying the things that they'd both said and done was easier than the alternative. Distracting himself couldn't last forever though. The memory of how it felt, sword cutting through into her, sent a shudder through his core. Even when he'd faced Elhin or Renyar they'd always worn armour. Did it always feel like that? Like running a knife over prepared meat? He couldn't understand how people could do that to another person. His stomach seemed ready to collapse in on itself as bile rose in his throat.

Thaun stood, hoping the vain hope that the sudden movement might leave his pain behind in the seat.

Whatever the other men had discussed, they stopped to look at him. He returned their stares for a moment before turning away.

"Thaun?" said Rufenrich. "What's wrong?"

"It's... nothing. I just need some air."

"Are you sure?" He frowned. "It's raining."

"I like the rain," Thaun said as he walked towards the door. "I won't go far." And, with that, he left before his uncle could object further.

Within the sooted glass of the night's first lanterns, flames flickered. Light had faded from the sky, leaving the steely clouds as dark as his mood. He saw fewer men now, the Outpost's occupants making excuses to stay in the dry.

Thaun fumbled to pull the hood up on his borrowed raincloak. The Fang's weight pulled at him as he drew the cloth forward. Like his uncle had said, the first few drops had started to fall only a short while before they'd entered the impromptu war room. A thick, earthy smell filled the air. Heavy but few, each drop exploded outwards in a ring as it impacted upon stone and wood. Soon the dull ground would be a uniform smooth darkness, but for now each damp speck stood as a lone island.

He hadn't realised how long they'd sat around that crude table.

Thaun wandered, paying little attention to either his path or his destination. Behind him, one of their few Royal Guardsmen followed at a discreet distance. He'd have rather walked alone, but he couldn't fault the man's sense of duty.

For years he'd spent his time wishing to be away from home, out from beneath the avaricious eyes of the nobility. Like so many youths he'd dreamed of freedom and adventure. Now, faced with the reality of those blinkered desires, he wasn't so sure of what he really wanted.

He wondered if the soldiers, labourers, and the rest of the Empire had the same motivations. In the shadows of politics and religion, their similarities were greater than their differences, even if few admitted such a truth.

Thaun halted near the yard's muddy centre, his boots sinking into the dirt that lined its cobbles. He paused for a moment, mind blank, and stared at nothing. Walking felt harder when he didn't know where he wanted to go anymore.

"Took you long enough." Sigren's gravelly voice undercut the murmuring rain. The Shadow grunted as he pulled tight the saddlebags across the back of a grey horse. Alongside his familiar crossbow, both an unstrung longbow and a steel siege arbalest hung from leather straps. "Nice of you to stop by, but you won't convince me."

Thaun rubbed rainwater from his eyes. "...Convince you of what?"

The Shadow barked a humourless laugh, refusing to look his way. "I should've known you wouldn't have figured it out."

Thaun staggered back as if struck. "What're... What're you talking about?" The question came out as a whisper.

"I told you." Sigren still didn't face him. "You did the right thing. People were hurting, but there were others around to share the burdens. You saw a way you could make a difference, and so you left."

"That's not..." He took a few steps towards his friend, but stopped out of reach. "I mean, I was just trying to do the best I could. It's just... it's hard."

"It's hard for all of us. We make our choices, and we live with them..." Bitterness filled the Shadow's voice. "Until we can't live with them anymore. It's up to those of us still breathing to keep making the hard choices."

Thaun shook his head. "I'm sorry, Sigren."

"I know you are. That doesn't bring her back though." He adjusted the same strap that he'd already tightened several times. "But thanks for saying it. I won't forget."

He arched an eyebrow and lowered his voice. "Why would you forget? That's an odd thing to say."

"I'm leaving, Thaun."

"Leaving? But you're meant to join Hastigr's other Shadows."

"Gimme a break." Dry humour and impatience danced together in Sigren's voice. "You always complain about people having expectations of you, but you're the first to do as you're told. Isn't it time that you start making your own decisions?"

"I–"

"I don't need to know the answer to that; it's something you need to work out yourself." The Shadow pushed a boot into a stirrup and swung up into the saddle. Looking down, some of the hardness left Sigren's face. He sighed. "I'm sorry. I know you don't let these things go, and I don't say this to hurt you. You can be better, Thaun. We should all be better."

The Crown Prince let out a little, awkward laugh. "Thanks, no pressure there." He shook his head, and tiny raindrops sprayed in all directions. "Wait, you haven't answered me. Where are you going?"

Sigren looked away, eyes settling on the Outpost's gates. "As much as I'd like to blame at least some of this on you, this is all happening because of Renyar. I'm going to kill him. Orders be damned."

"You can't!" Thaun exclaimed, shocked. As faces turned their way, he cleared his throat and lowered his voice. "How? The entire Palace couldn't stop him. He'll block anything you try, and then command you to help him, like he... like he did to Heizl."

"He's got to see me coming to do either of those. A quarrel through the eye doesn't care if he's channelling some dragon or not." Sigren turned his back and lowered his voice. "Besides, killing him isn't the hard bit." He left the words hanging in the air, as cold as the rain.

It took Thaun a moment to comprehend. Without cover or a means to escape, a lone bowman might still kill their mark. Their chances of escaping after though...

He bowed his head. Heizl would've found a way to both get her target and get away. He wished he had her way with words. She'd never known a responsibility she couldn't either shoulder or run from. They were all gone now though – Korten, Heizl, Lena, even Frida – and only Sigren remained. He couldn't help but feel like someone else should've stood there then, someone to share a word of reassurance, or a moment of sombre silence. Holding back tears, Thaun's vision settled upon the shield hanging from his left arm.

"Wait, Sigren." He took a deep breath. "How are you going to find Renyar by yourself?"

"Think about it, you barely go anywhere without someone to watch over and to tidy up after you." He waved a free hand towards the silent Royal Guardsman who stood a short distance away. "I don't need to find just him – there's an entire army with him leaving tracks."

"Okay, fine, but what if you get there too late? What if he crosses to Insel Drach before you find him?"

Sigren almost growled. "I give you a solution to all this, one where the only cost would be a single world-sick Shadow, and all you can offer in return are more problems. Every moment we spend discussing this is a moment less that I have to find him before it's too late."

Thaun's own response, voice raised and anger rising to meet his friend's, shocked even him. "But what if you didn't have to find him?! What if you didn't have to kill yourself for vengeance's sake?"

Before, the others that shared the Outpost's yard with them had at least pretended not to listen to their conversation. Now they fell quiet as they awaited Sigren's answer. Only the incessant rain accompanied the awkward silence. Somewhere in the distance, a dog howled.

"Everyone keeps talking about sacrifice," said Thaun, quieter now. "Uncle, Toland, even you. How with everything going on, people are going to get hurt, and that we need to accept it so that we can act. They're wrong. If we accept it, we won't try to care for as many as we can. It's an excuse." He bowed his head, the rainwater running down his face and from it like a spout. "It's easier. That's why you're doing this. You think it's an acceptable way to stop hurting. That pain's blinded you. Maybe it's blinded me before now too."

"Thaun..." Sigren shook his head, still looking down from his mount. "Just say what you wanted to say."

"You don't have to go out there to find him. He's going to come to us. We can dig in, and maybe face Renyar on our own terms."

"A lot of people might die if we do that."

"Maybe, but you won't be the only one trying. Together, maybe we can get out after."

"I can do this, Thaun."

"I know you can." He tried to laugh. "You can do anything. You always have been able to. But I won't let you do it alone."

Sigren's smile twisted as he failed to hide his own pain. "I wondered if you'd say something like that. I wondered what Lena would say too." He rubbed his face. "She sacrificed herself to protect us all, you included. What do you think she'd say if we risked throwing that gift away?"

Thaun rolled his shoulders. "I don't know. I'm not done though." He eyed his friend. "It's simple. Either you come with me, or I come with you. Whatever happens, I'm not losing someone else." On his arm, the Fang felt almost warm.

"Simple, huh?"

"Well, clear at least."

"I thought about preparing a second horse, you know. In case you decided to come with me."

"I would, if you wanted me to. You know that, right? But it's not our only option." Thaun considered saying more, but held his tongue. Some things were better left unsaid.

Sigren deflated, shoulders visibly falling. He didn't say anything for a moment either. Drifting rain punctuated their silence. In the distance, the muted sounds of men and women preparing to depart filled the gap.

Just as Thaun started searching for something else to say, convinced that he hadn't done enough, the Shadow finally spoke.

"Fine."

"Fine?"

"Yeah, fine," Sigren growled. "Lena wouldn't forgive me if I got you killed. I'll stay."

He breathed a little more easily. "You will? This isn't some way to just make me go away? Some way for you to sneak off later?"

"Sorry, you're stuck with me." The Shadow turned and almost smiled. His face remained in darkness. "We're still going to get him. Renyar, I mean. There's something we have to do before then, though."

Tooth and Nail – Chapter Twenty-Six

"Following the Crown Prince's death, and the civil war that followed, many whispered rumours of who had wielded the blade. Fjujhost, Seorsa, and Kuhlner. Demons, dragons, and elementals. Mages and assassins. I propose a greater question was ignored during this tumultuous time.

Who paid for the knife?"

Open letter to the Imperial Court,
Filip Daylen (401 I.Y.)

8th day of Ehnaln, 406th Imperial Year
17th Year of Emperor Rufenrich Konreig's Reign

No one could do it for him.

In a single week, Thaun had lost more than he had in his whole life. Family killed by his own hand. A friend sacrificed so that he might live. Untold souls slain following his orders.

He'd always known an emptiness within him that came and went, but not like this. Other faces, ones that he didn't quite remember, whispered in the darkness. A mother bleeding out as she birthed him. A father slain when he was still a child. A love that he'd never known.

Those around him couldn't see the pain that each loss formed. No one else could decide how he should grieve.

More than just people though, he'd lost... what? His confidence? His certainty? Neither word did it justice.

He'd always run away before, fleeing any expectation or responsibilities. Things had changed. He marched towards all those challenges now. While he'd fled, there was always the chance that things could eventually work out. The possibility of success, whatever that looked like, could be round the next corner if he didn't go looking for it.

Facing them head on though, he'd know soon enough. One way or another, he'd find out if what he'd always thought of himself was true or not. Everyone would find out.

"Come on," Sigren spoke softly, rousing Thaun as they walked. "Just because she's not going anywhere doesn't mean you have to take your time."

"It's not that." Thaun considered for a moment. No one could do any of this for him, but he wasn't entirely alone. "Sorry. It's not just that, I mean. I have to do this. I *want* to do this." At the break in his friend's stride, he thought a little harder. "No, not like that. I wish it hadn't come to this, but we should–"

"Thaun, you're babbling."

"Sorry." He took a deep breath. "What am I meant to do if someone recognises me?"

"What're you talking about?"

"It's my fault most of them are here." He gestured at the ordered rows of distant shapes. "They'll blame me. It's all so hard already. I don't know if I can face them."

Sigren slowed to walk more closely alongside him. "You might not be babbling anymore, but you're still overthinking it." His tone changed, hinting at something almost reassuring. "Noone's going to confront us. Honestly, probably the opposite."

"That's worse!" he hissed.

"How is that possibly worse?"

"I, uh." Thaun clenched his eyes shut in an effort to steady his thoughts. "They all expect so much from me. I'm only going to disappoint them. I'd rather they didn't notice us."

"Guess we'll never know – look." Turning back over one shoulder, Sigren tilted his head towards the nearest group of sentries. Leaning on a spear, one nudged another, and faces began turning their way.

Thaun held his breath and kept walking.

In time with the first man's salute, as if choreographed by some divine irony, the misty rain chose that moment to fall once more. Its chances of clearing the old mud from uniforms of so many of the Second was about the same as cleaning the stains from their mourning souls.

"This again?" Thaun muttered beneath his breath, offering a half-hearted salute in return.

"It's your own damn fault." Sigren was kind enough not to smirk too broadly. "I wanted to go find Renyar. You shouldn't have been so persuasive."

"If I'd realised it meant going through this, I might've agreed with you."

"Come on." The Shadow pushed past him, nodding to some of the guardsmen. "We should get a move on."

Royal and Shadow continued onwards, pausing at intervals to return the Second's scattered salutes. On all sides, the survivors' attention followed them with barely a word.

The troops that had travelled to Insel Drach with them overnight had shown the sort of grudging respect he'd come to expect. They'd moved out of his way, but always with the impatience of those inconvenienced by others.

The Second reacted differently though. Since returning, they'd treated him in a way he hadn't experienced before. Sincere salutes, genuine smiles, and friendly – if weary – faces. A few had even clapped him on the back, or offered him space at their cookfires.

It had been like that since getting off the ship. Thaun didn't understand. He hadn't earned their respect. Lena had given her life to give them the chance at beating Elhin. Toland's timely arrival had halted the Thalan pursuit. Under cover of darkness, Sigren had killed half the mages arrayed against them.

All Thaun had done was pick up a shield.

They'd left most of the horses behind on the mainland to save space on the ships. Thaun and his uncle had ridden to the ruins, but scouts had taken the mounts now to cover more ground as they watched for Renyar's advance. A part of him wished they'd kept the beasts, to move past the Second's surviving members more quickly. Instead, they now walked beneath the burden of their stares.

The guardsmen that ignored their passing weighed more heavily on Thaun's thoughts.

Around them, hundreds of graves lay in rough ranks. Scratched out of Insel Drach's shallow soil, their comrades had raised cairns over each to keep scavengers from disturbing their rest. Dozens more remained beneath the stones upturned by Thalan sorcery less than a mile away. One way or another, rock now covered all those that had given their lives here.

Those that remained from Thaun's battalion had placed markers on many of the plots. As he walked, he lost track of the variety. An arsenal of the fallen's weapons, helms, and shields denoted most. Personal belongings distinguished others, be they jewellery, trophies, or trinkets. A thief could earn their fortune walking these rows, if not for the scores of soldiers – all now veterans if they weren't before – tending to those they'd lost.

The defeated Thalans lay beneath a single, freshly-raised barrow to the north. A handful of reluctant guardsmen, their uniforms marking them as members of the First Army, stood sentry nearby. Practicality and grudging respect had seen these worthy foes buried, but tensions remained high. It'd be all too easy for a grieving soldier, control loosened by drink, to do something regrettable.

No mourners paid their foes their respects, and no memorials distinguished the soldiers lying there. If not for the reined anguish smouldering within him, Thaun might've felt some melancholy at that thought.

He followed after Sigren in silence. Behind them, trailing at a respectful distance, several of the Second shadowed them. The mage and Shadow that had accompanied him since the Palace didn't seem to know how to react. He pretended not to see any of them.

Their impromptu procession might've walked for a few minutes, or they might've walked for an hour. Either way, it felt like a lifetime, weighed down by the attention of a hundred expectant mourners. Ahead, at the end of a row of graves, lay a stack of stones. A familiar, shattered shield leant upon it, a silvery chain depicting three stars hanging from the wood.

Sigren came to a halt, feet together in near attention. A few paces later, Thaun reached his side. Staring down on the makeshift grave, neither spoke for a moment.

Every gouge and splinter upon that shield should've struck someone else, but Lena had taken it upon herself. The healer's flesh and bones had twisted and swollen in unimaginable pain to prevent others' suffering. A Highmage couldn't have done better, but their friend, as much a surgeon as a soldier, had fought Elhin almost to a standstill. Where soldiery and technology had failed, she had stood against her.

And for what? A draconic relic burdening Thaun just as much as the lives that now rested upon his shoulders. A few extra days of life before a foreign army reached them, a tyrant at its head. Even if his uncle stopped Renyar's summoning, almost all of them would end up dead beneath Seorsan steel soon enough.

He knew that he should say something, but the words wouldn't come. What could be said to give sacrifice meaning? It wouldn't help Lena, and it wouldn't help the others lying beneath piled stones all around them.

Unable to so much as look at Sigren, Thaun turned away. His gaze fell upon the next closest grave. A lantern burned upon its flat stones, its glass blackened almost to opacity, with a row of oil flasks lined up ready to refill it.

"It's empty," Sigren whispered. "A lot of them are. Some of the scouts are still finding bodies, but I don't think many are holding out hope of putting them to rest." The Shadow cleared his throat. "Fairly sure Korten's just a stream of dust on the wind now. Kinda fitting, don't you think?"

"What about Lena? Is she... in there?"

"She is. A lot of the Second were buried with their uniforms. Didn't seem much point in keeping them for the next batch of recruits." Sigren eyed him sidelong before turning back to the healer's grave. "We couldn't bury her with her armour in the end. It wouldn't fit. She might've liked that though. She was more than just a soldier."

Thaun couldn't voice a response to that. *All of them were.* He'd felt it in that moment, marching with the Second to face Elhin. Soldiers, each and every one of them. Labelled and numbered by those that would use them, but they were used gladly. Some might've originally joined for the steady pay and a full belly, but in doing so they'd become something else. A line separating the vulnerable from those that would prey upon them. Lena hadn't just done what she had to, but had stepped into a gap and taken responsibility for other people's wellbeing. At his order, they all had.

"I wish it wasn't this way," Thaun choked, wiping his eyes clear of burgeoning tears.

"I doubt you could find a single person here, breathing or otherwise, who wished otherwise," said Sigren in a flat tone. "But it is. Plans fail, but there's still a job to do, and so we keep on going."

"You sound a bit like her. Lena, I mean."

He shrugged. "She was the best of us. We could all stand to be a bit more like her."

"Yeah…" Thaun nodded, and the silence drew out. "And now it's just you and me."

Sigren grunted in laughter. "Even if it wasn't for a madman trying to resurrect an elder god, the Empire would still be in trouble with just us looking out for it. Good job your uncle's still around."

He was right, of course. Ever since the Civil War, by all accounts, Rufenrich had held everything together. The Konreig line would've ended there and then if not for him. Lands and power had left the hands of so many nobles, even those that hadn't outright stood with the Kuhlner-rebels, to be redistributed to the loyal and the talented.

His uncle had all but raised him and Heizl. Thaun could barely remember his actual father, murdered when they'd been just children. He couldn't remember much of the war that had followed either, but that was probably for the best. They were the only family that he'd ever known. And now…

"What is it?"

"Huh?"

"That face you're pulling. It's the one you make just before we'd get worried about you."

Thaun steeled himself. "I don't know. Heizl said some things."

The Shadow glanced at the guards standing a respectful distance away. Even so, he lowered his voice. "What sort of things?"

"Strange things. Bad things. She wasn't herself."

"She was always a bit strange. Sorry, I didn't mean it like that."

"It's fine, I get it." Thaun made himself smile. "There was no one else quite like her. It wasn't that though. The way she talked, she was so certain. More so even than usual. I think she genuinely believed what she said."

"She was always confident in her choices. She'd have got into less trouble if she'd been a little more uncertain."

"Not like this. She said that I shouldn't trust our uncle."

Sigren pitched his voice lower still. "Thaun, careful. I'm with you, and I know there's a lot going on, but people could get the wrong idea with that sort of talk."

"I know, I know. I'm not trying to do anything stupid. I just... I don't know."

"Have you spoken to His Majesty about it?"

"Not about this. I'm not sure I can. He's doing so much already. I don't want to make things worse."

"Not the worst decision you've made." The Shadow turned back towards Lena's grave. "If you're wrong, talking to him could be a bad idea. You might distract from greater threats. It'd spark rumours, whether treason or madness. People could get hurt."

Thaun's stomach tightened at the thought. Needles tingled through his fingertips. "And what if Heizl was right? What then?"

"Well," Sigren said slowly, picking his words with care. "If he is doing something we don't know about, but it's for the best, then that's basically fine. Everyone does that all the time. Parents with their kids, officers with the troops, the gods with all of us. We might not like being kept in the dark, but it happens.

"And if he's wrong..." Sigren shook his head. "Thaun, we could get in trouble just talking about this." Still facing Lena's resting place, he continued. "We could fight it. Whatever *it* is. You're his heir – plenty of people would stand with you. If it's you, I would too. We'd have another war. More people would suffer. We might still win though.

"Or we can support him. Not like that, not like pushing some motive that we don't know enough about. You're close to him. You're *family*. He'll listen to you. You can take your time, learn more, and help guide him if necessary. We might have a chance to make things better for a lot of people."

Thaun closed his eyes. In the darkness behind his eyelids, colours swirled. He'd seen those patterns a thousand times before. Whether rubbing away tears or fending off wordless fears, they so rarely appeared on his good days.

"The real question though is what difference does it make right now? No, I'm serious. What difference does it make?"

He opened his eyes again. "What difference would the Emperor being involved in some conspiracy make?"

"Yeah. Renyar's still out there. He's on his way here. He's killed dozens." He gestured towards the next grave. "It's because of him that Korten's dead. He caused an uprising that probably got hundreds killed and affected thousands.

"Voids, because of him, there's a hostile army marching halfway across the Empire. Do you know how many people are going to suffer when winter rolls in? Do you know how long that sort of thing takes to mend? We've still not fully recovered from the Civil War, and that was years ago. Even if his goals can be twisted into something worthwhile, he has to be held accountable for his actions.

"But worst of all?"

At the hint of a sidelong glance, Thaun turned away, not yet ready to lock eyes with his friend. Even like that, he could feel the anger radiating from him. So far at least, the Shadow had restrained himself from an outburst like before.

Sigren let out a final whisper. "He killed Lena. He might not have stabbed her himself, but this is on him."

He was right. At least, he wasn't entirely wrong. Sigren meant every word that he said. He'd put words to Thaun's fears, but that didn't make things any easier.

Not so long ago, Thaun had thought he knew where things would go. It had all seemed inevitable. Join the Court. Get married off to secure some alliance. End up on the throne. Continue the family legacy.

So much could happen when you weren't looking though. Only a few days had passed, and nothing seemed so certain now. He wished he could trust some higher power, but he lacked the faith. He wished someone could give him the answers and simply tell him what to do.

After all that had happened, for all the things he'd learned, he still didn't know what to do.

"Well," said the Shadow around a deep breath. "At least the rain's eased some."

"Yeah," Thaun replied, still looking down at the pair of graves before them. He was grateful for the change of subject. "The footing will still be treacherous when Seorsa gets here, though."

"You've not seen the positions? The Guard's digging in and collapsing some of the entrances. Numbers and magic won't make such a difference down there. Just a couple of chokepoints and overlapping lines of sight."

"I guess that makes sense. Renyar won't risk collapsing tunnels if it means he can't get into the ruins himself."

"And he wants to get in." Sigren's reaching into a pocket for a small, battered flask – undercut the edge creeping back into his voice. "So I'll be waiting." He took a mouthful, and offered it to Thaun.

"You won't be the only one." He accepted it, nodding his thanks. "But there's gonna be a whole load of Seorsans between you and him. There might be a hundred fighters in the way, and that's before thinking about his magic."

"I'll only need a clear shot once."

Thaun didn't know how to respond to that. In face of his own despair, he wouldn't describe his friend's attitude as hopeful. Single-minded or thick-skulled, but not hopeful.

In spite of standing there with him, Thaun suspected that Sigren still had his doubts. He hadn't voiced too many arguments on their way to Insel Drach. Awkward silences, just like this one, had blossomed more often than he liked. Even at the best of times, Thaun had little love for discussing serious, even life-threatening, matters.

With a sigh, he took a swig from the Shadow's flask, momentarily registering having seen it once before in a rain-soaked command tent not far from where they now stood.

The alcohol struck the back of his throat like the rake of flaming talons. Sharp vapours flowed up the back of his nose, burning the whole way. He suppressed a slight cough as he swallowed. Beside him, Sigren cast a sidelong glance his way, the slightest hint of a smile flickering upon his cheeks.

"Thanks for coming with me," said Thaun.

"I told you before, I'm not here for you. I'm here for Lena."

"In that case–" He lay a hand on his friend's shoulder, ignoring the awkward sensation that came with it. "–I'll try to be here for you."

"You're the worst, you know that, right?" Sigren reached up, placing his gloved hand upon Thaun's shoulder for a second longer than necessary before removing it again.

"Yeah, maybe…" He trailed off, feeling that brief moment of camaraderie fading.

"No, Thaun, I was just–"

"I broke a promise to her."

"What?"

"To Lena. After we lost Korten." He tracked to the bare pile of stones nearby. "I promised I'd talk to her about things. How I was feeling. About everything that was happening."

"I doubt she held that against you. With everything else going on, she probably didn't even remember."

"That's not the point though, is it? I told her that I'd do it, and I didn't. I couldn't help her against Elhin. I wasn't even there when she..."

"She'll have understood." Sigren nodded once as he slipped the flask away again. "She was a Spire Legacy. She knew what it was like to put family first."

"Do they know?"

"Does who know what?"

"Lena's family, do they know that...?" He gestured to the broken shield. "Voids, Korten's too? Everyone else buried here?"

"...I don't know. Lena only had her grandmother left. She was stationed up north, I think. Tarnac, or assisting the Vigil. And Korten? I wouldn't be surprised if he'd sprang into existence from a burst of smoke or something."

After a halfhearted chuckle, silence fell again. Though his eyes remained upon his friend's grave, Thaun saw nothing but the inside of his own mind. The last he'd seen of Lena, she'd still fought on, healing the maladies that she'd inflicted upon herself. He hadn't seen her pass away. Few had. A foolish voice within him suggested that she'd reappear when they needed her most. Axe in hand, she'd arrive to protect them like she always had.

Thaun shook his head. It didn't work that way. She'd made her choice, and faced its consequences. Such childish wishes to the contrary had no place here.

The same had befallen Heizl. He'd seen her death though. Bloodied and bruised after facing Vandel and Hastigr, the pained look of betrayal remained woven into Thaun's memory of her.

He'd killed her. As simple and as heartbreaking as that.

At his side, almost forgotten beyond his thoughts, Sigren's grunt dragged Thaun back to the field of fallen.

"Ugh. Is that what it felt like?" said the Shadow.

"What's that?"

"When Heizl spoke to you at a distance. Like at your party."

"Who's speaking to you?" Thaun paused for a second. "Wait, you knew about that?"

Rubbing his temple, Sigren smirked. "Lena worked it out months ago. We talked about it, but we thought it might be good for you to relax a little."

"Oh."

"You didn't think it was odd that we gave you so much space at things like that? You're not that good a liar, Thaun." The Shadow stayed quiet at that. "Anyway, Hastigr says that we should come back. The general recall is going to sound shortly. Advance Seorsan elements have made contact with the scouts' outer perimeter."

Thaun swallowed. "Are they sure?" Even as it left his mouth, he burned with shame at the question. Of course this was all happening. They all knew it would happen sooner or later.

His friend frowned a little at him, but didn't bite. "That's the order. Come on, Your Highness, let's go get a good seat for the end of the world."

Guiding Thaun back around, both men walked away from the graves. Imperial Guardsmen dressed in the Second's blue and gold uniform fell in at a respectful distance behind. Nobody had asked them to provide an escort, but they'd taken responsibility for it anyway.

They'd almost reached the edge of the fresh graveyard when the horns sounded. One by one, soldiers and camp followers said their farewells to those left in the ground. Some lay down mementoes and offerings, others snatched such trinkets up in an attempt to protect them from scavengers. A few of those already trailing Thaun threw conflicted glances back, perhaps considering doing the same.

As they left, and the day dimmed towards dusk, the lantern upon Korten's grave flickered in amber reflection of the blue-green Comet peeking through the clouds above.

Tooth and Nail – Chapter Twenty-Seven

> *"Take the gemstone. Most see its singular colour, its simple value. Some know the labour and skill required to reveal it to mortal eyes. It is those few who observe each cut face as part of a greater whole that truly appreciate its beauty.*
>
> *It is the same in war. Citizens see the clean lines between us and them. Soldiers know the sacrifices made in the name of duty. Only the greatest of leaders observe the complete theatre, and understand the bonds between one front and the next."*
>
> A Melech's Wisdom,
> Vinen of Thala (349 I.Y.)

8th day of Ehnaln, 406th Imperial Year
17th Year of Emperor Rufenrich Konreig's Reign

His arm trembled. So often before, panic kindling in his belly had expressed itself like that, smouldering outwards even as he tried to suppress the sickening sensation. Thaun knew it well, but this felt different.

Tilting his head back, his helmet touched the cut stone that he leant against. He could sense it now. Who knew how much rock, flesh, and sky separated them from the Comet as it neared its peak. It didn't matter. Cinched tight to his arm, the Fang reacted to it. He could almost make out distinct words as it whispered to him.

Other voices drowned it out. Shouts and cries, sobs and laughter, stone and steel.

The Imperial Guard held the tunnels at the heart of Insel Drach. It had started several bells before, but the passage of time grew more difficult to judge with each passing moment.

By the light of day, skirmishers had traded shots with Renyar's Seorsan vanguard before retreating down the two entrances that their sappers had left clear. Hastily-dug pits, deadfalls, and fire traps had taken their toll, slowing the advance, but the inevitable had come.

Guardsmen – reinforcements from the Fourth – held two narrow chokepoints, little wider than the Great Hall's doors, lit by lantern light. Shields and spears formed the frontline, those holding them rotating out periodically with fresher troops. Medics and cutters dragged the injured back when they could, as much to keep footing clear for those still standing as to try and save the wounded.

Further back, but still closer to the front than Thaun, soldiers too hurt to stand for long held crossbows or manned the handful of heavy mounted arbalests that the Imperials had assembled. Twice already, Renyar's force had penetrated the infantry line, but the answering volleys had stopped them from progressing further. The Fourth would run out of those healthy enough to fight long before they exhausted their ammunition.

In a straight line, a hundred paces separated the two Imperial shield walls in their respective passageways. Twisting corridors, collapsed ceilings, and heaps of rubble complicated the movement and communication between the two fronts. Though a relief force – Royal Guardsmen, Toland's Pinions, and several other fresh units – held the central chamber, they'd struggle to arrive in time to defend this location if the Fourth lost their footing. A hurried retreat would be the best the Imperials could hope for.

Rumour held that Vandel had arrived not long before the fighting had started. Now he fought on the other front at the Emperor's direct command. People's morale swelled with each mention of the Champion's name. After the tales of how he'd scared Renyar away, and after seeing how he'd held his own against Heizl and her Fragment at the Royal Docks, Thaun could believe it.

With Hastigr's attention elsewhere, Vandel would have no one to deflect hostile magicks from him this time. It still seemed the best explanation for how the old veteran had fought Heizl so effectively.

Leaning against a stone wall crafted centuries ago by inhuman hands, Thaun eyed Sigren. The Shadow periodically glanced out of the room's empty doorway, watching the clashing soldiers. A handful of officers shared the small chamber with them, while messengers ran back and forth as they coordinated the defence.

His uncle had nominally left Thaun in charge of their eastern front, but he'd ceded that responsibility to the guardsmen here with him almost as soon as fighting had begun. None of them had arrived on the island with him all those days ago, and so they hadn't hesitated to take command from an untested Royal. Had more of these troops been veterans from the Second, he couldn't help but feel they'd have argued the point.

The thought of drawing either blood or steel still twisted his gut into a knot, but Thaun kept his breathing held steady. Deep, slow, and calming. He didn't know if he'd made the decision to come here or if someone had made it for him, but this was where he now stood.

Renyar terrified him. He wouldn't deny that. Rumours whispered through the men and women huddled in the darkness with him. Of the attack on the Palace, of Heizl's brief rebellion. No one would blame anyone there for fleeing if the Thalan appeared in the flesh, but Thaun didn't think any of them would.

He wouldn't either. Things had changed since flames and smoke had filled his home. For a moment, the Fang's whispers increased, their meaning just beyond reach. Oh, his uncle would like to keep him safe and far from any fighting if he could, standing silently at his side as Hastigr studied the Rift. The shield offered too many advantages though, even if Thaun himself didn't. If Renyar showed his face, they could now answer his Fragment with one of their own.

"Hey," said Sigren. "Wipe that look off your face."

"Huh?"

"That frown. You'll worry the troops."

"Oh. Sorry."

"Fine." From where he stood, he gestured to something out of Thaun's line of sight. "Fewer heavies hitting us right now. Think they're attacking Vandel's front?"

He shrugged. Thaun had overheard a few of the messengers speaking to the officers huddled in the room with them. The first few times that a Seorsan elite had appeared, armour shining and magic erupting alongside their blades, they'd thought that Renyar himself had arrived. He'd rarely seen Sigren move so quickly, and had struggled to keep up. No one had stopped long enough to identify the individuals, but it seemed a safe assumption that members of Seorsa's sorcerous nobility had been swayed to the Thalan's side.

They died the same as anyone else. Before the Imperial's ordered retreat, the direct fire of a dozen crossbows would cut them down sooner or later. Thaun had yet to face one directly, but suspected that the Fang would handle their magicks just fine. If it could neuter Korten, it'd stop them.

"Or they're gathering for a big push." Thaun stretched, both arms above his head. "We'll be hard pressed if more than a couple of their heavies attack at once."

"Then we fall back, and let the Highmage get involved."

Thaun smiled. "Think he's noticed you've left yet?"

"Probably not." The Shadow gazed out of the room still. "Last I saw, he was focused on the Rift. Books and charms out, circles drawn on the floor, that sort of thing. Dunno what it involves, but he's seen better days – looked like he'd taken a beating already. Pretty sure your uncle saw me leave, but he kept quiet."

"That makes a change."

Sigren didn't reply for a moment. When he spoke, it was to change the subject. "Do you still think waiting for him here was the right thing to do?"

"Waiting for Uncle?"

"Waiting for Renyar," he said, rolling his eyes.

"Oh. That makes more sense." He considered for a moment. "I'm not sure." He thought for a moment longer. "I'm not sure I'm sure of anything."

"Hey, something's happening." As Sigren straightened, Thaun pushed off from the wall. At their movement, the officers fell quieter still. "The light's changed. The fighting's eased off too."

"Think it's another Seorsan mage?"

"If so, they're not like the others." Sigren glanced down, checking his crossbow. "This might be it. I'm gonna get into position."

"Wait," said Thaun, arriving at his side and clamping a hand down on his friend's shoulder. "Are you sure?"

Cradling the weapon in the crook of an arm, the Shadow gestured beyond the doorway as he stepped aside. "See for yourself. Slowly now."

Thaun nodded, checked his helmet's chinstrap, and leant around the corner.

A familiar sight greeted him. Familiar in colour and style, if not in magnitude. Green light bathed the Imperial ranks with a sickly glow, turning the soldiers into twisting silhouettes. Men and women planted their feet and raised their shields even as their foes made an ordered withdrawal. As the last Seorsan ducked back and out of sight, the leading edge of an emerald sphere crawled forwards.

At home, with smoke and flame on all sides, Renyar had wrapped himself in such sorcery. This time, so close to his goals, he'd stretched himself further. The sphere, green surface marbled with swirls of white, filled the corridor from wall to wall.

The sounds – mutters, challenges and curses, mostly – changed as Renyar closed. Blocking the flow of musty air, echoes faded, and breaths grew thick and charged like the moments before a storm.

A guardsman, braver or more foolish than her comrades, lunged forwards as the massive sphere came closer. Well-trained muscles contracted, her iron-sheathed spear darted out to strike the green shell. Like hitting stone, the metal point dug a fraction of an inch into the rolling surface before skittering and bouncing away. In the weapon's wake, the slender gouge closed and the shield reformed.

"Time to go," Sigren whispered. "Like we discussed, remember?"

Thaun swallowed, not trusting himself to speak. With a nod, the Shadow disappeared into the milling soldiers and out of sight.

One step at a time, Thaun moved out from the side chamber, painfully aware of the officers whispering behind him.

Between him and the sphere's unrelenting advance, a few more soldiers tried their luck with no more success than their comrade. None yielded willingly, but Renyar gave them no choice. No matter how much they pushed, hammered, or dug their heels in, the jade wall edged closer.

Thaun walked towards his foe, flinching as crossbow bolts whipped past his head. A distant part of him wondered if Sigren's shot made up part of the volley, but he paid it little attention. Here and there, a tiny crack appeared in the ward, only to fill again a moment later.

"Renyar!" he called, wincing at the tremble that filled his own voice. The impenetrable wall came closer, and he shouted again. "Renyar! I am Thaun Konreig, Imperial Crown Prince, and I demand to speak with you!" Speaking the clumsy words aloud, he still wished that they'd come up with a better plan.

Unrelenting, the sphere paid him less attention than the nervous soldiers on either side did. Its advance continued. The hail of projectiles hammering against it slowed before halting completely.

On either side, shields still raised between them and it, the frontline separated around Thaun as the guardsmen withdrew. A few hesitated as they passed, unwilling to leave the Royal to face it alone.

"Renyar!" Thaun wasn't sure what else to say. With an anxious snarl, he stepped forward, sword leaping free of its scabbard. He didn't know why he did it. The Fang's growl in the recesses of his mind pushed him to continue.

A second later, and the dark iron met Renyar's defensive wards.

Where the veterans' weapons had done little more than superficial damage, his swing had a more noticeable effect.

He wished he could take the credit for it himself, but Thaun had started to suspect that the Fragment had more subtle effects than consuming the forces striking it. Ever since returning home, he'd caught glimpses of its possibility. A strength not quite his own, his wounds and stamina recovering more quickly than it should have. He didn't want to think too
hard about it.

Even uncharged by the Fang, Thaun's muscles tensed and burned with the effort, the impact reverberating up his arm as iron protested. The sorcerous shell fared worse. Sharp, emerald shards shattered outwards. Like a ripple on water, the field fractured and broke. Within half a dozen heartbeats, an opening wide enough for two men abreast opened at the corridor's centre.

Though the edges flickered as the sphere regrew before him, Thaun didn't see. His gaze held on Renyar, where he stood with one raised, empty hand.

With a dismissive shake of his head, the Thalan lowered his arm, and his spell faded. Since the flames that had engulfed the Palace, a single image had dominated Thaun's mind. Imposing and controlled, a physical presence like few others. The Patriarch now seemed almost small. Like something had diminished within him, a visible weariness wrapped around Renyar. Dirt marred his clothes, and the strange mantle he'd worn before was now gone, but an argent fire still burned in his eyes.

"Crown Prince." He glanced past Thaun to the rows of levelled crossbows. In the green-hued gloom behind him, Seorsans, Thalans, and a mix of mercenaries drew bows in return, but none loosed. Renyar spoke as if oblivious to the growing tension. "I was eager to speak with you in your home, but events conspired against us."

"Well," he swallowed down his nerves, "I'm here now. Talk."

"I was expecting... something else. Have you come to threaten me? To join me? To beg?"

He paused, holding Renyar's steady gaze. "I've come for answers."

"Answers require questions, Your Highness." He took a step closer. "And I've some of my own. Why come to me now? When your late cousin accepted my offer, she didn't surprise me, but you? What I learned of you suggested you'd be less cooperative."

"You don't get to talk about Heizl." He fought the sudden urge to raise his sword. "It's your fault she's dead."

"It's regrettable." Renyar edged closer still, silver eyes locked with Thaun's own. "I'd heard rumours of her loss. For what it's worth, I valued our short time together. Had she done as she promised, this could've all turned out better for everyone."

"Promised?" His eyes opened wide in disbelief. "You tricked her. You lied to her!"

"She made her own choices. All of us suffer the consequences of our decisions."

"Heizl wouldn't have done what she did if not for your orders."

"I give no orders anymore. Only requests. It might serve you to consider them."

"It's pretty hard to take you seriously when you keep spouting shit like that."

"This sounds less and less like you want to talk."

"Honestly? I'd rather punch you in the mouth than share another word with you, but..." Thaun hesitated, doing his best to hold his expression still. If anyone there caught wind of what he and Sigren had planned, there'd be no more time for questions. "But I need answers, and apparently I'm not likely to get them from anyone else."

Renyar gave an infuriating smile. "And why should I tell you the things that I've dedicated myself to learning?"

Thaun rolled his eyes at the ridiculous claim. "I figure you've nothing to lose, what with the world about to end."

"I have no intention of letting this world burn."

"Sure, why ruin your own home, after all?"

Renyar smiled. "Your cousin said something very similar, once."

"I told you that you don't get to talk about Heizl," snapped Thaun, feeling his anger welling up. Grief had buried it long enough, and now it threatened to burst out all at once. Breathing in through tight lips, the air shuddering from his lungs as he fought to control himself. Forgetting why he'd come here would dash their hopes more certainly than attempting to fight the entire Seorsan army by himself.

"My work with your family was a necessary evil." The Thalan's gaze dipped to where Thaun had strapped the Fang to his arm. "The same cannot be said for Elhin's death."

"I guess we've all lost someone."

Renyar ignored the barb, anger and sadness drifting across his face showing a world-weariness that he hadn't shown a moment earlier. "How did she die?"

Seeing the grief on the other man's face, Thaun almost apologised before he got a grip on his emotions. "She tried to face down an army."

Something like a smile passed over Renyar's expression. "I see that you haven't learned from the mistakes of the Fang's previous bearer." He gestured to the troops gathering closer behind him.

"I told you, I came here to talk." Where was Sigren? Thaun didn't know what else to say. Every moment gave the Shadow longer to prepare, true, but the Seorsan vanguard recovered with each heartbeat too.

"Then talk, Crown Prince. Ask the questions worth risking yourself for."

"Why are you doing this?" Thaun waved round with both hands. "Why attack our home? Why hurt so many people? Why summon Urathear?"

"I had expected you to be misguided, yet still it pains me to see. Why do so many of you Imperials fail to understand what I am trying to do for this world?"

"Can't you just tell me to understand? You've enthralled others with your words before, why not now?"

"I relinquished the Tongue." He shrugged. "It was the cost to attain the help of four Seorsan Councillors. Where one man and a Fragment would fail, the force of arms might succeed."

"Might succeed to do *what?!*" Thaun threw up his arms. "I ask to talk, and you just speak in riddles. I'm finally questioning what's actually going on, and you answer with condescension. I don't know why, but I expected you to actually know how to hold a conversation, what with having had a dragon's tongue and all."

"Your uncle made jokes to deflect from serious matters as well," Renyar mused. "A foolish habit, and one that seems all too common among your people."

"Well my uncle is going to make you regret ever getting involved with us."

"Trust me when I say, Your Highness, that I sincerely regret my dealings with your entire family."

"I bet you do."

The Thalan continued as if he hadn't heard him speak, his grey eyes taking on a distant look. "If I hadn't attempted to recruit the Emperor to my side, he never would have learned of Urephor's Heart."

"And then he couldn't have stopped you."

Renyar's gaze narrowed on Thaun. "And then he couldn't have planned to summon it himself."

Thaun hesitated. No one else spoke for a moment. Nearly every man and woman faced him regardless of their allegiance, and he felt the weight of expectation settle upon his shoulders. Renyar stared as if awaiting some reaction.

He sighed. Just because he'd agreed to hold the Seorsans collective attention didn't mean he felt comfortable beneath all those hostile gazes. Sigren had better be in position by now. A lot of this plan rested on the Shadow being as good a shot as he always claimed. Thaun couldn't remember ever having witnessed his friend miss, but a lot had happened recently. Fatigue didn't care how skilled a person was.

"...Your Highness?" Renyar asked, head bowed slightly. "I had expected some kind of interruption or outburst, not for you to fall speechless."

Thaun flinched at the words. He bit back an instinctive apology. "Did you tell Heizl the same thing? What else did you tell her?"

"May I speak about her now?" His grin spoke of mockery, even if his words didn't. "Merely that I am but concerned for your wellbeing, and that of the world."

"You must realise how ridiculous you sound. Who in their right mind would trust you?" He almost smiled at his own words. It was probably best not to think too hard about his own mental clarity right now.

"Why do you not believe me, Your Highness? You speak of questioning the ways of the world, yet you ignore my answers. Seorsa has allied itself with me. Your uncle listened, even if it was only to turn against me. Your cousin gave her life for–"

Renyar inclined his head a fraction of a degree as he came closer. Behind them both, their respective allies held their breath. Arms trembled as they held bows drawn. "Your Highness. Thaun. You need to listen carefully. An ancient power is on the verge of returning to our material world, and it must be stopped."

"And that's why I'm meant to believe that you're fighting Urathear now?"

"I'm not talking about Urephor. Daericani, what few that remain, hold little relevance upon the world stage. There are more dangerous forces awakening than you or your people know. Forces that ruled lands centuries before your Empire's conception. Creatures that beggar your gods. Sources of power that your mages and scholars haven't even begun to uncover."

"I think I read this one," Thaun drawled. "Is it the one where the captain sails the ship into the monster's head?"

"Please, take this seriously," said Renyar earnestly. "After the Comet has passed, I will gladly discuss this with you at length. I will reveal to you histories lost to men, and teach you how to control the Fragment that you bear. Now though? Stand aside. This conversation is over. I go to stop your uncle."

"Wait, you're..." Thaun's face wrinkled in concern. For a moment, all plans to delay Renyar disappeared from his mind. He could almost hear the Fang's growl. "I can't tell if you're lying, insane, or something else. Don't start thinking that I trust you or anything, but what are you talking about?"

"My people have watched you, Crown Prince. I've learned about you. Your denial of your talents. Your wilful refusal to take your place in the world." Over the armies' murmurs that came from all sides, Thaun could scarcely hear Renyar's whisper. "Your inability to trust the words of those around you that just want to help. We dismissed you in favour of other potential allies, and perhaps that was a mistake." He paused, but Thaun had no reply. "Surrender, Your Highness. Protect the lives of those that follow you. Come with me before the Emperor, hear his lies for what they are."

"I can't."

"I understand, Thaun. Just answer me one thing before this escalates. There are few who can see the fates of life's many choices, but what do you think would be different if you had accepted the reassurances of those around you? If you'd questioned those around you rather than simply suffering under their expectations? If you fulfilled your duties sooner?"

Thaun opened his mouth to respond, but a lump rose in his throat, silencing any response. Not that he knew what to say.

"What would be different, Your Highness, if you trusted the right people now?"

He stood almost in a duelist's stance, with feet planted and sword in hand. Still he reeled. What would have changed? What would change now? Too many ifs, shoulds, and buts. Heizl had tried to tell him. He should've listened. Lives might not have ended, losses might've been avoided, souls could've been saved. The mere thought, that smallest glimpse of different possibilities, paralysed him.

"...I can't tell if you're lying to me or not."

"I am afraid that I don't have time to indulge you further." Sympathy and regret drained from Renyar's features. "Surrender the Fang and command your soldiers to stand down. You will be kept in our custody until after your uncle's ritual is prevented." On both sides, feet shuffled and grips tightened as men and women prepared to resume fighting.

"No, Renyar. Let's say that I believe you. I need to know more, before–"

So close to comprehension, a crossbow bolt cut short any attempt at further understanding. From where he stood, Thaun didn't know if Sigren had finally found a clear shot, or if some soldier's nerves had got the better of them.

The quarrel struck Renyar in the upper chest with a subdued flash of green and a sound not unlike an axe striking wood. Its leather fletching stuck out between silvery chainlinks, but it disappeared from sight as a glowing green globe enveloped the wounded Thalan.

A volley of projectiles echoed the shot a second later. Arrows, quarrels, and even a handful of siege bolts filled the air. Chaos joined them – Imperial Guardsmen and Seorsan troops rushing in from both sides – but Thaun saw little of it.

Catching the briefest glimpse of cracks forming in Renyar's sorcery, Thaun ducked behind the Fang. The impact of a dozen Seorsan missiles felt as gentle as falling rain upon its bronze surface. Sickening power flowed up one arm and down the other as his blade burst to life with unholy fire.

Edging his head out beyond the shield's rim, he barely brought it round in time to receive Renyar's assault.

His emerald sphere, no longer filling the whole corridor, launched towards Thaun like a boulder down a hill. Its frayed surface opened just enough to afford a glimpse of the injured Thalan. The remains of Sigren's quarrel remained in his chest, but he moved as if unencumbered.

Shifting his weight to swing the destructive force clinging to his sword, Thaun staggered back as Renyar projected his sorcery outwards. Before he could land a blow, a piece of his emerald ward connected forcefully with Thaun's blade. Darkness, riven with violet, blossomed in the tunnel.

The blast threw armoured soldiers from their feet without discrimination. Imperial and Seorsan alike hit the stone floor, punctuating the clash that surrounded them.

Caught unawares, Thaun staggered. His foe had expected it though. Renyar's green shields weathered the worst of the blow. In the flash of green and black he slid around Thaun's flank, curved blade slicing over leather and steel. The armour held, if only just.

Dodging back beyond the reach of Thaun's answering slash, Renyar adjusted the grip on his sword as he shifted his stance.

"Renyar, I'm sorry! I should've listened sooner!"

As if anticipating Sigren's second shot, the Thalan's ward burst outwards again, and the quarrel ricocheted away.

"Please! Renyar, you have to tell me—"

"You must realise how ridiculous you sound." The Thalan spoke in a mock Imperial accent. "Who in their right mind would trust you?"

"Look, I'm sorry." Thaun found himself shifting to face him, shield snapping upwards. At the edges of his vision, soldiers clambered back to their feet. "We can talk this out. If Uncle's doing something, then he'll have a good reason for it."

"I don't care. He betrayed my trust, and now his ambition threatens not just your Empire, but the world beyond. Had you not designed to assassinate me, or attacked my allies, I might have believed you, but now..." Renyar shook his head, a hint of regret tainting his anger. "You leave me no choice. I will take the Fang from you in hope that it proves enough for me to halt this evil."

"But—"

The Thalan's sudden attack stopped Thaun mid-sentence. His blade became a blur, faint green traces hanging behind it in the air before dissipating like morning mist. Thaun barely got his own sword up in time to turn the attack aside.

He yielded ground as quickly as he could, parrying another blow as Renyar flowed after him. Dodging right, he raised his shield to block a swing, fully expecting to feel the black fire pour through him. Nothing happened. The Thalan had halted an inch from connecting before wheeling back. Braced to receive the blow, Thaun found himself stumbling off balance.

Renyar exploited the opening, his single-edged longsword slashing along Thaun's flank. Within the armour, he felt the impact, its force driving up from his side to push the air from his lungs. Coughing, his chainmail weathered two more swings before he recovered.

He continued backpedalling beneath Renyar's relentless assault. His own blade danced before him. Every time he attempted to use the Fang though – whether to block a strike, or to push his foe back – the Thalan anticipated it, dodging away before connecting with its scratched, bronze surface. What few counterattacks Thaun managed to lash out with met shimmering green shells.

"I trained with Elhin daily after she gained the Fang," Renyar said between elegant swings. "I learned beneath Inurta's Aspects themselves, as well as a dozen generations of swordmasters. Yield and I shall make your death painless."

Thaun didn't feel the need to respond to his taunts and threats. He could believe every claim. In spite of the wound in his chest, the Thalan carried an economy of movement that he couldn't begin to match. He hadn't even noticed his opponent shift his blade into his left hand, though he didn't know if he had done this to better avoid the Fragment Thaun carried, or to favour his uninjured side.

Throwing aside his vain attempts to level the field with the Fang's abilities, Thaun allowed a swing to connect. He felt a wash of heat and pain as something tore in him and chainlinks scattered to the muddied ground. Still, now within Renyar's reach, he stepped in further.

His blade, a gift of Tszerrichan iron from Toland, impacted the Thalan's side, bending the mail there inwards and eliciting a pained grunt. Thaun didn't stop, leaning into the follow-through to strike high.

He'd practiced the motion a hundred times before while training with Lena. It had worked once against Elhin and even Renyar himself, during that fateful night in the Imperial Palace. As he thrust, Thaun remembered how that last incident had ended.

Green wards appeared from nowhere, locking on either side of the blade and halting his attack a hair's breadth from his foe. The shimmering arcs screeched as iron ran across them, swirling cracks forming beneath his lunge's Fragment-enhanced strength.

The Thalan flinched for the briefest second before composing himself. Motionless, close enough to breathe upon Thaun's weapon, he waved his free hand and more of the barriers grew up around his prey's arm.

Thaun struggled to break free as emerald enveloped his wrist, before it moved up his arm and shoulder like some virulent growth. Cold, unyielding surfaces appeared on all sides, trapping him as surely as any vice.

Satisfied that his magic held his foe securely, Renyar sighed and inspected his own sword for damage. "I truly am sorry that it must come to this, Your Highness, but your duplicity leaves me little choice. I would have preferred to resolve this peacefully, and to forge a new future as allies. Be assured that I will strive to protect your people in your absence."

Thaun would have shook his head if it hadn't been held in place. Instead, through the T-shaped hole of his helmet, he whispered. "I'm sorry too."

Flexing his fingers as far as the wards allowed him, he squeezed the short bar that ran the length of his sword's hilt. Something clicked within the crossguard, and the weapon shuddered. He'd heard the noise of Toland's rifles before, but it did little to prepare him for such a loud cracking sound so close at hand. The pipe running the blade's reverse side barked as smoke and fire leapt from its open end.

Eyes clenched shut against the bright flash, Thaun staggered sidewards, suddenly freed as the crystalline shields dissipated. He steadied himself, stomach turning, and looked around.

Renyar's body lay unmoving upon his back. A faint tendril of smoke rose from the gaping, bloody hole that had appeared at the base of his throat. Another of Sigren's heavy quarrels stuck out from his gut. The Thalan's pale grey eyes stared up at the stone ceiling, not seeing a thing.

Thaun sagged, unable to stop his hands from trembling. Fighting the urge to throw Toland's gift to the ground, he instead slammed it back into its scabbard. What parts of him didn't feel sick ached beneath the storm of blows that the late Renyar had hammered down upon him.

Seorsa gave him no time to process this though. Unperturbed by the loss of their ally, armed soldiers threw themselves forwards.

To either side, cracking noises filled the air as strong hands dragged him back.

Pinions stepping up to join the battered guardsmen, Toland shook him. Behind them, their attackers faltered beneath the sudden onslaught before backing away up the corridor to regroup.

"Sorry I'm late." The noble smiled. "Come on, we should get back. Once they recover, Seorsa will make another push. They've come too far not to."

"Toland?" Thaun's head spun. "You're here? I thought you were back in reserve?"

"We were." He shrugged. "Figured we'd be more helpful up here. Most of my men are still back with the Emperor."

Sigren appeared alongside them, helping to pull Thaun back towards safety. "Did we get him?"

"...Pretty sure we killed him," Thaun replied through a haze.

"Then we won?" The noble's grin widened.

"I'm not so sure." Thaun shook his head before shaking free of his friends' grips. "I don't think I should put off speaking to my uncle any longer."

Tooth and Nail – Chapter Twenty-Eight

> *"Even the most ancient of lines may be consigned to history's footnotes. Such was the fate of the Kuhlners. The assassination of its heirs, the loss of its allies, and the execution of Rhaekeiran himself. All this and more saw them cast into obscurity. Our people will not share their fate."*
>
> An address to the Baras,
> Cylarid of Oaks (407 I.Y.)

8th day of Ehnaln, 406th Imperial Year
17th Year of Emperor Rufenrich Konreig's Reign

"What in the Void has got into you?"

Thaun ignored the noble as he strode through the ruin's depths. If not for the various injuries on the soldiers he passed, he would've sworn that he'd walked this way already. All the passages looked so similar.

"Thaun!" Toland grabbed him by the arm, and almost fell from his feet as Thaun dragged him along for several steps. He still hadn't grown used to the strength that the Fang lent him. Only when Sigren obstructed his path did he stop.

"What did he say to you?" the Shadow said, one hand pressed against Thaun's chest as he stared at him. "Did he make any commands?"

"No, stop it." Thaun shrugged away from both his friends.

"Then what's going on?"

"I need to go."

"Thaun, stop." Toland moved alongside Sigren, speaking slowly and calmly. "Slow down. Breathe. Talk to us."

"I..." He sighed, feeling his resolve fade with it. "Sorry."

"It's fine. What's going on? Why do you need to see His Majesty so urgently? Messengers will let him know that Renyar's dead soon enough."

"He said something."

"Renyar? Are you sure he hasn't enthralled you or anything?" Sigren gripped his crossbow with one hand where it hung from its strap, its groove empty.

"Nothing like that, no. He didn't even have the Tongue anymore."

"You're certain?" Toland asked, grasping Thaun once more.

"I'm not certain of anything, but I think so. I could feel something when Heizl was around, when she had the Claw. Like a, I don't know, a presence. A weight. I didn't notice anything like that just now."

"Then what is it?"

"I don't know, but... so much has happened. I don't know the words. I should've listened more. I should've paid more attention. I should've asked more questions, and not just blindly done what everyone else expected. I've got to, I don't know, do something," he finished weakly.

"Thaun?"

"Sorry. Look. I need to talk to my uncle. I've left things too long. Maybe I'm worried about nothing, maybe I'm wrong, but I have to hear it from him."

Both other men glanced at one another. For a moment, only the distant sounds of pain and conflict filled the air.

"Well," Toland spoke first. "I don't know if I agree with you on all this. Or your uncle, for that matter... but I'm coming with you. I don't think this is something you should do by yourself. Maybe I can be there to help do the right thing."

"I should come too," said Sigren, nodding.

"I think you should hang back," said the noble before Thaun could say anything more. "You're tired, and I don't think you've slept properly in days. You don't even have any shots left for your crossbow."

The Shadow looked down at his crossbow and the empty quiver at his hip as if for the first time. He nodded once. "Maybe. I should still be there though."

"Thaun?" Toland turned towards him. "What do you think?"

"...I don't know. Maybe he's right. If nothing happens, you won't have missed anything, but... I don't want you to get hurt. Not after losing everyone else."

Sigren shrank, his shoulders slumping and his head bowing forwards. "Fine."

"I know it's hard," Thaun continued. "Thank you."

"I'll catch you up after I resupply."

"That's not quite what... alright."

"Come on, Thaun." Toland nodded to the Shadow as he checked his own weapons, and gave Thaun a reassuring smile. "Let's go and find out how all this is going to be fine."

For a second, he considered rebuking his friend's overdramatic optimism. Instead, he shook his head, threw Sigren a hurried salute, and pushed on.

It felt harder now. More real, somehow. Putting words to his thoughts and emotions had made them solid. The face he wore for others, reluctantly maintaining their expectations, was cast aside. For now, at least.

Thaun took a breath – feeling the way it cooled his throat and expanded his chest – and walked. Without hesitation, Toland fell in beside him, matching pace, and the noble's Pinions followed behind.

"When we get there," Toland spoke in a low voice, "What do you need me to do?"

"I don't know. I kind of expected you to ask more questions."

"You sound more certain than you think. It's not often that I've heard you speak like that. I figure I should take the opportunity to see how it turns out." From the corner of Thaun's vision and by the light of their guards' lamps, his friend looked almost as anxious as he felt. "Or maybe it's the duty of people like us to do the hard things. To protect as many as we can, no matter the cost."

"Thank you, Toland." They turned a corner, and the uneven firelight grew, joined by the faintest of shifting, arcane colours as they neared the ruins' central chamber. "Just try to make sure no one interrupts Uncle and me. If I can just talk to him, we can work out whatever's going on."

The noble didn't reply.

Side-by-side, they rounded a corner. He'd seen the shadows and signs from a distance, but the change in light still came as a shock. Thaun had his shield raised before his eyes against the brightness in an instant. Pale flames, fed by lime or some alchemists' trick and magnified by mirrors, lit the length of the bare passageway. An attacker would find no cover on this approach.

Angered voices assaulted his ears. Though obscured by both darkness and light, his mind's eye could almost imagine the ranks of Royal Guardsmen blocking the corridor, weapons levelled. Behind them, the sounds of Pinions cocking rifles sent a shiver down his spine.

"Stand down!" Toland's voice rose over the soldiers' challenges. "In the name of the Crown Prince, let us through!" Some of the shouts quietened. Only when the noble pushed Thaun's shield down, revealing his face, did they all fall to murmurs. "Well? Let us pass, Void-damn you!"

After a tense moment, Thaun's eyes not quite adjusted to the limelights' blaze, a captain stepped forward and waved them through. Sidling between the soldiers, Toland in his wake, he ignored the hard stares exchanged between Pinions and Royal Guardsmen. Petty rivalry would wait.

His vision failed again as soon as Thaun stepped past their perimeter. His eyes, having adjusted to the brightness, struggled at the sudden change. Lanterns illuminated the massive central chamber beyond, but still he was forced to stand blinking until he could see again.

The place had changed since he'd last stood here. Murals, collapsed doorways, and faint shapes remained, but so much had joined them. Guardsmen in royal blue guarded entrances, manning barricades and pintle-mounted arbalests. No Seorsan or Thalan had penetrated this far yet, but the Imperial defences stood ready to meet them.

Scattered throughout, Thaun made out the subdued colours of Pinions, their red and blue so dark he could scarcely distinguish them from the occasional Imperial Shadow. At his back, the rest of Toland's men spread out around the room.

Overhead, like oil on water, the Rift rippled in the air, casting feeble shadows from those below. For a second, Thaun's gaze lingered on its unnatural shape. He could almost feel the energy cresting out from it. Another world, another place, where dead gods bided their time.

On his arm, the Fang trembled as if in anticipation.

He dragged his attention away, eyes settling on the figure knelt beneath the sorcerous portal. Feet moving beneath him almost of their own will, it took Thaun a few steps to recognise the prone man. Pale beard and dark skin, an old brown robe hanging over a bent but stout frame, and dozens of charms hanging from his wrists to rest upon the stone floor. Even engrossed in his trance, Hastigr looked deflated somehow. His clothes singed, his flesh sallow.

A handful of lesser Spire Mages worked nearby, drawing triangular glyphs around the Highmage, ferrying essence-filled items to him, and making gestures as they wove their own spells.

Focused on the old man and vision still burnt with the aftereffects of bright light, Thaun didn't see the last figure. Dressed head-to-toe in black cloth and with a short blade at their hip, they dashed from the darkness.

Rufenrich wrapped his arms around Thaun in a tight embrace, halting him midstride. With a brief squeeze, his uncle stepped away. He looked so different now from the image of him in Thaun's mind. The simple grace and poise had gone, replaced by creases, sweat, and weariness. Deep wrinkles framed his eyes.

"What are you doing here?" A hint of anger seeped into his voice. "You're meant to be commanding the eastern approach."

"Sorry," Thaun muttered as much out of habit as anything. "They don't need me there though. We got him. We got Renyar."

"He's dead? Vandel found him?"

"No, Vandel is still out there I think. Renyar came to my side. We fought."

"You did? Are you hurt?" The Emperor looked him up and down, seeking signs of any injury. "What happened? No, never mind. You shouldn't be here – it's still dangerous. Go resume command."

"Uncle, it's not like that, I need to–"

"Thaun!" At his raised voice, soldiers flinched away and heads turned. Even Thaun took a step back. "I was used to this from Heizl, but you?" He opened his mouth as if to say more, before closing it again and letting out a frustrated breath. "We can discuss all this later." As if seeing Toland for the first time, he nodded once. "Master Acquiel, please escort my nephew back to the First."

"No," Thaun replied before his friend had the chance, doing his best to match the certainty in his uncle's tone. "Toland's helped me more than you could know. I want him here, and I want to talk about things *now*."

"Thaun..."

"Renyar said some things to me. No, not like that. I don't think he had the Tongue anymore. I don't know if I'd still be standing if he had."

"This needs to wait." Some of the authority had left Thaun's voice, and the Emperor struggled to meet his eye, glancing instead towards Hastigr.

"Uncle Rufenrich... what's going on?" He gestured with one hand towards the Rift and the Highmage beneath it. "Renyar's defeated, he can't summon Urathear now. His army is still out there though. Wouldn't it be better to have Hastigr supporting the front? He might not be a battlemage, but he can still make a difference." As anxiety seeped into his stomach, worse than anything he'd felt while fighting, he could hear his own voice rising unbidden. "If it's so dangerous here, why send both me and the Champion away? Why are we still here at all and not retreating? Or mounting a sortie?"

"I'm sorry, Thaun, but it's not that simple."

"You said that it was Renyar behind this summoning... but it's not, is it?" Despite the pain reaching for him, he pressed on. "What's Hastigr doing? What haven't you told me?"

"You should—"

"No more, Uncle!" Thaun shouted. More heads turned their way. "No more half-truths, no more dodging questions or sending me away. Heizl said not to trust you, and I should've believed her." Though he fought the urge, Thaun could feel his right hand edging towards the blade at his hip. "Say what you've been keeping from me. Now."

"I'm sorry," Rufenrich shook his head. "It's for your own sake. For the good of our family."

"No excuses, Uncle! Not from you, and not from me either. There are things wrong with me, but I'm not hiding behind them now."

"It's not an excuse!" the Emperor all but screamed back. "Our Empire, our legacy is in jeopardy! More than just Urathear, more than just Renyar, more than just Seorsa. Gods and monsters have shaped this world before, and soon they'll come back!"

"I..." In the face of such passion, Thaun faltered.

"They'll come back, but if we have Urathear's Heart, and everything else up there with it—" he waved one hand in the Rift's direction, "—Then we'll be fine! They'll try to change things, but we can stand strong! We can take something wrong and make things right with it!"

Silence filled the chamber as his echoing voice faded. The whispers of soldiers filled the quiet, but Thaun heard nothing past his pounding heartbeat in his ears.

"Thaun, you can't stay here. Hastigr's not finished yet, but before then—"

Shouts cut him short. From the other fortified entrance, soldiers shouted their challenges once again. They only lasted a moment, as another voice barked something at them, unintelligible from the clamouring echoes. Long shadows shifted, dancing with those cast by the Rift like reunited lovers.

Thaun glanced between Toland and his uncle, before facing the disturbance, hand still near his sheathed blade. None of them said anything as the line of Royal Guardsmen separated to let a figure through. He didn't know who he'd expected, so few commanded such respect, but the sight of the towering figure stepping through into the chamber tied his stomach into complex knots.

A sword, amber in the lamplight and as long as some soldiers were tall, dragged behind him, gripped in one hand. Shreds of a uniform hung from his broad frame, rent and scorched. In the gloom, Thaun saw no injuries on any exposed flesh; just mud, dirt, and soot.

"One Fang, a Claw, two Scales, a Wing, Bone, and..." Vandel's gravelly voice ground to a halt as his hard grey gaze tracked from Thaun to the flickering Rift overhead, and the Highmage beneath it. As if in answer to his arrival, the portal twisted and grew, like a beast fighting against chains. "What...?"

"Champion, I order you to—" Rufenrich failed to finish his own sentence either as the old soldier lifted his heavy blade to point it at the other men.

"What is this?" he demanded.

"Champion, Vandel, great." Through his nerves, Thaun still felt a flicker of relief. Someone else, someone who knew how to take command, had arrived. Toland had stood with him, but now they didn't have to confront this alone. "Uncle is about to do something dangerous! Take him into, I don't know, custody or something. We can fix this."

"Quiet." The veteran took a step closer, shifting his weapon into a two handed grip. "I should've known something was happening. This is what I get for tolerating your commands." One inexorable pace after another, he gradually closed with the Emperor. "You plan to undo what we did? Stupid."

"Vandel?" Thaun found himself edging forwards, shield raised between him and the Champion. Behind him, Toland edged sideways, pulling free his sidearm. "I don't know what you're talking about, but–"

"You and your Fragment's time will come soon enough, boy."

"Thaun," said Rufenrich, eyes locked on the Champion. "Be careful!"

The warning came even as Vandel surged forwards. Mottled blade swung faster than Thaun could track, but his raised shield caught the weapon with a screech. Flames gripped his own sword, barely free of his scabbard, and leapt halfway up his arm. Whether in his hands or Elhin's, he'd not seen anything like it. Ancient bronze bent at the impact. A shining streak flashed to life upon its surface as the sword gouged through the tarnish. The impact took Thaun's balance, one foot leaving the ground as he flailed and fought to find his balance.

Before a follow-up could separate his arm from his shoulder, Toland's shot barked from behind him. Vandel grunted as the projectile connected with his wrist, his flinch so imperceptible as to be meaningless.

The shouts and movements of the assembled guardsmen muted as his vision shrank to a single point. Thaun found his stance again, flames still clinging to him, and stared at Vandel. Pausing for a moment, the Champion glanced down at his bare arm, where soot ringed a red circle from Toland's shot.

As the noble reloaded, the way that the veteran's grey eyes settled murderously upon Toland filled Thaun's gut with ice.

At that moment, Rufenrich lunged. The Emperor had trained as a Shadow in his youth, when only second in line to the throne. His attack, the knife in his hand pitifully small, looked slow and clumsy in comparison to the man he attacked.

As Vandel twisted, massive blade still between him and Thaun, the Champion stepped into the lunge and raised his weapon to strike. Rufenrich's dagger skittered across torn armour and dirty flesh.

Neither god nor sage could quite explain what happened then. Where armies, firearms, and mages had failed to do more than slow the old veteran, the short blade drew blood, slicing between ribs. Letting out a yell, as much shock as pain, Vandel staggered sideways.

His swing, already started, continued its deadly arc, the ancient blade connecting with Thaun's Fang-fed black fire. The resulting explosion – fierce as anything Korten had drawn upon – threw Champion, Emperor, and Prince aside as it buckled stone.

Thaun had only experienced the Fang's direct effects a handful of times as its bearer. Each blast – the force of another's strike consumed and redirected – had washed over him like destruction's own tide. Instinct and training had risen within him, muscles bracing against the power. He'd felt its push, threatening to take his balance, but always a weak echo compared to what others suffered.

The Fang, it seemed, could only protect him from so much.

Rising from the smoke, hands reached towards Thaun. He pushed aside the pair of guardsmen who rushed to help. Clambering upright, he glanced aside.

"Where are the rest of you?" He demanded, but neither soldier answered. Thaun looked around, spotting more men and women as the dust settled. Those that had reached his side first now lay unmoving in a rough ring around them. Thaun's blast had repaid their loyalty in the most brutal way. Toland and his Pinions had fared better, standing at a distance, but some of them lay among the bodies too. Others stood further away, steel in hand as they stared past the explosion's aftermath.

He followed their gazes, taking in his developing surroundings. Thaun barely touched upon those closest – Vandel clutching his open wound as he struggled to rise, and Rufenrich cradling one arm as he crouched – as the pulsing Rift dragged his attention upwards.

Vandal's crimson blood climbed from the wound in his side like tar dripping from a cracked vessel. It didn't fall though. Instead, it formed a faint, broken tendril through the air that reached towards the portal growing above. The Rift's oil-on-water effect no longer rippled, now raging as if blown by tempest winds.

As Hastigr rose to his feet, the slick, intangible waves parted.

Thaun's darkest nightmare had painted scenes of monstrous, scaled forms coalescing from the darkness to loom over humanity. For all that the opening Rift looked like a leviathan shape breaking the surf, this resembled such thoughts poorly. The end of the world wasn't so obvious.

Depthless night poured into the chamber.

"Uncle!" Thaun all but screamed, scooping up his sword from where it had fallen. Eyes wide with barely restrained fear, Toland appeared at his side. "Stop this!"

Rufenrich didn't turn. He simply stood, holding an arm against his chest and favouring one leg. Blood trickled from a dozen places. Tears marked his once pristine uniform. Though it had let him cut Vandel when others had failed, his knife had lent him little resilience against the blast.

As Hastigr's ritual blossomed, the Emperor answered in a pained voice. "We've done it, Thaun. We'll be safe now, and can save others too." A smile came to his lips. "It'll be our legacy. When I pass, it'll be your legacy. Now—" He took a breath. "—We think it might react with your Fragment. Master Acquiel, please escort the Crown Prince to a safe distance."

At the clicking sound of the noble cocking his weapon, Thaun turned to see his friend stepping away, firearm levelled. "Toland...?"

Neither man looked up as a stale breath flowed from the Rift, and the dark surface trembled.

No dragon or god came through the portal as it yawned open further. Like stars winking to life in the sky, a dozen objects rained down. Weapons and tools, metal and hide, each emerged in turn. One after another, they impacted the fractured floor so far below. Metal struck stone in a cacophony of uneven sound, each note twisting out of tune. The Fang on Thaun's arm trembled, its shaking growing as more of them appeared. It ended almost as soon as it had started, one final object striking the floor with a thud, not a ring.

Rufenrich edged closer to where they'd fallen, as Hastigr stumbled as if awaking from sleepwalking.

"I'm sorry, Thaun." Tears welled in Toland's eyes. "I never thought it'd come to this."

"It doesn't have to." His voice trembled. The words tasted sick in his mouth. "You don't have to do what anyone tells you. Just do the right thing."

The noble smiled weakly. "All I've ever wanted was to do the most good for the most people."

Thaun clenched his eyes shut. Toland's pistol barked as he fired, the muzzle flash briefly breaching his eyelids. The shot never reached him.

At the sound of a pained grunt beside him, Thaun opened his eyes again. Smoke rose from the barrel, but not aimed at him.

Instincts coming to life, he lunged forwards. Closing the gap in three quick steps, Thaun slammed his shield into his friend, sending him sprawling. Even without any of the Fang's fiery strength coursing through him, he knocked

Toland from his feet. Risking a glance behind him, the sickening fire in his belly turned to ice.

Rufenrich dropped to his knees, clutching at a fresh wound in his upper chest. With his bloody arm, he strained to crawl forwards.

Reacting to their leader's shot, Pinions opened fire all around the room.

Diving towards his uncle as much as away from Toland, Thaun hit the floor with a grunt. Projectiles cracked and lanced through the chamber above his head. Royal Guardsmen, Shadows, and Spire Mages alike shouted in alarm as the gunmen turned. A handful along the chamber's outer edge dropped into cover, but dozens of the most loyal died in the opening salvo.

Green shields flashed into existence around Hastigr. A fraction of the size and half as bright as any Renyar had conjured, no shot found him. Nonetheless, he fell back to his knees halfway towards the largest thing that had fallen from the Rift.

As the loyal guardsmen that had survived the Pinions' opening volley began to answer with bowfire, violence blossomed to life on all sides.

Lancing through the air towards Thaun, shots lurched into the Fang's surface. Strapped tight to his arm, it did little more than whisper with each impact, but he felt the energy flowing from it. Clamping down on that sickening heat, willing it to stay within, dark flames still burst from his sword. As more projectiles connected, their force kindled the black fire until the blade's iron glowed.

Other rounds hit closeby, showering him with knifelike shards of ancient stone. Flagstones that had lay untouched for centuries shattered, their pieces striking his armour. Ignoring their sharp pains, he crawled to Rufenrich's side to drape himself across the man.

Even with all the Fang's power – the attacks of a hundred men magnified by a piece of an elder god – he was helpless. Sword held out and away so as to prevent any accidental contact from unleashing all it now held, he crouched over Rufenrich.

Inches from Thaun's face, his uncle coughed up blood. Hands stained red where he clutched at his bullet wound, the Emperor opened pained eyes and locked them onto his nephew.

"It wasn't meant to—" another shot found the older man, burrowing deep into his leg, and cut him short. Overhead, the Rift roared like a squalling sea, drowning out the sounds of battle for a few breaths.

Staring at Rufenrich, Thaun saw none of it, the whole world drawing down to a point. "It's alright," he said between tears. "Don't speak, save your strength."

"I only ever wanted..." He sobbed through gritted teeth. "It's not too late, Thaun."

"Uncle, don't. We'll get a healer, we'll get out of here."

"No, we won't." He clenched his eyes shut against the pain, but nonetheless managed a weak smile. "But you might. Live, be strong, and pro... protect our..." He trailed off. The Rift drowned out any other words he might have said.

Thaun hesitated, feeling the swelling of emotions threaten to close his throat. He opened his mouth to speak, but no sound escaped. His tears more than made up for his silence, streaming down his face to drip onto his uncle's.

Rufenrich didn't move, but then, Thaun hadn't expected him to. More urges flickered through his mind than he could respond to in a lifetime, twisting his thoughts this way and that. Each felt more hopeless than the last, whether begging his uncle to open his eyes, or banging upon his lifeless chest.

With stolen power and flame flowing through his flesh, Thaun rose. A snarl escaped his lips as he turned towards Toland.

The noble found his feet less steadily, staggering as if six wines deep. Clutching at several of the burnt and tarnished objects that had fallen from the Rift, his friend turned a wild gaze upon Thaun.

"Toland!" His snarl grew into a ragged shout. Another Pinion's shot struck the Fang. "How could you?!"

"Thaun..." the noble slurred, struggling to focus as Thaun bore down upon him.

"You killed him! We could've talked him down. It didn't have to come to this!"

"It was always going to happen. One way or another." He blinked several times. "You weren't strong enough to stop him. You wouldn't be strong enough to face whatever comes next."

"I thought... I..." Words failed him, their meaning eclipsed by the primal anger within him. Left arm high, the Fang absorbing shots as more Pinions turned towards him, he pointed with his right. Wreathed in black and grey, he looked down his blade's barrel.

The eyes that looked back at him weren't his friend's. Not anymore. Had he ever truly known the man? Always so sure of himself, and his own course of action. Toland now wielded that certainty against Thaun. How much of everything that had passed between them had served some ulterior motive? Just how naive had Thaun been?

Taking one step towards Toland, he didn't know the answer. At the back of his mind, a weak voice called for him to flee, to hide from the missiles now thrown his way. Louder yet less distinct, the Fang whispered over it, urging him to cut down the man before him and to reap his vengeance.

Thaun's grip trembled as he aimed the Fragment's growing tempest at the noble. That same pitiful voice, the one that sounded so much like his own thoughts, begged him to stop. To not do anything so impersonal. Even with everything that had happened, Toland deserved that, didn't he?

Thaun ignored it, and pulled the trigger.

His mind's eye painted an image of flames launching out like Urathear's own breath. He saw fire consuming the man that had just killed his uncle, erasing him and all his acts from existence.

Nothing happened. Beneath the sounds of battle, he only just heard the metallic click ring out from the weapon.

Straightening, Toland smiled at him, humour and sadness mingling upon his face. "Sorry, Thaun. Those old prototypes only held one round at a time."

The noble pointed straight back at him, his own sidearm raised while balancing the relics of people long past in the crook of his other arm.

Toland's shot arced towards the Fang, but never quite connected over the short range. Chain and plates protested as it took Thaun in the chest, lead screaming on steel. Metal bent but didn't break as he rolled with the impact.

Grunting at the pain, Thaun spun, ready to slash the noble apart from hip-to-shoulder, just in time for Toland's next attack.

He didn't know where the sword had come from. No Imperial smith had forged this top-heavy, hooked length of rusted iron that Toland now held. Arcing upwards, the air shimmering around its silvery edge, instinct saved Thaun then. A hundred lessons missed in favour of a duelling ring, he thrust both burning blade and draconic shield into its path.

The resulting explosion shook the room. Every ounce of power, stolen by the Fang and fed to his hand, erupted all at once. At point blank range, Thaun blacked out as flesh and mind shrieked in agony.

Striking the fractured flagstones shoulder-first pulled him back to consciousness a second later. Pain bolted through him as bone crunched against bone, and acid rose in his throat.

Thaun came to a halt a dozen paces from where he'd started. Dust fell and smoke rose. Shrill silence gripped his ears, the sounds of gunfire slowly returning to him as his head spun.

His vision focused long enough to see Toland standing over him. The noble admired the rusted blade that he still held.

It took Thaun a moment to realise his eyes didn't play tricks upon him, as he watched metal crawl over his erstwhile friend's body. Like beetles upon a corpse, jewellery and armour crept into place as if with a mind of its own. A shield, so similar to the Fang if not for the deep gash bisecting its bronze face, crawled from the ground near Toland's feet, its straps snaking out to pull itself onto his arm.

"I really am sorry, Thaun. For everything." The noble's voice came to him as if from faraway. "We were never going to be able to protect everyone. Like this at least, I can protect some of them. In another life, you might understand, you might even thank me. I don't ask for forgiveness now though. What I do is terrible, even if it is right. I wouldn't ask anyone else to make such a sacrifice." As bronze-rimmed cheek-guards wrapped around Toland's face, obscuring him, the briefest hint of a tear caught the light. "There's one more thing for me to be sorry for. I'm going to need your Fang now, too."

With a roll of his shoulders, a leathery cape hanging from one that hadn't a moment earlier, Toland hefted the sword up high.

Its rust-kissed blade fell, but never reached Thaun.

A dark cloud, marbled by purple lightning, struck Toland from behind. As he tumbled through the air, it pushed further, driving him forwards like some colossal tendril.

Thaun didn't see where Toland landed, hearing the traitor's impact as little more than a whisper. Propping himself up onto his elbows, he stared across the chamber.

Perhaps he'd hit his head harder than he thought. It was the only way he could make sense of what he saw.

The figure stood like something from a dream or nightmare. Choking dust closed back around them after a moment, but Thaun knew them in an instant. Different yes, with clothes shredded and scathe clawing around much of her neck and face now, but still the same person.

Heizl.

Tooth and Nail – Chapter Twenty-Nine

> *"Thanks be to the Judge, for her light guides our fates.*
> *Thanks be to her Word and Spirit, for they awaken us to the paths before us.*
> *Thanks be to the Saints, for they tip the scales towards our salvation."*
>
> The Blessing of Saint Wealmaer
> (297 I.Y.)

6th day of Ehnaln, 406th Imperial Year
17th Year of Emperor Rufenrich Konreig's Reign

Fear flashed through her body as she awoke. At the instinctive intake of breath, fresh pain stabbed into her side. Her reaction, lurching away, served only to make things worse. Heat and cold strobed through her. Darkness claimed Heizl once again.

The second time that she awoke was no better. Agonising consciousness accompanied her a little longer though, enough that she caught fleeting details of her surroundings. Nothing clear, just the sight of dark mist and the taste of stagnant river water coating her tongue.

A day could've passed while she knew only blackness, or just a few minutes. Awakening for the third time – that she remembered at least – Heizl clenched her jaw and pressed her left hand tight against her side.

Pain smothered her senses at the contact, and she adjusted her position upon the uneven floor just enough to think clearly. As memories rose into view, the thought of sinking back into insensate darkness grew more appealing.

She didn't know where she now lay, but she remembered where she'd last stood. A wooden jetty damp and slick with spray, facing a foe she couldn't beat.

Heizl wrapped her other arm around herself, bringing the Claw's beaten bronze with it. She hadn't realised she still held it. Her hand ached with how tightly she gripped the shaft. It brought scarce comfort. All that destructive power deep within its core, and Vandel had resisted her. All her talents turned to twisting souls and threads, and she'd walked into that fight blind to who or what she faced. All the might that she'd wielded to usurp her uncle, to lead an uprising in the very seat of her family's power, and she might as well have thrown harsh words at the old veteran.

It didn't make sense. He didn't make sense. Not yet, anyway. That hadn't stopped her though.

Rolling onto her back, Heizl allowed a pained smile to touch her lips. She hadn't needed to harm the Champion to put an end to his bloody rampage. Jilia would hear about her feat, wouldn't she?

Eyes opening to narrow slits, the mage stared up at the grey mist only just out of reach. Jilia, that most special and precious of people, would be safe. Only their most loyal supporters had witnessed her working with Heizl and Renyar. The loyalty of their Strahl troops had relied upon it.

Heizl would hardly have described her own circumstances as safe right now.

With a grunt and a wince, she rose onto her elbows, and inspected her surroundings. An old blanket of coarse-knit wool crumpled into a creased heap in her lap. It might've fallen further if not for her hand still pressed against the wound in her side. She couldn't think about that injury right now. There was more than one sort of pain.

Heizl didn't recognise the green clothes that she wore beneath the blanket. She'd much preferred the grey outfit she'd worn in the Palace, but suspected that it hadn't survived the incident at the docks unscathed. At least she still had the Claw.

Looking further beyond, she glanced over a neat stack of wrapped packages, and at the all-encompassing mist. Her eyes watered looking at that shifting wall for too long. Above, below, and all around, she might've been in a single room, or the middle of a field for all she knew. The floor that she lay upon felt solid enough.

Two lanterns burned bright with fresh oil just out of her reach. Through their soot-darkened glass, they cast uncertain shadows, but even they recoiled from the dim, sourceless light that permeated the air. The slightest of stale smells lingered, of damp and dust, of smoke and rot, and the whole world felt muted.

A place of quiet and solitude. Thaun would love it, away from everyone else. Maybe that was why he'd attacked her. One less person to put pressure upon him. She knew that wasn't really it, but her thoughts flinched away from the painful truth.

Few people understood her cousin, but he didn't much understand himself either, Heizl was sure. He didn't see his own value or worth, couldn't appreciate his own qualities.

She loved him dearly, and still regretted having locked him away. Thaun had made a mistake though, misunderstanding her as much as he misunderstood himself. Why couldn't he have just stayed safe where she'd put him?

Too many questions, and never enough answers. Well, she didn't expect any to stumble over her lying here, wherever she was. She'd work it out, whether anyone else wanted or expected her to. Some things never changed.

Shifting her weight, Heizl took a grip on the thick blanket that covered her.

"I wouldn't remove that if I were you," came a familiar, deep voice. In a rush, Heizl remembered; more than just Vandel and Thaun had opposed her. Hastigr. He sat not a dozen paces away, half-obscured by the strange mist. She hadn't noticed him there, but such an omission was far from the strangest thing to happen in the Highmage's company.

"You brought me here, didn't you?" she asked. In her hand, the Claw felt hot, its sickly radiance spreading through her.

"Sent you, more accurately." Despite their surroundings, a genuine kindness reached his eyes as he smiled. "Somewhere safer, where no one's likely to find you. Where you can't cause too much trouble, either."

She rolled her eyes. "Where is this place, anyway?"

"You'll ask me that again shortly."

"Just when I think you can't be any more annoying... Fine. What should I ask you until then? Why you're siding with Uncle? Why I should stay under some ratty sheet? Why I shouldn't blast you back into that Void-damned fog of yours?"

"It's not mine, though I suppose our line has more claim to it than most."

"Our line?" She arched an eyebrow. "Wait, are you saying–"

"No, nothing like that. Our relationship isn't one of blood. I'm suggesting that it's not the sheet you should keep close."

"What? Even by your insane standards you're talking nonsense."

"It's not the sheet. It's what's on it. Look more closely."

"I swear..." Heizl risked another glance down at the blanket as she adjusted how it lay. Her wound flared with every knitted rustle. Indignation faded into curiosity as she inspected the crude triangular shape daubed upon it, and the splatters crossing each line. "It's a... rune? A sigil? I didn't go to that class."

"I suspect you don't appreciate the poetic symmetry of 'sigil.' No, the term I prefer is 'glyph.' You'd have struggled to attend such lessons. The Spire hasn't run them since long before you joined."

"Spit it out, old man. It doesn't have to be this complicated."

"Just another source of magic, Heizl. Few enough practise sorcery, and only a fraction of those have the gifts to fuel a glyph. There'd be little benefit in teaching you how to write one correctly when you lack such talent."

"Yeah, well, you and Uncle still sent me to all the other lectures."

"A well-rounded education is important. Many assume that what they believe they know is all that there is to learn. Understanding the threats posed by sources other than your scathe may prove advantageous."

"I don't think I'm going to ask you about what this place is now." Heizl shook her head. "It's obviously just another classroom."

Hastigr barked a gravelly laugh. "Very good. I assure you that these things are important. Like keeping that blanket close."

"Worried I'm gonna catch a cold?"

"Few things could catch you, child. No, the glyph I scribed upon it promotes healing. Perhaps not as efficiently as a dedicated healer might, but when combined–"

"Right, fine, you can stop there. In the last couple of weeks I've heard stranger things than a magic blankie that'll keep me alive."

"Heizl," said the Highmage, shaking his head. "You are wounded in more than just the flesh. Body, mind, heart, soul – we all carry unseen injuries. Even before your recent exertions, and your bonding to that Claw, you hurt. Let me help you with this small pain, at least."

"Small pain?" She scoffed. "You know I got stabbed, right? And that was after your buddy, Vandel, threw me around."

"I'm aware. Had I reached you any later, I doubt we'd be having this conversation. If you hadn't drowned, you'd have bled out. The Claw would've sought a new bearer by now."

"Am I meant to thank you?"

"Ask your prior question, Heizl," he said, dismissing her outrage with a gesture. "Ask about this place."

"If you're so all knowing, do I have much other choice?"

"Not really, no."

"You would say that. Fine. Where've you sent me?"

The old man didn't answer straight away. Grunting and groaning, he rose from where he sat, leaning hard upon his cane. At his wrists, a score of silver charms rattled. Adjusting his moth-eaten robe, he shuffled around the clearing, never quite touching the mist.

"...Um, Hastigr? I asked–"

"Do you remember how my Nexus works?"

"Vaguely? Two beacons, objects bonded to one another, and you send people back and forth along that bond."

"Broadly, yes. The Nexus' beacons bridge distant locales." He gestured with one hand. "This is a part of the depths that lie beneath those bridges."

"Void-damn it, will you ever explain things clearly?"

"Void-damned, indeed. A Void, anyway. An endless stretch of mist and shadow, where once there was cloud and sky. Not of our world or above it, but sharing the same space, just in a different way. A battleground slain when myths were young."

"Poetic," she drawled.

"Perhaps. Truth needn't be fact."

"I dunno if you noticed, between your poetry and knitwear–" Heizl lay herself back down as gently as she could, careful to keep the glyph over her abdomen. "–But I'm not in much of a shape for discussing arcane theory, religion, or whatever this is."

The Highmage nodded. "You're right. Forgive me. I should be leaving, anyway, before my absence is missed."

"Oh yeah? Had enough of me already?"

"The bond between master and pupil is a valuable one, Heizl, but it's not always easy." He halted, standing almost directly over her. "There's food and water in the packs. Eat. Drink. Rest. I'll return soon."

"Y'know," she slurred, feeling the welcome grip of sleep reaching towards her once more. "It's usually me sneaking away while someone is half-asleep and the worse for wear…"

Eyes closed, Heizl didn't see the Highmage leave, but she sensed his magicks. The waft of sulphur, the ripple of stale air, and her ears popping. As he left, warmth grew. She hadn't noticed the chill. Too much recently, she'd felt cold.

Dreams, distorted by darkness and destruction, faded as she awoke again. The lanterns had died, leaving just the mist's ephemeral light casting faint shadows. In this sunless place, Heizl had no way to tell how long had passed. She didn't feel the need to sit up this time.

Beyond its soft weight upon her, she sensed nothing from the glyph knitting her flesh back together. Her pains had faded to a dull ache at least.

Using the Claw to drag the nearest package closer, Heizl devoured its contents. Bread, fruit, and honey, but she'd have probably eaten anything at that moment. She opened the second parcel more slowly, following it with tepid water from a corked skin. Clenching tight, her stomach protested at the sudden meal, but she didn't care. Only spite and stubbornness kept it all down.

"Well." She didn't know why she said it. That lone sound faded into the mist on all sides. It felt like a risk, as if some inhuman presence yearned to find her. Heizl could only care so much, lying there beyond the ends of the world. It wasn't like she could do much from here anyway. "I guess this is it. Just me and you."

Adjusting the blanket, she leant back with fingers laced behind her head and turned to eye the Claw. "A broken elder god, and a bastard mage. There must be other Claws out there somewhere. Do you miss them?"

No answer.

"I would, I think. Others like you, those you could trust, laugh and cry with… Or maybe it wasn't like that. Maybe Urathear just compared you to them, and your imperfections meant you always came up short."

Heizl didn't speak for a moment, as tumultuous, wordless thoughts tumbled through her mind. Was it poetic, tragic, or arrogant comparing herself to such a legend? She didn't know. She didn't know so much these days, not even how certain she could be about it all. What sort of life was it, when you couldn't trust your own mind?

"I'd feel a lot less like there's something wrong with me if you were to reply, you know. I guess you wouldn't be a Claw then though, right? You'd be a... I dunno, a mouth or something." Heizl considered for a moment. "I mean, not a Tongue though, unless Urathear had more than one. Renyar has that. Had it? I think... he was going to trade it for an alliance or something, right?" Another moment passed. "But what do you care? You're just a chunk of bone."

She sighed. "Yeah, I know. You're not going to actually say anything. Maybe I am mad, or maybe it just helps me think. Thaun was always the unstable one, not me. Well, maybe I was too, but in a different way. If I was stable, I probably wouldn't have done half the things I've done. I don't quite remember if I was like this before I took you off...what was he called? Okuaak's brother? Oh, Naqtuqa.

"Was he the same? Stumbled upon power, and tried to do the best for people? You abandoned him when we beat him. You wouldn't be with me now if you hadn't. So why didn't you leave me when Thaun kicked me into the river? When Hastigr trapped me here? I can feel it, you know. How you want to be with the rest of you. How you want to feel whole again. I guess neither of us will get that, trapped here."

Turning her gaze away from the motionless Fragment, Heizl felt the tears welling in her eyes. Enough to blur her already misty vision, but not yet running down her face. Trapped and abandoned in a place no person should find themselves. The weight of it threatened to crush her.

She'd die here.

"No." Eyes closed against the tears, the words came out unbidden. Not a shout or a growl, but a simple statement. That simple protest, weak and fragile, was all she had left.

Not quite all. She had her regrets, and time to reflect on her failures. So many of them. Every ambition met with disappointment. Every opportunity snatched from her. Every achievement ignored. Even her coup, that single sacrifice to try and protect everyone, ended with her hurt and abandoned.

Could she have done anything better? *Would* she have done anything better? None of those she'd aspired to impress would've expected anything more from her.

Had it always been about what others thought of her? Their approval, respect, and love? That line of thinking stung almost as much as her half-healed injury. Admitting that others' attention had inspired all her actions had a bitter taste to it.

Stretching herself just to impress Hastigr and the Spire in some vain hope of recognition. Mocking and performing before the courts to get her uncle to look her way, even if only to scold her. Twisting minds and leading hundreds to their deaths in the name of Renyar and his promises. Even Jilia... No, she didn't want to think about her right now.

Thaun though... Had he ever judged her? Probably. Her cousin had his own issues. But she'd reached into his soul before. Heizl had seen that collection of injuries and neuroses that moulded him. When he had looked at her that way, it was always because he wanted her to do better. Not for his benefit, no. But for her own sake.

The opinions of those others didn't matter now, here at the end of things. Thaun though... He only attacked her because he didn't understand. He'd have thought he did the right thing. He wouldn't let people get hurt, even if he hated every minute of it. That sort of person, someone trying to do the right thing even when weak and exhausted, maybe they mattered.

Heizl grunted as she sat up. Her cousin might not have the strength to keep going, but she did. Sure, if she tried she might only end up falling further and harder next time, but it wasn't like things could get much worse than here.

"Come on," she said, still as much to herself as anything, as she stretched out and wrapped fingers around the Claw. "We're not done yet." Rolling to put both hands beneath her, Heizl pushed herself to her knees. Her flesh protested, but that didn't matter right now. "Yeah, I know. It hurts. We can't rest yet though." Another push, and she rose, leaning hard upon the spear. Her head spun, and the metal beneath her grip pulsed and twisted like a serpent. "What do you mean, what work? We can, I don't know, do things that others can't. We can make a difference. If we can, we should, so let's not stick around here longer than we have to."

Heizl looked around with fresh eyes. A dim island in the midst of impenetrable fog. A broken Fragment, a moth-eaten sheet, and a heap of supplies her only company. She couldn't stay here.

With a quiet grunt, she draped the blanket over her shoulders. Setting her jaw, she took a step towards the wall of mist.

"I'd advise against straying far," Hastigr's gravelly voice broke her stride. As she turned, the last remnants of sulphurous darkness tore itself apart and he stepped from his black sphere. "A featureless sky, without even the stars for guidance... I fear you'd lose yourself."

She stood leaning on the bronze spear, even as her mentor stood with both hands upon his cane in crude reflection. "Do you really? And why should I listen to you?"

"Because I've been here before. More than once. This domain might as well be infinite, for all the good exploring would do. Two wanderers could spend their whole lives here and never see a trace of the other. Should you step into the unknown, you might never find your way back."

"Fine, I'll stay here. For now," she growled, and tilted the Claw towards him almost imperceptibly. "You need to start talking though."

"I've long strived to improve your education, Heizl." He smiled and scratched at his jaw, the silver charms upon his wrist jangling musically. He looked more weary than when she'd seen him last. How long had she slept for? "I will answer what I can, but I have obligations elsewhere. This was to be a simple visit to check upon you." The Highmage cocked his head. "Honestly, I'd expected you to still sleep."

"I don't care what you expect," she replied, though with less venom than she'd hoped. Her curiosity overshadowed any such vitriol. "You'll answer anything?"

"I'm not all-knowing, but I've always been truthful with you. I'll try to answer."

"Yeah, truthful maybe, but that's not the same as honest, is it?" She shook her head. "Fine. Why are you doing this? Helping my uncle, I mean."

"Out of loyalty. No, not to Rufenrich. Not directly, at least. His and my goals align. He wishes for the power to protect his legacy. A power he believes he'll find in Urathear's Heart."

"And what about you?"

"I am less interested in the Heart, and more in he who banished it to this place."

Heizl's head spun. "Right. And just who's that?"

"My own teacher. Just one facet of a being as elder as Urathear, and one who could bring order back to this chaotic world."

"You're talking about..." She struggled to remember. "You're saying that one of the tyrants that defeated Urathear, that's the guy who taught you to be this frustrating?"

Hastigr nodded once. "Indeed. He found me, a pariah by my chimeric heritage, and accepted me. He rests, undying, somewhere in this realm, clutching the Heart, and surrounded by the Fragments his siblings cast here."

"Siblings? You mean that story. An undying god, ripped up by others? God-kings ruling over continents."

"Broadly speaking, yes."

"And you're just a guy? A Highmage, sure, but you're not a...?"

"A god?" he chuckled. "No, far from it."

"Then why's it fallen to you to find him? Why not one of these siblings?"

"Family is complicated."

"Ain't it just."

"They believe in different paths. There's more than one route to mastery." He sighed. "A long time ago, when we both wore different faces, I proposed such a rescue to one of them. We disagreed. Dramatically. I, unfortunately, did not have a river to drop him. Nor did he underestimate me as he did you."

"A river?" Heizl's eyes widened in realisation. "Wait, Vandel–"

"Correct. Another Aspect of Imes. It was quite clever, really, the way Rufenrich kept him close but unaware. Your uncle is quite an exceptional man."

"That's a pretty risky move."

"His whole plan to protect your Empire has had its risks. Without Vandel, or another Aspect, it would be for naught though. His bond to my mentor, the blood that they share, gives us an opportunity to locate him that we would struggle to find elsewhere."

"Is that really going to make a difference if you can't get that blood from his veins? I don't know if you noticed, but even this didn't do so much." She shook the Claw.

"Indeed. Precisely why Rufenrich went to such lengths to secure a method to harm him. All it'll take is a drop."

Something clicked within her. "Are you talking about that dagger of his? Oh, or the Champ's oversized sword?"

Hastigr smiled. "Your uncle's blade is related, at least. 'Osteel' – a failed imitation of a broken Fragment, made long ago. It lacks many of your Claw's attributes, but should prove sharp enough, particularly with Vandel's habit of overestimating his immortality."

"Right. So what about the Champ? He's got to have one, right? Pretty sure I'd have at least dented his scimitar or something if it was a normal weapon. Is it another copy or something?"

"No. A trophy, taken from a vanquished deity. Intrinsically connected to glyphs, but unmarked by them."

Heizl didn't say anything immediately. It was all so much to take in. Gods and their pieces, the woven threads of plans and motives, she struggled to make sense of it all. Even if she had a better grip on her anger, she doubted she'd have thought any more clearly.

"Why tell me all this?"

"You asked."

"Sure, but why answer? I guess I'm grateful, but you don't have to indulge me like this. You must know that I don't like the sound of all this, that I'm likely to try and stop you. Are you really so sure about yourself? It sounds like the Champ's not the only one who thinks he's invulnerable."

"Hardly. I am all too aware of my own fallibility."

"That still doesn't answer me."

He sighed. "Nothing is certain, but I've explored our most likely choices, both yours and mine. Whether you leave this place under your own power or not, you are likely to go on to do great things." Hastigr smiled and cocked his head. "The greatest of those are most likely when you understand the greater scope of events."

"Right. And in all these fortunes, how many involved me stopping uncle from summoning the Heart? From you finding your tyrant-teacher?"

"Few."

Heizl didn't ask any more questions. The Claw's blast, laced with violet lightning, leapt from the spear towards the Highmage.

Green wards flashed before Hastigr, deflecting the brunt of the assault to one side as she drove him backwards. For a second he staggered, dissipating that destructive energy out and away from him. Before reaching the misty wall, he swung one hand in an arc before him.

Like the metallic sound of hot coins dropped on glass, the air screeched. The shriek faded, and suddenly the Claw's blast struck only fog.

Relenting, Heizl looked up. Four Hastigrs stood around their island within the Void.

"I'm sorry," the Highmage's deep voice came from all four figures, arriving staggered upon her ears. Each shuffled and shifted separately from the others, as if true individuals. "I do this for your own good. You'll be safe here."

"I don't care," she bit back. Before her, the four figures walked, circling her but not striking.

"That's not true, Heizl."

She paused. "Huh. Yeah, I guess you're right."

Eyelids flickering, she fell within. Bonds reached out from her like tendrils, linking her with each of her mentor's projections. Echos of every lesson, every joke and shared experience. Bittersweetness dripped from them like saltwater from rigging.

Swatting away anger and distraction, she spared little time on the threads themselves. Instead, she plunged towards their end points. Hastigr's soul, or something like it at least. Four identical versions, with nothing to distinguish one from the next.

Could she strike all of them at once? Maybe if rested, but now? She didn't know. Before Norjhost and the Claw, she couldn't have struck even one. She'd have resorted to twisting attention away from her and running, for all the good that would've done. Maybe she could've done more back then, if she'd turned up to more lessons.

Heizl's eyes narrowed. Hastigr had taught her to manipulate others' focus. He knew better than most how people thought.

Shifting her grip, she hurled the spear. Not at an illusion or trick, but off to one side. One of the few spaces not between her and a decoy.

A brief flash of dull emerald rewarded her as the Claw glanced from Hastigr. Deflected by his defences at the last possible instant, still its ivory head tore cloth and flesh before clattering to the floor beyond him. The old mage spun away, dropping to the floor. His echoes lasted a dozen heartbeats longer before fading, revealing a silver, glyph-covered charm where each had stood.

"I'd rather be lucky than good." Heizl straightened from her throw. "But all your talk about choices got me thinking. It's an old trick, isn't it? Getting someone to buy into the options you give them." She couldn't help but smile a little. "There's always another choice."

Sprawled but still clutching his cane, Hastigr looked up at her and smiled in return. Pain gripped his features as tightly as he held his side. "Wise words. Wise words indeed."

"Oh, shut the Void up." Weight still on the Claw, and blanket draped over her shoulders, she reached down and hauled the old man to his feet. She almost blacked out at the effort. Still gripping him by the collar, she held him at arm's length. "It's over. You're going to stay here with me until the Comet passes. No Heart, no tyrant."

"Heizl, I'm sorry."

"Not as sorry as you will be."

"That's not what I mean." She couldn't tell if the tears in his eyes were from pain or regret. "Like you say, there's always another choice."

As the rippling black sphere rose up around Hastigr's feet like a flame consuming kindling, she let out a string of colourful words as complicated as any sanguine spell. Fabric tore as she recoiled from its dark path. Stumbling, she hit the floor, a scrap of the Highmage's collar falling from her grip as she flailed.

So similar to all the times she'd seen it before within his Nexus, Hastigr disappeared.

Heizl screamed. No words or pleas, just the primal release of mental anguish and all-too-physical pain.

Darkness faded and, not for the first time, she stood alone within the Void. One more failure to add to the list.

It felt little different to before, but the stubborn spark within her lingered. She'd done enough counting of failures recently. Sure, someone like Thaun would probably have started listing their regrets again, but, much as she loved her cousin, she wasn't him.

It hurt, getting back to her feet. She ached to her bones, the pain in her half-healed wound held at bay by a thin layer of stained cloth and gritted teeth. It wouldn't stop her though.

Limping, Heizl collected the Claw. She hated it and everything it represented. It wasn't even a good conversationalist. A whisper of her wanted nothing more than to hurl it far into the mist. She knew she'd never do it though. Even if it didn't offer her its cracked wellspring of power, a visceral part of her needed it close. Someday, she might rid herself of it, but not today.

She breathed. Long, slow, and intentional, the musty air filled her battered lungs before she released it again. Calm would serve her better than any of the Fragment's destructive urges.

Hastigr had left. Probably to rejoin her uncle, to perform this ritual of theirs. They'd wait for the Comet's peak, draw out Vandel's blood, and use it to find both tyrant and dragon. She didn't know what would happen then, with elder powers returning to the world, but she doubted it'd end well.

"There's always another choice," she whispered, looking down at the Claw, unsure if she spoke to it or herself. Making a decision was all well and good, but useless if she couldn't act upon it. Words required action. Without a way to follow Hastigr, she might as well have stayed lying down.

Lowering herself to the floor with her meagre supplies, Heizl pulled the blanket around her midsection before tying it off. Claw balanced in the crook of one arm, she chewed lazily, savouring the sweet taste on her tongue, and let her mind work.

She had to get home. Not that she had much of one after all that had happened, but anywhere had to be better than here. Even if the Empire didn't hang in the balance, she wouldn't want to stay here.

Norjhost had felt the same. The weariness of dealing with traitorous old men and the trapped sensation that came with it. She'd escaped though. It had taken the unfiltered power of the Claw, and Hastigr's Nexus beacons, but she'd done it.

Only one of those things was available to her now. Well, two counting herself. Voids, she was probably the one thing she could count on.

It had been different back then though. Starting in the same plane of existence helped things. Not that she could know for certain, but it didn't feel like an unreasonable assumption.

Sat there, she closed her eyes and dredged through what Hastigr had taught her about his Nexus. It had changed things within the Empire, altering the way information flowed. Without it, the Civil War might never have happened. Or it could've killed even more. She had no way of knowing that either.

Even before the Claw, Hastigr had told her she had the potential to run something like it. Not as wide-reaching as his Nexus, but still. She hadn't paid much attention to the specifics. Would she have done things differently since then if she'd known how?

Heizl shook her head. She didn't have an answer for that.

Right. Focus. Beacons. That was the important bit. Two objects linked on a deeper level than most could even begin to understand. They were made, not found, but not just from anything. A pre-existing bond, focused and strengthened with layers of enchantment.

Her own threads flickered at the edge of her vision. Their far ends disappeared into the mist, but she knew where each reached as well as she knew the people they represented. Thaun, her uncle, Jilia, even the likes of Hastigr, Zecht, and Renyar.

With them physically before her, some of those threads felt as broad as roads. The thought of walking down one of those wasn't so daunting. A circus performer would struggle to balance upon one of the ones before her now.

A memory rose within her like a knock at the door, unexpected and jarring. The smells of sulphur and smoke, gardens and starlight, and crowds and distractions. Those didn't matter.

Back then, Hastigr had crossed a city to her side with just her hair between his fingers. He'd said she'd appreciate learning it was possible, or something like that. Did he really know that this would happen? Even with all his talk of different futures and paths, she didn't really believe that. If she did, she'd have tossed the idea away as much out of spite as anything.

Still, she didn't have a better idea. Not yet, anyway. She didn't have one of his hairs either, but that wouldn't stop her.

With Hastigr's blanket scraping the misty floor, Heizl crawled on hands and knees. Only a few paces away, she stopped. Cold sweat coated her at even that exertion.

She rolled onto her back, and looked up at the torn piece of cloth between her fingers. The Highmage's collar.

It seemed almost poetic to her weary mind, the threads woven by some tailor's hand, each wrapped around the next to give them form. Not a hair, and certainly not a prepared beacon, but what other option did she have?

She found its strand. A faint, lightless thing, but present nonetheless. It lacked the obvious path that she'd seen with Hastigr's beacon back in Norjhost. Even with the strength she could draw from the Claw, she didn't know if it'd be enough.

Words of recrimination rose against her fragile ego. Circumstance snatched from them the chance to bloom into anything more destructive. In an instant, her senses erupted.

She'd never seen anything like it. A needle rewarded with spouting blood as it thrust through skin. The call and response of operatic lovers singing to one another. Untold leviathans rising in answer to a fishermen's meagre bait.

Like the sea rushing through a breached hull, it pulled upon her. Heizl resisted, fearing where that flow might take her. Desires warred within her. She couldn't stay here, but faced with the looming unknown fear rose in her throat. She wanted to escape, but not like this. Uncertainty might be as bad as staying trapped.

As suddenly as the sorcerous tempest had sprung to life, it dwindled again.

Cracking open one eye, she found herself rolled into a foetal position, clutching the Claw. The air lay as stale and motionless as it had when she'd first awoke. Her senses cried out still, drawn to that unseen hole within the Void.

Her sorcery sang with the promise of freedom. Risking a glance within, she saw dancing threads reach out from her towards that shadow. Whispers in the darkness spoke of some unknown place beyond.

Her threads reacted, snaking towards the Rift torn in the arcanosphere. Each, so faint before, glowed a little brighter, as if their far ends were almost within reach. As her senses adjusted, one seemed more solid than the others.

Hastigr's collar. An object yearning to be whole again. Not a true beacon, but close enough.

For a heartbeat she wondered at the circumstance. Had the Highmage foreseen this moment too? Thinking too hard about such fates and paths would only waste time.

Breathing heavily, Heizl pushed to her feet. She caught herself as she tripped, one foot treading upon the corner of the blanket tied roughly around her waist. Scowling, she swept the Claw's head through the cloth, cutting it down to size. Her impatient kick sent the fabric drifting through the musty air, but before it had drifted back to the ground she had set to gathering up food and water.

Holding the spear in one hand and her supplies in the other, Heizl returned to her magicks. Edges swirling with faint blue fire, her sorcerous sight saw clearly now what her physical eyes had missed. A path towards freedom.

Setting her jaw, Heizl willed herself forwards. Grasping the thread that reached from Hastigr's torn shirt into the strange portal's depths, she pulled.

A second later, uncontrolled darkness wrapped around her feet, rising to envelop her in sable fire.

Tooth and Nail – Chapter Thirty

> *"Conspiracy says more about those speaking it than it does those that they speak of."*
>
> Erna Pohl,
> Imperial Shadow (390 I.Y.)

8th day of Ehnaln, 406th Imperial Year
17th Year of Emperor Rufenrich Konreig's Reign

She hit solid stone a heartbeat later. As acid rose in her throat, she let old reflexes take over. Nervous attention turned her way, strangers' eyes cast in her direction as the black sphere tore itself to shreds. With a brutish shove, she pushed their threads away before their owners' could focus on her fully.

Swearing, Heizl thrust her hands beneath her and rose into a crouch.

Unfamiliar, uneven flagstones. Fallen masonry as large as most houses. Flickering torchlight and alarmed voices. The oily shimmer of a sorcerous Rift roaring high above her head. It looked different from this side.

She didn't know where she'd brought herself, but it had to be better than Hastigr's Void. Despite the half-swallowed vomit in her mouth and the stale sulphur filling her nostrils, the air felt cool and clean.

Head still spinning, Heizl moved up against the nearest chunk of broken cover. Sinking into the shadows, the threads of those within the chamber felt lighter beneath her touch, easier to turn aside. The pressure of their attention upon her easing, she adjusted her makeshift sash and risked raising her head above the stone.

The air cracked in a staccato rhythm on all sides as men and women levelled strange weapons at figures in the Royal Guard's blue. Here and there, a pitiful handful of Spire Mages returned fire, but for every bolt of flame or lance of energy, a dozen mundane projectiles leapt their way.

Familiar flashes drew her eye. Emerald wards burst to life around Hastigr's crawling form as shots turned his way. The Highmage draped himself over a desiccated body. If not for her scathe seeing past flesh and bones, she would've taken it for a corpse, but weak life flickered within.

Her attention didn't linger as a dark explosion rocked the room. An armoured figure rocked back, absorbing the bulk of the blast. Another, more familiar, man fared little better, staggering back to sprawl to the ground.

Thaun.

She didn't catch the words that the figure spoke. Primal instinct growled to life within her before she could consider the assailant's identity.

The destruction within the Claw leapt forth at her slightest encouragement. Purple lightning lit the interior of the grey cloud as it punched into her target's back. The man spiralled through the air, pursued by Heizl's attack, to slam into an already cracked pillar.

As she limped forwards, her cousin scrambled back to his feet to meet her halfway. Soot marred his armour's torn steel, but she saw only wide, brown eyes.

"Heizl?!" He turned as he came close, raising his shield. Projectiles struck its surface, ebony flames licking the blade in his other hand. "How? I killed you!"

"Not for lack of trying!" She swept the Claw's blast past him. Flicking its strand from one projectile to the next in rapid succession, she destroyed more shots before they reached either of them.

"I'm so sorry, but you were righ–"

"Yeah, yeah, I know," she growled, grabbing Thaun with one arm and pulling him towards cover. As Royal Guardsmen fell, more and more weapons were aiming their way. "You can apologise later – now, get down!"

Tears ran through the grime upon Thaun's cheeks. "Heizl, it's over, it's too late, we–"

"Just *shut up* for one second, alright?!" Splinters of ancient masonry rained down on them as shots struck uncomfortably close. "Take a deep breath, calm that damn voice inside you down, and tell me what I need to know." She placed one hand on his trembling shoulder. "Please. For now, start with who's trying to kill us."

"Toland." His voice cracked as he said it. "He shot uncle, but it didn't stop the Rift opening. I don't know why he did it. Then he and his Pinions..."

She felt like someone had punched her in the gut. How was she meant to feel? She'd tried to oust Rufenrich from power, would've willingly killed him herself, but... "Well, maybe he should've shot Hastigr instead. I understand the urge either way. Why are his men still shooting though?"

"I don't... I think he took it, the Heart, I mean, and whatever else came out with it."

"A Fang, a Scale, a Wing, and some other stuff, I bet?" Heizl snorted. "Right, then we deal with your buddy first. You can fill me in afterwards, and I'll tell you all about where I ended up. Agreed?"

"Heizl, I–"

"You're sorry, I get it."

"No, let me say it." He wiped away a tear and set his jaw. "I should've listened. I was wrong, and I'm sorry." A half-smile grew then. "You were at least a bit wrong too though. If we'd actually listened to one another, then between us..."

"Thaun, I know." She gave his shoulder a brief squeeze and turned away. "I'm sorry too. Really, I am. Now though, it's time to put that sword of yours to use on someone other than me."

She didn't hear her cousin's response as she fell within herself. Disrupting the aim of those attacking them, she rose from cover. The men's – Pinions, was it? – shots went just wide enough. Ignoring the sound of projectiles missing, but only just, Heizl levelled the Claw. Rubble shifted as Toland's hulking, armoured shape found his footing again.

No longer with his back to her, he saw the attack coming this time. A shield, similar to Thaun's own, came up in front of his helmeted face in time to weather the worst of the blow.

Heizl couldn't take credit for the way Toland broke his own line of sight with that manoeuvre. Willingly blinding himself to her in exchange for blocking her assault, he couldn't see as she shifted the stream upwards. Just because she didn't have a river to dump the noble into didn't mean she had to attack him where he was strongest.

Rubble collapsed as she targeted the pillar directly, hammering him with ancient stone and forcing him to his knees. Toland's shield, another Fang by the way his curved blade blossomed into darkness, came up to intercept. She rewarded him by altering her aim again, blasting his unguarded midsection.

Feeling the heat leaving her flesh, Heizl relented, her blast diminishing before fading. Somewhere off behind her, she was vaguely aware of the sounds of combat as her cousin reached the nearest group of Pinions. His initial blast, his own Fragment having consumed the shots of a dozen men, drowned out the first few metallic rings and grunts as his sword came into play.

She didn't spare Thaun any more attention as Toland lurched out of the dust clouds to close the gap between them.

Her Claw leapt to meet his blade almost of its own volition. That ruinous instinct, bleeding from the spear into her, almost killed her. Metal clashed against metal, both weapons slamming to a halt. The impact unleashed the flames wreathing Toland's sword.

Heizl flew backwards, sprawling clumsily to the floor. Hard stone grazed her outstretched hands as she steadied herself.

Everything hurt. Vision spun, ears sang, and flesh screamed. The stench of burning hair filled her lungs. Grime and soot stung as it mingled with blood.

Pain clouded her thoughts. Heizl watched, helpless, as Toland reached Thaun. She didn't know if it was better or worse that he'd chosen to ignore her. Appearing at her cousin's flank, she couldn't follow their exchange.

Thaun's counter against the Pinions' volleys halted as swiftly as it had begun.

Forced onto the defensive immediately, he held his own for a dozen blows, blade and shield intercepting Toland's furious strikes. Threads burned across her vision like staring at the sun. She struggled to distinguish between soul and substance. Too many sources of light fought for her attention. Too many Fragments to comprehend, Toland's jagged iron blade among them.

A faint smile came to Heizl's cracked lips as she saw Thaun slip his own thrust in among the fierce assault. She knew firsthand how much a stab like that hurt. Her hope dwindled as their onetime friend barely slowed.

Bursts of dark candescence punctuated their duel as the two Fangs traded strength. Exchanging well-practised swings for a dozen heartbeats more, Thaun buckled under the bestial strength thrown against him.

Heizl didn't know what blow had weaved through his guard, but in an instant her cousin collapsed backwards, one leg disappearing out from under him.

That was that then. She could survive burning palaces, uncivilised wilderness, and drowning in a river, but this was how they'd die. At least she wouldn't have to mourn Thaun for long this way, for what small comfort that was worth.

They'd make it into the history books, she suspected. Even if just a footnote in some secondary account, someone would remember them. An Empire fallen, a dozen ancient Fragments returned to the mortal world, and even an ancient tyrant released. Worthy company, perhaps.

She'd have preferred to be noticed for her own efforts.

The strand between Toland and Thaun pulsed and flared as both struggled with conflicting emotions. Heizl wondered if her cousin's bright soul had looked like this when he'd attacked her, but that didn't matter now. Even hidden within that ancient, wretched armour, she could sense Toland's hesitation fading. The noble's corrupted thoughts, assaulted by so many Fragments, presented him with only one path forward. It didn't include any vestige of the ruling family surviving this place.

Teeth clenched tight together, she rose to a sitting position, head still spinning. The collection of pains that now formed her body had nothing left with which to muster any intervention. Her new vantage rewarded her with a view of Toland as he raised his iron Claw over Thaun.

No doubt remained in Heizl's mind that he would've killed her cousin then, and that she'd follow not long after. Muscles protesting, she lacked the strength to react as he was interrupted.

Lost to the gloom, something struck Toland in the side of the head. He recoiled, clutching at the slit in his visor, as a stout quarrel bounced along the stone.

Thaun forgotten for the moment, the noble spun, seeking this new attacker.

A second shot emerged from the darkness, striking towards the weak point between neck and breastplate, but it didn't come alone. Dozens more bolts and arrows lancing from one of the larger passageways hammered Toland and the nearest of his Pinions. Though his Fang absorbed many, more sank home, skittering over iron mail.

Soldiers followed at a jog, battered shields raised before their formation. As they split, squads scattering outwards to avoid the Pinions' return fire, another volley erupted out from behind them.

Confusion filled the chamber. More shots forced Toland back, his Fang unable to catch them all. Heizl watched as the noble flinched as another bolt, more accurate than the rest, bounced from helmet.

Tracking back along its path, Heizl saw a dark figure dropping his empty weapon to accept a loaded crossbow from a bandage-wrapped guardsman. She struggled to make sense of it all, and, as the Shadow turned to aim in her direction, recognition finally slid into place.

Sigren's shot skipped close enough to her that she felt its passing. Behind her, an unseen Pinion fell to the ground, doubled up around the bolt's leather fletching.

Heart pounding, Heizl crawled. The Shadow reached Thaun's side, along with a handful of blue and yellow guardsmen a few torturous moments before she did. As she came close, she found the crossbow levelled at her.

"Wait, don't!" Thaun hissed, resting his weight on Sigren's shoulder as he found his feet. Shields raised, the soldiers formed a wall around them. "It's okay, she's... we're all in this together."

"Last I heard, she'd turned traitor and got killed for it," the Shadow snapped as he loosed a bolt to cover their retreat.

"Things have changed," said Thaun, shoving Heizl behind an all-too-familiar heap of rubble before limping after her.

"Where's the Emperor?"

"Dead."

"Then who–"

"Look," Heizl interrupted. "We don't have time for all of this. Ugh, I think I broke a rib. Toland's over there, holding onto whatever pieces of Urathear just dropped into this place and it seems he'd very much like to kill anyone here not wearing his colours."

"Thaun?" asked Sigren after a moment.

"Pretty much," he sniffed, and wiped his face. "I don't know why he's doing it. I don't know if he planned this, or it's an accident, or if he decided something in the moment." He shook his head. "We can't stay here."

"And we can't go yet either," she said. "Whatever his motives, if we leave the pretty boy with the Heart, he's only gonna get more dangerous. These Fragments take some getting used to. This might be our only chance to do something about him."

"We can't beat him! You saw what he did."

"Leaving the Heart anywhere but the Void isn't an option, Thaun."

"It took, I dunno, some god-king or something to get rid of it before."

"If I can offer some feedback?" said Sigren as he loosed another quarrel. A limping soldier at his side dutifully handed him a fresh crossbow and began to reload. "You look like half a lizard could knock you over right now, Heizl. Voids, you look *like* half a lizard."

"I know, I know." She couldn't think of a better response. Still wincing at the sting of fresh blood on her face, she risked a glance over the rubble.

Lit by the weak, flickering light of torches and lanterns, Pinions and guardsmen fought. Men and women fell in service of causes they didn't understand. How many of them could truly comprehend the weight of events? The trust in one's leaders could be a terrible thing.

Toland had recovered, and now fought a full squad of the Imperial Second. Soldiers reached him in formation, as if facing an opposing army. Spears and blades came at him from all directions, though few did more than scrape ancient iron. In return, his rusted Claw lashed in all directions, periodically erupting with flame as dark as any shadow.

Through the chaos, Heizl saw no sign of Hastigr, nor of Vandel. She hadn't really expected to, but had held out hope at the chance to have a few more words with her mentor. The Highmage could be halfway across the Empire by now. It didn't bear thinking about.

Eyes tracking upwards, Heizl stared into the Rift. Clusters of Pinions and guardsmen fought upon the coiling staircase beneath it.

A thin stretch of fabric separating real and unreal, forced open from this side by the Comet's passing and an immortal's blood. The Heart had fallen from it, as had she. Had it grown bigger? How long would it remain open? Those memories of lying within the Void already seemed fainter. Something though, some glimmer of an idea, fought against her spinning thoughts.

"Heizl?" Thaun shook her by the shoulder and pulled her back around. He stood a little straighter now, she thought. It suited him. "Are you listening?

We're leaving. If we're quick, we can punch through Seorsa before they regroup."

"No."

"What? We have to. We've lost too many. Sigren agrees." He sounded a little less uncertain now. "If we limit our losses now, we can, um, try again with a better plan later."

"Pull it together, Thaun." She smiled, hoping it looked more confident than she felt. "You know this is on us."

"I–"

"Uncle's gone. You don't just inherit the Empire now, you get his responsibility too." She waved a hand at the Rift. "And he did this."

"How're we–"

"You said it yourself, things have changed. Do you trust me?"

He scrunched up his face as if pained. "I think so?"

"Good. What about you, Sigren? I'm a mage without a Shadow, and I'm about to do something really, *really*, stupid." She didn't give him time to reply. "Great. In that case, you heavies, make us some space. Deal with those Pinions."

The lone officer who had stayed with them, a middle-aged man with an arm in a sling, eyed her for a moment before turning to Thaun.

"Sir?"

"...Heizl, are you certain you want to do this?"

"Not in the least," she laughed, feeling a touch of mania creeping into her voice, "But I'm going out there anyway. Are you coming with me, or are we going our separate ways again?"

"Dammit. You're the worst." Thaun shook his head, and turned to the officer. "Colonel Halig, can the Second handle those Pinions?"

"It's Captain Halig, sir."

"Not if we make it out of this alive it's not." Thaun winced at the sound of an all too close explosion. Without either Claw or Fang to distract him, Toland was making his presence known.

If the captain had straightened any more, he'd have stuck out from cover. "We're with you, sir."

"Atta boy," said Heizl. "Thaun, you're with me. We're going straight down the dragon's throat."

"We tried that already."

"Not together we didn't."

"We've only got a Fragment each. There's no telling how many he's carrying now."

"Maybe," she shrugged. "But Toland's no mage, and I bet he paid attention in lessons that didn't involve swinging a sword around. Most people only really pay attention one way at a time."

"Heizl…"

"You're better than him, Thaun," she said. "Voids, you're better than you think you are."

"Hate to say it, but she might be right," Sigren drawled as he checked his weapon. "I don't like it, but we might not get another chance at this. Where do you want me?"

With a grunt, she untied the blanket around her waist. Pain flooded through her. "You, my friend, are going to make one more shot, and this time it's going to stick."

Tooth and Nail – Chapter Thirty-One

> *"If you judge a person by their enemies, then I must be a domineering piece of–"*
>
> Reported last words of Aepoli, Seorsan Inquisitor (376 I.Y.)

8th day of Ehnaln, 406th Imperial Year
Final Day of Emperor Rufenrich Konreig's Reign

"I can't believe I let you talk me into this."

"Let me?" Heizl scoffed, pulling out another heel of Hastigr's bread and tearing off a dry chunk. "I don't know what you're talking about. It's not like I've talked you into worse things." She didn't feel the levity her words suggested, but she did her best anyway as she moved up on Thaun's left.

"Name one." Her cousin moved more slowly than she'd have liked. Torn mail and battered plates could only protect bruised flesh for so long.

"How about that time with your language tutor? I'd rather deal with Frida again than face this upstart."

Thaun neither replied nor moved towards Toland. At a horn blast, the last of the Second still facing the noble attempted an ordered retreat. One, slower than the rest, suffered for their loyalty.

"Yeah," she said, the single word lacking any hint of humour. "I wish we'd a better option. Still, gotta try, right?"

He sighed, and shifted his weight a fraction. "Seems that way."

"Well, no time like the present!" Swallowing her mouthful, Heizl edged out to the side, wishing she didn't limp so much. "We do this together, remember? Don't hesitate, and we'll be fine."

Her cousin snorted as he advanced towards their foe. "Yeah? We haven't won yet."

Three steps in and Toland turned to them, wiping the crude, iron Claw on a bloodied uniform at his feet. At that stare, heavy as any of the chamber's cyclopean columns, all three of them paused. He glanced from one to the other and back again.

"It's been a while, Heizl." Through the greathelm that he now wore, Toland's voice sounded dull and out of tune, as if his tongue didn't quite fit in his mouth. "I heard you drowned."

"Drowned? Only thing I've drowned in recently is men who think they know what's best for everybody else. Uncle, Hastigr, Renyar, and now you too? It's like you get a free dose of arrogance with every pair of balls."

"There's no need to be uncivilised." He rolled his shoulders. "I understand how it might look that way, but we can only act on our own beliefs. Not anyone else's. There's only one difference between my actions now and your family's. I didn't plan all of this. I'm simply trying to protect my people. Even now, you're only trying to do what you think is the most good for the most people. Exactly the same as I'm doing."

"You're wrong." Heizl risked another bite, speaking with her mouth full. "Preach whatever you want, but none of your justifications are any better than anyone else's. Me though? I'm not so sure that this is the only way. You see, Toland, there's always another choice."

"You might be right, if only because we're friends." He gestured, Claw and Fang out to either side as if encompassing the whole chamber. "You don't have to do this. Put a stop to the fighting. Throw down your weapons."

"You're seriously gonna make an offer like that?"

"It's the right thing to do."

Heizl paused, glancing at Thaun. She could see the nervous trembling that he tried to clamp down upon, though his duelist's stance had yet to waver. He was different to so many of those that had led to all this... but not so different.

"I can't believe I nearly fell for it!" she exclaimed, her unguarded laughter spraying crumbs out before her. "You're stalling. You're *scared!*"

Almost imperceptibly, Toland bowed, the sour twist of a smile audible in his voice. "Pretty sure we should all be at least a bit scared right now, shouldn't we? Far from light, deep in some forgotten ruin, beneath a wound in our world itself, about to bring ancient relics to bear... Sounds pretty terrifying to me."

She didn't have a good response to that. "Well, yeah, I guess."

"Besides, I prefer the term 'practical' to 'scared.'"

Heizl didn't have a reply for that either. Not one made of words at least.

Fear in her belly and sorcery in her veins, time slowed. Thaun's tiniest movement at the corner of her sight launched her forwards, still choking down a last mouthful.

For all the sickening strength that she felt with the Claw in hand, her cousin's attack left her behind. She'd hoped, if they'd reached Toland together, that they could exploit openings left by the other. Instead, she arrived a beat behind Thaun.

With a ferocious parry, Toland locked his iron blade with Thaun's as his own Fang dropped into Heizl's path. A heartbeat from unleashing the wellspring of destruction deep within the Claw, her spear scratched along the shield's surface. Though Toland's boots skidded a handspan backwards beneath the blow, it couldn't compare to the burst of eldritch darkness from his own Fragment.

Thaun reeling from the sudden blast, the mage found herself facing Toland alone for a torturous second.

She didn't follow how he slid up the Claw's shaft, scarcely catching the sight of his shield slamming into her face. Colourful darkness filled her vision as she felt something crack. Blood filled her mouth.

Instinct saved her then. It didn't matter that the noble now stood well within the reach of her inexpert lunge. Any other person wielding a spear would've had no options left to them.

Heizl didn't need any more of an excuse to remind people that she wasn't just anyone else.

Like a sheet of lightning beneath storm clouds, power flooded from the Claw. Head, shaft, even its half-rotted leather grips, Heizl tied its power indiscriminately to her foe.

If she'd bought more into the church's teachings, she might've described that strike with metaphor or allegory. Ulora's own light. Urathear's argent fury. Magic beyond mortal ken. For Heizl though, it didn't need defining.

The broad, grey front hammered into Toland like a cresting wave. Old, forgotten armour – another Fragment? – creaked beneath the impact as plates and chains sparked.

Toland stumbled off-balance just enough, his slash striking only air as Heizl pushed past blindly.

Her vision cleared as Thaun arrived. Grimacing, she gave herself to the melee.

To her, sight fading in and out to both sorcery and pain, their fight could've stretched between bells. She'd later learn from others the difficulty in keeping a solid grip on time under such pressures. Terror twisted memories, and confusion bled into perception, tainting her reality.

She'd recall some parts more clearly than others.

The way that Thaun fought. His grace in the face of true mortal danger, moving as effortlessly as if he stood in the training ring. She lost count of how often he intercepted blows aimed for her, or the number of times his strange blade connected to not-enough effect.

Emotions and fears filled her mind. Her attempts blurred into one, whether physical lunges with the Claw's preternaturally sharp point, or unleashing scathed sorcery upon the noble.

The bile rising in her throat and the strength seeping from her flesh remained the only constant. For all she knew, the fight raging on all sides of them, of loyalist guardsman versus cultish Pinion, might fill songs and poems, but her world narrowed down to a single deadly sphere.

Throwing herself backwards beyond Toland's reach, his own Claw, iron and jagged, tore through her shirt, scraping skin beneath. That flash of heat and pain brought with it a glimpse of clarity.

Violent movement on all sides, of steel, lead, and sorcery. One source of motion though, indistinct in the shadows, called to her.

"Here's hoping..." she muttered in spite of herself and to no one in particular. Binding the Claw and Heart together, inexhaustible energy writhed towards Toland.

Before the blast could cross the full distance, Thaun stepped into its path. For a second, Heizl's weary, green eyes widened. She hadn't meant to...

"Ohhh." The smallest of smiles formed at the corner of her mouth. "I didn't think of that."

She relented, the grey cloud fading, and her cousin's blade breathed into new life. Dark flames poured from its steel. A familiar purple lightning flickered through the blackness.

Power overflowing, it didn't fade with Thaun's initial backswing. Perfect despite the weariness that he must feel, his feet almost left the floor with the effort. Iron struck iron, energy bursting outwards as he brought down his sword on Toland's helmeted head.

Her cousin's follow-up, leaning his weight into the still-glowing blade, met the dazed noble's block with his shield.

Heizl had waited for that opening. The idea might've only come to her a few moments before, but she felt like she'd aged decades in that span. Time had slowed through terror's lens as she'd fought. Now though, she willed those gaps between heartbeats to grow longer.

As power crept from Thaun's strange sword and up the noble's arm she found Toland's Fang. So similar to those of her own Fragment, Heizl felt the shield's threads. The same primal energies, the same predatory force, but contained in a different vessel.

It resisted her touch for a second, before yielding to her sorcery.

Tempted by the promise of ruin, she bound it to Thaun's blade. She grasped at the similarities between sword and shield. Iron to bronze, she twinned the two together – even if only for a second.

Slender threads of connection wove together to form rope. Subtle relationships formed links in a chain. It'd have to be enough.

Heizl turned back to the web entangling them all.

It all passed in no time at all. As the echo of Thaun's last slash flowed through Toland and into his Claw like frozen lightning, the noble stepped in, thrusting upwards.

She pushed and pulled, scrambling to gather up the jagged blade's bonds. It took only the slightest twist. Had it demanded anything more, well, in her condition it didn't bear thinking about.

As if holding Thaun's Fang in one hand and Toland's Claw in the other, she redirected the blade the width of a coin one way and her cousin's Fragment the other.

They met. Explosively.

Power and energy flowed in a circle, growing with no release. Wheeling through, from blade to shield, shield to blade, and back again, it swelled in a vicious cycle. Fragments that had absorbed, redirected and amplified deadly blows now fed one another.

Tying fresh threads to bind the two swordsmen together, Heizl fought to keep up as strands snapped and burst with the fury filling them.

Sunk so deep within her own magic, any fuel left in her belly now long gone, Heizl fell blind to all else. Even if she hadn't, she might've missed the short crossbow bolt that lanced to join the growing conflagration.

Iron slammed into Toland's visor, pushing itself half an inch into the helmet's bent eye slit. Ensnared within, the noble's head snapped back at the impact, and he let out an almost bestial scream.

A single piece of cloth, torn unevenly and still smelling of sulphur, hung from the crossbow bolt.

What little of it that she sensed, Heizl ignored. She might come to regret it, but her waning focus clung to only one thing. Not the noble and his collection of Fragments, nor her cousin as he struggled to hold Toland there. Not even the bloodshed on all sides, or the Shadow preparing for a second shot.

For a moment at least, a strip of fraying, grey cloth was the only thing in her world. A piece of fabric, taken from a moth-eaten blanket daubed with glyphs. A twisting banner now close enough to their foe. A traitor's blanket that lay in another world, upon a source of arcane power that she didn't truly understand.

Reaching out, thin as gossamer, a thread stretched towards the chamber's vaulted ceiling. It stopped short though, disappearing as it met the Rift above, even as that whorl in reality shrank with the fading of a Comet's passing. Glinting in the light of souls and sorcery, that thread was enough. It had to be.

The link from one end to another, between two pieces of a whole, shone to her. She didn't see the black sphere, rough and anguished, as it rose up from the floor to consume Toland. One by one, she felt the threads binding him to Thaun snapping as the dark shell grew, cutting each in turn.

Lacking Hastigr's experience and finesse, Heizl poured the Claw's raw power into widening the portal. It flowed into her and out again, tearing parts of her away with it. Flickering shadow grew at the edges of her sight as her body gave way to the forces acting upon it. Teeth clenched hard enough that it hurt, she held on.

The sphere grew, breaking and reforming as Toland struggled to free himself. She felt every blow as if they landed upon her own flesh.

With a last push, blood vessels bursting within one eye and her scathe spreading further round her neck, Heizl screamed.

Black as night and hard as onyx, the orb closed upon Toland, Urathear's Heart, and all.

As it began tearing itself apart, the man within it stretched across two spaces at once, all would've ended well, had it ended a second sooner.

Battered Fang still strapped to its bracer, one arm burst out. Toland's armoured fingers dug into the tears on Thaun's armour. Both men screaming, voices rough, obsidian magic bulged outwards, consuming the pair.

Heizl didn't see it. Consciousness wavering as strength left her, even the Claw feeling weary within her grip, the mage cast both of them into the Void.

Darkness, sour and infinite, claimed her.

She awoke an unknown length of time later to coarse hands lifting her jaw, dried blood beneath their cracked fingernails. Vision still blurred, she moaned and lashed out, breaking the grip, and rose into a sitting position.

Just that exertion almost sent her back into dreamless oblivion. She tried falling within, to draw upon her own talents, or the fires within the Claw, but couldn't even summon that effort.

Wracking coughs shook her body, and, still half-blind, she twisted onto her side.

"Take it easy."

The words came to her muted, her muddled mind struggling to make sense of them. She continued coughing, uncaring for how defenceless she felt, or how little she wanted to *take things easy*.

She forced slow, deep breaths into her lungs. Her head spinning, her coughs faded. Eyes still closed, she didn't speak.

"Are you done?" She recognised the voice this time, memory catching up to where she now lay.

"Sigren? Did it work? Did we get him?"

"Here." The nudge of a wineskin against her ribs helped ground her. "Halig's cutter was going to try and get some into you, but you can do it yourself now."

Rolling onto her back, Heizl came up against something hard. The floor beneath her moved slowly, like the seat of a carriage. Weak light filtered through her eyelids. "What's going on?"

She heard his grunt as he lowered himself to sit alongside her. "I'd hoped you could tell me. First, drink. Small sips. There's food too, when you're ready."

"Ugh, blacking out this much must be worse for me than I thought. It almost sounds like you're being kind to me."

"It's the training. You're the only mage around, so keeping you alive is down to me." She smiled at that, feeling her dry lips crack and sting. Heizl held out a hand palm up to take the drink, and slowly opened her eyes.

As the weight settled between her fingers, her vision adjusted to the light.

By any other standards, the daylight would've felt weak and dull, but the grey clouds overhead almost overwhelmed her senses. On all sides, sailors and soldiers moved, pulling ropes, seeing to injuries, and doing all those other things that such people did. Fitful wind tugged at canvas overhead, moving the ship who-knew-where.

Pain rising as she turned her head, Heizl saw the officer that had come to their aid. Even out of his armour, she couldn't mistake him for anything but a soldier. His stained surcoat over padded clothing gave her enough of a hint. He stood near the ship's rear, where he spoke with a better-dressed sailor. She didn't recognise anyone else there, but the blue and yellow of the Imperial Second comforted her.

Eyes closed against the muted scene before her, Heizl fumbled with the wineskin's stopper before putting it to her mouth. Cheap, sour, and diluted, she'd had worse, but not by much. Even without Sigren's advice, she wouldn't have drank more than a mouthful.

"Where's Thaun?" she asked, head tilted back as she suppressed the urge to gag.

"He..." For a second, his voice cracked before disciplined control clamped back down. "He didn't make it."

Too tired to do anything else, a tear welled up behind closed eyelids. A different sort of nausea threatened her insides now, but she forced another mouthful down to hide her feelings if nothing else. "What happened?"

"Why don't you tell me what you remember?" Though the Shadow's training kept his tone level, she could hear the slipping grasp he held upon his own grief.

"I... We... It must've worked. Thaun locked Toland down, you landed the shot, and I used that as a beacon to send him into the Rift."

"More or less. Toland dragged Thaun with him. They're gone, both of them."

Silence, accompanied by another tear.

What could she say to that? "I'm sorry."

"Yeah, well, me too."

"No, not like that." Heizl opened her eyes, and risked a glance to the Shadow sat alongside her. Her Shadow now? That didn't bear thinking about. Greying bags under bloodshot eyes revealed a weariness that she hadn't heard. "This is genuinely my fault. All of it."

"You might not have his name, but you're as bad as Thaun was," grunted Sigren. "He carried the weight of the world on his shoulders too. I get it, you made choices, and you regret them. A lot of us did."

"You can't just dismiss it. If I'd stopped Uncle sooner, it wouldn't have got this far. If I'd beaten Hastigr, he couldn't have completed his ritual. If..." She trailed off.

"Maybe, and if I'd broken Toland's jaw a week ago, maybe he wouldn't have been there to pull the trigger. We don't get to know how it would've turned out."

"I guess."

Not-quite-silence rose between them again then. Creaking ropes, waves crashing against the hull, and sailors calling to one another prevented true peace from forming.

"You still look like shit, by the way." False humour tugged at the Shadow's mouth.

"I bet you say that to all the girls."

"If I had a mirror, you'd see. Your scathe's got worse. It makes you look part-dragon."

Wincing at even that small effort, Heizl scratched the back of her neck, feeling hard, lumpy skin. "Gee, thanks. It happens sometimes, when I exert myself. Don't worry about it. It'll fade." She didn't give the conversation a chance to develop into another awkward gap. "What else happened? How long have I been out for?"

"Where should I start?"

"Just get on with it."

"Fine. Toland's Pinions retreated not long after you fainted."

"I didn't *faint*. I was... I fell unconscious."

"Yeah, they have a word for that already."

"And where are we now?" she continued, ignoring the jab.

Sigren coughed. At least, that's what she thought it was. Heizl couldn't imagine the dour marksman laughing much right now. Or anytime, for that matter. "We got out before things got worse."

"Worse? I thought those, what were they, Pinions? I thought you said they ran."

"They did, but we don't know how far. And then there's Seorsa. Their advance forces were far from beaten without Renyar. The rest of them are probably turning up on Insel Drach sometime now." Sigren took a breath. "Me and Halig, we figured it was best if you didn't wake up in the midst of a siege, so he led a break-out with as much of his company as could walk. A few that probably shouldn't have walked too, for that matter. Bloody work, but better than the alternative."

She couldn't remember her cousin's Shadow having ever said so many words at once around her. "Smart move, I guess. Where are we going now then?"

"Yeah." He lowered his voice. "Right now, we're just trying to stay ahead of the news. When word of what's happened gets out..."

"Huh. Right." She didn't feel the need to put words to that. An Empire without an experienced Emperor would've been bad enough. Thaun, the only legitimate heir, disappeared on the same day too... a third, anxious sickness grew within her, mingling with grief and poor wine.

In spite of Rufenrich summoning the Heart, they'd stopped things spiralling fully out of control. Oh, he'd paid for thinking only of his legacy, and Hastigr had disappeared in the chaos, but they'd halted whatever Toland had attempted. She wished she could remember better what he'd claimed. Power to protect, or some other self-serving mania.

If the Rift hadn't closed yet, it wouldn't stay open for much longer. Sheltz's Comet would pass soon. Urathear's Heart, and all those other Fragments along with it, would stay out of reach. For now, at least.

"Me and Halig were wondering..." Sigren started.

"What is it?"

"With Thaun gone, and the Emperor dead, we didn't know if...?"

"If..?"

"If you might, y'know. Don't make me say it."

"Oh!" Heizl almost laughed. "If you'd asked me a month ago, I'd already be measuring for a more comfortable cushion. I tried it though. I don't think me and the Throne would be a good fit anymore."

"I don't know if that's the answer I wanted to hear or not."

"Me neither." She shrugged. "I'm not saying Thaun would've been a great choice either, but I'm pretty sure I'd only make things worse if I was in charge."

"Someone else will make a move for it then. A governor, a general, or someone. Maybe another civil war."

"Nothing civil about all that." Heizl let a smile dawn on her face. "It might not be all that bad, anyway. I spent a little time in the Void, even if unintentionally, and I made it back more or less in one piece. Who's to say we can't bring Thaun back?"

"Do you really believe that?" The slightest note of hope played in Sigren's tone.

"Maybe? I'd have to give it some thought. I'm pretty beat, I don't even know what I think right now. It's not like that's our only option though."

"You sound dangerously like you have a plan."

"I dunno about that. A plan needs someone to take charge of it. I'm not so sure I'm cut out for that. I might manage a plot or a scheme though, if we're lucky."

"Heizl..." The Shadow growled, frustration playing into his voice.

"Tell you what." She smiled, closed her eyes again, and lay her head sideways onto Sigren's shoulder. At the touch, he flinched before softening. "Let me sleep for five minutes... maybe ten, and then we can talk it out. Oh, I'll need some food though. You might want to call your officer friend. Maybe find us all a change of clothes too..."

"You don't sound so sure."

"Not in the slightest, but I'd rather head towards something than simply run from what happened back there. I, uh, know a guy."

"Right you are," Sigren paused, and she could almost hear his thoughts grinding inside his skull. After a moment, he added a single word that she hadn't realised she longed to hear. "Sir."

Heizl smiled. The sun might as well have broken through the clouds at that moment. As the weariness in her bones spread to the rest of her body, she felt a lightness growing in her belly.

"I know I've said before that I wanted to be taken more seriously, to be in charge, to have more responsibility, but I don't know how I feel about being called that." The Shadow grunted wordlessly in response. "Is this what it feels like, to win? I'm not talking about banishing a god or whatever, this, right now. Getting what you thought you wanted."

"I wouldn't know."

"If it is, let's not make a habit of it? Victory's not all it's cracked up to be."

Tooth and Nail – Epilogue

"The responsibility of the noble ruler, the parent, and the poet is the same. To bring truth, wisdom, and hope to those in their charge whether they like it or not."

Rufenrich Konreig (387 I.Y.)

Toland opened one eye and stared up at nothing. Greyish smoke lingered in the air just beyond his reach. The right side of his vision held only blackness.

Pushing himself upright, he yanked free the quarrel protruding through his helmet's grille. A scorched, stained scrap of cloth hung from its leather fletching.

With a growl, he tossed it aside. It bounced across the soft ground to halt mere inches from a matching piece of fabric.

At a sudden, faint whisper, Toland spun. Nothing. No one. Turning a slow, cautious circle, he inspected his new surroundings.

Grey floors and endless grey sky. Waving an arm through the air, the thin smoke shifted around its path before coalescing in its wake. Beyond his reach, he could see nothing but the wall of smog.

Passing by the bloody crossbow bolt, he scooped up his Claw. Its beautiful, iron blade shone like marbled silver, annealed by the black flame that it had birthed. Toland tracked down its length to his arm.

Every plate, chain, and rivet gleamed the same way, spreading past his shoulder to flicker across his chest armour like tongues of flame. Soot-marred tendrils twisted around bright swirls as if at random. For all the power he felt from them even now, these pieces of an elder god weren't invulnerable. Thaun and Heizl had shown that with their own Fragments.

No sign of either of them now. Or anyone else for that matter. Other than the whispers.

He hadn't wanted it to end how it had. The Court had whispered of rivalries between him and Thaun since their youth, but he'd never taken them seriously. His friend had always run from the same Imperial responsibilities that so many nobles desired. Heizl too. Not Toland though. Such mundane ambitions didn't concern him, nor his father.

Had Thaun survived? Toland's memory felt as thick as the fog that now surrounded him. He could remember fighting, and the trembling certainty that had consumed him. The fear that had come with that torn, black, sphere still lingered. In that moment, holding tight to a friend had been the most natural thing in the world.

Even with the power of a dozen Fragments flowing through him, Toland had struggled to fend the Prince off. He almost felt pride at Thaun's swordsmanship. No, not pride. Pride implied ownership, of taking credit.

Thaun was gone now. He wished he could tell him how impressed he'd been. He wished they could talk, so he could explain the secrets that his father had taught him. He wished he knew why he'd not had any answer other than violence.

Toland sighed. Any chance of that had left when they'd drawn swords against one another.

Sliding the jagged blade back into its cracked scabbard, he walked. Bruised muscles protested the movement, with freshly knitted flesh threatening to tear at every step. Though weary from his fight, the Fragments felt as light as breath.

Leaving Sigren's bolt and the scraps of cloth in his wake, the ground undulated gently beneath Toland's feet. No hidden holes or coarse brush snagged at his boots, a far cry from Insel Drach's surface. Could this be that blasted island? He doubted it. He hadn't expected any fog bank or strange weather there, nor did he see any sign of his loyal Pinions.

With no landmarks to go by, Toland saw little choice but to keep walking. Sooner or later he'd find some clue as to wherever he'd ended up. Hadn't his father told him a story like that? Of a Daericani saint crossing a desert until he found an accepting people? Those tales seemed such a blur now.

Had he succeeded? It was hard to tell. Urathear was coming, their entire hidden faith knew it. When the dragon arrived, all but the purest would burn to ashes. His homeland, so many people that he cared for, none would survive. Failure would spell the end of the Empire, and the world beyond it. He couldn't have failed. He wouldn't let himself.

Drawing in a sharp breath through the grille of his ancient helmet, Toland lengthened his stride. Things couldn't end now, not like this. He'd find out where he was, and he'd find a way home. People depended on him.

After half a dozen paces, the noble smiled. The blackness behind his right eye didn't seem so dark anymore.

* * *

The old building trembled, amber leaves drifting from its wooden roof at the violent impact. Its frame shook again as Vandel slammed the Highmage into the wall a second time.

"I should kill you here and now," the veteran growled only inches from Hastigr's face.

"But then," wheezed the mage, "You'd be stuck like this."

The Champion shook him almost casually, teeth rattling inside his skull. "Know your place." With a twist, Vandel threw him across the room. Dry dust and half-rotted straw scattered as he bounced and rolled across the floor. "I won't be baited like that. You don't matter to me."

Hastigr pushed himself up, feeling bones grind together with the effort. It'd take time, but it would heal. Not that that did anything for the pain right now. "Yet you haven't killed me."

"Yet. I haven't killed you *yet*." He began pacing, any sign of his recent injury long faded. "You ruined everything! Kwen was safe, but you brought him back. He couldn't do any more damage there. I was rebuilding!"

"Please, old friend, you don't see this for the victory it truly is."

"Victory? I should've executed you last time." Vandel took a step closer to loom over the Highmage. "Give me one decent reason not to break every bone in your body before–"

Sable flame enveloped them both for an instant. A sulphurous heartbeat later and both men reappeared within the room, their positions changed. Hastigr stood, leaning heavily on the cane now in hand, a thin shell of green wards before him. He couldn't manage anything more.

The Champion barely stumbled as he turned from where he'd landed near the window.

"Vandel, stop, listen." He risked a glance over one shoulder to where an emaciated body lay. If not for the occasional arrhythmic wheeze, anyone would've taken him for a corpse. "You have options now, all of you. Kwen's back. You can be together again."

"And I'm supposed to think you managed all this by yourself? Some irrelevant, chimeric bastard long past his prime?"

"I played my part," said Hastigr, his face painted in ghostly green light. "But so did your sister."

For a heartbeat, Vandel looked like he'd strike the sorcerous wards between them. "...You're lying."

"You know better than I do that she's still alive."

"I've not seen her since before Razeen got himself locked away."

"I know, but she's kept tabs on you."

"I should've seen you for who you are sooner." Fists uncurled as he glared murderously at him. "I might still decide to kill you."

A weak smile graced Hastigr's lips. "It wouldn't be the first time that you tried."

"Kwen's in no state to protect you this time."

"He'll recover. Eventually. Your sister said a family reunion was in order."

"...What else did she say?"

* * *

"...And so I implore you to support my father. In these turbulent times, only by a strong hand and a strong faith can our great peop–"

The carriage bucked as it struck a pothole, and Jilia's pen scratched across the letter's surface. She sighed. At least this was only a draft. Blotting the excess ink, she lay the sheet down on a loose stack consisting of dozens more incomplete ideas. She'd got further with this one at least.

For a while, the young noble stared out the window. The night hid all but the occasional guard's lantern or the glimmer of a distant homestead. Still, she'd long grown accustomed to her carriage's gilded interior.

It bounced along an uneven backroad now. For every dip down into a wheel rut or puddle, it rose over a broken branch or jagged stone. She felt each rut tremble through her bones. In better times they'd have followed a more well-trod path, heading to their destination by a more direct route. People expected that – it was what everyone else did, after all.

The finest woods and the most expensive clothes, craftspeople had toiled over the carriage's elegant form. Its cost could've fed a family for a year. She'd have sold the whole thing if it meant travelling through the Nexus one more time.

But no, that wasn't an option. It no longer functioned, the Spire as broken and scattered now as the Empire's hopes and safety. Her informants would find out in time what had happened, but right now it didn't matter.

Instead, they hid and crept between villages, avoiding tradeposts and population centres. Their meagre escort of house guards and mercenaries formed a thin perimeter. Against the chaos that now grew within Imperial borders, they'd pose little resistance.

Under other circumstances she might've enjoyed the trip, but she'd hardly describe the royal family's disappearance as normal.

Getting home could take weeks, and so much would change in that time. The fractures in the Empire had already begun widening.

Jilia closed her eyes and breathed deep. Swearing wouldn't do her any good, even if it might make her feel a little better.

She turned her attention back towards the task at hand and selected a fresh sheet of parchment. Her resources were few, but she had ideas, she had her training, and she had time. By the time they reached Kragiv-Stal, she'd have a letter for every conceivable possibility. Whatever challenges arose, she'd rise with an answer in hand.

The Courts whispered occasionally of unlicensed, radical mages who'd made a fortune from selling glimpses of the future's possible paths. She didn't know if she believed in such gossip, but only a fool would discount the uses of such knowledge. Still, until she could exploit such information, she'd do what she could by herself. Effort and intellect could take a person far.

Before ink touched paper again, the carriage door opened, letting in a gust of cold night air. A shadowy figure, garbed in the gold and bronze colours of House Strahl, stepped in as if blown on the wind.

"Now's not a good time," said Jilia, pen hovering an inch from the blank page.

The man settled into the seat opposite her, rainwater seeping into the expensive cushions. "You don't get to put it off again," Zecht growled. "I did my part and got you outta the city. I went into the Forge and got what you asked for. You owe me."

"And you'll be repaid," the noble soothed, looking up through long eyelashes at the Shadow. She might've found him attractive if he wasn't so insufferable. How Heizl tolerated him for so long, she didn't know. "There are greater forces at play than you and your sister."

"Maybe." He shrugged, and one corner of his mouth turned upwards. "They're not sitting here with a knife, are they?"

Jilia smiled in return, a touch of amused affection tinging the expression, and leant forwards to place a hand on his knee. "No, but a political power vacuum is just as dangerous to both of us. Zecht, as soon as we're safe, I promise that we'll turn resources to finding your sister."

"...Fine, but I'm staying close." The Shadow crossed his arms over his chest, but mischief glinted in his narrowed eyes. "I don't want you trying anything."

"I wouldn't dream of it." Her smile gentled as she sat back in the carriage's rocking seat. "So, did you get them all?"

"All what?"

"The reports I requested, Zecht. From the Forge."

"Oh, them. O' course." From a satchel he began pulling out rolls of wax-sealed papers. "Some are copies, but I figured that'd be fine. Homegrown governors, Thalan Melechs, runaway mages; I got 'em all. Grabbed a few things too that other people seemed to think were important. Bunch of Oesel gibberish to me, but thought you might get something from it."

"You didn't mention Baron Gildur." She drew each syllable out. "Or any of my father's Boyars."

"Ah. About that."

"Go on."

"I kinda forgot."

Jilia took a moment as she attempted to maintain her composure. "Let's hope that we don't come to regret your oversight."

"Great. So, it's a long way to go." He grinned suggestively. "What do we do now?"

"Now..." She reached out, picking back up her pen. "I have some work to do."

"Well, that's boring."

"I can see that." She didn't look up from the paper. "Nobody enjoys waiting, but there'll be more excitement soon enough."

Leaning back against the wooden boards, Zecht clicked his tongue several times, but didn't say anything. A moment later, he closed his eyes.

Jilia dipped the pen into her wide-based ink well, touched it to the page, and began writing.

"An open letter to the Imperial Church; The Empire is shattered, and the Konreig line gone. Without words of guidance the people will fall to chaos, but faith can take the place of order..."

* * *

Ryuko stood upon the chalk cliffs, alone. Waves struck its rocky base far below as the morning seabirds took to the sky. A gusting breeze played in her straight hair and the heavy folds of her plain dress, drying the tears from her red and white skin. The cloud's eastward edges bore the mottled light of a sun not yet risen, and salt lingered upon the cold air.

A beautiful final morning.

Others should've stood with her, but then, if they had it wouldn't be her last day. A husband and son lost to war, a daughter lost to childbirth. The ancestors were ever greedy for more to join their number. She'd become one with them herself, soon enough.

She leant heavily upon her spear as its chitinous point glimmered in the dawnlight. It had served her better than she'd served her people. Such a loyal weapon didn't deserve the same ignoble fate as her. Gritting her teeth, Ryuko wrapped calloused fingers around its smooth, familiar shaft, and thrust its butt into the soft clifftop. Her touch lingered as she withdrew, leaving it standing upright. Kamii deserved a sentinel that wouldn't tire and fail them.

Rolling her shoulder to loosen an old wound, she looked inland. The overgrown ruins there would witness her end. Those she'd left behind at home would care about as much as these ancient stones. Raised by monstrous hands and felled by hubris, the rounded blocks and weathered spires had seen death enough already over the centuries – what was one more?

Her people were a superstitious folk. Ryuko couldn't admit to being any different. Would they blame her disappearance upon their ever-present ancestors? Or the ghouls that elders whispered of? Perhaps someone would even name the unspeakable interlopers of generations past. They'd all be wrong.

Sighing, the veteran turned, wincing as she felt the cold seep into stiff joints. Something made her pause midway. A hint of movement, a whiff of brimstone, a change in air pressure. Old instincts struggled to wake, like a beast rising from slumber, and her eyes narrowed.

Obscured by monolithic stones, something dark flared and disappeared within the haunted ruins. A wave of prickling heat washed over Ryuku, exorcising the morning's chill. For a brief moment, she considered drawing her spear from its resting place. What was the point? She came here to die. Why fight it?

Moving with a practised grace in flowing, shallow steps, she crept down the gentle slope. The further she went, the stronger the dry, rotting smell grew. It took only a score of heartbeats before Ryuko pressed her back to a broken stone arch, and peered around its rounded corner.

A dark figure lay sprawled upon the uneven ground. Beneath its still form, the coarse grass stalks withered as if thrown into a raging forge. Tattered and burnt cloth hung over glistening chains and blackened steel. A broken, twisted blade of iron rested smoking in a nearby patch of coarse grass, just beyond its reach. That single piece of metal was probably worth more than her whole village.

The breath caught in her throat at the unexpected sight, but she edged forwards regardless. Had the inhuman interlopers returned? The monks and mystics said that they had come through in this desecrated place once before, so why not again?

Through the damage and darkness, it took Ryuko a moment to realise that it wore strange, alien armour. She'd mistaken most of the iron and steel for scale and horn. Past scorched metal, skin shone with blisters and scars. It would've looked inhuman if not for the pale flesh peeking past what remained of its helmet.

She flinched back as it moaned and rolled onto its back revealing a battered bronze disc strapped to its arm. Had it spoken some eldritch word? There was no way to tell.

Ryuko uncurled her fists. She'd planned on dying today, but she couldn't leave a monster like this alive. Stories whispered of the damage that they'd caused in times long past.

As she moved closer, preparing to strangle the life from the injured creature, she paused. Its brown eyes had fluttered open without her noticing.

By some twist of fate, the sun peeked over the eastern horizon. Long shadows reached past her, bathing the ruins, cliff, and interloper alike with its amber glow. Light glinted from the being's slitted eyes.

All too human eyes, even if surrounded by strange-coloured flesh, but that wasn't what stopped her. Old familiarity held her back as surely as any shackle. Memories of her son – smiling sadly the day he left for war – assaulted Ryuko then, and a tear rolled down her cheek.

In that moment of hesitation, she realised that the interloper couldn't be anything but human. She had so many questions, but none mattered. Her child had never worn such armour – not even their greatest leaders owned anything so valuable – but she couldn't deny the uncanny resemblance.

Ryuko couldn't have said what guided her decision. Motherly instinct, a grief-shaped hole in her heart, or the ancestors themselves. Edging closer, she leant in and raised the interloper's head into her lap. Her spear would remain as a reminder, but she'd return home with a reason to continue.

***

Tilting back under a god's weight, the chair creaked a perfect tone. Its maker had stopped asking questions after agreeing to a most generous fee. Few customers wanted their every shifting muscle to herald their discomfort. Fewer still would outright pay for it.

The oblivious carpenter would've had more questions if he'd known his client's identity. It helped that they knew him by a different name in these parts.

Leaning forward, Haber untied the laces upon his worn, scuffed boots. With a lazy flick, he hung his broad-brimmed hat upon its peg. Three other caps ruffled alongside it as they settled, each as flamboyant as the last.

He was done, adequately satisfied by what he'd witnessed. Every journey came to an end, and he should know.

Beyond the vellum-thin door to the office, his followers worked. They didn't know his identity either. Not in full, anyway. Only a few accepted the wage he offered them. The rest served not out of any divine reverence, but from a sense of debt to the mad benefactor that had helped close so many of their stories.

Haber watched his boots fall to the floor. He'd watched so many of those involved in recent events, even if they'd occurred on the other side of the world. One of them lay close by now, his story entangled with that of a grieving local. Neither knew it, but Haber's interference, that gentlest nudge from one Juncture to another, had likely saved them both from the fates they'd arced towards. His domain might not have been as flashy as Fire, Darkness, or Illusion, but he'd never questioned his duty.

His chosen family had their own issues with one another. Rivalries and history strained relationships among the helpless, let alone when gods became involved.

He'd watched the bastard mage's awkward reunion with her even more awkward brother. The lack of conflict there had disappointed him, but he could appreciate the pathos involved. It might've ended differently if the grieving Shadow hadn't already left her company, but he didn't know for sure. Not yet, at least.

Haber sighed.

He'd seen it before. Oh, with different people in different places, but tales only came in so many flavours. Sure as Death, all came to an end one way or another. All stories had been told before, and they'd be told again.

Glossary

Arcanosphere (*aa·kay·no·sfeeuh*) – A term for general background magic levels and how they interact with one another.

Arcanotype (*aa·kay·no·tipe*) – A term for one of four broad styles of magic that a mage is able to manipulate.

Aspect (*a·spekt*) – A term used to describe the legendary personifications of a broken god that ruled Trissk'thala as tyrant-rulers.

Bara (*bah·rah*) – A small group of Yrgol families, often semi-nomadic.

Birka (*buh·kuh*) – A city in southern Fjujhost.

Daericani (*deuh·ruh·kaa·nee*) – A group of related sapient draconic species.

Daqin (*da·keen*) – A nation far to the south of Thala, known for their bureaucracy and alchemy.

Fitz (*fits*) – A derogatory term for someone with unknown parentage, predominantly used within the Konreig Empire.

Fjarl (*fyaal*) – A Fjujan title that loosely translates as warden.

Fjujhost (*fyoo·ho·st*) – The most recently occupied province of the Konreig Empire, currently in open rebellion against the Throne.

Imperial Civil War (*im·peeuh·ree·uhl si·vl waw*) – A conflict within the Empire headed by the Konreig and Kuhlner families, both attempting to claim the Imperial Throne. (386 -391 I.Y)

Kragiv-Stal (*krag·eev stal)* – A western province of the Konreig Empire known for the purity of their metal deposits. Currently governed by the Strahl family.

Lairz (*leuhz*) – A Tszerrichan title that loosely translates to landowner.

Melech (*meh·lek*) – A Thalan title that loosely translates to lieutenant or assistant.

Norjhost (*naw·ho·st*) – A region to the north of Kragiv-Stal populated by nomadic herders and fisherpeople.

Oesel (*o·sehl*) – A fallen nation situated in the Trilithik Isles. Houses Seorsa and Tszerrik both survive as nation-states, while the Yrgol eke out a living as travellers. Other Houses, including Oeska and En'templa, disappeared long ago.

Scheltz's Comet (*shelts ko·muht*) – A celestial body that reappears approximately every twenty-nine years.

Seorsa (*see·or·sa*) – A kingdom in name only, a nation occupying much of the Trilithik Isles. Ruled by a hereditary council of wealthy nobles.
Saedura (*say·duor·ah*) – A magically-altered ape, shaped with sorcerous sigils to form a living siege weapon.
Shadow, Imperial (*sha·dow, im·peeuh·ree·uhl*) – Secret police of the Konreig Empire. Publicly, partnered with Spire mages to protect them from anti-magic prejudice, and to protect the populace from them.
Spire, Imperial (*spai·uh, im·peeuh·ree·uhl*) – An Imperial institution dedicated to training and controlling mages.
Snake of Birka (*snayk of buh·kuh*) – The name given to a group of loyalist Imperial refugees fleeing Fjujhost during the recent rebellion.
Tarnon (*taa·non*) – A northern province of the Konreig Empire.
Takuq (*ta·kuk*) – A Norjan spirit.
Thala (*thah·lah*) – A collection of loosely-allied city-states built on the ruins of ancient Trissk'thala.
Radical (*ra·duh·kl*) – An Imperial term for mages unaffiliated with the Spire.
Reiget Trade Guild (*ray·get trayd gild*) – A group of merchants, mostly Imperial, that cooperate towards mutual profit.
Trilithik (*tril·li·thuhk*) – An archipelago south of the Konreig Empire and north of Thala.
Trissk'thala (*trisk·thah·lah*) – An ancient nation ruled by tyrant god-kings near present day Thala, destroyed by Urathear.
Tszerrik (*seh·ruhk*) – A theocratic nation occupying multiple isles in the southern Trilithiks.
Ulora (*uh·luh·rah*) – Principle Imperial deity, the Judge.
Urathear (*uh·ra·feeuh*) – One of four elder gods, associated with purity, destruction, and dragons.
Urlungenlied, The (*uh·luhng·uhn·leed*) – A pre-Imperial epic poem.
Velast (*vel·ast*) – A Fjujan city.
Wealmaer, Saint (*weel·mehr*) – An Uloric saint, originally from an unknown Yrgol Bara.
Yrgol (*eeuh·gohl*) – A defunct Oesel house. Presently itinerant nomads of both the Empire and Trilithik Isles.

For updates, behind-the-scenes insights, and shameless self-promotion, follow at:

Instagram: huw.mungous
Facebook: H. Carrington - Author
www.huwcarrington.co.uk

Printed in Great Britain
by Amazon

ba933bd4-40af-4eca-a066-de8343ccc4efR01